EVA IBBOTSON

The Morning Gift

YOUNG PICADOR

First published in Great Britain 1993 by Random Century Group

This edition published 2007 by Young Picador
an imprint of Pan Macmillan Limited
20 New Wharf Road, London N1 9RR
Basingstoke and Oxford
Associated companies throughout the world
www.panmacmillan.com

ISBN 978-0-330-44499-6

5 7 9 8 6

A CIP catalogue record for this book is available from
the British Library.

Typeset by Intype Libra Ltd
Printed and bound in the UK by CPI Mackays, Chatham ME5 8TD

PROLOGUE

Vienna has always been a city of myths. Before the First World War there was the ancient Kaiser, Franz Joseph, who slept on an iron bed, never opened a book, and ritually washed the feet of twelve old gentlemen on Maundy Thursday.

'Is nothing to be spared me?' the Emperor had asked – and indeed not very much was. His wandering, neurotic wife was stabbed to death by a mad anarchist on the shores of Lake Geneva; his son, the Crown Prince Rudolf, shot himself and (after a larger interval than was suitable) his mistress, in the hunting lodge at Mayerling. Tragic events, all, but the very stuff of legend and excellent for the tourist trade.

This was the Vienna from which thirteen nationalities were governed; the city of parades and pageants where the world's most dashing soldiers in blue and white and silver could be seen each night crowding the standing parterre at the opera, for every serving officer had the right to hear music free. The Vienna of the Lippizaners, the city's darlings, stabled in an arcaded palace, who turned the death-dealing movements of war into an equine ballet and were followed by solemn men with golden shovels who scooped their noble droppings from the perfectly raked sand.

The carnage and wretchedness of the Great War brought this era to an end. Yet somehow the city survived the death of Franz Joseph, the abdication of his nephew, Austria's crashing defeat, the loss of her empire. And new myths, now, were assembled for the visitors. Professor Freud, on good days, could be pointed out drinking beer on the terrace of the Café Landtmann. Arnold Schönberg, the inventor of atonal music, gave concerts which might not be comprehensible but were obviously important, and while no one knew exactly what logical positivism was, it was understood that the philosophers who were inventing it were bringing acclaim to the city.

Leonie Berger's family had lived in Vienna for a hundred years and her myths were her own.

'Personally I never meet Professor Freud in the Landtmann,' she said to an enquiring visitor. 'All I ever meet in the Landtmann is my Cousin Fritzi with those spoilt children of hers running between the tables.'

Her father, descended from prosperous Moravian wool merchants, owned a big department store in the Mariahilferstrasse, but Leonie Berger had married into the intelligentsia. Kurt Berger was already in his thirties, a lecturer at the university, when he crossed the

2

Stephansplatz and heard, from underneath a multitude of hungry pigeons, the cries of a desperate young girl. Beating back the predatory birds, he discovered a scratched and very pretty blonde who threw herself weeping into his arms.

'I wanted to be like St Francis of Assisi,' wailed Leonie, who had bought six whole packets of corn from the old man who sold pigeon food.

Kurt Berger had not expected to marry, but he married now, and could blame no one but himself when he discovered that Leonie, so to speak, would never proffer one bag of corn where six would do.

As for Leonie, she adored her husband, who in turn became Professor of Vertebrate Zoology, a Director of the Natural History Museum and Adviser to the Government. She orchestrated his day with the precision of a Toscanini, herself handing him his briefcase and silver-handled umbrella as he left at eight, serving lunch within five minutes of his return, stilling the servants to silence while he took his afternoon nap. The amount of starch in his collars, the movements of his intestine, were known to Leonie within millimetres; she guarded him from importunate students and carried his favourite mineral water to their box at the opera in a silver flask. None of which prevented her from also attending to the ailments, birthdays and love affairs of innumerable relatives whom she entertained, visited and succoured, often more than once a day.

The Bergers lived in the Inner City, on the first floor of a massive apartment house built round a courtyard with a chestnut tree. The Professor's aged mother was hived off in two of the twelve rooms; his unmarried sister, Hilda, an anthropologist who specialized in the kinship systems of the Mi-Mi in Bechuanaland, had her own suite. Leonie's Uncle Mishak, a small balding man with a romantic past, lived in the mezzanine. But, of course, they wouldn't have been truly Viennese if they hadn't, on the last day of the university term, departed for the mountains. For the Crownlands of the old Habsburg Empire were left to the Austrians: the Tyrol, Carinthia, Styria . . . and the rain-washed Salzkammergut where, by a deep green lake called the Grundlsee, the Bergers owned a wooden house.

The preparations for the 'simple life' they lived there involved Leonie in weeks of planning. Hampers were brought up from the basement and filled with crockery and china, with feather beds and linen. City suits were laid up in mothballs; dirndls were washed, loden coats and alpen hats brought out of storage and the maids sent on by train.

And there, on a verandah overlooking the water, the Professor continued to write his book on *The Evolution of the Fossil Brain*, Hilda composed her papers for the Anthropological Society and Uncle Mishak fished. In the afternoons, however, pleasure erupted. Accompanied by friends, relatives and students who came to stay, they took excursions in rowing boats to uncomfortable islands or walked ecstatically across flower-filled meadows exclaiming '*Alpenrosen!*' or '*Enzian!*' Since a number of doctors, lawyers, theologians and string

4

quartets also had houses along the lake, some extremely high-powered conversations often grew up between one clump of flowers and the next. Midges bit people, splinters from the bathing huts lodged in their feet, bilberries stained their teeth – and each evening they gathered to watch the sun set behind the snow-capped mountains and shriek '*Wunderbar!*'

Then on the last day of August the dirndls were put away, the hampers packed – and everyone returned to Vienna for the first night of the Burg Theatre, the opening of the Opera, and the start of the university term.

It was into this fortunate family that – when the Professor was already approaching his forties and his wife had given up hope of a child – there was born a daughter whom they called Ruth.

Delivered by Vienna's most eminent obstetrician, her arrival brought a posse of *Herr Doktors, Herr Professors*, University Chancellors and Nobel Laureates to admire the baby, poke at her head with scholarly fingers and, quite frequently, quote from Goethe.

In spite of this roll call of the intelligentsia, Leonie sent for her old nurse from the Vorarlberg, who arrived with the wooden cradle that had been in the family for generations, and the baby lay under the chestnut tree in the courtyard, lulled by the sweet and foolish songs about roses and carnations and shepherds that country children drink in with their mother's milk. And at first it seemed that Ruth might turn into just such an Austrian *Wiegenkind*. Her hair, when it grew at last, was the colour of sunlight; her button nose attracted freckles, she had a wide, sweet smile. But no goose girl ever clasped the sides of her cot with such fierce resolution, nor had such enquiring, life-devouring dark brown eyes.

'A milkmaid with the eyes of Nefertiti,' said an eminent Egyptologist who came to dinner.

She adored talking, she needed to know everything; she was an infant fixer convinced she could put the world to rights.

'She shouldn't know such words,' said Leonie's friends, shocked.

But she had to know words. She had to know everything.

The Professor, a tall grey-bearded and patriarchal figure accustomed to the adulation of his students, nevertheless took her himself through the Natural History Museum where he had his own rooms. At six she was already familiar with the travail and complications that attend the reproductive act.

'Sex is a little bit sad, isn't it?' said Ruth, holding her father's hand, surveying the bottled wind spiders who bit off their partners' heads to make them mate faster. 'And the poor octopus . . . having to hold on to a female for twenty-four hours to let the eggs go down your tentacles.'

From her unworldly Aunt Hilda, who was apt to depart for the university with her skirt on back to front, Ruth learnt the value of tolerance.

'One must not judge other cultures by the standards

6

of one's own,' said Aunt Hilda, who was writing a monograph on her beloved Mi-Mi – and Ruth quite quickly accepted the compulsion of certain tribes to consume, ritually, their grandmothers.

The research assistants and demonstrators in the university all knew her, as did the taxidermists and preparators in the museum. At eight she was judged fit to help her father sort the teeth of the fossil cave bears he had found in the *Drachenhöhle* caves and it was understood that when she grew up she would be his assistant, type his books and accompany him on his field work.

Her little, bald-headed Uncle Mishak, still grieving for the death of his wife, led her into a different world. Mishak had spent twenty dutiful years in the personnel department of his brother's department store, but he was a countryman at heart and walked the city as he had walked the forests of Bohemia as a child. With Mishak, Ruth was always feeding something: a duck in the Stadtpark, a squirrel . . . or stroking something: a tired cab horse at the gates of the Prater, the stone toes of the god Neptune on the fountain in Schönbrunn.

And, of course, there was her mother, Leonie, end-lessly throwing out her arms, hugging her, scolding her . . . being unbearably hurt by an acid remark from a great-aunt, banishing the aunt to outer darkness, being noisily reconciled to the same aunt with enor-mous bunches of flowers . . . Carrying Ruth off to her grandfather's department store to equip her with sailor suits, with buckled patent leather shoes, with pleated

7

silk dresses, then yelling at her when she came in from school.

'Why aren't you top in English; you let that stupid Inge beat you,' she would cry – and then take Ruth off for consolation to Demels to eat chocolate eclairs. 'Well, she has a nose like an anteater so why shouldn't she be top in English,' Leonie would conclude, but the next year she imported a Scottish governess to make sure that no one spoke better English than her Ruth.

And so the child grew; volatile, passionate and clever, recommending birth control for her grand-mother's cat, yet crying inconsolably when she was cast as an icicle instead of the Snow Queen in the Christmas play at school.

'Doesn't she ever stop talking?' Leonie's friends would ask – yet she was easily extinguished. A snub, an unkind remark, silenced her instantly.

And something else . . . The sound of music.

Ruth's need for music was so much a part of her Viennese heritage that no one at first noticed how acute it was. Ever since infancy it had been almost impossi-ble to pull her away from music-making and she had her own places, music-places, she called them, to which she gravitated like a thirsty bullock to a water hole.

There was the ground-floor window of the shabby old *Hochschule für Musik* where the Ziller Quartet rehearsed, and the concert hall by the fruit market – the Musikverein – where, if the janitor had been kind enough to leave the door open, one could hear the Phil-harmonia play. One blind fiddler of all the beggars that

8

played in the streets would halt her, and when she listened she seemed to turn pale with concentration, as children do in sleep. Her parents were sympathetic, she had piano lessons which she enjoyed, she passed her exams, but she had a need of excellence which she herself could not provide.

So for a long time she had listened with wide eyes to the stories about her Cousin Heini in Budapest.

Heini was a scant year older than Ruth, and he was a boy in a fairy story. His mother, Leonie's stepsister, had married a Hungarian journalist called Radek and Heini lived in a place called the Hill of the Roses high above the Danube in a yellow villa surrounded by apple trees. A Turkish pasha was buried in a tomb further down on the slope of the hill; from Radek's balcony one could see the great river curling away towards the Hungarian plains, the graceful bridges and the spires and pinnacles of the Houses of Parliament like a palace in a dream. For in Budapest, unlike Vienna, the Danube flows through the city's very heart.

But that wasn't all. When he was three, Heini climbed onto his father's piano stool.

'It was like coming home,' he was to tell reporters afterwards. At the age of six, he gave his first recital in the hall where Franz Liszt had played. Two years later, a professor at the Academy invited Bartók to hear him play and the great man nodded.

But in fairy stories there is always grief. When Heini was eleven, his mother died and the golden *Wunderkind* became almost an orphan, for his father, who edited a

9

German language newspaper, was always working. So it was decided that Heini should continue his studies in Vienna and be prepared there for entrance to the Conservatoire. He would lodge with his teacher, an eminent Professor of Piano Studies, but his spare time would be spent with the Bergers.

Ruth never forgot the first time she saw him. She had come in from school and was hanging up her satchel when she heard the music. A slow piece, and sad, but underneath the sadness so right, so . . . consoled.

Her father and aunt were still at the university; her mother was in the kitchen conferring with the cook. Drawn by the music, she walked slowly through the enfilade of rooms: the dining room, the drawing room, the library – and opened the door of the study.

At first she saw only the great lid of the Bechstein like a dark sail filling the room. Then she peered round it – and saw the boy.

He had a thin face, black curls which tumbled over his forehead and large grey eyes, and when he saw her, his hands still moving over the keys, he smiled and said, 'Hello.'

She smiled too, awed at the delight it gave her to hear this music in her own home, overwhelmed by the authority, the excellence that came from him, young as he was.

'It's Mozart, isn't it?' she said, sighing, for she knew already that there was everything in Mozart; that if you stuck to him you couldn't go wrong. Two years earlier she had begun to attend to him in her daydreams, keeping him alive with her cookery and care long after his thirty-sixth year.

'Yes. The Adagio in B Minor.'

He finished playing and looked at her and found her entirely pleasing. He liked her fair hair in its old-fashioned heavy plait, her snub nose, the crisp white blouse and pleated pinafore. Above all, he liked the admiration reflected in her eyes.

'I musn't disturb you,' she said.

He shook his head. 'I don't mind you being here if you're quiet,' he said.

And then he told her about Mozart's starling.

'Mozart had a starling,' Heini said. 'He kept it in a cage in the room where he worked and he didn't mind it singing. In fact he liked it to be there and he used its song in the Finale of the G Major Piano Concerto. Did you know that?'

'No, I didn't.'

He watched the thick plait of hair swing to and fro as she shook her head.

Then: 'You can be *my* starling,' Heini said.

She nodded. It was an honour he was conferring; a great gift – she understood that at once.

'I would like that,' said Ruth.

And from then on, whenever she could, she settled quietly in the room where he practised, sometimes with her homework or a book, mostly just listening. She turned the pages for him when he played from a score, her small, square-tipped fingers touching the page as lightly as a moth. She waited for him after lessons, she

11

took his tattered Beethoven sonatas to the bookbinder to be rebound.

'She has become a handmaiden,' said Leonie, not entirely pleased.

But Ruth did not neglect her school work or her friends, somehow she found time for everything.

'I want to *live* like music *sounds*,' she had said once, coming out of a concert at the Musikverein.

Serving Heini, loving him, she drew closer to this idea.

So Heini stayed in Vienna and that summer, preceded by a hired piano, he joined the Bergers on the Grundlsee.

And that summer, too, the summer of 1930, a young Englishman named Quinton Somerville came to work with the Professor.

Quin was twenty-three years old at the time of his visit, but he had already spent eighteen months in Tübingen working under the famous palaeontologist Freiherr von Huene, and arrived in Vienna not only with a thorough knowledge of German, but with a formidable reputation for so young a man. While still at Cambridge, Quin had managed to get himself on to an expedition to the giant reptile beds of Tendaguru in Tanganyika. The following year he travelled to the Cape where the skull of *Australopithecus africanus* had turned up in a lime quarry, setting off a raging controversy about the origin of man, and came under the influence of the brilliant and eccentric Robert Broom

12

who hunted fossils in the nude and fostered Quin's interest in the hominids. To avoid guesswork and flamboyance when Missing Link expeditions were fighting each other for the 'dragon bones' of China, and scientists came to blows about the authenticity of Piltdown Man, was difficult, but Quin's doctoral thesis on the mammalian bone accumulations of the Olduvai Gorge was both erudite and sober.

Professor Berger met him at a conference and invited him to Vienna to give the Annual Lecture to the Palaeontological Society, suggesting he might stay on for a few weeks to help edit a new symposium of Vertebrate Zoology.

Quin came; the lecture was a success. He had just returned from Kenya and spoke with unashamed enthusiasm about the excitement of the excavations and the beauty of the land. It had been his intention to book into a hotel, but the Professor wouldn't hear of it.

'Of course you will stay with us,' he said, and took him to the Felsengasse where his family found themselves surprised. For it was well known that Englishmen, especially those who explored things and hung on the ends of ropes, were tall and fair with piercing blue eyes and braying, confident voices which disposed of natives and underlings. Or at best, if very well bred, they looked bleached and chiselled, like crusaders on a tomb, with long, stately noses and lean hands folded over their swords.

In all these matters, Quin was a disappointment. His face looked as though it needed ironing; the high forehead crumpled at a moment's notice into alarming furrows, his nose looked slightly broken, and the amused, enquiring eyes were a deep, almost a Mediterranean brown. Only the shapely hands with which he filled, poked at and tapped (but seldom lit) an ancient pipe, would have passed muster on a tomb.

'But his shoes are handmade,' declared Miss Kenmore, Ruth's Scottish governess. 'So he is definitely upper class.'

Leonie was inclined to believe this on account of the taxis. Quin, accompanying them to the opera or the theatre, had only to raise the fingers of one hand as they emerged for a taxi to perform a U-turn in the Ringstrasse and come to a halt in front of him.

'And there is the shooting,' said Ruth, for the Englishman, at the funfair in the Prater, had won a cut-glass bowl, a goldfish and an outsize blue rabbit and been requested by the irate owner of the booth to take his custom elsewhere. And what could that mean except a background of jolly shooting parties on breezy moors, disposing of pheasants, partridges and grouse?

The reality was different. Quin's mother died when he was born; his father, attached to the Embassy in Switzerland, volunteered in 1916 and was killed on the Somme. Sent back to the family home in Northumberland, Quin found himself in a house where everyone was old. An irascible, domineering grandfather – the terrifying 'Basher' Somerville – presided over Quin's first years at Bowmont and the spinster aunt who came to take over after his death hardly seemed younger. But if there was no one to show the orphaned boy affection, he was given something he knew how to value: his freedom.

'Let the boy run wild,' the family doctor sensibly advised when Quin, soon after his arrival, developed a prolonged and only partly explained fever. 'There's time for school later; he's bright enough.'

So Quin had his reprieve from the monotony of British boarding schools and furnished for himself a secret and entirely satisfactory world. Most children, especially only ones, have an invisible playmate who accompanies them through the day. Quin's, from the age of eight, was not an imaginary brother or understanding boy of his own age; it was a dinosaur. The creature – a brontosaurus whom he called Harry – stretched sixty feet; his head, when he put it through the nursery window, filled the room and its heart-warming smile was without menace for he ate only the bamboo in the shrubbery or the moist plants in the coppice which edged the lawn.

An article in *The Boy's Own Paper* had introduced him to Harry; Conan Doyle's *The Lost World* plunged him deeper into the fabled world of pre-history. He became the leader of the dinosaurs, a Mowgli of the Jurassic swamps who learnt to tame even the ghastly tyrannosaurus rex on whose back he rode.

'I must say, you don't have to spend time amusing him,' said his nurse, not realizing that nothing could compete with the dramas Quin enacted in his head.

From the dinosaurs, the boy went backwards and forwards in time. He read of the geological layers of the earth, of lobe-finned fishes and the mammals of the Pleistocene. By the time he was eleven, he was risking his life almost daily, scrambling down cliffs and quarries, searching for fossils embedded in the rock, and had started a collection in the old stables grandly labelled 'The Somerville Museum of Natural History'. As he grew older and Harry became dimmer in his mind, the museum was expanded to take in the marine specimens he found everywhere. For Quin's home looked out over the North Sea to the curving, sand-fringed sweep of Bowmont Bay whose rock pools were his nursery; the creatures inside them more interesting than any toy.

Quin would have been surprised if anyone had told him he was 'doing science' or becoming educated, but later, at Cambridge, he was amused by the solemnity with which they taught facts which he had learnt before his eleventh year, and the elaborate preparations for field trips to places he had clambered up and down in gym shoes.

He got a First in the Natural History Tripos with embarrassing ease, but his unfettered childhood made him reluctant to accept a permanent academic post. Financially independent since his eighteenth birthday, he had managed to spend the greater part of his time on expeditions to inaccessible parts of the world, yet now he fell in love with Vienna.

Not with the Vienna of operettas and cream cakes, though he took both politely from the hands of his hostess, but with the austere, arcaded courts of the university with its busts of old alumni resounding like a great roll call of the achievements of science. Doppler was there in stone, and Semmelweis who rid women of puerperal fever, and Billroth, the surgeon who befriended Brahms. In the library of the Hofburg, Quin spun the great gold-mounted globe which the Emperor Ferdinand had consulted to send his explorers forth. And in the Natural History Museum, he found a tiny, ugly, pot-bellied figurine, the Venus of Willendorf, priceless and guarded, made by man at the time when mammoths and sabre-toothed tigers still roamed the land.

When the university term ended, the Bergers begged him to join them on the Grundlsee.

'It's so *beautiful*,' said Ruth. 'The rain and the salamanders – and if you lie on your stomach on the landing stage you can see hundreds of little fishes between the boards like in a frame.'

He was due back in Cambridge, but he came and proved an excellent bilberry picker, an enthusiastic oarsman and a man able to shriek '*Wunderbar!*' with the best of them. If they enjoyed his company, he, in turn, took back treasured memories of Austrian country life: Tante Hilda in striped bathing bloomers performing a violent breaststroke without moving from the spot . . . The Professor's ancient mother running her wheelchair at a trespassing goat . . . And Klaus Biberstein, the second violin of the Ziller quartet, who loved Leonie but had a weak digestion, creeping out at midnight to feed his secreted *Knödel* to the fish.

17

Of Ruth he saw relatively little, for in one of those wooden huts so beloved of Austrian musicians, her Cousin Heini practised the piano and she was busy carrying jugs of milk or plates of biscuits to and fro. Once he found her sitting by the shore with a somewhat surprising collection of books. Krafft-Ebing's *Sexual Pathology*, *Little Women* and a cowboy story with a lurid cover called *Jake's Last Stand*.

It was the Krafft-Ebing she was perusing with a furrowed brow.

'Goodness!' he said. 'Are you allowed to read that?'

She nodded. 'I'm allowed to read everything,' she said. 'Only I have to eat everything too, even semolina.'

But on the night before he had to leave, Miss Kenmore could no longer be gainsaid and Quin was informed that Ruth would recite Keats' 'Ode to a Nightingale' for him after supper.

'She has it entirely by heart, Dr Somerville,' she said – and Quin, repressing a sigh, joined the family in the drawing room with its long windows open to the lake.

Ruth's fair hair had been brushed out; she wore a velvet ribbon – clearly the occasion was important – yet at first Quin was compelled to look at the floor and school his expression, for she spoke the famous lines in the unmistakable accent of Aberdeen.

Only when she came to the penultimate verse, to the part of the poem that belonged personally to her, for it was about her namesake, did he lift his head, caught by something in her voice.

Perhaps the self-same song that found a path
Through the sad heart of Ruth, when, sick for home,
She stood in tears among the alien corn . . .

Hackneyed lines, lines he had grown weary of at school, they still had power to stir him.

Yet no one there, not one of the people who loved her, not Quin, not Ruth herself, enjoying the poem's sadness, were touched by a single glimmer of premonition. No hairs lifted on the nape of any necks; no ghosts walked over the quiet waters of the lake. That this protected, much-loved child should ever have to leave her native land, was unimaginable.

The next day, Quin left for England. The family all came to see him off and begged him to come back soon – but it was eight years before he returned to Vienna and then he came to a different city and a different world.

1

On the day that Hitler marched into Vienna, Professor Somerville was leading his not noticeably grateful expedition down a defile so narrow that overshadowing precipices blocked out all but a strip of the clear blue sky of Central Asia.

'You can't possibly get the animals down this way,' a Belgian geologist he had been compelled to take along had complained.

But Quin had just said vaguely that he thought it might be all right, by which he meant that if everyone nearly killed themselves and did exactly what he told them, there was a chance – and now, sure enough, the chasm widened, they passed the first trees growing wherever roots could take hold, and made their way through forests of pine and cedar to reach, at last, the bottom of the valley.

'We'll camp here,' said Quin, pointing to a place where the untroubled river, idling past, dragged at the overhanging willows, and drifts of orchids and asphodels studded the grass.

Later, when the mules were grazing and the smoke from the fire curled upwards in the still air, he leant back against a tree and took out the battered pipe which many women had tried to replace. He was thirty years old now, lines were etched into the crumpled-looking forehead and the sides of the mouth, and the dark eyes could look hard, but at this moment he was entirely happy. For he had been right. In spite of the gloomy prognostications of the Belgian whose spectacles had been stepped on by a yak; in spite of the assurances of his porters that it was impossible to reach the remoter valleys of the Siwalik Range in the spring, he had found as rich a collection of Miocene fossils as anyone could hope for. Wrapped now in woodwool and canvas, more valuable than any golden treasure from a tomb, was the unmistakable evidence of *Ramapithecus*, one of the earliest ancestors of man.

There were three weeks of travelling still along the river valley before they could load their specimens onto lorries for the drive down to Simla, but the problems now would be social: the drinking of terrible tea with the villagers, bedbugs, hospitality . . .

A lammergeier hung like a nail in the sky. The bells of browsing cattle came from a distant meadow, and the wail of a flute.

Quin closed his eyes.

News of the outside world when it came at last was brought by an Indian army officer in the rest house

21

above Simla and was delivered in the order of importance. Oxford had won the Boat Race, an outsider
named Battleship had romped home at Aintree.

'Oh, and Hitler's annexed Austria. Marched into
Vienna without a shot being fired.'

'Will you still go?' asked Milner, his research assistant and a trusted friend.

'I don't know.'

'I suppose it's a terrific honour. I mean, they don't
give away degrees in a place like that.'

Quin shrugged. It was not the first honorary degree
he had been awarded. Persuaded three years ago to take
up a professorship in London, he still managed to
pursue his investigations in the more exotic corners of
the world, and he had been lucky with his finds.

'Berger arranged it. He's Dean of the Science Faculty
now. If it wasn't for him I doubt if I'd go; I've no desire
to go anywhere near the Nazis. But I owe him a lot and
his family were very good to me. I stayed with them one
summer.'

He smiled, remembering the excitable, affectionate
Bergers, the massive meals in the Viennese apartment,
and the wooden house on the Grundlsee. There'd been
an accident-prone anthropologist whose monograph on
the Mi-Mi had fallen out of a rowing boat, and a pigtailed little girl with a biblical name he couldn't now
recall. Rachel . . .? Hannah . . .?

'I'll go,' he decided. 'If I jump ship at Izmir I can con-
nect with the Orient Express. It won't delay me more
than a couple of days. I know I can trust you to see the

22

stuff through the customs, but if there's any trouble I'll sort it out when I come.'

The pigeons were still there, wheeling as if to music in this absurdly music-minded city; the cobbles, the spire of St Stephan's glimpsed continually from the narrow streets as his taxi took him from the station. The smell of vanilla too, as he pulled down the windows, and the lilacs and laburnums in the park.

But the swastika banners now hung from the windows, relics of the city's welcome to the Führer, groups of soldiers with the insignia of the SS stood together on street corners – and when the taxi turned into a narrow lane, he saw the hideous daubings on the doors of Jewish shops, the broken windows.

In Sacher's Hotel he found that his booking had been honoured. The welcome was friendly, Kaiser Franz Joseph in his mutton chop whiskers still hung in the foyer, not yet replaced by the Führer's banal face. But in the bar three German officers with their peroxided girlfriends were talking loudly in Berlin accents. Even if there had been time to have a drink, Quin would not have joined them. In fact there was no time at all for the unthinkable had happened and the fabled Orient Express had developed engine trouble. Changing quickly into a dark suit, he hurried to the university. Berger's secretary had written to him before he left England, explaining that robes would be hired for him, and all degree ceremonies were much the same. It was only necessary to follow the person in front in the manner of penguins.

All the same, it was even later than he had realized. Groups of men in scarlet and gold, in black and purple, with hoods bound in ermine or tasselled caps, stood on the steps; streams of proud relatives in their best clothes moved through the imposing doors.

'Ah, Professor Somerville, you are expected, everything is ready.' The Registrar's secretary greeted him with relief. 'I'll take you straight to the robing room. The Dean was hoping to welcome you before the ceremony, but he's already in the hall so he'll meet you at the reception.'

'I'm looking forward to seeing him.'

Quin's gown of scarlet silk, lined with palatine purple, was laid out on a table beside a card bearing his name. The velvet hat was too big, but he pushed it onto the back of his head and went out to join the other candidates waiting in the anteroom.

The organist launched into a Bach passacaglia, and between a fat lady professor from the Argentine and what seemed to be the oldest entomologist in the world, Quin marched down the aisle of the Great Hall towards the Chancellor's throne.

As he'd expected in this city, where even the cab horses were caparisoned, the ceremony proceeded with the maximum of pomp. Men rose, doffed their caps, bowed to each other, sat down again. The organ pealed. Long-dead alumni in golden frames stared down from the wall.

24

Seated to the right of the dais, Quin, looking for Berger in the row of academics opposite, was impeded by the hat of the lady professor from the Argentine who seemed to be wearing an outsize academic soup tureen.

One by one, the graduates to be honoured were called out to have their achievements proclaimed in Latin, to be hit on the shoulder by a silver sausage containing the charter bestowed on the university by the Emperor Maximilian, and receive a parchment scroll. Quin, helping the entomologist from his chair, wondered whether the old gentleman would survive being hit by anything at all, but he did. The fat lady professor went next. His view now unimpeded, Quin searched the gaudily robed row of senior university members but could see no sign of Berger. It was eight years since they had met, but surely he would recognize that wise, dark face?

His turn now.

'It has been decided to confer the degree of Doctor of Science, Honoris Causa on Quinton Alexander St John Somerville. The public orator will now introduce Professor Somerville to you.'

Quin rose and went to stand facing the Chancellor, one of whose weak blue eyes was partly obscured by the golden tassel hanging from his cap. While the fulsome platitudes in praise of his achievements rolled out, Quin grew increasingly uneasy – and suddenly what had seemed to be an archaic but not undignified attempt to maintain the traditions of the past, became a travesty, an absurd charade mouthed by puppets.

The oration ceased, leaving him the youngest professor in the University of Thameside, Fellow of the Royal Society, Gold Medallist of the Geographical Association and the Sherlock Holmes of pre-history whose inspired investigations had unlocked the secrets of the past.

Quin scowled and climbed the dais. The Chancellor raised his sausage – and recoiled.

'The chap looked as though he wanted to kill me,' he complained afterwards.

Quin mastered himself, took the scroll, returned to his place.

And now at last it was over and he could ask the question that had haunted him throughout the tedious ceremony.

'Where is Professor Berger?'

He had spoken to the Registrar whose pale eyes slid away from him.

'Professor Berger is no longer with us. But the new Dean, Professor Schlesinger, is waiting to greet you.'

'I, however, am not waiting to greet him. Where is Professor Berger? Please answer my question.'

The Registrar shuffled his feet. 'He has been relieved of his post.'

'Why?'

'The Nuremberg Laws were implemented immediately after the Anschluss. Nobody who is not racially pure can hold high office.' He took a step backwards. 'It's not my fault, I'm only –'

'Where is Berger? Is he still in Vienna?'

The Registrar shook his head. 'I don't know. Many Jews have been trying to emigrate.'

'Find me his last address.'

'Yes, Professor, certainly, after the reception.'

'No, not after the reception,' said Quin. *Now.*

He remembered the street but not, at first, the house. Then a particularly well-nourished pair of caryatids sent him through an archway and into the courtyard. The concierge was not in her box; no one impeded him as he made his way up the wide marble staircase to the first floor.

Professor Berger's brass plate was still screwed onto the door, but the door itself, surprisingly, was ajar. He pushed it open. Here in the old days he had been met by a maid in a black apron, but there was no one there. The Professor's umbrella and walking sticks were still in the stand, his hat hung on its hook. Making his way down the passage with its thick Turkey carpet, he knocked on the door of the study and opened it. He had spent many hours here working on the symposium, awed by Berger's scholarship and the generosity with which he shared his ideas. The Professor's books lined the wall, the Remington, under its black cover, stood on the desk.

Yet the silence was eerie. He thought of the *Mary Celeste*, the boat found abandoned in mid-ocean with the cups still on the table, the uneaten food. A double door led from the study into the dining room with its massive table and tall leather-backed chairs. The Meissen plates were still on the dresser; a cup the Professor had won for fencing stood on the sideboard. Increasingly puzzled, he moved on into the drawing room. The paintings of alpine landscapes hung undisturbed on the walls; the Professor's war medals lay in their cases under glass. A palm tree in a brass pot had been watered – yet he had never sensed such desolation, such emptiness.

No, not emptiness after all. In a distant room some-one was playing the piano. Hardly playing, though, for one phrase was repeated again and again: an incongru-ous, chirruping phrase like the song of a bird.

He was in the rooms facing the courtyard now, open-ing more doors. And now a last door, and the source of the sound. A girl, her head cradled in the curve of her arm as it lay on the piano, the other hand touching the keys. In the moment before she noticed him, he saw how weary she was, how bereft of hope. Then she lifted her head and as she looked at him he remembered, suddenly, her name.

'You must be Professor Berger's daughter. You must be Ruth.'

It was a certain triumph, his recognition, for much had happened to the pretty, prattling child with her flaxen pigtail. A kind of Rapunzel situation had developed with her hair; still blonde, but loose to below her shoul-ders and shot through with colours that were hard to name . . . ash . . . bronze . . . a sort of greenish gold that was almost khaki. Inside its mass as she waited, perhaps, for a prince to ascend its tresses, was a pale triangular face with dark smudged eyes.

'What were you playing?' he asked.

She looked down at the keys. 'It's the theme of the last movement of the G Major Piano Concerto by Mozart. It's supposed to be based on the song of a starling that –' Her voice broke and she bent her head to vanish, for a moment, into the privacy accorded by her tumbled hair. But now she, too, recalled the past. 'Of course! You're Professor Somerville! I remember when you came before and we were so disappointed. You were supposed to have sunburnt knees and a voice like Richard the Lionheart's.'

'What sort of a voice did he have?'

'Oh, *loud*! Horses used to kneel at his shout, didn't you know?'

Quin shook his head, but he was amazed, for she had pushed back her hair and smiled at him – and in an instant the beleaguered captive in her tower vanished and it was summertime on an alp with cows. It was not the eyes one noticed now, but the snub nose, the wide mouth, the freckles. 'Of course, it was the degree ceremony today, wasn't it? My father tried to contact you while he was still allowed to telephone. Did it go all right?'

Quin shrugged. 'Where is your father?'

'He's in England. In London. My mother too, and my aunt . . . and Uncle Mishak. They went a week ago. And Heini as well – he's gone to Budapest to pick up his visa and then he's joining them.'

29

'And left you behind?'

It didn't seem possible. He remembered her as, if anything, over-protected, too much indulged.

She shook her head. 'They sent me ahead. But it all went wrong.' It was over now, the pastoral time on the alp with cows. Her eyes filled with tears; one hand clenched itself into a fist which she pressed against her cheek as though to hold in grief. 'It went completely wrong. And I'm trapped here now. There is nobody left.'

'Tell me,' said Quin. 'I've plenty of time. Tell me exactly what happened. And come away from the piano so that we can be comfortable.' For he had understood that the piano was some special source of grief.

'No.' She was still the good university child who knew the ritual. 'It's the Chancellor's Banquet. There's always a dinner after the honorary degrees. You'll be expected.'

'You can't imagine I would dine with those people,' he said quietly. 'Now start.'

Her father had begun even before the Anschluss, trying to get her a student visa.

'We still hoped the Austrians would stand out against Hitler, but he'd always wanted me to study in England – that's why he sent me to the English School here after my governess left. I was in my second year, reading Natural Sciences. I was going to help my father till Heini and I could . . .'

'Who's Heini?'

'He's my cousin. Well, sort of . . . He and I . . .'

Sentences about Heini did not seem to be the kind she finished. But Quin now had recalled the prodigy in his wooden hut. He could attach no face to Heini, only the endless sound of the piano, but now there came the image of the pigtailed child carrying wild strawberries in her cupped hands to where he played. It had lasted then, her love for the gifted boy.

'Go on.'

'It wasn't too difficult. If you don't want to emigrate for good, the British don't mind. I didn't even have to have a J on my passport because I'm only partly Jewish. The Quakers were marvellous. They arranged for me to go on a student transport from Graz.'

As soon as her departure was settled, her parents had sent her to Graz to wait.

'They wanted me out of the way because I'd kicked a Brown Shirt and –'

'Good God!'

She made a gesture of dismissal. 'Anyway, after I went, my father was suddenly arrested. They took him to that hell hole by the Danube Canal – the Gestapo House. He was held there for days and no one told me. Then they released him and told him he had to leave the country within a week with his family or be taken to a camp. They were allowed to take just one suitcase each and ten German marks – you can't live for a day on that, but of course nothing mattered as long as they could get away. I'd gone ahead on the student transport two days before.'

'So what happened?'

'We got to the border and then a whole lot of SS people got on. They were looking for our Certificates of Harmlessness.'

'Your *what*?'

She passed a hand over her forehead and he thought he'd never seen anyone so young look so tired. 'It's some new piece of paper – they invent them all the time. It's to show you haven't been politically active. They don't want to send people abroad who are going to make trouble for the regime.'

'And you hadn't got one?'

She shook her head. 'At the university there was a boy who'd been to Russia. I'd read Dostoevsky, of course, and I thought one should be on the side of the proletariat and go to Siberia with people in exile and all that. I'd always worried because we seemed to have so much. I mean, it can't be right that some people should have everything and others nothing.'

'No, it can't be right. But what to do about it isn't always simple.'

'Anyway, I didn't become a Communist like he was because they kept on calling each other "Comrade" and then quarrelling, but I joined the Social Democrats and we marched in processions and had fights with the Brown Shirts. It seems childish now – we thought we were so fierce. And, of course, all the time the authorities had me down as a dangerous radical!'

'So by the time they took you off the student train your parents had gone?'

32

'No, they hadn't actually. I phoned a friend of theirs because they'd cut off our telephone and she said they were off the next day. I knew that if they realized I was still in Austria they wouldn't go, so I went to stay with our old cook in Grinzing till they left.'

'That was brave,' said Quin quietly.

She shrugged. 'It was very difficult, I must say. The most difficult thing I've ever done.'

'And with luck the most difficult thing you'll ever have to do.'

She shook her head. 'I think not.' The words were almost inaudible. 'I think that for my people, night has come.'

'Nonsense.' He spoke with deliberate briskness. 'There'll be a way of helping you. I'll go to the British Consulate in the morning.'

Again that shake of the head, sending the blonde, absurdly abundant hair swinging on her shoulders. 'I've tried everything. There's a man called Eichmann who runs something called the Department of Emigration. He's supposed to help people to leave, but what he really does is make sure they're stripped of everything they own. You don't know what it's like – people weeping and shouting . . .'

He had risen and begun to walk up and down, needing to think. 'What a huge place this is!'

She nodded. 'Twelve rooms. My grandmother had two of them, but she died last year. When I was small I used to ride round and round the corridors on my tricycle.' She followed him. 'That's my father in the

33

uniform of the 14th Uhlans. He was decorated twice for bravery – he couldn't believe that none of that counted.'

'Is he completely Jewish?'

'By birth, yes. I don't think he ever thought about it. His religion was to do with people . . . with everyone trying to make themselves into the best sort of person they could be. He believed in a God that belonged to everyone . . . you had to guard the spark that was in you and make it into a flame. And my mother was brought up as a Catholic so it's doubly hard for her. She's only half-Jewish, or maybe a quarter, we're not quite sure. She had a very Aryan mother – a sort of goat-herding lady.'

'So that makes you . . . what? Three-quarters? Five-eighths? It's hard to believe.'

She smiled. 'My snub nose, you mean – and being fair? My grandmother came from the country – the goat-herding one. My grandfather really found her tending goats – well, almost. She came from a farm. We used to laugh at her a bit and call her Heidi; she never opened a book in her life, but I'm grateful to her now because I look like her and no one ever molests me.'

They had reached a glassed-in verandah overlooking the courtyard. In the corner beside an oleander in a tub, was a painted cradle adorned with roses and lilies. Over the headboard, painstakingly scrolled, were the words *Ruthie's cradle*.

Quin set it rocking with the toe of his shoe. Beside him, Ruth had fallen silent. Down in the courtyard a single tree – a chestnut in full blossom – stretched out its arms. A swing was suspended from one branch; on a washing line strung between two posts hung a row of red-and-white checked tea towels, and a baby's shirt no bigger than a handkerchief.

'I used to play down there,' she said. 'All through my childhood. It seemed so safe to me. The safest place in the world.'

He had made no sound, yet something made her turn to look at him. She had thought of the Englishman as kind and civilized. Now the crumpled face looked devilish: the mouth twisted, the skin stretched tight over the bones. It lasted only a moment, his transformation into someone to fear. Then he laid a hand lightly on her arm.

'You'll see. There will be something we can do.'

Ruth had not exaggerated. There were no words to describe the chaos and despair the Anschluss had caused. He had arrived early at the British Consulate but already there were queues. People begged for pieces of paper – visas, passports, permits – as the starving begged for bread.

'I'm sorry, sir, I can't do anything about this,' said the clerk, looking at Ruth's documents. 'It's not the British refusing to let her in, it's the Austrians refusing to let her out. She'd have to re-apply for emigration and that could take months or years. The quota's full, as you know.'

'If I was willing to sponsor her – to guarantee she wouldn't be a burden on the state? Or get her a domestic work permit? My family would offer her employment.'

'You'd have to do that from England, sir. Everything's at sixes and sevens here with Austria no longer being an independent state. The Embassy's going to close and they're sending staff home all the time.'

'Look, the girl's twenty years old. Her entire family's in England – she's alone in the world.'

'I'm sorry, sir,' the young man repeated wearily. 'Believe me, the things I've seen here . . . but there's nothing that can be done at this end. At least nothing you'd consider.'

'And what wouldn't I consider?'

The young man told him.

Oh, bother the girl, thought Quin. He had a sleeper booked on the evening train; the exams began in less than a week. When he took his sabbatical, he'd promised to be back for the end of term. Letting his deputy mark his papers was no part of his plan.

He turned into the Felsengasse and went up to the first floor. The door was wide open. In the hallway, the mirror was smashed, the umbrella stand lay on its side. The word *Jude* had been smeared in yellow paint across the photograph of the Professor shaking hands with the Kaiser. In the drawing room, pictures had been ripped off the walls; the palm tree, tipped out of its pot, lay sprawled on the carpet. The silver ornaments were missing, the Afghan rug . . . In the dining room, the doors were torn from the dresser, the Meissen porcelain was gone.

On the verandah, Ruth's painted cradle had been kicked into splintered wood.

He had forgotten the physical effects of rage. He had to draw several deep breaths before the giddiness passed and he could turn and go downstairs.

This time the concierge was in her box.

'What happened to Professor Berger's apartment?'

She looked nervously at the open door, behind which he could see an old man with his legs stretched out, reading a paper.

'They came . . . some Brown Shirts . . . just a gang of thugs. They do that when an apartment is abandoned. It's not official, but no one stops them.' She sniffed. 'I don't know what to do. The Professor asked me to look after his flat, but how can I? A German diplomat is moving in next week.'

'And Fräulein Berger? What happened to her?'

'I don't know.' Another uneasy glance through the open door. 'I can't tell you anything.'

He was halfway down the street when he heard her cracked old voice calling him – and as he turned she came hurrying up, still in her foulard apron.

'She gave me this to give you. But you won't say anything, will you, *Herr Doktor*? My husband's been a Nazi for years and he'd never forgive me. I could get into awful trouble.'

She handed him a white envelope from which, when he opened it, there fell two keys.

2

Ruth had always loved the statue of the Empress Maria Theresia on her marble plinth. Flanked by her generals, a number of horses and some box hedges, she gazed at the strolling Viennese with the self-satisfied look of a good hausfrau who has left her larder full and her cupboards tidy. Every school child knew that it was she who had made Austria great, that the six-year-old Mozart had sat on her knee, that her daughter, Marie Antoinette, had married the King of France and lost her head.

But for Ruth the plump and homely Empress was something more: she was the guardian of the two great museums which flanked the square that bore her name. To the south was the Museum of Art – a gigantic, mock Renaissance palace which housed the famous Titians, the Rembrandts, the finest Brueghels in the world. To the north – its replica down to the last carved pillar and ornamented dome – was the Museum of Natural History. As a child she had loved both museums. The Art

Museum belonged to her mother and it was filled with uplift and suffering and love – rather a lot of love. The Madonnas loved their babies, Jesus loved the poor sinners, and St Francis loved the birds.

In the Natural History Museum there wasn't any love, only sex – but there were stories and imagined journeys – and there was *work*. This was her father's world and Ruth, when she went there, was a child set apart. For when she had had her fill of the cassowary on his nest and the elephant seal with his enormous, rearing chest, and the glinting ribbons of the snakes, each in its jar of coloured fluid, she could go through a magic door and enter, like Alice, a secret, labyrinthine world.

For here, behind the gilded, silent galleries with their grey-uniformed attendants, was a warren of preparation rooms and laboratories, of workshops and sculleries and offices. It was here that the real work of the museum was done: here was the nerve centre of scholarship and expertise which reached out to every country in the world. Since she was tiny, Ruth had been allowed to watch and help. Sometimes there was a dinosaur being assembled on a stand; sometimes she was allowed to sprinkle preservative on a stretched-out skin or polish glass slides for a histologist drawing the mauve and scarlet tissues of a cell, and her father's room was as familiar to her as his study in the Felsengasse.

In earlier times, Ruth might have sought sanctuary in a temple or a church. Now, homeless and desolate, she came to this place.

It was Tuesday, the day the museum was closed to the public. Silently, she opened the side door and made her way up the stairs.

Her father's room was exactly as he had left it. His lab coat was behind the door; his notes, beside a pile of reprints, were on the desk. On a work bench by the window was the tray of fossil bones he had been sorting before he left. No one yet had unscrewed his name from the door, nor confiscated the two sets of keys, one of which she had left with the concierge.

She put her suitcase down by the filing cabinet and wandered through into the cloakroom with its gas ring and kettle. Leading out of it was a preparation room with shelves of bottles and a camp bed on which scientists or technicians working long hours sometimes slept for a while.

'Oh God, let him come,' prayed Ruth.

But why should he come, this Englishman who owed her nothing? Why should he even have got the keys she had left with the concierge? Hardly aware of what she was doing, she pulled a stool towards the tray of jumbled bones and began, with practised fingers, to separate out the vertebrae, brushing them free of earth and fragments of rock. As she bent forward, her hair fell on the tray and she gathered it together and twisted it into a coil, jamming a long-handled paintbrush through its mass. Heini liked her hair long and she'd learnt that trick from a Japanese girl at the university.

The silence was palpable. It was early evening now; everyone had gone home. Not even the water pipes, not even the lift, made their usual sounds. Painstakingly, pointlessly, Ruth went on sorting the ancient cave bear bones and waited without hope for the arrival of the Englishman.

Yet when she heard the key turn in the door, she did not dare to turn her head. Then came footsteps which, surprisingly, were already familiar, and an arm stretched over her shoulder so that for a moment she felt the cloth of his jacket against her cheek.

'No, not that one,' said a quiet voice. 'I think you'll find that doesn't match the type. Look at the size of the neural canal.'

She leant back in her chair, feeling suddenly safe, remembering the hands of her piano teacher coming down over her own to help her with an errant chord.

Quin, meanwhile, was registering a number of features revealed by Ruth's skewered hair: ears . . . the curve of her jaw . . . and those vulnerable hollows at the back of the neck which prevent the parents of young children from murdering them.

'How quick you are,' she said, watching his long fingers move among the fragmented bones. And then: 'You had no luck at the Consulate?'

'No, I had no luck. But we'll get you out of Vienna. What happened back at the flat? Did you save anything?'

She pointed to her suitcase. 'Frau Hautermanns warned me that they were coming.'

'The concierge?'

'Yes. I packed some things and went down the fire escape. They weren't after me. Not this time.'

He was silent, still automatically sorting the specimens. Then he pushed away the tray.

'Have you eaten anything today?'

She shook her head.

'Good. I've brought a picnic. Rather a special one. Where shall we have it?'

'I suppose it ought to be in here. I can clear the table and there's another chair next door.'

'I said a *picnic*,' said Quin sternly. 'In Britain a picnic means sitting on the ground and being uncomfortable, preferably in the rain. Now where shall we go? Africa? You have a fine collection of lions, I see; a little moth-eaten perhaps, but very nicely mounted. Or there's the Amazon – I'm partial to anacondas, aren't you? No, wait; what about the Arctic? I've brought rather a special Chablis and it's best served chilled.'

Ruth shook her head. 'The polar bear was almost my favourite when I was small, but I don't want to get chilblains – I might drop my sandwiches. You don't want to go back in time? To the Dinosaur Hall?'

'No. Too much like work. And frankly I'm not too happy about that ichthyosaurus. Whoever assembled that skeleton had a *lot* of imagination.'

Ruth flushed. 'It was old Schumacher. He was very ill and he so much wanted to get it finished before he died.' And then: 'I know! Let's go to Madagascar! *The Ancient Continent of Lemuria!* There's an aye-aye there, a baby – such a sad-looking little thing. You'll really like the aye-aye.'

Quin nodded. 'Madagascar it shall be. Perhaps you can find us a towel or some newspaper; that's all we need. I'm sure eating here's against the regulations but we won't let that trouble us.'

She disappeared into the cloakroom and came back with a folded towel, and with her hair released from its skewer. There could be doubts about her face thought Quin, with its contrasting motifs, but none about her impossible, unruly, unfashionable hair. Touched now by the last rays of the sinking sun, it gave off a tawny, golden warmth that lifted the heart.

It was a strange walk they took through the enormous, shadowy rooms, watched by creatures preserved for ever in their moment of time. Antelopes no bigger than cats raised one leg, ready to flee across the sandy veld. The monkeys of the New World hung, huddled and melancholy, from branches – and by a window a dodo, idiotic-looking and extinct, sat on a nest of reconstructed eggs.

Madagascar was all that Ruth had promised. Ring-tailed lemurs with piebald faces held nuts in their amazingly human hands. A pair of indris, cosy and fluffy like children's toys, groomed each other's fur. Tiny mouse lemurs clustered round a coconut.

And alone, close to the glass, the aye-aye . . . Only half-grown, hideous and melancholy, with huge despairing eyes, naked ears and one uncannily extended finger, like the finger of a witch.

'I don't know why I like it so much,' said Ruth. 'I suppose because it's a sort of outcast – so ugly and lonely and sad.'

'It has every reason to be sad,' said Quin. 'The natives are terrified of them – they run off shrieking when they see one. Though I did find one tribe who believe they have the power to carry the souls of the dead to heaven.'

She turned to him eagerly. 'Of course, you've been there, haven't you? With the French expedition? It must be so beautiful!'

Quin nodded. 'It's like nowhere else on earth. The trees are so tangled with vines and orchids – you can't believe the scent. And the sunbirds, and the chameleons . . .'

'You're so lucky. I was going to travel with my father as soon as I was old enough, but now . . .' She groped for her handkerchief and tried again. 'I'm sure that tribe was right,' she said, turning back to the aye-aye. 'I'm sure they can carry the souls of the dead to heaven.' She was silent for a moment, looking at the pathetic embalmed creature behind the glass. 'You can have my soul,' she said under her breath. 'You can have it any time you like.'

Quin glanced at her but said nothing. Instead, he took the towel and spread it on the parquet. Then he began to unpack the hamper.

There was a jar of pâté and another of pheasant breasts. There were fresh rolls wrapped in a snowy napkin and pats of butter in a tiny covered dish. He had brought the first Morello cherries and grapes and two chocolate soufflés in fluted pots. The plates were of real china; the long-stemmed goblets of real glass.

'I think you'll like the wine,' said Quin, lifting a bottle out of its wooden coffin. 'And I haven't forgotten the corkscrew!'

'How did you *do* it all? How could you get all that? How did you have the time?'

'I just went into a shop and told them what I wanted. It only took ten minutes. All I had to do was pay.'

She watched him lay out the picnic, amazed that he was thus willing to serve her. Was it British to be like this, or was it something about him personally? Her father – all the men she knew – would have sat back and waited for their wives.

When it was finished it was like a banquet in a fairy story, yet like playing houses when one was a child. But when she began to eat, there were no more thoughts; she was famished; it was all she could do to remember her manners.

'Oh, it's so *good*! And the wine is absolutely lovely. It's not strong, is it?'

'Well . . .' He was about to advise caution but decided against it. Tonight she was entitled to repose however it was brought about.

'Where have your parents gone to?' he said presently, as they sat side by side, leaning their backs against a radiator. 'I mean, what part of London?'

'Belsize Park. It's in the north-west, do you know it?'

'Yes.' The dreary streets with their dilapidated

Victorian terraces, the cat-infested gardens of what had once been a prosperous suburb, passed before his mind. 'A lot of refugees live there,' he said cheerfully. 'And it's very near Hampstead Heath, which is beautiful.' (Near, but not very near . . . Hampstead, at the top of the hill, was a different world with its pretty cottages, its magnolia trees, and the blue plaques announcing that Keats had lived there, and Robert Louis Stevenson, and a famous Admiral of the Fleet.) 'And Heini will go there too?'

'Yes; very soon. He's in Budapest getting his emigration papers and saying goodbye to his father, but there won't be any trouble. He's Hungarian and the Nazis don't have anything to say there. He had to go quickly because he's completely Jewish. After the goatherding lady died, my grandfather married the daughter of a rabbi who already had a little girl – she was a widow – and that was Heini's mother, so we're not blood relations.' She turned to him, cupping her glass. 'He's a marvellous pianist. A real one. He was going to have his debut with the Philharmonic . . . three days after Hitler marched in.'

'That's rough.'

'Yes. He was absolutely frantic. I didn't know how to comfort him; not properly.'

She retreated momentarily into her hair.

'And you're going to get married?'

'Yes . . . Well, Heini doesn't talk a lot about getting married because he's a musician . . . an artist . . . and they don't talk much about bourgeois things like marriage – but we're going to be together. Properly, I mean. We were going to go away together after the concert, to Italy. I'd have gone earlier but my parents are very old-fashioned . . . also there was the thing about Chopin and the études.'

The fork which Quin had been conveying to his mouth stayed arrested in his hand. 'I'm sorry, I'm afraid you've lost me. How do Chopin études come into this?'

Too late, Ruth realized where she was heading and looked with horror at her empty glass, experiencing the painful moment when it becomes clear that what has been drunk cannot be undrunk. It had been so lovely, the wine, like drinking fermented hope or happiness, and now she was babbling and being indiscreet and would end up in the gutter, a confirmed absinthe drinker destined for a pauper's grave.

But Quin was waiting and she plunged.

'Heini had a professor who told him that Chopin thought that every time he made love he was depriving the world of an étude. I mean that . . . you know . . . the same energy goes into composing and . . . the other thing. A sort of vital force. And this professor thought it was good for Heini to wait. But then Heini found out that the professor was wrong about the way to finger the Appassionata, so then he thought maybe he was wrong about Chopin too. Because there was George Sand, wasn't there?'

'There was indeed,' said Quin, deeply entertained by this gibberish. It wasn't till they had finished the meal and Ruth, moving nimbly in the gathering darkness, had cleared away and packed up the hamper, that he said: 'I've been thinking what to do. I think we must get you out of Vienna to somewhere quiet and safe in the country. Then we can start again from England. I know a couple of people in the Foreign Office; I'll be able to pull strings. I doubt if anyone will bother you away from the town and I shall make sure that you have plenty of money to see you through. With your father and all of us working away at the other end we'll be able to get you across before too long. But you must get away from here. Is there anyone you could go to?'

'There's my old nurse. She lives by the Swiss border, in the Vorarlberg. She'd have me, but I don't know if I ought to inflict myself on anyone. If I'm unclean –'

'Don't talk like that,' he said harshly. 'And don't insult people who love you and will want to help you. Now tell me exactly where she lives and I'll see to everything. What about tonight?'

'I'm going to stay here. There's a camp bed.'

He was about to protest, suggesting that she come back to Sacher's, but the memory of the German officers crowding the bar prevented him.

'Take care then. What about the night watchman?'

'He won't come into my father's room. And if he does, he's known me since I was a baby.'

'You can't trust anyone,' he said.

'If I can't trust Essler, I'll die,' said Ruth.

At two in the morning, Quin got out of bed and wondered what had made him leave a girl hardly out of the schoolroom to spend a night alone in a deserted building full of shadows and ghosts. Dressing quickly, he made his way down the Ringstrasse, crossed the Theresienplatz, and let himself in by the side entrance.

Ruth was asleep on the camp bed in the preparation room. Her hair streamed onto the floor and she was holding something in her arms as a child holds a well-loved toy. Professor Berger's master key unlocked also the exhibition cases. It was the huge-eyed aye-aye that Ruth held to her breast. Its long tail curved up stiffly over her hand and its muzzle lay against her shoulder.

Quin, looking down at her, could only pray that, as she slept, the creature that she cradled was carrying her soul to the rain-washed streets of Belsize Park, and the country which now sheltered all those that she loved.

3

Leonie Berger got carefully out of bed and turned over the pillow so that her husband, who was pretending to be asleep on the other side of the narrow, lumpy mattress, would not notice the damp patch made by her tears. Then she washed and dressed very attentively, putting on high-heeled court shoes, silk stockings, a black skirt and crisply ironed white blouse, because she was Viennese and one dressed properly even when one's world had ended.

Then she started being *good*.

Leonie had been brave when they left Vienna, secreting a diamond brooch in her corset which was foolhardy in the extreme. She had been sensible and loving, for that was her nature, making sure that the one suitcase her husband was allowed to take contained all the existing notes for his book on *Mammals of the Pleistocene*, his stomach pills and the special nail clippers which alone enabled him to manicure his toes. She had been patient with her sister-in-law, Hilda, who was emigrating on a domestic work permit, but had fallen over her untied shoelaces as they made their way onto the Channel steamer, and she had cradled the infant of a fellow refugee while his mother was sick over the rails. Even when she saw the accommodation rented for them by their sponsor, a distantly related dentist who had emigrated years earlier and built up a successful practice in the West End, Leonie only grumbled a little. The rooms on the top floor of a dilapidated lodging house in Belsize Close were cold and dingy, the furniture hideous, the cooking facilities horrific, but they were cheap.

But that was when she thought Ruth was waiting for them in the student camp on the South Coast. Since the letter had come from the Quaker Relief Organization to say that Ruth was not on the train, Leonie had started being *good*.

This meant never at any moment criticizing a single thing. It meant inhaling with delight the smell of slowly expiring cauliflower from the landing where a female psychoanalyst from Breslau shared their cooker. It meant admiring the scrofulous tom cats yowling in the square of rubble that passed for a garden. It meant being enchanted by the hissing gas fire which ate pennies and gave out only fumes and blue flames. It meant angering no living thing, standing aside from houseflies, consuming with gratitude a kind of brown sauce which came in bottles and was called coffee. It meant telling God or anyone else who would listen at all hours of the day and night, that she would never again complain

51

whatever happened if only Ruth was safe and came to them.

By 7.30, Leonie had prepared breakfast for her family – bread spread with margarine, a substance they had never previously tasted – and sent Hilda, with red-rimmed eyes, off to her job as housemaid to a Mrs Manfred in Golders Green. If she hadn't been so desperate about Ruth, Leonie would have greatly pitied her sister-in-law, who was constantly bitten by Mrs Manfred's pug and found it impossible to believe that a bath, once cleaned, also had to be *dried*, but now she could only be thankful that Hilda would not be around to 'help' her with her chores.

At eight o'clock, Uncle Mishak, the English dictionary in the pocket of his coat, set off up the hill to join the long queue of foreigners in Hampstead Town Hall who waited daily for news of relatives, for instructions, for permission to remain – and as he walked, a tiny compact figure stopping to examine a rose bush in a garden or address an unattended dog, he was hailed by the acquaintances this kind old man had made even in the ten days he had been in exile.

'Heard anything yet?' asked the man in the tobacco kiosk, and as Mishak shook his head: 'There'll be news today, maybe. They're coming over all the time. She'll come, you'll see.'

The cockney flower seller with the feather in her battered hat, from whom Mishak had bought nothing, told him to keep his pecker up; a tramp with whom he'd shared a park bench one afternoon stopped to ask after Ruth.

And as Uncle Mishak made his way up the hill, Professor Berger, holding himself very erect, forcing himself to swing his walking stick, made his way downhill for the daily journey to Bloomsbury House where a bevy of Quakers, social workers and civil servants tried to sort out the movements of the dispossessed – and as he walked through the grey streets whose very stones seemed to be permeated with homesickness, he raised his hat to other exiles going about their business.

'Any news of your daughter?' enquired Dr Levy, the renowned heart specialist who spent his days in the public library studying to resit his medical exams in English.

'You've heard something?' asked Paul Ziller, the leader of the Ziller Quartet. He had no work permit, his quartet was disbanded, but each day he went to the Jewish Day Centre to practise in an unused cloakroom, and each night he dressed up in a cummerbund to play bogus gypsy music in a Hungarian restaurant in exchange for his food.

Left alone in the dingy rooms, Leonie continued to be good. There were plenty of opportunities for this as she set about the housework. The thick layer of grease where the psychoanalyst's stew had boiled over would normally have sent her raging down to the second-floor front where Fräulein Lutzenholler sat under a picture of Freud and mourned, but she wiped it up without a word. The bathroom, shared by all the occupants, provided almost unlimited opportunities for virtue. There was a black rim around the bath, the soaked bathmat was crumpled up in a corner . . . and Miss Bates, a nursery school teacher and the only British survivor at Number 27, had hung a row of dripping camiknickers on a sagging piece of string.

None of it mattered. Loving Miss Bates, hoping she would find a husband soon, Leonie wrung out the knickers, cleaned the bath. She had had servants all her life, but she knew how to work. Now everything she did was offered up to God: the Catholic God of her childhood, the Jewish God on whose behalf all these bewildered people roamed the streets of North-West London . . . any God, what did it matter so long as he brought her her child?

Then, at twelve o'clock, she renewed her make-up and set off for the Willow Tea Rooms.

'It's bad news, I'm afraid,' said Miss Maud, filling the sugar bowls and looking out of the window at Leonie Berger's slow progress across the square. Even at a distance it was easy to see how carefully she walked, with what politeness she spoke to the pigeons who crossed her path.

And: 'It's bad news,' said her sister, Miss Violet, carrying a tray of empty cups to Mrs Burtt in the kitchen, who took her arms out of the washing-up water and said that Hitler would have something to answer for if ever she got hold of him.

Miss Maud and Miss Violet Harper had started the

Willow Tea Rooms five years earlier when it was discovered that their father, the General, had not been as provident as they had hoped. It was a pretty place on the corner of a small square behind Belsize Lane and they had made it nice with willow-pattern china, dimity curtains and a pottery cat on the windowsill. Reared to regard foreigners as, at best, unfortunate, the ladies had stoutly resisted the demands of the refugees who increasingly thronged the district. The Gloriette in St John's Wood might serve cakes with outlandish names and slop whipped cream over everything, the proprietors of the Cosmo in Finchley might supply newspapers on sticks and permit talk across the tables, but in the Willow Tea Rooms, the decencies were preserved. Customers were offered scones or sponge fingers and, at lunchtime, scrambled eggs on toast, but nothing ever with a *smell* – and anyone sitting more than half an hour over a cup of coffee, got coughed at, first by Miss Violet, and if this was ineffectual, by the fiercer Miss Maud.

Yet by the summer of 1938, as the bewildered Austrians joined the refugees from Nazi Germany, the ladies, imperceptibly, had changed. For who could cough at Dr Levy, with his walrus moustache and wise brown eyes, not after he had diagnosed Miss Violet's bursitis – and who could help laughing at Mr Ziller's imitation of himself playing 'Dark Eyes' on the violin to an American lady with a faulty hearing aid?

And now there was Mrs Berger who had come in on her first day in England with her distinguished-looking husband and her nice old uncle, and praised the sponge fingers and showed them photos of her pretty, snub-nosed daughter. Ruth was coming, she was going to study here; soon her boyfriend, a brilliant concert pianist, would follow. The change in Mrs Berger since then had shaken even the General's daughters, used as they were to stories of loss and grief.

Leonie entered the café, navigated to the chair which Paul Ziller drew out for her, nodded at the actor from the Vienna Burg Theatre in the corner, at old Mrs Weiss in her feathered toque, at an English lady with a poodle . . .

Dr Levy put down his book on *The Diseases of the Knee* which he had understood intimately twenty years ago, but which came less trippingly in English from the tongue of a middle-aged heart specialist who'd had no breakfast.

'I have heard that many student transports are coming in now to Scotland,' he said, speaking English in deference to the lady with a poodle.

'Yes, thank you,' said Leonie carefully. 'My husband enquires.'

Miss Maud, unasked, set down Leonie's usual cup of coffee. The actor from the Burg Theatre – a fair-haired, alarmingly handsome man exiled for politics not race – said many people were escaping through Portugal, a fact confirmed by the couple from Hamburg at a corner table.

Paul Ziller said nothing, only patted Leonie's hand.

Lonely beyond belief without the three men with whom he had made music for a decade, he was remembering the comical, blonde child who had climbed out of her cot the first time the quartet had played for Professor Berger's birthday and come stamping down the corridor in a nightdress and nappies, refusing absolutely to be returned to bed.

Mrs Weiss, her auburn wig askew under her hat, now launched into an incoherent story involving a missing girl who had turned up unexpectedly on a milk train to Dieppe. The scourge of the Willow Tea Rooms, she was seventy-two years old and had been rescued by her prosperous lawyer son from the village in East Prussia where she had lived all her life. The lawyer now owned a mock Tudor mansion in Hampstead Garden Suburb, a fishpond, and an English wife who deposited her dreadful mother-in-law each morning in the café with a fistful of conscience money. The words 'I buy you a cake?' struck dread into the other habitués who knew that acceptance meant listening to Mrs Weiss's interminable lament about her daughter-in-law who did not allow her to fry onions, speak to the maids, or *help*.

When she had finished, the English lady, who for a year had refused to speak across the tables, said that if Leonie really was an Aquarian, the stars in the *Daily Telegraph* that morning had been entirely favourable.

'It definitely said that you can expect a pleasant surprise,' said Mrs Fowler, feeding a biscuit to the dog.

But when Professor Berger came in, weary from his

long walk up the hill, and then Uncle Mishak, it was clear that the stars in the *Telegraph* had not prevailed.

'Well, tomorrow, perhaps,' said Miss Maud, putting down the plate of bread and butter which was the Bergers' lunch.

'Yes, tomorrow,' echoed Miss Violet.

And Leonie said, yes, and thank you, and remembered to ask about the wedding of Mrs Burtt's niece, and the cat which had had kittens in an unsuitable linen basket in the ladies' flat above the shop.

Then Professor Berger picked up his manuscript on *The Mammals of the Pleistocene* and went with Dr Levy to the public library, and Paul Ziller went to play Bach partitas among the wash basins and lockers of the Day Centre, and the actor (who had declaimed Schiller from Europe's most prestigious stage) made his way to the casting offices in Wardour Street to see if someone would let him say *Schweinehund* in a film about wicked German soldiers in the Great War.

'We go to look for schnitzel?' said Mrs Weiss, cocking her raddled head at Leonie. And Leonie nodded and accompanied the old lady out into the street and into the shop of the nearby butcher with whom Mrs Weiss did daily battle – for helping Mrs Weiss to procure the delicate veal suitable for frying and thus confound her daughter-in-law was so time-consuming and so tiresome that it had – oh, surely – to be classed as Being Good.

Until the long day was done at last and Hilda returned with a hole in her skirt where she had caught it in Mrs Manfred's carpet sweeper, and Uncle Mishak changed into his pyjamas in his cupboard of a room and said, 'Good night, Marianne,' as he had said every night for eighteen years and not stopped saying when she died. And Leonie and her husband climbed into their lumpy bed, and held each other in their arms – and did not sleep.

But in the flat above the Willow Tea Rooms, a light still burned.

'I suppose we *could* serve some of those cakes of theirs,' said Miss Maud as the two ladies, in flannel dressing-gowns, sat over their cocoa.

'Oh, Maud! Not . . . strudels? I'm sure Father would not have wished us to serve anything like that.' Three years younger than her sister, Violet was less skeletally thin and, at forty-three, her hair still retained traces of brown.

'No, not strudels, I agree. That would be going too far. But there's one they all talk about. It begins with a G. Sounds like guggle . . . *Guglhupf* or something.'

Violet put down her cup. 'Buy it in from the Continental Bakery, you mean?'

'Certainly not. There is no question of anything being bought in. But I did just glance at the recipe when I was in the library,' said Miss Maud, blushing like someone admitting to a peep at a pornographic magazine. 'You need a mould, but it isn't difficult.'

There are many ways of helping. That early summer evening when Ruth was lost in Europe and the first air-raid sirens were tried out in Windsor Castle, the ladies of the Willow Tea Rooms let compassion override principle.

'Well, if you think so, Maud,' said Violet – and they put the cat in with the kittens, and washed up their cocoa cups, and went to bed.

4

The Franz Josef Station, at two in the afternoon, was relatively quiet. Only local trains left from platform seven. Here there were none of the tragic scenes of parting; weeping parents, children with labels on their coats being sent to safety abroad. The wooden third-class carriages were filled with peasant women carrying bundles and babies, or chickens in coops.

Ruth, leaning out of the carriage window, was dressed as they were in a dirndl and loden cape, a kerchief round her head. She had found an old rucksack in one of her father's cupboards and repacked her few belongings. With her unruly Rapunzel hair straightjacketed into two pigtails, she looked about sixteen years old and seemed to be in excellent spirits.

'And I can do the local dialect; you'll see, I'll be fine. Only you shouldn't have given me so much money.'

'Don't be silly, I can well afford it, I've told you.'

Quin had put off his departure for yet another day, determined to hear of her safe arrival, schooling his impatience as cables and telephone messages from England collected at Sacher's. Ruth had spent two nights at the museum; no one had given her away, not the cleaning lady, not the night watchman, and Quin, relieved that his task was nearly done, smiled at her with avuncular kindness.

'I think I must be the richest peasant girl in the whole of Austria,' she said. 'But I'll pay you back. On Mozart's head, I swear it.'

He made a dismissive gesture. 'No need to trouble the composer.'

The guard came by, doors were slammed. The self-important engine emitted clouds of steam, and under cover of the noise, Ruth leant over to speak into his ear.

'Please, when you go and see my parents will you tell them not to worry –'

'Of course.'

'No, I mean tell them I'll be with them *very soon*. In less than a month, I hope. I know exactly what to do.'

Apprehension seized him. 'What do you mean?'

The mail had been loaded now. A last door slammed – and Ruth's face came out of the steam, radiant and self-assured.

'I'm going to walk over the mountains into Switzerland,' she said. 'I've done it before when I was staying there. You go over the Kanderspitze; it's only a few hours. I did it with one of the boys from the farm and the guards didn't even turn round!'

'For God's sake, girl, that was before Hitler and all

62

his devilry. The Swiss are armed and on the alert. Next thing they'll shoot you for a spy.'

'No, they won't. I promise I'll be all right. Then when I'm safe in Switzerland I'll make my way to the French border and swim the Varne – it's a tributary of the Rhône and it's not at *all* wide; I've looked it up on the map. After all Piatigorsky swam the Sbruch with his cello over his head to get away from the Russians so I ought to manage with a rucksack. I'm a very good swimmer because of my Aunt Hilda . . . Do you remember she did this breast stroke where she never actually moved and I got used to pushing her across the lake. And once I'm in France all I have to do is contact my father's cousin. He's got a boat and he'll take me across the Channel, I know, so –' She broke off. 'What are you *doing*? You're *hurting* me! Let me go!'

Quin had opened the door; his hand gripped her arm; he was pulling her out of the train.

'Will you be *quiet*,' he said furiously. 'Climbing the Kanderspitze, swimming the Varne . . . you're like a child of ten. Do you think this is a girl's adventure story? "Ruth of the Remove"? The world's on the brink of – oh, to hell!'

She was down on the platform now. Tightening his grip as she struggled, he reached out for the rucksack which a peasant lady, approving of masterful males, had taken from the rack. The guard, scowling at the commotion, closed the door and raised his whistle to his mouth.

'You have no *right*,' said Ruth. Still fighting him,

twisting her head, she saw her train draw away, gather speed, and vanish.

'Get me a taxi,' Quin snapped at a grinning porter.

'I'll never forgive you for this,' she said.

'That is something I shall have to live with,' said Quin and pushed her into the cab.

It had been a mistake to introduce the word *morganatic* into a conversation that was already going badly. Quin had had a sleepless night and spent the last forty-eight hours bullying, bribing, cajoling and confronting a series of officials or he would not have done anything so stupid, the more so as they were speaking English. Ruth's Aberdonian accent was only vestigial now, she was entirely fluent, but over the concept of a morganatic marriage, this over-educated girl had clearly met her Waterloo.

'Who is he, this Morgan?' she asked.

'He isn't anyone,' said Quin, sighing. They were sitting in a café in the Stadtpark and he was almost certain that at any moment someone would start playing Strauss. 'The word morganatic comes from the Latin *matrimonium ad morganaticum* – a marriage based on the morning gift. It's a gift given the morning after the bridal night with which the husband, by bestowing it, frees himself from any liability to the wife. Like Franz Ferdinand. His wife didn't have any of his titles or responsibilities.'

If he had hoped to dispose of the subject by mentioning Austria's most unpopular archduke, he was unfortunate.

'But you say we wouldn't have a bridal night, so Morgan doesn't come into it.'

Quin drained his glass of schnapps and set it down. He was not a man for headaches, but he had one now. 'Yes, that's right. Ours would simply be a marriage in name only. A formality. I'm merely pointing out that there are many ways of dealing with marriage other than the conventional –' He broke off. It was as he had thought. At least a dozen ladies in braided uniforms had come on to the bandstand. Not just Strauss, but Strauss played by women dressed like Grenadier Guards.

'What's the matter?'

'Are they going to play Strauss?'

'Yes,' said Ruth happily. 'They're the All Girl Band from the Prater – they're terribly good!' And looking at him incredulously: 'Don't you *like* waltzes?'

'Not before tea.' He frowned, mastering his impatience. By day, he and Ruth, speaking only English, could pass for foreign visitors, but she was still sleeping in the museum and it was only a matter of time before someone gave her away.

'Look, Ruth, let's not waste any more time. I've got to get back to England, you want to go there. The consul here will marry us – it'll take a few minutes, it'll be a mere formality. Then you'll be put on my passport as my wife – in effect you become a British subject. When we get to London we go our separate ways and dissolve the marriage on the grounds of –' He stopped himself just in time. Non-consummation on top of morganatic marriage was not something he was willing to discuss to the sound of Strauss with this obstinate girl.

Ruth was silent, tilting the lemonade in her glass. 'It is a pity there is no Morgan,' she said. 'He could help one to choose the morning gift. It would have to be something very nice so that one would not mind not having responsibilities. A St Bernard dog, perhaps.'

'Well, there isn't. If there was, he would probably be a Welshman from Pontypool and a rugger blue.'

'A Welshman? Why is that?'

Quin leaned across the table and laid a hand briefly on hers. 'Listen, Ruth, we have finished with Morgan, right? The subject is closed. I'll fetch you at eleven from the museum; we'll be married at noon and by the evening we'll be on the sleeper.'

He had risen, but she did not follow suit. 'Don't you see, I can't let you do this,' she said in a low voice. 'There must be someone in England that you want to marry.'

'Well, there isn't. As for your Heini, surely he'd rather you were safe and reunited with him even if it means waiting a little while before you can be married? Think how you would feel if the positions were reversed?'

'Yes, I would do anything to be with Heini,' she said quietly. 'Only it isn't fair. I can't ask it of you and –'

But Quin was looking at the bandstand where the worst was happening. 'For heaven's sake, let's get out of here,' he said, pulling her to her feet. 'That trout in the helmet has raised her baton.'

'It's *Wiener Blut*,' said Ruth reproachfully, as the luscious waltz soared out over the park.

'I don't care what it is,' said Quin – and fled.

5

The night had been stormy, but now the sky was clearing and over Lindisfarne, the Holy Island, a thin strip of silver light appeared, widened . . . and the sea, which minutes before had been turbulent and dark, became suddenly, unbelievably blue. Three cormorants skimmed over the water, heading for the Farnes, and from the bird-hung cliffs came the incessant mewing of the nesting kittiwakes and terns.

But the elderly lady, formidably dressed in dark purple tweeds, her iron-grey hair concealed under a woollen scarf adorned with the bridles of horses and their whips, was not gazing either at the birds, nor at the round heads of the seals bobbing off Bowmont Point. Standing on the terrace of Bowmont, she trained her binoculars on the long, golden strand of Bowmont Bay. The tide was out, revealing the rock pools at either end, and the crescent of perfect sand ran for half a mile before the next headland, but polluting its emptiness, ruining its peace, were . . . people. Three; no, more . . .

A whole family, paddling and, no doubt, shrieking, though they were mercifully out of earshot. She could make out a man and a woman, and another woman . . . a grandmother. And a child. Not fishermen or village people going about their business.

'*Trippers*!' pronounced Miss Somerville. Her voice was deep, her outrage total.

They would have to go. They would have to be shooed away. It was happening more and more. People came up from Newcastle or down from Berwick. Holiday-makers, tourists, defiling the empty places, catching shrimps, wearing idiotic clothes . . .

Bowmont had been built on a promontory: an old peel tower to which, generations ago, had been added a wing of ochre stone. Lonely, wind-buffeted, its history was Northumbria's own – raided by the Danes from the sea, by the Scots from the land, besieged by Warwick the Kingmaker; ruined and rebuilt.

Turner had painted it in a turbulent sunset, a sailing boat listing dangerously at the base of its sea-lashed cliffs. St Cuthbert, on Lindisfarne, had preached to the eider ducks which still nested on Bowmont Point, and from the white needle of Longstone lighthouse, Grace Darling had rowed into legend, bringing rescue to the shipwrecked wretches on Harcar Rock. Quin, as a child, had known exactly where God lived. Not in the Holy Land as painted in his illustrated bible, but in the swirling, ever-changing, cloud-wracked sky above his home.

Frances Somerville had been forty years old, a

spinster still living at home, when old Quinton Somerville, the legendary and terrifying 'Basher', retired from the navy, had sent for her.

'I'm going to die soon,' the Basher had said. 'I want you to come to Bowmont and look after the boy till he's of age.'

Frances had refused. She disliked the old man, who had made no secret of the fact that as a plain, unmarried woman, she was entirely without consequence. Then Quin, aged ten, was sent for and introduced.

'I'll come when you're dead,' Frances said that evening – but she did not believe that the bucolic old reprobate was anywhere near his end.

She was wrong. The Basher was found dead on a garden seat not three months later, and in his own way he had played fair, for he had left her a comfortable annuity out of his admittedly vast estate. Since then she had been Bowmont's guardian and its chatelaine and with Quin so often away on his travels, that meant keeping it free from invaders, from the creeping stain of tourism and so-called modern life.

Now in her sixtieth year, big-nosed, tight-lipped, with sparse grey hair and fierce blue eyes, her opinion of the human race was low. An abandoned seal pup, a puffin with a broken wing, could count on Miss Somerville for help; a human in a similar plight would be lucky to get a cup of tea in the servants' quarters. Once, rumour had it, it had been different. She had been sought in marriage by a Scottish nobleman, despatched to his house to be looked over . . . but it had come to nothing, and the shy, plain girl became the formidable spinster, respected by all and loved by nobody.

A gardener's boy came across the terrace, carrying a rake.

'You! George!' called Miss Somerville, and the boy scuttled towards her and touched his cap.

'Yes, Miss Somerville.'

'Tell Turton there are trippers at the end of the bay. They must be removed.'

'Yes, miss.'

The boy hurried away and Miss Somerville turned her binoculars to the other side of the promontory. Here, in the relative shelter of the curving cliff there was a smaller bay, the sand dotted with rocks and dark drifts of seaweed. Anchorage Bay, it was called, and in the previous century boats had tied up at the little jetty, there had been fishermen living in the row of cottages and cobles drawn up on the beach.

Those days were gone and Quin had converted the boat-house and two of the cottages into a lab and dormitory for the students he brought up for his field course. More people who did not belong, she thought wearily, more defilement and chatter. Last year one of the girls had worn a two-piece bathing costume and Miss Somerville's early morning viewing through her binoculars had revealed the completely exposed midriff of a girl from Surbiton.

The gardener's boy reappeared.

'Please, miss, Mr Turton says as they're between the tides, so he can't shoo 'em off right now. And he says to tell you, miss, that Lady Rothley telephoned and she's coming at eleven.'

Miss Somerville tightened her lips. The tide-marks . . . the infuriating ancient law that decreed that the shore between low tide and high tide belonged to everyone. It was nonsense, of course. To get there they had come over Somerville land – the fields behind the bay all belonged to Quin and she made sure that the gates were kept locked.

For a moment, she felt old and discouraged. This was not her world. Beyond the point was ancient Dunstanburgh with a golf course now lapping its ruined towers. Trippers could creep in that way too and make their way to Bowmont. She was like King Canute, struggling uselessly against the defilement of the human race.

And Quin didn't really help her. Quin had ideas that she tried to understand but couldn't. Miss Somerville loved no one; it was a point of honour with her to have banished this destructive emotion from her breast, but Quin was Quin and she would have jumped off the cliff for him without further consideration. And yet from this boy, whom she herself had reared, came ideas and theories that she would not have expected to read even in the Socialist gutter press. Quin did not chase trippers off his land, merely requesting them to close the gates; he had acknowledged a right of way across the dunes to Bowmont Mill, and now there was talk of one day . . . not while she lived, perhaps . . . but one day, giving Bowmont to the National Trust.

The dreaded words made Miss Somerville shiver.

The sun had established full dominion now; the terns were white arrows against the indigo of the water; hare-bells and yarrow and clusters of pink thrift glowed in the turf, but Miss Somerville, usually so observant, saw only the spectre of the future. A car park in the Lower Meadow, refreshment kiosks, charabancs with stinking exhaust pipes unloading trippers in the forecourt. Poor Frampton had done it, given his home away, and there were vulgar little green huts at the gates of Frampton Court and men in caps like doormen punching tickets, and a tea room and souvenir stall. But Frampton had an excuse; he was bankrupt. Quin had no such excuse. The farm was in profit, the rents from the village brought in sufficient revenue to see to repairs, and his inheritance from the Basher had left him a wealthy man. For Quin to give away his heritage was irresponsible and mad.

She turned and went in through a door beside the tower, to a store room which she had turned into a kennel for her Labradors.

'How are they, Martha?'

'Fine, Miss Frances. Just fine.'

Martha had been sent to her as a lady's maid, but Miss Somerville, returning from her broken engagement on the Border, had refused any nonsense to do with dressing up and frippery, and Martha now looked after the dogs.

The puppies were sucking: five blissful, ever-swelling bags of milk whose mother thumped her tail in greeting and let her head fall back again onto the straw.

There was good blood there. Comely had been mated in Wales – Miss Somerville had taken her there herself and it had been a bother, but it always paid to get decent stock.

Oh, why couldn't Quin marry, she thought, making her way across the courtyard. Not one of those girls he brought up sometimes: actresses or Parisiennes who came down to breakfast shivering in fur coats and asked about central heating, but a girl of his own kind, a girl with breeding. Once he had a lusty son or two, he'd forget all this nonsense about the Trust.

Later, in the drawing room, the subject came up again. Lady Rothley was the closet thing to a friend which Frances Somerville allowed herself and there was no need to make a fuss when she came. No need to light a fire, no need to shoo the dogs off the chairs. Ann Rothley bred Jack Russells and all the tapestry sofas at the Hall were covered in short white hairs.

'I thought Quin would be back by now,' she said, lifting the *famille rose* cup and sipping her coffee appreciatively. Frances might dress like a charwoman, but she kept the servants up to scratch.

'He was delayed in Vienna,' said Miss Somerville. 'They gave him an honorary degree and he had to stay on to see to some business or other.'

Lady Rothley nodded. A dark, handsome woman in her forties, she did not object to Quin's scholarship. It happened sometimes in these old families. At Wallington, the Trevelyans were for ever writing history books.

'Well, I'm afraid you'll have to break it to him, Frances. I simply had to get rid of that German he landed me with. The opera singer from Dresden. I sent him to the dairy because all the indoor posts were filled and it's been a disaster. The dairy maid fell in love with him and he was useless with the cows.'

Miss Somerville nodded. 'A Jew, I suppose?'

'Well, he said he was, but he had fair hair. I can't help wondering whether some of them go round pretending to be Jewish just to get the benefits. The Quakers are giving away fortunes in relief, I understand. I didn't like to dismiss him, but the cows are *not* musical. There's almost nothing I won't do for Quin, but he must stop trying to get us all to employ these dreadful refugees. Poor Helen – he made her take a man from Berlin to act as a chauffeur and handyman and as soon as he's finished work he gets people in and they play chamber music. It's like lemons in your ears, you know – screech, screech. She's had to tell them to go and do it in an outhouse. I wish Quin wasn't so concerned about them. I mean, there are lots of other people to worry about, aren't there? The unemployed and the coal miners and so on.'

Miss Somerville agreed. 'Of course one cannot approve of the way Hitler carries on – he really is a very vulgar man. Not that one likes Jews. When they're rich they're bankers and when they're poor they're pedlars and in between they play the violin. I'm not having any of them at Bowmont while I'm in charge and I've told Quin.'

One of the Labradors yawned, jumped down from the chair, and rearranged himself across Miss Somerville's feet.

'Mind you, if there's a war we'll get evacuees from London,' said Lady Rothley. She spoke cheerfully and no one knew what it cost her to do so, for Rollo, her adored eldest son, was eighteen years old.

'Well, I'd rather have slum children than foreign refugees. One could keep them separate in the boat-house on mattresses with rubber sheets and take their food across. Whereas refugees would . . . mingle.'

There was a pause while the ladies sipped and the freshening wind stirred the curtains.

Then: 'Has he said any more about . . . you know . . . the Trust?'

That Ann Rothley, so forthright and uncompromising, spoke with hesitation was a measure of her unease.

'Well, I haven't seen him for months, as you know – he's been in India – but Turton said someone rang up from their headquarters and said Quin had asked them to send a man up later in the year. I think he means it, Ann.'

'Oh God!' Would the desecration never end, she thought wretchedly. Estates sold for building land, forests felled, townspeople gawping at the houses of one's friends. 'Isn't there any hope that he will see his duty and marry?'

Miss Somerville shrugged. 'I don't know. Livy saw him at the theatre twice with a girl before he went abroad, but she didn't think he was serious.'

'He never is serious,' said Lady Rothley bitterly. 'Anyone would think one married for pleasure.' She was silent, remembering the horror of her bridal night with Rothley. But she had not screamed or run away, she had endured it, as later she endured the boredom of his weekly visits to her bed, looking at the ceiling, thinking of her embroidery or her dogs. And now there were children and a future. Oak trees remained unfelled, parkland was tended because girls like her gritted their teeth. 'It is for England that one marries,' she said. 'For the land.'

'Yes, I know. But what more can we do?' said Frances wearily. 'You know how many people have tried . . .'

There was no need to finish the sentence. Girls of every shape and size had ridden through the gates of Bowmont on their thoroughbreds, climbed healthily up the turf path with their tennis rackets, smiled at Quin across dance floors in white organdie, in spangled tulle . . .

'You don't think he might be interested in someone who understood his work?'

'Not a student!' said Frances, horrified.

'No . . . but . . . I don't know; he's so clever, isn't he?' said Lady Rothley, trying to be tolerant. 'Only, I can't see a decently brought up girl knowing about old bones, so I suppose it's no good.' She rose to her feet, re-knotted her scarf. 'Anyway, give the dear boy my love – but tell him *absolutely no more refugees*!'

Left alone, Miss Somerville took her secateurs and

her trug and went through to the West Terrace, to the sheltered side of the house away from the sea. For a moment, she paused to look at the orderly fields stretching away to the blue humpbacks of the Cheviots: the oats and barley, green and tall, the freshly shorn flock of Leicesters grazing in the Long Meadow. The new manager Quin had engaged was doing well.

Then she crossed the lawn, opened a door in the high wall – and entered a different world. The sun ceased to be merely brightness and became warmth; bumble bees blundered about on the lavender; the scent of stock and jasmine came to meet her – and a great quietness as the incessant surge of the sea became the gentlest of whispers.

'I should hope so,' said Frances firmly to a Tibetan poppy which two days ago had dared to look doubtful, but now unfurled its petals of heavenly blue.

It was Quin's grandmother, the meek and silent Jane Somerville, who had made the garden. The daughter of a wealthy coal owner from County Durham, she brought the consolations of the Quaker faith to her enforced marriage with the Basher, and she needed them.

Jane had been two years at Bowmont when, to her own horror and amazement, she rose in the Meeting House at Berwick and found that she had been moved to speak.

'I am going to make a garden,' she said.

She never again spoke in Meeting, but the next day she gave orders for the field adjoining the West Lawn to be drained. She travelled to the other side of England to commandeer the old rose bricks of a recently demolished manor house; she planted windbreaks, built walls and brought in lorry loads of loam. The experts told her she was wasting her time; she was too far north, too close to the sea for the kind of garden she had in mind. The Basher, on leave from the navy, was furious. He made scenes; he queried every bill.

Jane, usually so gentle and acquiescent, took no notice. She sent roses and wisteria and clematis rioting up the walls; she brought in plants from places far colder and more inhospitable than Bowmont: camellias and magnolias from China, poppies and primulas from the Atlas mountains – and mixed them with the flowers the villagers grew in their cottage gardens. She set an oak bench against the south wall and flanked it with buddleias for the butterflies – and decades later, the Basher, who had fought her all the way, came there to die.

Miss Somerville knelt down by the Long Border, feeling the now familiar twinge of arthritis in her knee, and the robin flew down from the branches of the little almond tree to watch. But presently she dropped the trowel and made her way to the seat beside the sundial and closed her eyes.

What would happen to this garden if Quin really gave his house away? Hordes of people tramping through it, frightening away the robin, shrieking and swatting at the bees. There would be signposts everywhere – the lower classes never seemed to be able to find their way. And built against the far wall, where now the peaches ripened in the sun, two huts. No – one hut divided into two; she had seen it at Frampton. The lettering at one end would read *Ladies*, but the other end wouldn't even spell *Gentlemen*. Made over entirely to vulgarity, the second notice would read *Gents*.

'Oh, God,' prayed Frances Somerville, addressing her Maker with unaccustomed humility, 'please find her for me. She must be somewhere – the girl who can save this place!'

6

It had rained since daybreak: slanting, cold-looking sheets of rain. Down in the square, the bedraggled pigeons huddled against Maria Theresia's verdigris skirts. Vienna, the occupied city, had turned its back on the spring.

Ruth had scarcely slept. Now she folded the blanket on the camp bed, washed as best she could under the cloakroom tap, brewed a cup of coffee.

'This is my wedding day,' she thought. 'This is the day I shall remember when I lie dying –' and felt panic seize her.

She had put her loden skirt and woollen sweater under newspaper, weighed down by a tray of fossil-bearing rocks, but this attempt at home-ironing had not been successful. Should she after all wear the dress she had bought for Heini's debut with the Philharmonic? She'd taken it from the flat and it hung now behind the door: brown velvet with a Puritan collar of heavy cream lace. It came from her grandfather's department store:

the attendants had all come to help her choose; to share her pleasure in Heini's debut. Now the store had its windows smashed; notices warned customers not to shop there. Thank heaven her grandfather was dead.

No, that was Heini's dress – her page-turning dress, for it mattered what one wore to turn over music. One had to look nice, but unobtrusive. The dress was the colour of the Bechstein in the Musikverein – it had nothing to do with an Englishman who ran away from Strauss.

She wandered through the galleries and, in the grey light of dawn, her old friends, one by one, became visible. The polar bear, the elephant seal . . . the ichthyosaurus with the fake vertebrae. And the infant aye-aye which she had restored to its case.

'Wish me luck,' she said to the ugly little beast, leaning her head against the glass.

She closed her eyes and the primates of Madagascar vanished as she saw the wedding she had planned so often with her mother. Not here, but on the Grundlsee, rowing across to the little onion-domed church in a boat – in a whole flotilla of boats, because everyone she loved would be there. Uncle Mishak would grumble a little because he had to dress up; Aunt Hilda would get stuck in her zip . . . and the Zillers would play. 'On the landing stage,' Ruth had suggested, but Biberstein said no, he was too fat to play on a landing stage. She would wear white organdie and carry a posy of mountain flowers, and as she walked down the aisle on her father's arm, there would be Heini with his mop of curls and his sweet smile.

(Oh, Heini, forgive me. I'm doing this for us.)

Back in the cloakroom, she looked at her reflection once again. She had never seemed to herself so plain and unprepossessing. Suddenly she loosened her hair, filled the basin with cold water, seized the cake of green soap that the museum thought adequate for its research workers . . .

Quin, letting himself in silently, found her ready, her suitcase strapped.

'Does the roof leak?' he asked, surprised, for from the curving strands of her long hair, drops of water were running onto the floor.

She shook her head. 'I washed my hair, but the electric fire doesn't work.'

He saw the shadows under her eyes, the resolute set of her shoulders.

'Come; it'll be over soon – and it isn't as bad as going to the dentist.'

At the bottom of the staircase, as they prepared to leave by the side door, a small group of people waited to wish her luck. The cleaning lady, the porter, the old taxidermist on the floor below. They had all known she was there and kept their counsel. She must remember that when she felt despair about her countrymen.

She had expected something grand from the British Consulate, but the Anschluss had forced a reorganization of the Diplomatic Service, and the taxi delivered them in front of a row of temporary huts, on the tin roof of which the rain was still beating down. A disconsolate plumber in oilskins was poking at an overflowing gutter with an iron tool. Inside, in the Consul's makeshift office, the picture of George the Sixth hung slightly askew; out in the corridor someone was hoovering.

The Consul's deputy was there, but not in the best of tempers. He had pinkeye, an unpleasant inflammation of the conjunctiva, and held a handkerchief to his face. Though he had found Professor Somerville personally courteous, he could not approve of the way the Consul, presumably on the instruction of the Ambassador, was rushing this ceremony through. Procedures which should have taken days had been telescoped into hours: the issuing of visas, the amendment of passports. Someone, thought the deputy, whose origins were working class, had almost certainly been at school with someone else. Professor Somerville's father with the Ambassador's cousin, perhaps . . . There would have been those exchanges by which upper-class Englishmen, like dogs round a lamppost, sniff out each other's schooling – faggings at Eton, beatings at Harrow – and realize that they are brothers beneath the skin.

'Can I have your documents, please?'

Quin laid the papers down on the desk, and saw Ruth's knuckles tighten on the back of her chair. Scarcely twenty years old, and a child of the new Europe Hitler had made.

'We shall need two witnesses. Have you brought any?'

'No.'

The deputy sighed and went out into the corridor. The sound of hoovering ceased and a lady with a large wart on her chin, wearing a black overall, entered and stood silently by the door. She had cut a piece out of the sides of her felt slippers to give her bunions breathing space and this was sensible, Ruth appreciated this, and that someone whose feet were giving such trouble could not be expected to smile or say good morning. Then the plumber came, divested of his oilskins, and smelling strongly – and again this was entirely natural – of the drains he had been trying to clean and it was clear that he too was not pleased to be interrupted in his work – why should he be?

The Consul himself now entered, distinguished-looking, formally suited, with his finger in the Book of Common Prayer, and the ceremony began.

Quin had not expected what came next. 'It'll just be a formality,' he'd promised Ruth. 'A few minutes and then it'll be done.' But though the Consul was using a truncated version of the marriage service, he was still pronouncing the words that had joined men and women for four hundred years – and Quin, foreseeing trouble, frowned and stared at the floor.

'*Dearly beloved, we are gathered together here in the sight of God to join this Man and this Woman in holy Matrimony . . .*'

Beside him, Ruth moved uneasily. The lady with the cut-out bedroom slippers sniffed.

'*. . . and therefore is not by any to be enterprised,*

nor taken in hand unadvisedly, lightly or wantonly . . .
but reverently, discreetly, advisedly, soberly . . .'

It was as he had expected. Ruth made a sudden, panicky movement of her head and a last drop of water fell from her wet hair onto the bare linoleum.

The Consul listed the causes for which matrimony was ordained. The procreation of children brought an anxious frown to her brow; the remedy against sin worried her less.

It was only briefly that the plumber and the cleaning lady, neither of whom understood a word, were required to disclose any impediment to the marriage or for ever hold their peace and the Consul came to the point.

'Quinton Alexander St John, wilt thou have this Woman to thy wedded Wife . . .? Wilt thou love her, comfort her, honour, and keep her in sickness and in health; and, forsaking all other, keep thee only unto her, so long as ye both shall live?'

'I will.'

'Ruth Sidonie, wilt thou have this Man to thy wedded Husband . . .'

Her '*I will*' came clearly, but with the faint, forgotten accent of Aberdeen. A stress symptom, it would appear.

The Consul cleared his throat. 'Do you have a ring?'

Ruth shook her head in the same instant as Quin took from his pocket a plain gold band.

He too was pale as he promised to take Ruth for his wedded wife from this day forward, for better for worse, for richer for poorer, in sickness and in health. The ring, when he slipped it on her finger, was a perfect fit. Her hands were as cold as ice.

'*With this Ring I thee wed, with my Body I thee worship, and with all my worldly Goods I thee endow.*' His voice was steady now. The thing was almost done.

'We will omit the prayer,' said the Consul and allowed the final injunction to roll off his tongue with a suitable and sombre emphasis. '*Those whom God hath joined together let no man put asunder.*'

It was over. The register was signed, Quin paid his dues, tipped the witnesses, put a note into the collecting box for orphans of the Spanish Civil War.

'If you come back at four o'clock your passport will be ready with your wife's name on it, and her visa.'

Ruth managed to reach the gravelled driveway before she burst into tears.

'For God's sake, Ruth, what's the matter? It's all over now. Tomorrow evening you'll be with your family.'

She blew her nose, shook out her hair.

'You see, we shall be cursed!'

'Cursed! What on earth are you talking about? Could we have less of the Old Testament, please?'

'Ha! You see . . . Now you are also anti-Semitic.'

'Well, I do think this might be the moment to take after the goat-herding grandmother rather than some gloomy old rabbi. What do you mean, we shall be cursed?'

'Because of the words. Because we said those words before witnesses. I didn't think the words would be so *strong*. And you shouldn't have said that about with my worldly goods I thee endow because even if we were going to do the worshipping with the body, there would still be Morgan.'

'Ah, Morgan. I thought we hadn't heard the last of him. Look, Ruth, it doesn't become you, this kind of fuss. You know what Hitler is like, you know what had to be done.'

'I should have escaped over the border; I should not have let you swear things that are lies.'

Quin too was very weary. It was with difficulty that he repressed his views on her ascent of the Kanderspitze. 'Come, we'll go to the Imperial and have two whopping schnitzels. Because one thing you'll find it hard to come by in London is a decent piece of frying veal.'

'I can't go in these old clothes. And if I'm seen . . .'

Quin's arrogance was quite unconscious. 'Nothing can happen to you now. You are a British subject – and in my care.'

The schnitzels were a success. When they left the restaurant, her hair was dry and enveloped her in a manner that was disorganized, but cheerful. He had already gathered that it was a kind of barometer, like seaweed.

'We've still got three hours left. Where would you like to go on your last afternoon in Vienna?'

To his surprise, she suggested they take a tram to the Danube. He knew how little the wide, grey river, looping round the industrial suburbs of the city, actually concerned the Viennese. Gloomy Johann Strauss, with his dyed moustaches and inability to smile, might have written the world's most famous waltz in tribute to the river, but the Danube's vicious flooding had compelled the inhabitants, centuries ago, to turn their backs on it.

But when they stood on the Reich Bridge, it was clear that Ruth was on a pilgrimage.

'Do you see that little bay over there, just by the warehouse?'

He nodded . . .

'Well, my Uncle Mishak used to fish there – only he's my great-uncle really. That was years and years ago. Imagine it, the Kaiser was still on his throne and Austria and Hungary were joined up. One could take a barge down to Budapest – no passport, no restrictions. Anyway, Uncle Mishak had joined my grandfather in his department store, but he loved the open air and every Sunday he went fishing. Only on this particular Sunday, instead of a fish, he caught a bottle!' She turned to Quin, full of narrative self-importance. 'It was a lemonade bottle and inside it was a message!'

Quin was impressed, knowing how rarely messages in bottles are ever read.

'It said: *My name is Marianne Stichter, I am twenty-four years old and I am very sad. If you are a kind and good man, please come and fetch me*. And she'd put the address of the school where she taught. It was in a village on the river near Dürnstein – you know, where Richard the Lionheart was imprisoned.'

'Go on.'

'The school was run by her father and he was a sadist

and a bully. There was an elder sister who'd married and escaped, but Marianne was quiet and plain and shy, and she had a stammer, and he'd made her teach the junior class. Of course, the children all imitated her – every time she entered the classroom, she just wanted to die.'

Ruth paused and looked at Quin, savouring, on his behalf, what was to follow.

'Then one day she was giving a Geography lesson on the rivers of South America when the door opened and a small man in a dark suit and homburg hat came in, carrying a briefcase.

'The children started tittering but she didn't even hear them, she just stood and looked at the little man. Then my Uncle Mishak took off his hat – he was pretty bald by then, and he wore gold pince-nez, and he said: "Are you Fräulein Stichter?" He wasn't really asking, he knew, but he waited till she nodded and then he said: "I have come to fetch you." Just like that. "I have come to fetch you." And he opened his briefcase and took out the note from the bottle.'

'And she came?'

Ruth smiled and parted her hair with her fingers so that she could narrate unimpeded. 'She didn't say anything. Not a word. She picked up the duster and very carefully she wiped off the rivers of South America – the Negro and the Madeira and the Amazon. Then she put the chalk back into the box and opened a cupboard and took out her hat and put it on. The children had stopped tittering and started gawping, but she walked down between the desks and she didn't even see them; they didn't *exist*. At the door, Uncle Mishak gave her his arm – he didn't come much above her shoulder – and they walked across the play yard and down the road and got on the paddle boat for Vienna – and no one there ever saw them again!'

'And they were happy?'

Ruth put a hand up to her eyes. 'Ridiculously so. People laughed at them – plumping each other's cushions, pulling out footstools. When she died he tried to die too, but he couldn't manage it. That's when my mother made him come to us.'

Back in the Inner City, Ruth pointed out the balcony on which she had stood stark naked at midnight, at the age of nine, hoping that pneumonia would release her from disgrace and ruin.

'It was my great-aunt's flat and I'd just heard that I only got Commended instead of Highly Commended in my music exam. Oh, and look, here's the actual bench where my mother was overcome by pigeons and my father rescued her.'

'There seem to have been a lot of happy marriages in your family,' said Quin.

'I don't know . . . Uncle Mishak was happy, and my parents . . . but in general I don't think they thought of it as something that made you happy.'

'What then?'

Ruth was frowning. One ear turned colour slightly as she strangled it in a loop of hair. 'It was what you did . . . because you had set out to do it. It was . . . work;

it was like ploughing a field or painting a picture – you kept on adding colours or trying to get the perspective right. The women in particular. My Aunt Miriam's husband was unfaithful and she kept ringing my mother and saying she was going to kill him, but when people suggested divorce she was terribly shocked.' She looked up, her hand flew to her mouth. 'I'm terribly sorry . . . I don't mean us, of course. These were proper marriages, not ones with Morgan.'

Their last visit was to St Stephan's Cathedral, the city's symbol and its heart.

'I'd like to light a candle,' said Ruth, and he let her go alone up the sombre, incense-scented nave.

Waiting at the door, he saw across the square two terrified fair-haired boys with broad peasant faces being dragged towards an army truck by a group of soldiers.

'They're rounding up all the Social Democrats,' said a plump, middle-aged woman with a feather in her hat. There was no censure in her voice; no emotion in the round, pale eyes.

Making his way to where Ruth knelt, determined to take her out by a side door, Quin found that she had lit not one candle but two. No need to ask for whom – all roads led to Heini for this girl.

'Shall I ever come back, do you think?'

Quin made no answer. Whether Ruth would return to this doomed city, he did not know, but he and his like would surely do so, for he did not see how this evil could be halted by anything but war.

7

Heini had been ten days in Budapest. It was good to be back in his native city; good to walk along the Corso beside the river and look up at the castle on Buda hill; good to see the steamers glide past on their way to the Black Sea and to taste again the fiery *gulyás* which the Viennese thought they could make, but couldn't. There was a fizz, an edge of wit here that was missing in the Austrian capital, and the women were the most beautiful in the world. Not that Heini was tempted – he was finding it all too easy to be faithful to Ruth; and anyway one always had to be careful of disease.

His father still lived in the yellow villa on the Hill of the Roses; the apple trees in the garden were in blossom; they took their meals on the verandah looking down over the Pasha's tomb and the wooded slopes on to the Gothic tracery of the Houses of Parliament and the gables and roofs of Pest.

Heini did not care for his stepmother; she lacked soul, but with his father still editing the only liberal

German newspaper in the city, he had to be glad that there was somebody to care for him.

Nor was there any problem about securing a visa for entry into Great Britain. Hungary was still independent, there was no stampede to leave the country; the quota was not yet full. It would take a little longer than he expected – a few weeks – but there was nothing to feel anxious about.

Best of all, Heini's old Professor of Piano Studies at the Academy had managed to arrange a concert for him.

'I'd have liked to organize something big for you in the Vigado,' Professor Sandor said, mentioning the famous concert hall in which Rubinstein had played and Brahms conducted, 'but it's too short notice – and who knows, if you play here in the Academy, Bartók may come and that could lead to something.'

Heini had been properly grateful. He remembered the old building with affection; its tradition stretching back to Liszt and boasting now, in Bartók and Kodály and Dohnányi, as distinguished a group of professors as any music school in the world. It was to be an evening recital in the main hall; he was to get half the proceeds; all in all, Professor Sandor had been most helpful and generous.

But there was a snag. The Concert Committee had asked Heini to include in his programme the sonata that the third-year piano students were studying that term: Beethoven's tricky and beautiful Opus 99. Heini had no objection to this, but though he had the last ten

Beethoven sonatas by heart, this one he would have to play from the score – and that meant a page turner.

It was here that things had begun to go wrong. For Professor Sandor had a daughter, also a piano student, whom he had offered Heini in that role.

'You'll find her very intelligent,' the Professor had said proudly; and at Heini's first rehearsal Mali had duly appeared – and been a disaster.

Mali was not just plain – an unobtrusively plain girl would not have upset him – she was virulently ugly; her spectacles glinted and caught the light; she had buck teeth. Not only that, but she drove him nearly mad with her humble eagerness, her desperate desire to be of use, and though she could hardly fail to be able to read music, she was so hesitant, so terrified of being hasty, that several times he had had to nod at the bottom of the page. Worst of all, Mali *perspired*.

Heini had missed Ruth ever since he had come to Budapest, but in the days leading up to the concert his longing for her became a constant ache. Ruth turned over so gracefully, so skilfully that one hardly knew she was there; she smelled sweetly and faintly of lavender shampoo and never, in the years she'd sat beside him, had he found it necessary to nod.

Nor was his stepmother at all aware of the kind of pressures that playing in public put on him. Heini's hands were insured, of course, and taking care of them had become second nature, but a pianist used all his body and when he tripped over a dustpan she had left on the stairs, he could not help being upset.

'I'm not being fussy,' he said to Marta, 'but if I sprained my ankle, I wouldn't be able to pedal for a month.'

It had been so different in the Bergers' apartment, which had become his second home. Not only Ruth but her mother and the maids were happy to serve him, as he in turn served music.

But it was on the actual day of the concert that Heini's need for Ruth became almost uncontainable.

The day began badly, when he was woken at nine o'clock by the sound of the maid hoovering the corridor outside his room. He always slept late on the day of a concert, but when he complained, his stepmother said that the girl had to get through her work and pointed out that Heini had already spent ten hours in bed.

'In bed, but not asleep,' Heini said bitterly – but he didn't really expect her to understand.

Then there was the question of lunch. Heini could never eat anything heavy before he played and in Vienna Ruth always made a point of getting to the Café Museum early to keep a corner table and make sure that the beef broth, which was all that he could swallow, was properly strained and the plain rusks well baked. Whereas Marta seemed to expect him to play on a diet of roast pork and dumplings!

Leaving the house earlier than he had intended, Heini, walking down the fashionable Váci utca, faced yet another challenge: the purchase of a flower for his buttonhole. A gardenia was probably too formal for the

Academy, a camellia too, but a carnation, a white one, should strike the right note. Ruth, of course, had bought his buttonholes – he had watched her once, searching for a flawless bloom, involving the shop assistant, who knew her well, in the excitement of kitting him out.

Bravely now, Heini went in alone and found a girl to help him. It was only when he came out again, his flower safe in cellophane, that he realized that he did not have a pin.

In the hall of the Academy, Professor Sandor was waiting.

'It's an excellent attendance – almost full. Considering we had less than two weeks for the publicity and there's a premiere at the opera, we can be very pleased.'

Heini nodded and went to the green-room – and there was Mali in an unbelievably ugly dress: crimson crepe which clung unsuitably to her bosom and exposed her collar bones. The splash of colour would distract the eye even from the back of the hall. Ruth always chose dresses that blended with the colours of the hall, quiet dresses which nevertheless became her wonderfully.

'Do you have a pin?' he asked – and Mali did at least have that and managed, fumbling and nervous, to fasten the carnation in his buttonhole. 'I shall need to be quiet now,' he added firmly, and sat down as far away from her as possible.

Not that this ensured him the peace he craved. Mali

fidgeted incessantly with the Beethoven sonatas, checking the pages; she cleared her throat . . .

Ruth knew exactly how to quieten him during those last moments before a concert or an exam. She brought along a set of dominos and they played for a while, or she just sat silently with her hands folded and that marvellous hair of hers bright and burnished, but taken back with a velvet band so that it didn't tumble forward and distract the audience. Ruth made sure he had fresh lemonade waiting for him in the interval; he never had to think about his music, it was always there and in the right order. And now, glancing in the mirror, he saw that his carnation was listing quite noticeably towards the left!

'Five minutes,' called the page, knocking on the door.

'My handkerchief!' said Heini suddenly in a panic. The white one in the pocket of his dinner jacket was there, of course, but the other one, the one with which he wiped his hands between the pieces . . .

Mali flushed and jumped to her feet. 'I'm sorry . . . I didn't know that I . . .'

'It doesn't matter.' He found the one his stepmother had washed for him, but cotton, not linen. The Bergers' maids always laundered his handkerchiefs; they smelled so fresh and clean with just the lightest touch of starch: Ruth saw to that.

It was time to go. Professor Sandor put his head round the door. 'Bartók is here!' he said, beaming – and Heini rose.

The applause which greeted him was loud and enthusiastic for Heini Radek was an amazingly personable young man with his dark curls, his graceful body. This was how a pianist should look and in Liszt's city comparisons were not hard to make.

Heini bowed, smiled at a girl in the front row, again up at the gallery, gave a respectful nod in the direction of Hungary's greatest composer. Turning to settle himself on the piano stool he found that Mali, her Adam's apple working, was leaning forward in her chair. He had told her again and again that she had to sit back, that the audience must not be aware of any figure but his, and she jerked backwards. It was unbelievable – how could anyone be so gauche? And she had drenched herself with some appalling sickly scent beneath which the odour of sweat was still discernible.

But now there had to be only the music. He closed his eyes for a moment of concentration, opened them – and began to play.

And Professor Sandor, who had slipped into the front row, nodded, for the boy in spite of all was very, very musical and the persuasion, the work, he had put into arranging the concert had been worthwhile.

It was after three encores, after the applause and the flowers thrown onto the platform by an excited group of schoolgirls, that Heini thought of Ruth again. She always waited for him wherever he played – unobtrusive, quiet, but so very pretty, standing close by so that he could smile at her and claim her, but never crowding in when people wanted to tell him how much they had enjoyed the music. And afterwards she would take him back to the Felsengasse and Leonie would have his favourite dishes on the table, and they would talk about the concert and relive the evening till he was relaxed enough to sleep. Or if he was invited to a party, to people who might be useful to him, Ruth slipped quietly away without a word of reproach.

Whereas Mali now was waiting for praise, her eyes worried behind her spectacles. 'Was it all right?' she asked breathlessly. 'Everything was all right, wasn't it?'

'Yes, yes,' he said, managing to smile, and then returned to greet his well-wishers, and to receive their volatile greetings, so different from the well-bred handshakes and heel clicks of the Viennese.

But late that night, returning home, he realized again how bereft he was. That his father would be working late in his editorial office he knew, but his stepmother too had gone out. True she had left a note and a pot of goulash on the stove, but Heini had never had to return to an empty house.

He was out on the moonlit verandah when his father came through the French windows carrying two glasses of wine.

'How did it go?'

'Pretty well, I think.'

'I've heard good things already on the grapevine. You'll go far, Heini.'

Heini smiled and took his glass. 'I miss Ruth,' he said.

'Yes, I can imagine,' said his father, who had met Ruth in Vienna. 'If I were you, I'd marry her quickly before someone else snaps her up!'

'Oh, they won't do that. We belong.'

Beside him, Radek was silent, looking down at the lights of the city in which he had lived all his life. A man of fifty, he looked older than his age and troubled.

'How's it going with your visa?'

'All right, as far as I know.'

'Well, don't delay, Heini. I don't like the way things are shaping. If Hitler moves against the Czechs, the Hungarians will try and get a share of the pickings and that means kowtowing to the Germans. There aren't any laws against the Jews yet, but they'll come.' And abruptly: 'I've taken a job in Switzerland. Marta is going ahead next week to find us an apartment.'

Left alone again, Heini was filled with disquiet. For his father to leave his home and the prestige he enjoyed in Hungary meant there was danger indeed. Heini did not like the idea of England: *The Land Without Music*, the country of fogs and men in bowler hats who had done unmentionable things to each other at boarding school, but it looked as though he had better get himself there quickly. And he was going to Ruth, his starling, his page turner, his love. Humbly, Heini, staring down at the lights of a barge as it slipped beneath the Elisabeth Bridge, admitted that he had taken Ruth too much for granted. Well, all this was going to change. Not only would he make Ruth wholly his, physically as well as mentally, but he was ready – yes, he was almost ready now – to marry her. At twenty-one he was very young to be taking such a step and his agent in Vienna had advised against it. So much patronage at the start of a musician's career came from wealthy matrons and they were apt to look with a particular kindness on unmarried youths. But this did not matter. He was prepared to make the sacrifice.

On an impulse, he fetched a piece of paper and, lighting the lamp in the corner of the verandah, sat down to write a letter. He told Ruth of the concert and the disaster Mali had been, and wrote movingly and without hesitation of his love. Knowing, though, how practical Ruth was, how she needed to help, he wrote also of what he wanted her to do.

I shall have to have a piano as soon as I arrive, darling, wrote Heini. *I don't of course expect you to buy one – I know money may be a little tight till your family gets settled – only to rent one. A baby grand would be ideal, but if your parents' drawing room won't accommodate that, I'll make do with an upright for the time being. A Bösendorfer would be best, you know how I prefer them, but I'll be quite happy with a Steinway or a Bechstein, but if it's a Bechstein it must be a Model 8, not any of the smaller ones. Perhaps you'd better leave the tuning till the day before I come – and not an English piano, Ruth, not even a Broadwood. I'm sure I can leave it all*

to you, my love; you've never failed me yet and
you never will.

When he had signed the letter, Heini still lingered for a while, inhaling the scent of mignonette from the garden.

'I love you, Ruth,' he said aloud, and felt uplifted and purged and *good* as people do when they have committed themselves to another. He would have stayed longer, but for the whine of a mosquito somewhere above him. Once, on the Grundlsee, a midge had bitten him on the pad of his index finger and it had turned septic. Hurrying indoors, Heini closed the window and then went to bed.

8

It was not until she stood on the platform and looked up at the royal-blue coaches with their crests and the words *Compagnie Internationale des Wagons-Lits* painted over the windows, that Ruth realized they were travelling on the Orient Express.

Now, sitting opposite Quin in the dining car as the train streamed through the twilit Austrian countryside, she looked about her in amazement. She had expected luxury, but the Lalique panels, the rosewood marquetry of the partitions, the gilded metal flowers on the ceiling were sumptuous beyond belief. On the damask-covered table lay napkins folded into butterflies; a row of crystal glasses stood beside each plate; sprays of poinsettias, like crimson shields, glowed in the light of the lamp.

'Oh, I can't believe this,' said Ruth, trying to feel guilty and not succeeding. 'It's like a real and proper honeymoon. You shouldn't have done it.'

'It was no trouble,' said Quin, handing her the menu sheet.

But in fact the bribing and manoeuvring to get a compartment at such notice had been considerable. He'd done it, wanting to give her an interval of comfort between the days of hiding in the museum and the poverty which awaited her in London, and now, as she bent over the gold-lettered menu, he summoned the waiter and instructed him to pull down the blinds, for they were approaching the familiar country round her beloved Grundlsee.

'I ought to be a Hungarian countess,' said Ruth, looking round at the other diners. 'Or at least a spy.' She had taken one look at the people getting onto the train and unpacked the page-turning frock. Even so, she felt badly underdressed – whereas Quin, in the mysterious way of Englishmen who return from the wilds, was immaculate in his dinner jacket. 'Look at that woman's stole – it's a sable!' she said under her breath.

'I dare say she'd swop with you,' said Quin, glancing at their middle-aged neighbour with her heavily painted face.

'Because I'm with you, do you mean?'

'No, not because of that,' said Quin, but he did not elaborate.

'Do you think you might help me to order?' asked Ruth presently. 'There seems to be so *much*.'

'I was hoping you would suggest that,' said Quin. 'You see, I think we should pay particular attention to the wine.'

The wine, when it came, was presented by the sommelier who undid its napkin and held it out to Quin rather in the manner of a devoted midwife showing the head of a ducal household that he really has his longed-for son.

'Try it,' said Quin, exchanging a look of complicity with the waiter.

Ruth picked up her glass . . . sipped . . . closed her eyes . . . sipped again . . . opened them. For a moment it looked as though she was going to speak – to make an assessment, a comparison. But she didn't. She just shook her head once, wonderingly – and then she smiled.

All Ruth's acquaintances in Vienna knew that she could be silenced by music. It fell to Quinton Somerville, proffering a Pouilly-Fuissé, Vieux, to discover that she could be silenced too by wine.

'You know, I shall be sorry to relinquish your education,' he said. 'You're a natural.'

'But we can still be friends, can't we? Later, I mean, after the divorce?'

Quin did not answer. The wine seemed to have gone to Ruth's hair rather than her head: the golden locks shone and glinted, tendrils curved round the collar of her dress – one had come to rest in a whorl above her left breast – and her eyes were soft with dreams. Quin *had* friends, but they did not really look like that.

Ruth's vol-au-vents arrived: tiny, feather-light, filled with foie gras and oysters, and she had time only to eat and marvel and throw an occasional admiring glance at Quin, despatching with neat-fingered panache his flambéed crayfish. It was not until the plates were cleared and the finger bowls brought that she said: 'About our wedding . . . about being married . . .'

'Yes?'

'Would you mind if we didn't tell anyone about it? No one at all?'

Quin put down his glass. 'No, not in the least; in fact I'd prefer it; I hate fusses.' But he was surprised: the Bergers seemed a family singularly unsuited to secrets. 'Will you be able to keep it from your parents?'

'Yes, I think so. Later I suppose they'll find out because I'll have my own passport and it'll be British, but we'd be divorced by then.' She hesitated, wondering whether to say more. 'You see, they're very old-fashioned and they might find it difficult to understand that a marriage could mean absolutely nothing. And I couldn't bear it if they tried to . . . make you . . .' She shook her head and began again. 'They've been very good to Heini; he practically lived with us, but I don't think they altogether understand about him . . . my mother in particular. She might think that you . . . that we . . .'

No, she couldn't explain to Quin how she dreaded her parents' approval of this marriage, the gratitude which would embarrass him and make him feel trapped. To make Quin feel that he was still part of her life in any way after they landed would be an appalling return for his kindness.

The sommelier returned, beaming at Ruth as at a gifted pupil who has passed out of her confirmation class with honours. The wine list was produced again and consulted, and it was with regret that he and Quin agreed that in view of mademoiselle's youth it would be unwise to proceed to the Margaux he would otherwise have recommended with the guinea fowl.

'But there is a Tokay for the dessert, monsieur – an Essencia 1905 which is something special, *je vous assure.*'

'Is this how you live in your home?' asked Ruth when her new friend had gone. 'Do you have a marvellous cook and a splendid wine cellar and all that?'

He shook his head. 'I have a cellar, but my home is not in the least like this. It's on a cold cliff by a grey sea in the most northern county in England – if you go any further you bump into Scotland.'

'Oh.' It did not sound very inviting. 'And who lives in it when you aren't there? Does it stand empty?'

'I have an old aunt who looks after it for me. Or rather she's a second cousin but I've always called her aunt and she's a very aunt-like person. My parents died when I was small and then my grandfather, and she came to keep house after that. I'm greatly beholden to her because it means I can be away as much as I want and know that everything runs smoothly.'

'Were you fond of her as a child?'

'She left me alone,' said Quin.

Ruth frowned, trying to embrace this concept. No one had ever left her alone – certainly not her mother or her father or her Aunt Hilda or the maids . . . Not even Uncle Mishak, teaching her the names of the plants. And as for Heini . . .

'Did you like that?' she asked. 'Being left alone, I mean?'

Quin smiled. 'It's rather a British thing,' he said. 'We seem to like it on the whole. But don't trouble yourself – I don't think it would suit you.'

'No, I don't think it would. Miss Kenmore – my Scottish governess, do you remember her? – she was very fond of Milton and she taught me that sonnet where you do nothing. The last line is very famous and sad. *They also serve who only stand and wait.* I'm not very good at that.'

The dessert came – a *soufflé au citron* – and with it the Tokay in a glass as graceful as a lily . . . And presently a bowl of fresh fruit straight out of a Flemish still life, and chocolate truffles . . . and coffee as black as night.

'Oh, this is like heaven! If I was very rich I think I would spend my life travelling the world in a train and never get there. Never arrive, just keep on and on!'

'It's a dream many people have,' said Quin, opening a walnut for her and inspecting it carefully before he put it on her plate. 'Arriving means living and living is hard work.'

'Even for you?'

'For everyone.'

Ruth looked up, wondering what could be difficult for a man so independent, so successful, the citizen of a free and mighty land. 'It's odd, even before the horror . . . before the Nazis, people used to say to me, oh, you're young and healthy, you can't have any problems, but sometimes I did. It seems silly now when all one hopes for is to be alive. But you know . . . with Heini . . . I love him so much, I want to serve him, not by standing and waiting but by doing things. But sometimes I didn't get it right.'

'In what way?'

'Well, Heini is a musician. He has to practise most of the day and he likes me to be there. But I love being out of doors . . . everybody does, I suppose, only you can't play the piano out of doors – not unless you're in the Prater All Girls Band,' she glanced reproachfully at Quin who grinned back, unrepentant, 'and Heini isn't. So sometimes I used to get very resentful sitting there hour after hour with the windows tight shut because draughts are bad for pianos. It seems awful to think of now when I realize how lucky I was and that all of us were safe. Do you think we shall go back to being petty like that if the world becomes normal again?'

'If it is petty to want to be in the fresh air, then yes, I'm afraid we will,' said Quin.

But now it could not be postponed much longer, for the diners were leaving; the waiters were bowing them out and pocketing their tips – and it became necessary for Ruth to face that technically she was on honeymoon with Professor Quinton Somerville and must now go to bed.

'I'll stay in the bar for a while and smoke my pipe,' said Quin, and she rose and made her way down the train, through the dimly lit and silent corridors of the wagon-lits, and into Compartment Number Twenty-Three.

It was no good pretending that this bore the slightest resemblance to the kind of sleeping cubicles she had travelled in previously with their two bunks and narrow ladder. There was no question of climbing up and out of sight till morning, for confronting her were two undoubted beds, separated only by a strip of carpet. Had this been a proper honeymoon, she would have been able to stretch out her hand and hold her husband's in the night. And the steward had been busy. Quin's pyjamas, her own shamingly girlish cotton nightdress, were laid out on the monogrammed pillows and, above the marble wash basin, his shaving brush and safety razor rested beside her toothbrush in a manner that was disconcertingly connubial.

In other ways, though, the compartment was more like Aladdin's cave: the snow-white triangle of the turned down sheets, the pink-shaded lights throwing a glow on the dark panelling . . . Carafes of fluted glass held drinking water; a bunch of black grapes lay in a chased silver bowl.

She undressed, put on the nightdress she had packed for her ascent of the Kanderspitze – and for a lusting moment imagined herself in eau-de-nil silk pyjamas piped in black. No one would have *seen* them; she would have stayed entirely under the bedclothes, but she would have known that they were there.

Safely in bed, she turned off the lights to give Quin privacy, turned them on again so that he wouldn't fall

111

over things – and found that in this marvellous train there was a third alternative – a dimmer switch which caused the room to be filled with a soft, faint radiance like the light inside the petals of a rose.

When Quin came she would roll over to face the wall and pretend to be asleep, but as the train raced through the night, her tired brain threw up images of bridal nights throughout the ages . . . Of virgins brought to the beds of foreign kings, inserted in four-posters as big as houses to await bridegrooms seen only once in cloth of gold . . . The Mi-Mi had communal wedding nights; old ladies sang outside the hut of the married couple, young people danced and called encouragement through the wooden slats . . . And those poor Victorian girls in novels, told the facts of life too late or not at all, who tried to climb up window curtains or hide in wardrobes . . .

Would she have been looking for wardrobes if this had been a proper wedding night? At least she knew the facts of life – had known them since she was six years old. Now, moving restlessly between the sheets, Ruth wondered if she had pursued her studies a bit too zeal-ously, there on the Grundlsee. Kraft-Ebbing, Havelock Ellis, Sigmund Freud . . . There was so much that could go wrong, all the gentlemen had agreed on that. Frigidity, for example. Ruth had been particularly alarmed about frigidity, being a child who even then preferred fire to ice. But probably that wouldn't have happened here . . . not with someone who could always make her laugh.

It was an hour since she had left the dining car. Turning over, she closed her eyes and feigned sleep – but another hour passed, and another, and still he did not come.

She slept at last, only to be woken by a sudden jolt. The train had stopped, footsteps were heard outside, voices raised.

She was instantly terrified. It had happened. She was going to be taken off the train and turned back, as she had been turned back before. The bed beside hers was still empty. Unthinking, desperate, she ran out into the corridor.

Quin was standing by the window. He had pulled up the blind and was looking out at the moonlit landscape – and his pipe, for once, was actually alight.

'They're coming!' she cried. 'Oh, God, I knew it would go wrong! They're going to send me back!'

He turned and saw her, half-asleep still, but terribly afraid, and without thought he opened his arms as she, equally without thought, ran into them.

'Hush,' he said, holding her, manoeuvring so as to lay his pipe on the narrow windowsill. 'It's perfectly all right. There's something on the line, that's all. A cow, perhaps.'

'A cow?' She blinked up at him, made a negative, despairing movement of the head.

'One of those fat piebald ones, the kind you get on chocolate wrappers. Milk chocolate, of course; they're very good milkers, piebald cows.' He went on talking nonsense till the shivering grew less. Then: 'We're over the border,' he said. 'We're absolutely safe. We're in France.'

But she still couldn't believe it. 'Really?' she said, lifting her face to his. 'You're telling me the truth? But how did we get across – no one came to search us. Usually they come and –' She started to shiver again, knowing the brutality the border guards had shown to other refugees; the way they confiscated at the last minute even the few treasures they had been able to take.

'I left our passport with the *chef du train* – the border's only a formality for us.'

Our passport . . . The passport in which His Britannic Majesty's Secretary of State requested and required those whom it concerned to let the bearer pass without let or hindrance . . . For a moment, Ruth wanted nothing except to belong to this man and his world. With Quin, and those who protected him, one would always be safe. She would even live in a cold house on a northern cliff for that; even endure being left alone by his aunt.

Then, as the terror receded, she became aware that she stood in his arms in the corridor of a train in nothing but her nightdress – and not a suitable nightdress, a childish cotton one with a crumpled ribbon. That she had thrown herself at him and been entirely unashamed when all she owed him for ever and ever was to absent herself, to not make demands on him or claim even another minute of his time. Probably he thought – Oh God, surely not . . .

114

'I'm sorry, I've been an idiot,' she said pulling roughly away. 'You must think –'

'I don't think anything,' he said, but her fierce withdrawal had made him angry. Did she really think he would take advantage of her – a girl scarcely out of the schoolroom? Hadn't he made it entirely clear what this marriage was about? 'You'd better get back to bed,' he said abruptly – and she saw confirmation of her fears in his set face, and hurried back to the compartment and shut the door.

When she woke in the morning, he was lying fully dressed on the bed with his arms behind his head and his eyes open as he watched the rising sun.

They reached Calais two hours later. Seagulls wheeled above them, porters shouted on the quayside, cranes swung over their heads. This was a clean, white world, as different as could be from the enclosed luxury of the train.

'I'm really beginning to believe we'll get there,' said Ruth.

'Of course we'll get there.'

They went on board. Even for the short Channel crossing he had secured a cabin. 'You'll need another sweater,' he said, lifting her suitcase onto the rack. 'It'll be cold on deck and you'll have to pay your respects to the White Cliffs of Dover.'

She nodded and opened the case. On top, carefully packed, was a framed photograph which she had taken from the flat, kept in the museum . . . even packed, wrapped in her nightdress, in the rucksack with which she proposed to swim into France. Deliberately, she took it out and placed it in Quin's hands. Here was the chance to show him how committed she was to someone else; to make him see that she would never again forget herself as she had done the previous night.

'That's Heini.'

Quin did not doubt it. The photo, taken on the day of his graduation from the Conservatoire, was in colour and emphasized Heini's dark curls, his light grey, long-lashed eyes. He stood beside a Bösendorfer grand, one hand resting on the lid, and he was smiling. Across the right-hand corner of the picture, in large, spiky Gothic script, were the words: *To my little starling, with fondest love, Heini.*

'How do starlings come into it?' Quin wanted to know, remembering the distress that mention of these robust birds had caused her in the flat.

Ruth explained. 'Mozart had one. He bought it in the market for thirty-four kreutzers and he kept it in a cage in his room. It used to sing and sing but however loud it sang it never bothered him . . .' She told the story, her face alight, for she never forgot that first time when Heini had claimed her.

Quin listened politely. 'And what happened to it?' he asked when she had finished.

'It died,' Ruth admitted.

'It would,' commented Quin.

'What do you mean?'

'Well, they're not cage birds, are they? Perhaps Mozart didn't know that?'

'Mozart knew *everything*,' she flashed.

Quin grinned and left her. She put on an extra sweater and made her way onto the deck. As she emerged from the First-Class Lounge, she saw two fur-clad and unmistakably upper-class ladies, settled for sea sickness in reclining steamer chairs.

'Wasn't that Quin Somerville?' said one.

'Was it? I didn't see.'

'I'm pretty sure it was. That crinkly face . . . so attractive. I thought I saw him on the platform with a girl. One of those little peasants in a loden cape.'

'Goodness! Could he be serious?'

'I wouldn't have thought so, she hardly seemed his style. Not nearly soignée enough.'

A steward passed and the ladies demanded rugs.

'If he *is* serious, poor Lavinia will go into a decline. She still thinks she's going to get him for Fenella.'

'Well, you can't blame her. All that money and –'

Ruth drew back and went out by a different door. Quin was standing in the bows, his hair blown by the wind, absorbed in the pattern of the water as the ship drew away. I knew he was rich, of course, she thought: I must have known, and that the world is full of Fenellas waiting to marry him. Well, good luck to them – a man who sneers at Mozart and runs from Strauss as though the devil is at his heels.

'I suppose we won't see each other again after we land,' she said resolutely.

117

'I'd like to see you safe to Belsize Park, but after that it would certainly be best if we went our separate ways. If you want anything you have only to contact my solicitor – not just about the annulment, but about anything with which you need help. He's an old friend.'

Yes, she thought; your solicitor. Not you.

'I owe you so much,' she said. 'Not just that you got me out, but money. A lot of money. I must pay you back.'

'Yes, you must do that,' he said – and she turned to him in surprise. His voice was harsh and forbidding and she had not expected that. All along he had been so open-handed, so generous. 'And you know what that means?'

'That I must find a job and –'

'That's exactly what it doesn't mean! The most stupid thing you can do is to take some trumpery job for short-term gain. I can just see you being a shop assistant or some such nonsense. The only sensible thing to do is to get yourself back to university as soon as possible. If University College has offered you a place you couldn't do better. Remember there are all sorts of grants now for people in your position; the world is waking up at last to what is happening in Europe. Then when you've got a degree you can get a decent job and pay me back in your own good time.'

She digested this, but he noticed that she made no promise and he frowned, fearing some quixotic nonsense on her part – and Ruth, seeing the frown, remembered something else he had bestowed.

118

'What about the ring?' she asked. 'What shall I do with it?'

'Anything you like,' he said indifferently. 'Sell it, pawn it, keep it.'

Quelled, she looked down at her hand. 'Anyway I'd better take it off before my parents ask questions. Or Heini, if he's there already.'

She tugged at the ring, turned it, tugged again. 'It's stuck,' she said, bewildered.

'It can't be,' he said. 'It slipped on so easily.'

'Well, it is,' she said, suddenly furious.

'Perhaps your hands are hot.'

'How could they be? It's *freezing*!' And indeed they were well clear of the harbour now and in a biting wind.

He laid a hand lightly on hers. 'No, they seem to be cold, but I can't see any chilblains. Try soap.'

She didn't answer, but turned away and he watched her stamp off, her hair flying. She was away for a considerable time and when she returned and laid her hand on the rail once more, he was startled. Her ring finger was not just reddened, it looked as though it had been put through a mangle.

'Good God,' he said. 'Was it as bad as that?'

She nodded, still visibly upset, and, realizing that she had retreated into her Old Testamental world of omens and disasters, he left her alone.

When he spoke again, it was to say: 'Look! There they are!'

And there, indeed, they were: the White Cliffs of Dover, the hymned and celebrated symbol of freedom.

So much less impressive than foreigners always expected; not very high, not very white . . . yet Quin, who had made light often enough of this undistinguished piece of Cretaceous chalk, now found himself genuinely moved. After the horrors he had left behind in Europe, he was more thankful than he could have imagined to be home.

9

At the end of the Bergers' second week in Belsize Park, Hilda was sacked. She had climbed onto a stepladder to dust an ornament on the top of Mrs Manfred's bookcase, and the bookcase had fallen on top of her. It was the only one in the house, Mrs Manfred not being a reader, but glass-fronted, and a splinter had hit the dog.

No one was surprised, and no one blamed Mrs Manfred, but Hilda took it hard and stayed in bed, covered in zinc plaster, and wrote letters to the district officer in Bechuanaland enquiring after the Mi-Mi, which she did not post because she had no money for stamps and Leonie looked as though she would keel over if asked for anything at all.

Uncle Mishak, as the days passed and Ruth still did not come, got up at dawn and walked. He covered vast distances in his slow, countryman's gait and he knew that this was risky, for in one month, or perhaps two, his shoes would wear out, but he had to be out of doors.

Mishak's beloved wife was beyond hurt. He had

brought a handful of earth from her grave into exile, but he needed nothing to remind him of Marianne. She was inside his soul.

But to Ruth, in the nightmare world his country had become, there could befall unthinkable harm. Mishak had not wanted to come to the Felsengasse when Marianne died. He appreciated Leonie's kindness, but he had wanted to stay in the house he had built for his wife on the slopes of the Wienerwald. He had come to the flat to thank Leonie for her offer and to refuse it. But Leonie was out. It was the six-year-old Ruth, fresh from her bath, who had thrown her arms around him and said: 'Oh, you're coming to live, won't it be *wonderful!* You'll take me to the Prater, won't you – I mean the Wurstlprater, not the healthy part with fresh air – and can we go and see the llamas at Schönbrunn? Inge says they spit and make you quite wet. And you'll let me lean out of the window of the cable car when we go up to the Kahlenberg, won't you? *You* won't keep holding my legs?'

The blissful, self-seeking greed of a secure child who longs to gobble up the world was something he never forgot. Ruth was not sorry for him, she wanted him for her own purposes. Mishak changed his mind and came; they saw the llamas and more . . .

Now sitting in Kensington Gardens watching the children sail their boats, this quiet old man who preferred not to step on molehills in case there was someone at home, found that his knuckles had whitened on the sides of the bench, and knew that he

122

would kill without compunction anyone who harmed his niece.

Professor Berger said little about his lost daughter. He went to Bloomsbury House each morning, he worked in the library each afternoon, but no one, now, would have taken him for a man of fifty-eight. Then one morning he took a bus to Harley Street where his sponsor, Dr Friedlander, had his dental practice.

'I'm going back to Vienna,' he said. 'I'm going to find Ruth and I have to ask you to lend me the fare.'

No one knew what it cost him to ask for money. Since their arrival the Bergers had taken nothing from their sponsor in spite of frequent offers of help.

'You can have the fare and welcome,' said Friedlander. 'I'll lend it to you; I'll give it to you. The poor Englanders are so grateful for someone who doesn't pull out their teeth as soon as they sit down that they're beating a path to my door. But you're mad, Kurt. They won't let you out again and then what'll happen to Leonie? Is that what you imagine Ruth wants?'

'I can't do nothing,' said the Professor, 'it isn't possible.'

'Have you told Leonie that you mean to return?'

'Not yet. There's a big student transport coming on Thursday. I'll wait till then, but after that . . .'

Leonie, meanwhile, continued to be good. She approached the psychoanalyst from Breslau and tried to persuade that black-haired, gloomy lady to let her help with the cooking so as to ensure a less lingering death for the bruised vegetables that were Fräulein

Lutzenholler's diet. She fetched Paul Ziller's shirts from his room three houses down and washed them, and ironed his cummerbund, and she visited other émigrés in outlying suburbs. But at the end of the second week her body was beginning to take over. She had fits of dizziness, her skirt began to slip as she spectacularly lost weight. More frighteningly, she was finding it increasingly difficult to be good. She wanted to hit people, to throttle Miss Bates in her ever-dripping underwear. And if she stopped being good, the thin thread that bound her to a beneficent providence would snap and precipitate her daughter into hell.

Mrs Burtt, drying cups in the scullery behind the Willow Tea Rooms, was in a bad mood. She personally did not care for Jews, gypsies or Jehovah's Witnesses, and Commies, the world over, deserved everything they got. But the papers that morning had been even fuller than usual of nastiness – people in Berlin and Vienna being rounded up, old professors having to scrub the streets with toothbrushes – and though she didn't even know where the Polish Corridor was and didn't mind much what happened to the people in the Sudetenland, whoever they were, it was beginning to look as though something would have to be done about Hitler. Which brought her stomach lurching downwards yet again, because one of the people who would be doing it would be her nineteen-year-old son, Trevor, who that morning had said he fancied the air force.

The customers were in low spirits too, she could tell

even without going out in front. They weren't talking like they usually did, just reading the copies of *Country Life* the ladies now brought downstairs. It was odd how they fancied all those pictures of stately homes and the debutantes with the long necks who were going to marry the Honourable Somebody or Other. You wouldn't think they'd be so keen, all those professors and doctors full of degrees and learning.

Still, the guggle cake had turned out a treat. Miss Maud had baked it last night and Miss Violet had iced it, and though it didn't seem all that different to the rich sponge her auntie made except it was in a wiggly mould, the customers would be pleased. It had been Miss Violet's idea to wait till Mrs Berger came and let her have the first slice on the house: sort of like launching a ship – and the least you could do with what was happening to her daughter.

Only Mrs Berger, this morning, was late.

Mrs Burtt was right. There was a new hopelessness in the air. Everyone knew that Ruth had not been on the student transport and that Professor Berger intended to go back to Vienna. Now they faced the long weekend, so dreaded by exiles, when every place that could help them was closed and even the libraries and cafés which sheltered them were barred.

Paul Ziller, trying to immerse himself in an article about the oiling of field guns, had dreamt yet again about his second violin, the plump, infuriating, curly-headed Klaus Biberstein whose terrible jokes had sent the quartet into groans of protest, whose unsuccessful pursuit of leggy blondes was a byword – and who only had to tuck his Amati under his chin to become a god. Ziller missed his cellist, now playing in a dance band in New York, and his viola player who was entirely Aryan and had stayed behind, but missing Biberstein was different because he was dead. Hearing the storm troopers come up the stairs to his fourth-floor flat he had shouted to the passers by to clear the pavement, and jumped.

Dr Levy was playing chess with the blond actor from the Burg Theatre, but it was hard to concentrate for today he knew with certainty that he would never resit his medical exams in English. At forty-two he was too old to begin again – and even if he passed, they would find some other regulation for keeping him from practising. Not that he blamed the medical profession. In Vienna the doctors had been just as repressive, banding together against émigrés from the East.

'I'm going to take your knight,' he said to von Hofmann, who had not been allowed to say *Schweinehund* or anything else in a film about the Great War. The actor's union had objected, and anyway with another war perhaps on the way, no one wanted films about soldiers. They wanted Fred Astaire and Rita Hayworth and Deanna Durbin. They wanted ocean liners and Manhattan apartments furnished all in white – and who ever said *Schweinehund* in them?

The lady with the poodle entered, disappointing Mrs Weiss, with her bulging horsehair purse, who had hoped it was someone for whom she could buy a cake and tell about her daughter-in-law who that morning had forced open her bedroom window with some rubbish about rooms needing to be aired. Mrs Weiss had never allowed wet air into a room in which she slept and had told Moira so, and Georg (now called George) who should have taken his mother's part, had slunk off to the garage and gone to work.

At the table by the hat stand the banker and his wife from Hamburg sat in silence, each reading a magazine. In Germany they had been a successful and well-established *ménage à trois*, but Lisa's lover, a racially pure car salesman, had stayed behind and though he tried to take his place, the banker knew that he was failing. The walls of their small room were thin, the bed narrow – and afterwards, always, she sighed.

Then Leonie entered the café – and the sadness that was in all of them found a focus. There was no need to ask if there was any news. This was a Demeter who had given up all hope of rescuing her daughter from the Underworld. Ruth, like Persephone, was lost, and in the streets of North-West London, winter had come.

Supported by her husband and uncle, Leonie reached her table and sat down, but no one today did more than nod a greeting. Even a smile seemed intrusive.

In the kitchen, Miss Violet fetched the cake knife, Miss Maud cut a wedge from the virgin *Guglhupf*, Mrs Burtt fetched a plate – and the procession set off.

'With the compliments of the management,' said Miss Maud, setting the plate down in front of Leonie.

127

Leonie looked and understood. She took in the sacrifice of principle, the honour they did her. Then she breathed once deeply, like a swimmer about to go under. Her face crumpled, her shoulders sagged – and she burst into the most dreadful and heart rending sobs. It was weeping made incarnate: once begun it was impossible to stop. Professor Berger took her hand, but for the first time in her life, she pushed him away. She wanted to rid herself of tears and die.

In the café, no one else made a sound. Dr Levy did not offer professional help; von Hofmann, usually so gallant, did not proffer his handkerchief. And Miss Maud and Miss Violet looked at each other, horrified by what they had done.

Then suddenly Paul Ziller, at a table by the window, pushed back his chair.

'Oh dear!' said Miss Maud.

It was a mild remark, coming from the daughter of a general, for the damage was considerable. The coffee pot on the Bergers' table knocked over, staining the cloth, three willow-pattern plates broken . . . Mrs Berger's chair, as she pushed it back, had fallen on to Dr Levy's scrambled eggs. Nor had the poodle found it possible to remain uninvolved. Barking furiously, he had collided with the hat stand which had keeled over, missing the pottery cat but not the bowl of potpourri on the windowsill, nor the pretty blue and white ashtray the ladies had brought from Gloucestershire.

In the middle of the wreckage stood Leonie, holding

her daughter in her arms. Except that this wasn't *holding* it was fusion. The tears she still shed were Ruth's tears also; no human agency could have separated those two figures. Even for her husband, Leonie could not relinquish Ruth . . . could only draw him closer with a briefly freed hand. There had been joy in the moment of marriage, joy in childbirth – but this was a joy like no other in the world.

Uncle Mishak was the first member of the family to notice the devastation: Miss Violet dabbing at the tables, Miss Maud picking up pieces of crockery, Mrs Burtt on her knees. To add to the chaos, Aunt Hilda, who had leapt from her bed after redirecting Ruth to the café, had fallen over the bucket into which the ladies were wringing their cloths.

'I am so sorry,' said Leonie, emerging, and did indeed try hard to embrace the concept of sorryness and to calculate the damage.

It was now that Mrs Weiss rose. Her raddled face was bathed in an unaccustomed dignity, her voice was firm.

'I *will pay*!' she announced. 'I will pay for *everythink*.'

And she did pay. The ladies accepted her offer; everyone understood that the old lady had to be part of what was happening. Pound notes and half-crowns, shillings and sixpences tumbled out of the dreadful purse made of the scalped hair of East Prussian horses. She paid not for one coffee pot, but for two: not for three willow-pattern plates, but six. For the first time since she had come to England, the purse bulging with her daughter-in-law's conscience money was empty; the clasp clicked together without catching on the unshed largesse. It was Mrs Weiss's finest hour and not one person in the Willow Tea Rooms grudged it to her.

'So!' said Leonie, some twenty minutes later. 'Now tell us. How did you get here? How did you come?'

The tables had been cleared, clean cloths spread, fresh coffee brought. Though she found it necessary to sit so that her shoulder touched Ruth's, Leonie was now able to listen.

Ruth had rehearsed her story. Sitting between her parents, smiling across at Mishak and her friends from Vienna, she said: 'Someone rescued me. An Englishman who helps people to escape.'

'Like the Scarlet Pimpernel?' enquired Paul Ziller, impressed.

'Yes, a bit like that. Only, I mustn't ever get in touch with him again. None of us must. That was part of the bargain.'

'There was nothing illegal?' asked her father, stern even in the midst of his great happiness. 'No forged papers or anything like that?'

'No, nothing illegal; I swear it on Mozart's head,' said Ruth, and the Professor was satisfied, aware of the position the composer's head occupied in his daughter's life.

Leonie, however, was not satisfied at all. 'But this is awful! How can we thank him? How can we tell him what he has *done* for us?' she cried. A multitude of deeds she could have performed in gratitude – a plethora of baked cakes, embroidered shirts, letters of ecstatic appreciation – rose up before her. She wanted to rush out into the street after this unknown benefactor, to wash his feet as Mary Magdalene had done with Jesus.

'It has to be like that,' said Ruth, 'otherwise we might endanger other people that he could rescue' – and aware that her mother was having difficulties, she quoted Miss Kenmore's favourite sonnet. '*They also serve who only stand and wait*,' said Ruth, without, however, impressing Leonie who was not of the stuff that those who only stand and wait are made.

It was only now that Ruth, who had wanted to give her first moments wholly to her parents, dared to ask the question she had held back.

'And Heini?' she said.

It was all right. Not aware that she had crossed her hands on her breast in the age-old gesture of apprehension, she saw her father smile.

'All is well, my dear,' said the Professor. 'He's still in Budapest but we've had a letter. He is coming.'

It was very quiet in the café after the Bergers had left. One by one, the other customers got up to go, but the three men who had known the family in Vienna sat on for a while.

'So Persephone has returned,' said the actor.

Dr Levy nodded, but his face was grave and the

other two exchanged glances for the doctor had his own Persephone: a flaxen-haired, blue-eyed and silly girl whom he nevertheless loved. Hennie had been glad enough to marry the distinguished consultant she had ogled while still a junior nurse, but she seemed in no hurry to join him in exile.

'Perhaps a little celebration?' suggested Ziller, for it did not seem to him a good idea that Levy should return alone to his *The Diseases of the Knee*.

'We could just see what's on,' said von Hofmann.

And what was on, as they found when they had crossed the square and made their way uphill towards the Odeon, was Fred Astaire and Ginger Rogers in *Top Hat* – and without further consultation the three eminent gentlemen, none of whom could afford it, entered the cinema – and Elysium.

While back in the kitchen of the Willow Tea Rooms, Miss Maud and Miss Violet pronounced judgement.

'A very nicely behaved girl,' said Miss Maud.

'Father would have liked her,' said Miss Violet.

There was no higher accolade, but as so often Mrs Burtt managed to get the last word.

'And pretty as a peach!'

10

When he was not at Bowmont or on his travels, Quin lived in a flat on the Chelsea Embankment. On the first floor of a tall Queen Anne house, it had a trellised iron-work verandah from which one looked, over the branches of a mulberry tree, at London's river. The walls of his drawing room were lined with books, a Constable watercolour hung over the fireplace, Persian rugs were scattered on the parquet floor, but no one visiting Quin ever lingered over the furnishings. Without exception, they moved over to the French windows and stood looking out on the panorama of the Thames.

'You always live by water, don't you, darling?' a woman had said to him: 'Very Freudian, don't you think?'

Quin did not think. He liked Chelsea; the little shops in the streets that ran back from the river; greengrocers and shoemakers and picture framers, and the pubs where the bargees still drank, and though he did not go to his lectures at Thameside by boat, it amused him to think that it was possible.

Just as a man's friends are those who get there first and refuse to go away, so his servants are those who have installed themselves and become, for one reason or another, impossible to dismiss. Lockwood had been butler at Bowmont and should not have been shopping and cooking and valeting Quin, a job which meant a considerable loss of salary and prestige. Nevertheless, since Quin at the age of eight had brought his first discoveries up from the beach and demanded that the Somerville Museum of Natural History be set up in the stables, Lockwood had regarded the boy as his responsibility. This involved no show of amiability on the butler's part. He was a tall, thin man with a Neanderthal cranium and mud-coloured eyes and there were those who maintained that Quin's unmarried state was due to the fact that Lockwood had dismembered all aspiring Mrs Somervilles and thrown the pieces in the river.

Quin arrived in the middle of the afternoon, having dropped Ruth off in Belsize Park. Though he had been away five months, Lockwood's greeting was measured.

'Saw you on the newsreel,' he said, and carried Quin's suitcase to the bedroom.

But the furniture glowed with polish, the post was stacked in neat piles, there were fresh flowers in the vases, and now he returned with the tea tray and a plate of muffins.

'Will you be dining at home, then?' When he left

Bowmont, Lockwood had dropped the obsequious manner of an upper servant and now addressed Quin as if he was a wayward, but gifted, nephew.

'Yes, I will, Lockwood. That isn't *boeuf en daube* I can smell, by any chance?'

Lockwood bared his teeth in what he regarded as a smile and agreed that it was. Knowing that he had made his servant happy, for Lockwood was a formidable cook, Quin turned to the post. There were innumerable invitations from hostesses who were presenting their daughters, or giving dances for them, or making up little parties for Ascot and Henley, and the knowledge that he had missed most of these without the necessity of refusing, was pleasant. Though his professional mail went to the university, there was a letter from Saskatchewan offering him the Chair of Zoology and the usual missives from people who had found bones in their gardens and were sure they were mammoths or mastodons. Among the list of names of those who had telephoned, that of Mademoiselle Fleury, who was back from Paris, was prominent.

But it was not Claudine Fleury whom Quin now telephoned, though the thought of her brought a smile to his face; it was his long-suffering deputy and senior lecturer at Thameside, Dr Roger Felton.

Quin had not intended to accept an academic post. It was the journeys, the freedom to follow clues wherever they turned up that he valued in his professional life, and though he kept a room in the Natural History Museum, he had resisted all offers of a chair.

The man who had changed this was Lord Charlefont, the Vice Chancellor of Thameside, an enlightened despot who had changed Thameside from a worthy but undistinguished college of further education into a university with its own charter and a reputation throughout the country. Under Charlefont's reign, Thameside had merged with an art college in Pimlico, taken over the Institute of Natural Sciences and moved into a gracious Palladian building on the south bank of the river which he had wrested from the Ministry of Works.

'I know you don't need the job,' he had said, offering Quin the Chair of Vertebrate Zoology, 'but we need you. I want excellence; I want someone with an international reputation. There shouldn't be any trouble about going off on journeys – I can always find someone to fill in for a term or two – and I think you'd like teaching.'

So Quin had accepted, specifying a personal chair at a lower salary and no administration, and the arrangement had worked well. He found he did like teaching; in Roger Felton he had a willing and efficient deputy, and the field course he ran at Bowmont had become a model of its kind. Moreover, in Lord Charlefont he discovered not only the ideal employer but a friend. The Vice Chancellor's Lodge at Thameside was built into the main courtyard and Charlefont kept open house. A first-year student with problems was as welcome as the most eminent academic and Quin had enjoyed some of the best conversations of his life in the long drawing room with its terrace on the river.

But six months ago, just before Quin left for India, Charlefont had had a heart attack and died within hours. A good end for a strong and active man, but a blow to Thameside and to Quin. Of his successor, Desmond Plackett, who had spent ten years in the Indian Educational Service and been rewarded with a knighthood, Quin, as yet, knew nothing.

Now, dialling the university, he was put through at once to Felton in his laboratory. His deputy taught the Marine Biology course, as well as dealing with admissions: a friendly man, deeply concerned about the students, whose spectacle frames seemed to lighten or darken according to his mood.

'Oh, you're back, are you?' said Felton.

Since Quin himself had abolished the protocol and rank-pulling which still existed in so many university departments, he now had to endure some strong remarks about professors who left their underlings to mark their exam papers while they gallivanted about in foreign cities.

'It wasn't quite like that – but I'm sorry about the extra load. How have they done?'

'Oh, brilliantly on your questions, of course. I dare say you could teach Palaeontology to a chimpanzee and get him a First. The new intake looks promising too – numbers are up again.'

'You haven't had any applications from refugee

organizations, have you? University College is taking foreign students, I know.'

'Not so far.'

'Well, if you get any, accept them – it's hell over there, I can tell you. Even if it means putting them to work in a broom cupboard, say yes.'

'All right, I will. Though I don't know what the new VC will say; he doesn't seem to be much of a one for the huddled masses yearning to breathe free.'

'Plackett's a dud, is he?'

'He's one of those faceless men – adores committees. The paperwork's trebled since he came, but there's no harm in him; it's his wife that's the bother. Wants to improve the moral tone of the university and makes the college servants run her errands. She's a Croft-Ellis by birth – one of the Rutland Croft-Ellises. Mean anything to you?'

'Nothing earth shattering.'

'But that's not all,' said Felton ghoulishly. 'There's a daughter!'

'There usually is, I've found,' said Quin resignedly.

'Ah, but it's worse than that! She's coming to us to do a Zoology degree and she's going straight into the third year because she's covered most of the ground in India. I interviewed her last week and she was kind enough to tell me that she thought our course would be acceptable.'

'Good God,' said Quin.

'Exactly so.'

Quin spent the next two days in the Natural History Museum, supervising the disposal of the specimens which Milner had steered safely through the customs. Thameside he avoided, deciding to go up to Bowmont first and come back to prepare for the autumn term when the man who was filling in as visiting Professor had gone back to the States. Professor Robinson was prone to anxiety: he had worried because Quin's name was still on the door of his room, and about the length of his gown, and it seemed tactful to let him complete his tenure without interference.

But there was one chore which he intended to tackle before he went north: the undoing of his marriage.

The affairs of Bowmont were in the hands of a long-established and dozy firm of solicitors in Berwick-upon-Tweed, but for quick action in this highly personal matter, Quin had selected Dick Proudfoot, of Proudfoot, Buckley and Snaith, whom he had known in Cambridge.

Proudfoot was in his early thirties, a chubby, balding man whose amiable expression became considerably less amiable as Quin began to speak.

'You have done what?'

'I have married an Austrian girl to get her over here. She's partly Jewish and she was in danger – there was nothing else to do. Now I want you to get me a divorce as quickly as you can. I'll provide the evidence, of course. I imagine that business still works about being caught in bed in a hotel by the chambermaid?'

'Funny, I thought you were intelligent,' said Mr

Proudfoot nastily. 'I remember people saying it in Cambridge. What sort of quixotic idiocy is this? Even if it were possible for you to convince the judge that this kind of caper represents a genuine adultery – and they're getting very suspicious these days – it would hardly secure you a speedy divorce. You can't even begin to petition till three years after the marriage.'

Quin frowned. 'I thought the Herbert Act had changed all that? The poor man worked hard enough to get it through.'

'It has increased the grounds on which a divorce may be granted, but in this case the three-year clause still stands.'

'Well, it'll have to be an annulment then,' said Quin cheerfully. 'That was my first idea, but it sounded a bit ecclesiastical.'

Mr Proudfoot sighed and wrote something on a piece of paper. The laws on nullity were archaic and complex, and his subject was company law. 'What do you suggest? Nullity can be declared if one or both parties are under sixteen at the time of the ceremony, if there is a pre-existing marriage, if the parties are related by prohibited degrees of consanguinity, if there is insanity in one partner unknown to the other at the time of the marriage, or if the bride is a nun.'

Quin waved an impatient hand. 'Well, she's not my sister or a nun and she's not technically insane unless trying to swim out of Switzerland with a rucksack can be regarded as mental derangement. What else?'

140

'There is nonconsummation,' said Mr Proudfoot reluctantly, seeing minefields ahead.

'That's the one,' said Quin cheerfully. 'I spent our bridal night in the corridor of the Orient Express.'

'You may have to prove it.' The lawyer made another note, adding snarkily that he presumed Quin would plead wilful refusal to consummate rather than incapacity. 'And there's another difficulty.'

'What's that?'

'Well, you married this girl to give her British citizenship. But if you prove nullity *ex causa precedenti* – that is to say if you dissolve the marriage on grounds existing before it took place – then it is possible that the British citizenship which followed from the marriage could be imperilled. Of course, nonconsummation isn't in this category, but if she's under twenty-one we could be in trouble. The naturalization of minors is under review, but in my opinion we'd be unwise to go for nullity until her status as a British subject is confirmed and she has her own passport.'

Quin looked at his watch. 'Look, do what you can, Dick, and as quickly as possible. The girl's very young and she's in love with a soulful concert pianist. Oh, and write to her, will you, and say we're putting it through as fast as we can. Offer her any help she needs and charge it to me, but I think it's best if I don't see her again.'

'That isn't just best, it's absolutely essential,' said Mr Proudfoot. 'If there's anything that can scupper any kind of divorce or annulment, it's the three Cs.'

'The three whats?'

'Connivance. Collusion. Consent. Any suspicion that you've been fixing things between you and the courts will throw out the evidence then and there.'

'Good God! You mean they'd rather we parted in anger than sensibly and in accord?'

'That is precisely what I mean,' said Mr Proudfoot.

11

It was hot, the summer of 1938. In the streets of Belsize Park and Swiss Cottage and Finchley, the pavements glittered, the dustbins gave out Rabelaisian smells. In the ill-equipped kitchens of the lodging houses, milk turned sour and expiring flies buzzed dismally on strips of sticky paper. Children in buggies were pushed up the hill to Hampstead Heath to picnic in the yellowing grass or catch tiddlers in Whitestone Pond. In Spain, Franco's Fascists scored victory upon victory; in Germany, Hitler stepped up his tirades about the Sudetenland, ready to move against the Czechs. Mussolini started to ape, though less effectively, the Führer's measures against the Jews.

The British would have found it vulgar to let the ill-bred ravings of foreigners interfere with their pleasures. Trenches were dug in the parks, leaflets were issued giving instructions about the issue of gas masks; the fleet stood ready. But the rich left without signs of per-turbation for their grouse moors or houses by the sea.

The poor, as always, stayed behind and took the sunshine on their doorsteps or in their tiny gardens.

The refugees were poor and they stayed.

Ruth's arrival had enabled her family to try to reconstitute their lives. Professor Berger now left for the public library each morning with his briefcase, to sit between Dr Levy and a tramp with holes in his shoes who came to read the paper, and hid from Leonie, and partly even from himself, the knowledge that without the references and notes he had left behind, his book could only be a travesty of what he might have written. Aunt Hilda, having discovered that entry to the British Museum was free, spent hours wandering round the Anthropology section and found (among the exhibits from Bechuanaland) an error which caused her the kind of excited melancholy so common in scholars presented with other people's follies.

'It is *not* a Mi-Mi drinking cup,' she would say each evening. 'I am quite certain. The attribution is wrong.'

'Well then, go and tell someone, Hilda,' Leonie would suggest.

'No. I am only a guest in this country. I have no right.'

Uncle Mishak now had park benches he had made his own, and friends among the gardeners who kept London's squares and gardens tidy. Like a small boy, he would come home with treasures: a clump of wallflowers which still retained their scent, thrown onto a compost heap; a few cherries dropped onto a pavement from an overhanging branch. As for Leonie, once she'd accepted the miracle of Ruth's return, she began to repair the network of friends and relations, of good causes and lame dogs, that had filled her life in Vienna. Dispersed and scattered these might be, but there was still her godmother's sister, newly arrived in Swiss Cottage, a schoolfriend married to a bookbinder in Putney, and an ancient step-uncle from Moravia, a little touched in the head, who sat under the statue of Queen Victoria on the Embankment, convinced that she was Maria Theresia and he was still in his native city.

As for the ladies of the Willow Tea Rooms, they responded to the worsening of the situation in Europe with a gesture of great daring. They decided to stay open in the evening – to the almost sinfully late hour of nine o'clock. This, however, meant engaging a new waitress – and here they were extremely fortunate.

Ruth's first concern when she arrived had been to hide her marriage certificate and all other evidence of her involvement with Professor Somerville whom she could now only serve by never going near him or mentioning his name.

This was not as easy as it sounded. Number 27 Belsize Close was not a place where privacy was high on the list of priorities, nor had Ruth ever had to have secrets from her parents. Fortunately she had read many English adventure stories in which intrepid boys and girls buried treasure beneath the loose floor-boards of whatever house they lived in. Accustomed to the solid parquet floors of her native city, she had been puzzled by this, but now she understood how it could be done. The floor of the Bergers' sitting room, hideously furnished with a sagging moquette sofa, a fumed oak table and brown chenille curtains, was covered in linoleum, and her parents' bedroom next to it was obviously unsuitable. But in the room at the back, with its two narrow beds, which Ruth shared with her Aunt Hilda, the floor was covered only by a soiled rag rug. Dragging aside the wash-stand, she managed to prise open one of the splintered boards and make a space into which she lowered a biscuit tin decorated with a picture of the Princesses Elizabeth and Margaret Rose patting a corgi dog, and containing her documents and the wedding ring which she meant to sell, but not just yet.

Next she went to the post office and secured a box number to which all mail could be sent, and wrote to Mr Proudfoot to tell him what she had done. After which she settled down to look for work. It was nearly two months before the beginning of the autumn term at University College and though she had heeded Quin's admonitions and was looking forward very much to being a student once again, she intended to spend every available second till then helping her family.

Jobs as mother's helps were easy to come by. Within a week, Ruth found herself trailing across Hampstead Heath in charge of the three progressively educated children of a lady weaver. Untroubled by theories on infant care, she felt sorry for the pale, confused, abominably behaved little creatures in their soiled linen smocks, desperately searching for something they were not allowed to do. When the middle one, a six-year-old

146

boy, ran across a busy road, she smacked him hard on the leg which caused instant uproar among his siblings.

'We want it done to us too. Properly,' said the oldest. 'So that you can see the mark, like with Peter.'

Ruth obliged and soon the walks became extremely enjoyable, but, of course, the money was not very good and it was Ruth's announcement that she intended to spend her evenings as a waitress in the Willow Tea Rooms which brought Leonie's period of saintly virtue to a sudden end.

For several days after Ruth was restored to her, Leonie had kept to her vow never again to argue with Ruth or speak a cross word to her. Just to be able to touch Ruth's hand across the table, just to hear her humming in the bath, had been a joy so deep that it had precluded ever crossing Ruth's will again. This, however, was too much.

'You will do nothing of the sort!' she yelled. 'No daughter of mine is going to have her behind pinched by old gentlemen and take tips!'

But Ruth was adamant. 'If Paul Ziller can play gypsy music in a cummerbund, I can be a waitress. And anyway, what about you doing the ironing for that awful old woman across the road?'

Leonie said it was different and canvassed the inmates of the Willow Tea Rooms for support which did not come.

'Of course, when she begins university it will be another matter, but now she will want to help,' said Ziller, meaning – as did Dr Levy, and von Hofmann from the Burg Theatre and the banker from Hamburg – that the sight of this bright-haired girl bearing down on them with a tray of an evening was a pleasure they did not think it necessary to forego.

So Ruth became a waitress at the Willow and was undoubtedly good for trade. For the weary, disillusioned exiles, Ruth was a sign that there was still hope in the world. She had been rescued mysteriously by an Englishman and that in itself was a thought that warmed the heart. And not only was Ruth young and sweet and funny, but she was in love!

'I have had a letter!' Ruth would say, and soon everyone in the Willow Tea Rooms and the square knew about Heini, everyone asked about him. The news that Heini's visa was almost through made them as happy as if the good fortune was their own – and they all understood that it was essential that when Heini arrived, he had his piano.

It was the matter of Heini's piano which disposed of the last remnants of saintliness still adhering to Leonie. For there was only one place where it could possibly go: in the Bergers' so-called sitting room – and Leonie was perfectly correct in saying that it would make the place impossibly crowded.

'All right, he can sleep on the sofa till he has his own place, but Heini *and* the piano – Ruth, be reasonable.'

But when has love been reasonable? Seeing her daughter's distress, Leonie consulted her husband, sure that his strictness would prevail. But the week in which they had believed Ruth lost had changed the Professor.

'We shall manage,' he said. 'I work in the library in any case and we can take one of the chairs into our bedroom.'

So Ruth had put a jam jar on the windowsill, with a label on it saying *Heini's Piano*. It was an entirely British jam jar, which gave her satisfaction, having contained Oxford marmalade and been retrieved from the dustbin of the nursery school teacher on the ground floor, but it was not filling up very quickly. Ruth had made enquiries about the deposit on the kind of piano Heini required and it was two guineas even before the weekly rental and there was a delivery charge as well. She gave her wages from the progressive lady weaver to her mother and had hoped that the money from the Willow Tea Rooms would help, but there always seemed to be an emergency: Aunt Hilda needed throat pastilles, or the teapot broke its spout. Though she bought nothing for herself during those long hot weeks of summer, not a hair ribbon, not an ice cream on the most sizzling day, the heap of coins at the bottom of the jar remained pitifully small.

If Heini's letters were shown to everyone and were matters for rejoicing, the letters from Mr Proudfoot, arriving secretly at Ruth's post office box, were another matter. Mr Proudfoot had seen fit to lay the conditions of nullity before Ruth, who found them daunting.

'Are you *sure* there's no insanity in the family?' she asked her puzzled parents. 'What about Great-Aunt Miriam?'

'To believe that the Kaiser was a reincarnation of

Tutankhamen may be eccentric, but it is not insane,' said her father firmly.

But if the immediate prospects for annulment were poor, Mr Proudfoot was helpful about getting her British naturalization confirmed, sending her forms in prepaid envelopes and continuing to offer assistance. That Quin himself never wrote or sent a message was only what she had expected and did not disappoint her in the least.

By the middle of August, the crisis over Czechoslovakia began to dominate the newspapers. Hitler's rantings grew more demented; newsreel pictures showed him strutting about with his arm round Mussolini or shaking his fist at anyone who dared to interfere with the concerns of Eastern Europe. Cabinet ministers abandoned their grouse moors and began to shuttle back and forth between London and Paris, between Paris and Berlin. The Czechs appealed for help.

Great Britain's increasing preparations for war affected the inhabitants of Belsize Park in various ways. Mrs Weiss looked up at a large grey barrage balloon floating above her, said, '*Mein Gott*, vat is zat?', fell over a hole in the pavement and was conveyed to Hampstead Hospital for stitches in her nose. Uncle Mishak, passing a poster which urged him to *Keep Calm and Dig*, did just that, excavating a vegetable patch in the rubble-strewn garden behind the house. In the Willow Tea Rooms, Miss Maud pored anxiously over a leaflet giving instructions for the assembling of a prefabricated air-raid shelter and received much good advice from the male customers who professed to understand them. Mrs Burtt stopped singing over the washing up because her Trevor had been passed fit for the air force, and Dr Levy, though he had made it perfectly clear that he was not entitled to practise medicine, was pulled into a neighbouring house to resuscitate a man with a weak heart whose wife had sought to amuse him by coming to bed in her gas mask.

For Ruth, the crisis meant only the dread of separation from Heini. She emptied the jam jar and sent frantic cables to Budapest, but his emigration papers, though expected at any moment, still hadn't come through. There was one matter, however, on which she sought enlightenment from Miss Maud and Miss Violet who, as general's daughters, could be expected to know about the army.

'Would someone aged thirty, or a bit over, be called up?'

'Only if the war went on for a long time,' Miss Maud replied.

It was during these dark days that Ruth received news which would normally have caused her the deepest disappointment. University College had given her place on the Zoology course to another refugee. They were now full up and could not admit her in the coming year.

'It was a muddle,' she said, holding out the letter. 'When I wasn't on the student transport, the Quakers got in touch with them and they had so many people begging to come that they accepted someone else.

They're going to see if they can get me into another college, but they're not very hopeful as it's so late.'

After the first shock, however, she made the best of it. 'It doesn't matter,' she said. 'I want to go on working anyway, to help you and to help Heini when he comes.'

'It matters a great deal,' said the Professor sternly.

For him and his wife, Ruth's rejection was a bitter blow. Like parents the world over, they would accept any tribulation if their child could go forward into a better future. Ruth must not live in the twilit world of the refugees, the world of menial jobs, of anxiety about permits and poverty and fear.

'I wonder if I should get in touch with Quinton Somerville,' said the Professor that night when Ruth had gone to bed. 'I feel sure he would help.'

'No, I wouldn't do that.'

The Professor looked at her in surprise. 'Why not?'

But Leonie, who seldom found a use for logical thought and was pursuing a hunch so nebulous that it could not possibly be uttered, just said that she thought it was a bad idea – and in the days that followed nobody had time to think of their personal lives.

All the clichés written later about the Munich crisis were true. The world did hold its breath, the storm clouds did gather over Europe, strangers did stop each other in the street and ask for news. Then Neville Chamberlain, that obstinate old man who had never been in an aeroplane before, flew to meet Hitler, flew home again, and back once more . . . to return at last with a piece of paper in which he believed wholly and which he held up to his people with the words 'Peace in our time.'

There were many who cried appeasement and many – and the refugees, of course, among them – who knew what Hitler's promises were worth, and that the Czechs had been betrayed, yet who could want war? As the crowds cheered in front of Buckingham Palace, Ruth waltzed with Mrs Burtt among the pots and pans in the Willow Tea Rooms kitchen because Heini could come now and Mrs Burtt's Trevor sleep safe in his bed.

It was in this time of renewed hope, when the chrysanthemums glowed gold and russet in the flower seller's basket and little boys called at Number 27 for the conkers Uncle Mishak collected in his wanderings, that Professor Berger came home to find Ruth reading a letter – and was startled by the radiance in her face.

'From Heini?' he asked. 'He is coming?'

She shook her head. 'It's from the University of Thameside. They've offered me a place, straight away. I start next week.'

He took the letter she held out to him. It was signed by the Admissions Tutor, but no one was deceived by that.

'This is Somerville's doing,' said the Professor, and felt a weight lift from his heart because it had hurt, the belief that his young protégé had forgotten them. 'He's Professor of Zoology there. And sternly to Ruth: "You will be worthy of his kindness, I know."

She had retired into her hair, trying to still the

confusion in her mind and remained in it, figuratively speaking, till late that night when her Aunt Hilda's snuffling proclaimed her to be asleep, and she could lean out of the window, breathing in the sooty air, and try to think things out.

Why had he done it? Why had Quin, who had made it so clear that they should never meet again, accepted her as a student? What had made him override his decision and ignore the warnings of his solicitor about collusion and consent and heaven knew what else, to give her this chance?

But what did it matter why? He had done it, and the future lay bright and shining before her. She would be the most studious student they had ever seen at Thameside. She would work till she burst, she would get a First – she would get the best First they had ever had – and she would do it without ever making him speak to her, without even once looking his way.

That her acceptance had nothing to do with Quin, that he did not even know of it, was something which could not have occurred to Ruth or to her family, accustomed as they were to the formal working of Austrian academic life, yet it was so. Quin always left the admissions, indeed most of the administration, to his second in command, Dr Felton, and was himself not only not in London, but not even in his Northumbrian home.

Believing in the inevitability of war, he had taken himself off to a naval base in Scotland to evoke the revered name of his appalling grandfather, Rear Admiral 'Basher' Somerville, and get himself into the navy.

To talk himself into the corridors of power had been relatively easy; to talk himself out of them, as the threat of war receded, was taking longer.

Professor Somerville was going to be late for the beginning of term.

12

'What do you mean, he isn't back? Term begins next week. Do you intend to allow this kind of behaviour from your staff?'

Lady Plackett was annoyed. Since her husband had assumed his new position as Vice Chancellor of Thameside, she had taken a great deal of trouble planning suitable occasions at which the staff would be received. Their predecessor, Lord Charlefont, had been lackadaisical in the extreme and the position of the Lodge, marked off only by its Doric columns and Virginia creeper from the Arts Block which ran along the river, lent itself to the kind of haphazard coming and going which she had no intention of permitting. She had already had a *Private* notice put on the flagged path which led from the main courtyard to their front door, and instructed the college servants to erect a chain-link fence to keep their part of the river terrace free from students who seemed to think they had a right to sit there and eat their sandwiches.

To insist on one's privacy was essential, as it was essential to restore the high moral tone of the university; students holding hands or embracing could not, of course, be tolerated. But Lady Plackett also meant to *give* . . . to enrich college life with her hospitality and make the Lodge a place where good conversation and good breeding could be relied upon. To do this, however, she had to separate the sheep from the goats and find out what material was to hand, and to this end she had planned a series of organized entertainments for the beginning of term. First the professors to sherry, properly labelled, of course, with their names and departments, for unlabelled gatherings were never satisfactory – then the lecturers to fruit juice . . . and lastly, in batches of twenty or so, the students to play paper and pencil games.

Now ticking off the labels on safety pins against the names of the senior staff, she found opposite Professor Somerville's name the words: 'Unable to attend'.

'He's up in Scotland,' said Sir Desmond. A pale man with pince-nez, he had the kind of face it is impossible to recall within five minutes of seeing it, and owed his appointment to the fact that all the other candidates for the Vice Chancellorship had enough personality to acquire enemies. 'Apparently the Foreign Office tried to enrol him for some secret work in Whitehall – code breaking or some such thing. Somerville thought it would mean sitting in a bunker all through the war so he went up to try and get himself into the navy.'

'Well I hope you mean to have a word with him,'

said Lady Plackett. She was taller than her husband, with a long back, a long face and the close-set navy-blue eyes which characterized the Croft-Ellises. Having done several Seasons without, so to speak, a matrimonial nibble, Lady Plackett had accepted the son of an undistinguished chartered accountant and set herself to advancing his career. It had not been easy. Desmond, when she met him, did not even know that Cholmondely was pronounced Chumley, but she had persevered and now, after twenty-five years, she could honestly say that she was no longer ashamed to take him home to Rutland.

'No, dear, I don't think that would be wise,' said Sir Desmond mildly. 'We need Professor Somerville rather more than he needs us.'

'What do you mean?'

'He's a very eminent man; they're constantly offering him positions abroad and Cambridge has been trying to get him back ever since he left. Charlefont had quite a job persuading him to take the Chair and Somerville took it on condition he could get leave for his journeys. The college has done pretty well out of him – there's always money for Palaeontology because of his distinction and the field course he runs at his place in Northumberland is supposed to be the highlight of the year.'

'Northumberland?' said Lady Plackett sharply. 'Whereabouts in Northumberland?'

Sir Desmond frowned. 'I can't remember the name. Bow something, I think.'

'Not . . .' She had flushed with excitement. 'Not *Bowmont?*'

'That's right. That's what it was.'

'Bow something' indeed! Not for the first time, Lady Plackett felt the loneliness of those who marry beneath them. 'You mean he's *that* Somerville? Quinton Somerville – the owner of Bowmont? Old Basher's grandson?'

Sir Desmond said his name was Quinton, certainly, and asked what was so unusual about Bowmont, but this was a question it was impossible to answer. Those who moved in the right circles knew why Bowmont was special, and to those who didn't one couldn't explain. 'I know his aunt,' said Lady Plackett. 'Well, slightly. I shall write to her.' And eagerly to her husband who was leafing through the book of staff addresses: 'He isn't married yet, is he?'

Sir Desmond looked for the M opposite married members of staff, found it absent and said so.

Without hesitation, Lady Plackett dropped the label with Professor Somerville's name into the wastepaper basket. This man did not belong in large gatherings of people eating canapés. Professor Somerville would come to one of the intimate dinner parties with which she meant to put Thameside on the map and there he would find, in the gracious setting of her home, his intellectual equal, his future student and a girl of his own background. Would find, in short, Verena.

The Placketts' only daughter was twenty-three years old and had inherited not only her mother's breeding but her father's brains. From the age of four, when she made it clear that she preferred her abacus to her dolls, it was evident that Verena would grow up to be an intellectual. The great Dr Johnson, of dictionary fame, had been told by his mother to repeat what she had taught him immediately to the next person he met, and if it was the milkman, no matter.

'In that way you always remember it,' she had said to her son.

There was no need for Lady Plackett so to instruct her daughter. Verena took in information and gave it out with equal efficiency. In India they had surrounded her with tutors and at nineteen she had enrolled in the European College at Hyderabad. It had been a brave step for her parents to take: true, the students and staff were all white, but it meant giving Verena an unusual amount of freedom.

Verena had not abused it. Science was her preferred subject, and it was without difficulty that she came top in every exam she took. Even so, when she had taken her basic degree, her mother insisted on sending her ahead to do the Season with her Croft-Ellis cousins from Rutland.

Lady Plackett's intentions were good, but the plan was not a success. Verena stood five foot eleven in her socks and it is difficult to do the Season in socks. Nor did Verena make any secret of the fact that the vapid young subalterns and stockbrokers at the tops of whose heads she gazed on the dance floor, bored her beyond belief. As soon as her parents returned from India, she

160

announced her intention of taking an Honours Degree, and taking it at Thameside.

About this, her mother had been uneasy. Though she had intended to look among the intelligentsia for a husband for Verena, it had been among Nobel Laureates or Fellows of the Royal Society that she had expected to find someone suitable, not among the corduroy-clad and bearded professors who so often did the actual teaching. Now, though, it looked as though Verena's instinct had been right and it was with a light step that she made her way up to her daughter's room.

'Verena, I have something to tell you!'

Her daughter sat at her tidy desk, a large text book illustrated with diagrams of bones open in front of her, a propelling pencil and a notebook on her right, a ruler on her left.

'Yes?'

Verena had inherited not only her mother's height, but her close-set, downward curving eyes and Roman nose. Now she looked up without rancour at the interruption, though she had reached a difficult chapter and would have preferred to be alone.

'I've just been speaking to your father and it turns out that Professor Somerville – the head of the Zoology Department – is *Quin* Somerville, the owner of Bowmont. Frances Somerville's nephew.'

'Yes, Mother. I know.'

Her mother stared at her. 'You know?'

Verena nodded. 'I made it my business to find out. That's why I decided to do Zoology Honours. His reputation is second to none. I shall take his option, of course.'

Not for the first time, Lady Plackett marvelled at her daughter's perspicacity. Verena had spent the summer with her cousins in Rutland, yet she was already better informed than her parents.

'I'm going to invite him to dinner as soon as he gets back,' she said. 'A really carefully chosen group of guests. You will be seated next to him, of course, so that you have time to talk.'

Verena returned to her book.

'Professor Somerville will find me ready,' she said.

Ruth walked through the gates of Thameside College, greeted the porter in his lodge, and looked with delight at the closely mown grass, the ancient walnut tree, the statue of someone *not* on horseback.

Thameside was beautiful. She knew it to be one of the oldest buildings in London, but she had not expected the cloistered peace, the flowerbeds lapping the grey walls – and through a wide arch on the far side of the quadrangle, a breathtaking view of the river and the soaring dome of St Paul's on the other bank. The University of Vienna was larger, more formal, but Ruth, passing the windows of booklined rooms and lecture theatres, was in a familiar world.

The statue, when she reached it, turned out to be of William Wordsworth, which was entirely suitable for he had stood on Westminster Bridge and said that *Earth has not anything to show more fair*, with which, having just crossed the river, she absolutely agreed. And there was a late rose, a golden voluptuous rambler curling round the railings of the Students' Union which seemed to hold all the fragrance of the dying year.

She came as Vienna's representative to the Groves of Academe and carried with her not only the good wishes of everyone at Number 27 and the Willow Tea Rooms, but their gifts in a straw basket pressed on her by Mrs Burtt. Though term did not begin for another two days, her father had insisted she take the magnifying glass he had had since his student days; Dr Levy had bequeathed his old dissecting kit rolled in a canvas pouch – and setting up a delicious rustle under her woollen skirt was the Venetian lace petticoat Leonie had worn when she was presented to the Austrian Chancellor.

Her appointment with Dr Felton was for 2.30; glancing at the clock which topped the archway to the river, she saw that she was ten minutes early. About to make her way towards the water's edge, she was arrested by a sound of unutterable melancholy coming from the basement of the Science Building on her left. Letting go of the rose she had been smelling, she turned her head. The noise came again and this time it was unmistakable. Somewhere down there, in a state of apparent distress and abandonment, was a sheep.

Picking up her basket, Ruth made her way down the stone steps, pushed open a door – and found herself in a dusty, unlit laboratory. A Physiology lab, instantly familiar from her days in Vienna when she had ridden her tricycle through the animal huts of the university, watched by the pink eyes of a thousand snow-white rats. There were indeed rats here, and the big bins holding the flaky yellow maze they fed on, a pair of scales, microscopes, a centrifuge . . . and in one corner, staring from a wooden pen, the pale face and melancholy, Semitic snout of a large white ewe.

'Ah yes, you're lonely,' said Ruth approaching. In the deserted room, she spoke in the soft dialect of Vienna. 'But you see I musn't touch you because you belong to Science. You're an experimental animal; you're like a Vestal Virgin dedicated to higher things.'

The sheep butted its head against the side of the pen, then lifted it hopefully to gaze at her with its yellow eyes. It seemed to be devoid of tubes or other signs of experimentation – seemed in fact to be in excellent health – but Ruth, well-trained as she was, kept her distance.

'I can see that you aren't where you would choose to be,' she went on, 'but I assure you that right now the world is full of people who are not where they would choose to be. All over Belsize Park and Finchley and Swiss Cottage I could show you such people. And you belong to a noble race because you are in the psalms and St Francis chose you to preach to and I can see why because you have listening eyes.'

The sheep's butting became more frenzied, but its mood was lifting. The string of bleats it was emitting seemed to be social rather than despairing. Then quite suddenly it sat down, sticking out one hoof and extending its neck like someone listening to a lecture.

'Very well, I will recite some Goethe for you which you will like, I think, because he is an extremely calming poet, though somewhat melancholy, I do admit. Now let me see, what would you like?'

In his room on the second floor of the Science Building, Dr Roger Felton blew the contents of a pipette into a tank of sea slugs and frowned. There should have been wreaths of translucent eggs now, hanging on the weeds, and there were not. He could get more slugs from the zoo, but he had set his heart on breeding his own specimens – not just for the students in his Marine Biology class, but because the *Opisthobranchia*, with their amazingly large nerve cells, were his particular interest.

All round the room, in salt-water tanks cooled and aerated by complicated tubes and pumps, a series of creatures swam or scuttled or clung to the sides of the glass: sea urchins and brittle stars, prawns and cuttle fish, and an octopus currently turning pink inside a hollow brick. Dr Felton loved his subject and taught it well. The nuptial dance of the ragworm on the surface of the ocean, the selfless paternity of the butterfish, entranced him as much now as it had done when he first beheld it fifteen years ago, but there were problems, not least of them the new Vice Chancellor who had made it clear that it was publications that counted, not teaching.

Dr Felton was aware that he ought to spend more time on his research and less on the students, but someone had to see to them with the Prof so much away. Not that he grudged Quin his journeys – having a man of that calibre in the department made all the difference. If Felton had any doubts they would have been stilled by the two terms during which Professor Robinson had done Quin's teaching and the sound of laughter vanished from the common room.

Still, instead of getting ready to stimulate the posterior ganglion of the slug he had placed in readiness on a Petri dish, he now had to interview the new student wished on them by University College who had made a mess of things. Moving over to his desk, he took out Ruth Berger's particulars and glanced through the eulogy provided by Vienna for the benefit of UC and now passed on to him. She certainly seemed to be well up to the standard of the third years and able to take her Finals in the summer. Her exam results were excellent and her father was an eminent palaeontologist. Even without the Prof's instructions to accept refugees at all costs, he would have tried to find a place for her.

A knock at the door made him look up, ready to receive Miss Berger. But the figure who strode into the room, filling it with her bulk, her Nordic blondeness and Valkyrie-like strength, was Dr Elke Sonderstrom, the Lecturer in Parasitology, who worked in the room next to his.

'Come downstairs a minute, Roger. But quietly – don't say anything.'

Dr Felton looked enquiring, but Elke, grasping a tube of liver flukes in her mighty hand, only said: 'I went down to the basement to use the centrifuge and – well, you'll see.'

Puzzled, he followed her down two flights of stairs, to be met by Humphrey Fitzsimmons, the tall, skeletally thin physiologist.

'She's still there,' he whispered, putting a finger to his lips.

The Physiology lab was bathed in Stygian gloom, yet at the far end of it they could make out a gleam of brightness which revealed itself as a girl's abundant, loose and curling hair. She was draped over the side of the sheep pen, entirely absorbed, and at her feet was a straw basket which somehow suggested cornucopias and garlands and the flower-picking orgies of Greek girls on the slopes of Parnassus.

But it wasn't the shining hair, the girl's bent head, which held them. It was not even the unusual attitude of the listening sheep. No, what kept the three silent watchers transfixed, was the girl's voice. She was reciting poetry and she was doing it in German.

All of them, to some extent, were familiar with the German language. It came daily from the wireless in Hitler's obscene and hysterical rantings. As scientists they had waded through pages of it in various *Zeitschriften*, hoping to be rewarded, after interminable clauses, by a single verb.

But this . . . That German could sound so caressing, so lilting, so . . . loving. Dr Elke closed her eyes and was back in the wooden house on the white strand of Öland while her mother arranged harebells in a pottery jug.

167

Humphrey Fitzsimmons, too upper class to have seen much of his mother, recalled the soft eyes of the water spaniel he'd owned as a boy. And Dr Felton remembered that his wife, whose red-rimmed eyes followed him in incessant reproach because they couldn't start a baby, had once been a snowflake in the Monte Carlo Ballet with a borrowed Russian name and an endearing smile.

The girl's voice grew ever softer, and ceased. She picked up her basket and bade the sheep farewell. Then, turning, she saw them.

'Oh, I'm sorry,' she said in English. 'But I swear I haven't touched her – not even with one finger. I swear by Mozart's head!'

'It doesn't matter,' said Fitzsimmons, still bemused. 'She's not being used for anything. She was supposed to be part of a batch to use for a government feeding trial, but they cancelled it after Munich and the rest of the animals never turned up.'

'What was the poem?' Dr Elke asked.

'It's by Goethe. It's called "The Wanderer's Night Song". It's a bit sad, but I suppose great poems always are and it's a very *rural* sort of sadness with mountains and birdsong and peace.'

Dr Felton now came down to earth and assumed the mantle of Senior Lecturer, Tutor for Admissions and Acting Head (in the continuing absence of his Professor) of the Department of Zoology. 'Are you by any chance Miss Berger? Because if so, I've been expecting you.'

*

168

Half an hour later, in Dr Felton's room, the technicalities of Ruth's admission were under way.

'Oh, it will be lovely!' she said. 'Everything I like! I've always wanted to do Marine Zoology. In Vienna we didn't do it because there was no sea, of course, and I've only been to the Baltic which is all straight lines and people lying in the sand with nothing on reading Schopenhauer.'

Her arms flew upwards, her cheeks blew out, as she mimed a portly nudist holding a heavy book above his head.

'Well, that's settled your basic subjects then,' said Dr Felton. 'Parasitology, Physiology and Marine Biology. Which leaves you with your special option. With your father's record I imagine that'll be Palaeontology?'

For a moment, Ruth hesitated and Dr Felton, already aware that silence was not Miss Berger's natural state, looked up from the form he'd been completing.

'Professor Somerville teaches that himself,' he went on. 'It's usually oversubscribed but I think we could squeeze you in. He's a quite brilliant lecturer.'

'May I take it, then? Would it be all right?'

'I'm sure it will be. There's a field course too; we usually have it in the spring, but with the Professor having been away we're holding it in October.'

He frowned because the field course was officially full, the last place having been taken by Verena Plackett a few days before, but Dr Felton did not intend to let this stop him. There were no nudists reading

Schopenhauer on the curving, foam-fringed sands of Bowmont Bay.

'I don't think I'll be able to go to that. The Quakers are paying my fees but there won't be anything extra for travel. My parents are very poor now.'

'Well, we'll see,' said Dr Felton. There was a hardship fund administered by the Finance Committee on which he sat, but it was better to say nothing yet.

'You are so kind,' she said, lacing her fingers in her lap. 'You can't imagine what it means to be here after . . . what happened. I remember it all so well, you know. The smells and everything: formalin and alcohol and chalk . . . I didn't think I should come to university, I thought I should work for my parents, but now I'm here I don't think anything could get me away again.'

'It was bad?'

She shrugged. 'One of my friends was thrown down the steps of the university and broke his leg. But here it is all going on still, people trying to understand the world, needing to know about things . . .'

'Sea slugs,' said Dr Felton a trifle bitterly. 'They won't even reproduce!'

'Ah, but that's difficult . . . compatibility.' She glanced up, testing the word, and he marvelled again at her command of English. 'Even in people it's difficult and if one is both male and female at the same time that *cannot* be easy.'

Dr Felton agreed, obscurely comforted, and sent her to the Union where one of the third years was waiting to show newcomers round. When she had left, accom-

170

panying her handshake with that half-curtsy which proclaimed the abandoned world of Central Europe, he drew her form towards him and looked at it with satisfaction. Quin was always complaining that students these days were without personality. He'd hardly be able to level that charge at his new Honours student. Quin, in fact, would be very pleased. Whether he would feel the same about Verena Plackett, whose application form lay beneath Ruth's, was another matter.

'Vell?' said Mrs Weiss, and cocked her head in its feathered toque at Ruth, determined to extract every ounce of information about her first day at college.

'It's going to be wonderful,' said Ruth, setting a pot of coffee in front of the old lady, for she had not yet given up her evening job at the Willow Tea Rooms.

Everyone was in the café, including her own family, for Ruth's return to her rightful place among the intelligentsia demanded celebration and discussion. They had heard about the niceness of Dr Felton, the majesty of Dr Elke and her parasites, the beauty of the river and the Goethe-loving sheep.

'And Professor Somerville?' enquired her father, who had only just arrived, for on Fridays the library stayed open late.

'He isn't back yet. He went to Scotland to try and join the navy,' said Ruth, frowning over the slice of guggle she was bringing to Dr Levy. She had been certain that a man of thirty should not have to go to war. 'But everyone says he is the most amazing lecturer.'

The lady with the poodle now arrived, and in deference to her the conversation changed to English.

'You haf met the students?' Paul Ziller enquired.

'Only one or two,' said Ruth, vanishing momentarily into the kitchen to fetch the actor's fruit juice. 'But there's a girl starting at the same time as me – Verena Plackett. She's the daughter of the Vice Chancellor and I expect she could choose any course she liked, but she's doing the Palaeontology option too which shows how good it is.'

Ziller put down his cup. 'Wait!' he said, raising a majestic hand. 'Her I haf seen!'

The eyes of the entire clientele were upon him.

'How haf you seen?' enquired Leonie.

Ziller rose and made his way to the wicker table on which lay the piles of magazines which the Misses Maud and Violet, bowing to the need of the refugees for the printed word, now brought downstairs. Ignoring *Woman* and *Woman's Own* provided by the poodle-owning lady, and *Home Chat*, the contribution of Mrs Burtt, he sorted through the copies of *Country Life*, selected the issue he wanted, and began to turn the pages.

Considerable tension was by now generated, and Mrs Burtt and Miss Violet came out of the kitchen to watch.

'Hah!' said Ziller triumphantly, and held up the relevant page.

In the front of *Country Life* there is always a full-page photograph of a girl, invariably well bred, frequently about to marry someone suitable, but whether engaged or not, presenting a prototype of upper-class womanhood. Here are the Fenella Holdinghams who, in the spring, will marry the youngest son of Lord and Lady Foister; here the Angela Lathanby-Gores after their victory in the Highlingham Steeplechase . . . And here now was Verena Plackett – daughter of the newly appointed Vice Chancellor of Thameside – and not just Verena Plackett, but Verena Plackett gowned for presentation at Their Majesties' courts in flesh-coloured satin with a train embroidered in lover's knots of diamanté, and ostrich feathers in her hair.

Ruth, putting down her tray, was awarded first look, and studied her fellow student with attention.

'She looks intelligent,' she said.

Passed round, Verena seemed to give general satisfaction. Ziller liked her long throat, von Hofmann praised her collar bones and Miss Maud said she'd have known her anywhere for a Croft-Ellis by her nose. Only Mrs Burtt was silent, giving a small sniff which it was easy to attribute to class hatred.

But it was Leonie who looked longest at the picture and who, when she left the café, asked if she could borrow the magazine.

'I'm not a snob,' she said to her husband, who smiled a wise and matrimonial smile, 'but to have Ruth back where she belongs . . . Oh, Kurt, that is so *good*.'

It was not till Ruth had gone to bed that Leonie set up her ironing board for she did not want her daughter to know how long she worked, or for how little money. But as she smoothed the fussy ruffles and frills on Mrs Carter's blouse, she was humming a silly waltz she'd danced to in her girlhood and presently she put down the iron and once more examined Verena's face.

She did not look particularly affable, but who did when confronted by a camera, and if her mouth turned down at the corners, this was probably some inherited trait and did not indicate ill temper. What mattered was that Ruth was back where she belonged. The daughter of a Vice Chancellor was an entirely suitable companion for the daughter of an erstwhile Dean of the Faculty of Science.

Not I but thou . . . the refrain of all cradle songs, all prayers with which parents, ungrudging, send their children forth to a better life than their own, rang through Leonie's head. Verena and Ruth would be the greatest of friends – Leonie was quite sure of it – and nothing, that night, could upset her; not even the smell of burning lentils as the psychoanalyst from Breslau began, at midnight, to cook soup.

13

Within three days of the beginning of term, Ruth was thoroughly at home at Thameside. To reach the university, she had to walk across Waterloo Bridge and that was like getting a special blessing for the coming day. There was always something to delight her: a barge passing beneath her with washing strung across the deck, or a flock of gulls jostling and screeching for the bread thrown by a bundled old woman who looked poor beyond belief, but was there each day to share her loaf – and once a double rainbow behind St Paul's.

'And it always smells of the sea,' she told Dr Felton, who was becoming not only her tutor but a friend. 'The rivers in Europe don't do that – well, how could they with the ocean so far away?'

Dr Felton was a fine teacher, an enthusiast who shared with his students the amazing life of his creatures.

'Look!' he would cry like a child as he found, under the microscope, a cluster of transparent eggs from a brittle star, or the flagellum with which some infinitely small creature hurled itself across a drop of liquid. As she prepared slides and made her diagrams, Ruth was in a world where there was no barrier between science and art. Nor could anyone be indifferent to the extraordinarily successful lives led by Dr Elke's tapeworms, untroubled by the search for food or shelter – living, loving, having their entire being in the secure world of someone else's gut.

But if the staff were kind, and the work absorbing, it was her fellow students who made Ruth's first days at Thameside so happy. They had worked together for two years, but they welcomed her without hesitation. There was Sam Marsh, a thin tousle-haired boy with the face of an intelligent rat, who wore a flat cap and a muffler to show his solidarity with the proletariat, and Janet Carter, a cheerful vicar's daughter with frizzy red hair, whose innumerable boyfriends, of an evening, fell off sofas, got their feet stuck in the steering wheels of motor cars and generally came to grief in their efforts to attain their goal. There was a huge, silent Welshman (but not called Morgan) who was apt to crush test tubes unwittingly in his enormous hands . . . And there was Pilly.

Pilly's name was Priscilla Yarrowby, but the nickname had stuck to her since her schooldays for her father was a manufacturer of aspirins. Pilly had short, curly, light brown hair and round blue eyes which usually wore a look of desperate incomprehension. She had failed every exam at least once, she wept over her dissections, she fainted at the sight of blood. The discovery that Ruth, who looked like a goose girl in a fairy tale, knew exactly what she was doing, filled Pilly with amazement and awe. That this romantic newcomer (with whom Sam was already obviously in love) was willing to help her with her work and to do so tactfully and unobtrusively, produced an onrush of uncontainable gratitude. Within forty-eight hours of Ruth's arrival, it became almost impossible to prise poor Pilly from her side.

To the general niceness of the students there was one glaring exception. Verena Plackett's arrival for the first lecture of term was one which Ruth never forgot.

She was sitting with her new friends, when the door opened and a college porter entered, placed a notice saying *Reserved* in the middle of the front bench, and departed again, looking cross. Since the lecture was to be given by Dr Fitzsimmons, the gangling, rather vague Physiology lecturer and was attended only by his students, this caused surprise, for Dr Fitzsimmons was not really a puller-in of crowds.

A few minutes passed, after which the door opened once more and a tall girl in a navy-blue tailored coat and skirt entered, walked to the *Reserved* notice, removed it, and sat down. She then opened her large crocodile-skin briefcase and took out a morocco leather writing case from which she removed a thick pad of vellum paper, an ebony ruler, a black fountain pen with a gold nib and a silver propelling pencil. Next, she zipped up the writing case again, put it back into the briefcase, shut the briefcase – and was ready to begin.

Dr Fitzsimmons had decided to start with an outline of the human digestive system. Moving slowly from the salivary glands of the mouth to the peristaltic movements of the oesophagus, he reached the stomach itself which he drew on the blackboard, occasionally breaking the chalk. And as he spoke, or drew, so did Verena follow him. There was no word that Dr Fitzsimmons uttered that she did not write down in her large, clear script; no 'and' or 'but' she omitted. Then, at five minutes to ten, she wound down the lead of her propelling pencil, screwed on the top of her fountain pen, opened the briefcase, unzipped the morocco leather writing case . . . But even when all her belongings were back in place, Verena did not at once follow the other students into the practical class, for she knew how gratifying it must be for a member of staff to have the Vice Chancellor's daughter in the audience – and approaching the dais where Dr Fitzsimmons, lightly covered in chalk, was obliterating the human stomach, she stepped towards him.

'You will have gathered who I am,' she said, graciously holding out her hand, 'but I feel I should thank you on behalf of my parents and myself for your interesting lecture.'

It was not till she entered the Physiology lab that Verena was compelled to communicate with her fellow students. Waiting on the benches were a number of coiled rubber tubes, each with a syringe on one end, and

178

a slightly daunting set of instructions. *Swallow the tube as far as the white mark and remove the contents of the stomach for analysis*, they began.

The demonstrator, a friendly young man, came forward helpfully. 'You will have to work in pairs,' he said. And to Verena: 'Since you're new, Miss Plackett, I thought you might like to work with Miss Berger who's started this year also.'

Ruth turned and smiled at Verena. She would have preferred to work with Pilly who was looking at her beseechingly, or with Sam, but she was more than ready to be friendly.

Verena, in silence, stood and looked down at Ruth. There had been a row in Belsize Park after Ruth's acceptance at Thameside. Leonie had announced her intention of selling the diamond brooch she had secreted in her corset and kitting Ruth out for college, and Ruth had refused to hear of it. 'There'll be much more important things to spend money on,' she'd said firmly.

This morning, accordingly, Ruth wore a lavender smock printed with small white daisies to protect her loden skirt – the property of Miss Violet who had a number of such garments in which to serve tea at the Willow. It was not what Ruth would have chosen to wear in a laboratory, but she had accepted gratefully, as she had accepted the virulently varnished pencil box decorated with pink hearts which Mrs Burtt had bought for her from Woolworth's. Also in Ruth's straw basket was her lunch – a bread roll in a paper bag – and a

179

bunch of dandelions she had picked to give the sheep in the basement; and her hair, piled high on her head for purposes of experimentation, was bound by a piece of Uncle Mishak's gardening twine.

At this extremely unscientific apparition, Verena stared for a few moments in perhaps justifiable distress.

Then she said: 'I think it would be inadvisable for two newcomers to work together.'

The snub was unmistakable. Ruth flushed and turned away, and Verena proceeded to don a snow-white and perfectly starched lab coat before she decided on the partner of her choice. The group round Miss Berger was obviously unsuitable and a possible candidate – a handsome, fair-haired young man – moved away to another bench before she could catch his eyes. But hovering rather flatteringly near her was a nicely turned-out youth, tall and thin, with sandy hair which he kept short and under control.

'What about you?' she said to Kenneth Easton.

She had made an excellent choice. Kenneth, who watched birds (but only if they were rare) was a conscientious, painstaking young man who now saw his career take off under this august patronage and moved eagerly to her side.

'I hope she chokes to death,' said Sam viciously, looking across at Verena. But of course she didn't. While the sycophantic Kenneth stood beside her, ready to receive the contents of her stomach, Verena lifted the rubber tube to her mouth – and calmly, competently, in a series of python-like gulps, she swallowed it.

Because there were so many more men than women at Thameside, and because they were so very disposed to be friendly, Ruth told everyone early on about Heini: that he was coming, that he was incredibly gifted, that she meant – after she got her degree – to spend her life with him.

'What's he like?' asked Janet.

'He's got curly dark hair and grey eyes and he plays like no one else in the world. You'll hear him when he comes – at least you will when I've got the piano.'

Heini's existence was a blow to Sam, but he took it well, deciding to play a Lancelot-like role in Ruth's life which would be better for his degree than a public passion – and he, and all Ruth's friends, quite understood that if Ruth only joined those clubs that were free, or refused to come to The Angler's Arms after college, it was because any spare money she might collect in tips at the Willow had to go into Heini's jam jar. And soon even Huw Davies (the Welshman who was not called Morgan) could be seen staring into the windows of piano shops, for there is nothing more infectious than involvement in a noble cause.

Afterwards, Ruth wished that there hadn't been that week at the beginning of term when Quin was not yet back from Scotland. She heard too much about Professor Somerville's achievements, his intelligence, the wonderful things he had done for his students.

'I'd give my soul to be taken on one of his trips,' said Sam, 'but I haven't a chance; not even if I got a First. There's always a queue of people waiting to go.'

Even Janet, who had such a poor opinion of the male sex and continued to bite the heads off her unsuccessful suitors in the manner of the wind spider in the Natural History Museum, spoke well of him.

'His lectures are really good – he sort of opens up the world for you. And there's absolutely no side to him. It makes my blood boil to hear Verena go on as though she owns him – she hasn't even *met* him!'

But it was from Pilly that Ruth heard most about Professor Somerville. Priscilla might be unable to grasp the concept of radial symmetry in the jellyfish, but her loving heart made her perceptive and skilful where the needs of her friends were concerned, and she now decided that Ruth was not getting enough lunch.

This was true. Ruth had told Leonie that lunch in the refectory was free. She then got off the tube three stops early, used the tuppence she saved to buy a bread roll, and ate it by the river. Ruth was entirely satisfied with this arrangement, but Pilly was not, and on Ruth's third day at Thameside she asked if she might bring a picnic and join her.

'Wouldn't you rather go into the refectory?'

'No, I wouldn't. The food doesn't agree with me,' lied Pilly.

She then went home and consulted her mother. Mr Yarrowby did not just make aspirins, he made a great many of them. Priscilla was driven to college in a Rolls-Royce which dropped her two streets away because she was shy about her wealth, but her mother was a down-to-earth Yorkshire woman. Mrs Yarrowby had never been overcome by pigeons in the Stephansplatz, but she and Leonie were sisters under the skin.

'Oh dear!' said Pilly, opening her lunch box on the following day. 'I can't possibly eat all that – and if I leave anything my mother will be so *hurt*!'

That was a cry to which Ruth couldn't help rallying. Leonie's desperate face when she stopped at one helping of sauerkraut had been a feature of her childhood. She shared Pilly's flaky meat patties, the hard-boiled eggs, the parkin, the grapes . . . and even then there were crusts over to throw to the greedy birds which gave Ruth a special happiness.

'Oh, Pilly, you can't imagine how *lovely* it is to be able to feed the ducks again. It makes me feel like a real and proper person, not a refugee.'

'You'd always be a real and proper person,' said Pilly staunchly. 'You're the most real and proper person I've ever met.'

But it was as they sat leaning against the parapet with Ruth's loden cloak wrapped round their shoulders against the wind, that Ruth learnt how much Pilly dreaded the onset of the Palaeontology course.

'I'll never get through,' she said miserably. 'I can't even tell the difference between Pleistocene and plasticine.'

'Yes you can . . . But, Pilly, why do you have to take that option? I mean, there are rather a lot of names.'

Pilly looked depressed and threw another crust into the water. 'It's to do with Professor Somerville.'

There was a pause. Then: 'How is that? How is it to do with him?'

'My father thinks he's the perfect Renaissance man,' said Pilly. 'You know, he does everything. My father saw him on a newsreel about three years ago when he came back from Java with the skull of that Neanderthal lady and some other time when he was riding through Nepal on a yak. Or maybe it was a mule. You see my father had to go into a factory at fourteen and he never had a chance to do a degree or travel – that's why he's pushing me through college though I told him I was too stupid. And Professor Somerville is the sort of person he wants to have been.'

'I see.'

'He cuts all the articles about him out of the *National Geographic*. And then there's the sailing – Professor Somerville won some race in a dinghy with the sea banging about over his head and my father liked that too. And he's a Great Lover, like the Medicis, though I don't suppose he poisons people so much.'

'How do your parents know he's a Great Lover?'

Pilly sighed. 'It's in the papers. In the gossip columns. An actress called Tansy Mallet chased him all over Egypt and now he's got some stunningly beautiful Frenchwoman he takes to the theatre – and everyone's always trying to get him to take them on field trips. You wait till he gets back – his lectures are always absolutely packed with people from the outside. They pay the university ten pounds a year and they can go to any lecture,

184

but it's his they go to.' She bit into her sandwich. 'And there's Bowmont too.'

'What's Bowmont?'

'It's where Professor Somerville lives. You'll see when we go on the field course.'

'I'm not going on the field course,' said Ruth. 'But what's so special about Bowmont? I thought it was just a house with no central heating?'

Pilly shook her head. 'It can't be because Turner painted it.'

'Well, he painted a lot of things, didn't he? Cows and sunsets and shipwrecks?'

'Maybe – but everyone wants to go there all the same. Oh, Ruth, I'll never do it. All those names – Jurassic and Mesozoic and on and on . . .'

'You will do it,' said Ruth, setting her jaw. 'We'll make lists – a list for the bathroom, a list for the lavatory . . . I expect you've got a lot of bathrooms so you can have a lot of lists and I'll hear you every day. They're only *names* like people being called Cynthia or George.'

The weather was fine that first week at Thameside and for Ruth everything was a delight. Dr Felton's lectures, the first rehearsal of the Bach Choir which cost nothing to join and sent the sound of the B Minor Mass soaring over the campus. She coached Pilly, she made friends with a Ph.D. student in the German Department and persuaded him that Rilke, when properly spoken,

185

was not a madman but a poet – and she was faithful to the sheep.

Yet if her happiness was real, it could be fractured in an instant by a reminder of the past. One afternoon she was crossing the courtyard on the way back from a seminar when she heard, coming from a window of the Arts Block the sound of the Schubert Quartet in E flat. She stood still for a moment, making sure that she was right, that it *was* the Zillers who were playing, and it was: they always took the Adagio with that heavenly slowness which had nothing to do with solemnity. And now the second violin lifted itself above the others to repeat the motif and she could see Biberstein's dark curls standing on end and his chin pressed against his fiddle as he looked into the eye of Schubert, or of God.

Then she ran across the grass, through the archway, up the stairs . . . She knew, of course, before she opened the door of the Common Room, she knew it was impossible. Time had not run backward, she was not crossing the Johannesgasse towards the windows of the Conservatoire where the Zillers practised. But there were a few seconds while her body believed what her brain knew to be impossible – and then she saw the horn of the gramophone and the members of the Music Club sitting in a circle – and knew that the past was past, and Biberstein was dead.

It was on the following day that Verena was gracious enough to inform her fellow students that Professor

Somerville would be back to give his Palaeontology lecture on Monday.

'Are you sure?' asked Sam.

'Certainly I'm sure,' said Verena. 'He is to dine with us that night.'

14

'My God, Ruth, what is the matter with your hair?' said Leonie as her daughter appeared for breakfast on the morning that Professor Somerville was due to give his first lecture.

'I have plaited it,' said Ruth with dignity.

'Plaited it? You have tortured it; you will be *skinned*, pulling it back like that.'

But Ruth, in pursuit of a total unobtrusiveness, said that she felt quite comfortable and asked if she could borrow Hilda's raincoat which was black, mannish and in its dotage. With the collar turned up and a beret jammed on her head, she felt certain she could escape Professor Somerville's notice until he wished to acknowledge her, and ignoring her mother, who said that she looked like a streetwalker in an experimental film by Pabst, she made her way to college. There she came under attack again. Janet pointed out that it wasn't raining, and Sam asked sadly if her hairstyle was permanent. But if Ruth's appearance was odd, her behaviour was odder.

'Are you all right?' asked Pilly as Ruth edged into the lecture theatre like the musk rat Chu Chundra in Kipling's *The Jungle Book*, who never ventured into the middle of a room.

'Yes, I am. Well, I feel a bit sick actually, so I think I'll sit in the back row today in case I have to go out. But you go on down and get a good seat.'

This was a stupid remark. Where Ruth went, there Pilly went too, and presently Janet, Sam and Huw came to join them.

'It doesn't matter,' said Sam, resigning himself to being a long way from his idol. 'You can always hear what he says.'

The lecture theatre was packed. Not only students from other years but from other disciplines had come to listen, and the external students Pilly had described: housewives, old ladies, and a red-faced colonel with a handlebar moustache.

'Ah, here comes Verena,' said Janet. 'Could those curvaceous sausages on her forehead be in honour of the Prof?'

Verena did indeed have a new hairstyle, though the suit she wore was tailor-made as always, and the high-necked blouse severe. Descending the tiered lecture theatre with her crocodile skin briefcase, she found herself faced with an unexpected hitch. Her seat in the centre of the front row was filled.

There had been some unpleasantness about the

college porter who was supposed to place the *Reserved* notice for Verena before lectures. He had complained to the bursar, saying that this was not part of his duties, and the bursar, who was probably in the pay of the unions, had supported him. So far this had not mattered since everyone now understood what was due to her, but today, with the place full of outsiders, the entire row was packed.

Anyone else might be deterred, but not Lady Plackett's daughter.

'Excuse me,' she said – and holding the briefcase aloft, she passed along the row, stopping at the point where she was directly under the rostrum and facing the carafe of water. This was where she always sat and where she intended most particularly to sit today.

With her behind poised expectantly, Verena waited, ready to sink into her appointed place – and did not wait in vain. Such was the authority, the breeding exerted even by her posterior, that the woman on the right edged closer to her neighbour, the student on the left, with only a mutter or two, pushed himself against his friend – and with a polite 'Thank you', Verena sat down, opened her briefcase, took out the vellum notepad and the gold-nibbed fountain pen, and was ready to begin.

Quin entered the lecture theatre, put a single sheet of paper on the desk, moved the carafe out of the way, looked up to say 'Good morning' – and instantly saw Ruth, sitting as low as it was possible in the back row.

She was partly obscured by a broad-shouldered man in the row in front of her, but the triangular face, the big smudged eyes, stood out perfectly clearly, as did an area of nakedness where her hair wasn't. For an instant he thought she had cut it off and felt an irregularity in his heart beat as if his parasympathetic nerves had intended to send a message of protest and thought better of it, partly because it was none of his business, and partly because she hadn't. Evidently she expected rain, for he could see the pigtail vanishing into her coat, and was reminded of the museum in Vienna and the water dropping from her hair the day he fetched her for their wedding.

These thoughts, if that was what they were, lasted a few seconds at the most, and were followed by another, equally brief, as he wondered why University College was sending their students to his lectures and made a note to stop them doing so. Then he picked up a piece of chalk, went to the blackboard – and began.

Ruth never forgot the next hour. If someone had told her that she would follow a lecture on ancestor descendant sequences in fossil rocks as though it was a bed-time story – as riveting, as extraordinary, at times as funny, as any fairy tale – she would not have believed them.

The subject was highly technical. Quin was reassessing the significance of Rowe's work on Micraster in the English chalk, relating it to Darwin's theories and the new ideas of Julian Huxley. Yet as he spoke – never raising his voice, making only an occasional gesture with those extraordinarily expressive hands, she felt a contact that was almost physical. It was as if he was behind her, nudging her forward towards the conclusion he was about to reach, letting her get there almost before him, so that she felt, yes . . . yes, *of course* it has to be like that!

All around Ruth, the others sat equally rapt. Sam had laid down his pen; few of the students took more than an occasional note because to miss even one word was unthinkable – and anyway they knew that afterwards they would read and read and even, somehow, make the necessary journeys . . . that they would become part of the adventure that was unfolding up there on the dais. Only Verena still wrote with her gold-nibbed pen on her vellum pad – wrote and wrote and wrote.

Halfway through, pausing for a moment, raking his hair in a characteristic gesture of which he was unaware, Quin found himself looking once more directly at Ruth. She had given up her Chu Chundra attitude and was leaning forward, one finger held sideways across her mouth in what he remembered as her listening attitude. The pigtail, too, had given up anonymity: a loop had escaped over her collar like a bracelet of Scythian gold.

Then he found his word and the lecture continued.

At exactly five minutes to the hour, he began on the recapitulation, laid the unravelled controversy once more before them – and was done.

He had not taken more than a few steps before he

was surrounded. Old students came to welcome him back, new ones to greet him. The red-faced colonel reminded him that they had met in Simla, shy house-wives hovered.

Verena waited quietly, not wishing to be lost in the crowd. Only when the Professor finally made his way to the door did she intercept him with a few powerful strides and gave him news which she knew must please him.

'I am,' she said, 'Verena Plackett!'

'What do you mean, you've admitted her?'

Dr Felton sighed. He'd been so pleased to see the Professor a couple of hours ago. Somerville's arrival lifted the spirits of everyone in the department; the breeze of cheerfulness and enterprise he brought was almost tangible, yet now Felton rose, as if in respect to Quin's rank, and wondered what was supposed to be the matter.

'I've told you . . . sir,' he began – and Quin frowned, for the 'sir' meant that he had put Roger down harder than he had intended. 'University College gave her place to someone and they rang round to see if anyone could have her. I thought we might squeeze her in and I knew you were in favour of taking refugees wherever pos-sible.'

'Not this one. She must go.'

'But why? She's an excellent student. You may think that being pretty and having all that hair and talking to the sheep –'

'Talking to the *sheep*? What sheep?'

'It was sent down by the Cambridge Research Institute and now they don't want it back.' He explained, trying to work out why the Prof, who had come in in the morning in the best of tempers, was now so stuffy and irascible. 'It's lonely and Ruth recites poetry to it. Goethe mostly. There's one called "The Wanderer's Night Song" it likes particularly, only it sounds different in German, of course.' And catching sight of the Professor's face: 'But what I'm saying is that though she's original and . . . and, well, emotional, she's very good at her work. Her dissections are excellent, and her experimental technique.'

'I dare say, but you'll have to get her transferred.'

'I can't. There isn't anywhere. UC tried all sorts of places before they came to us. And honestly I don't understand what all this is about,' said Roger, abandoning respect. 'The whole of London is riddled with refugees you've found work for – what about the old monster you wished on the library of the Geographical Society – Professor Zinlinsky who looks up the skirts of all the girls? And your aunt called in when she was here for the Chelsea Flower Show and she says it's just as bad in Northumberland – some opera singer of yours trying to milk cows – and now you try and turn out one of the most promising students we've had. Of course it's early days, but both Elke and I think she has a chance of beating Verena Plackett in the exams. She's the only one who's got a hope.'

'Who's Verena Plackett?'

'The VC's daughter. Didn't she come and thank you for your excellent lecture?'

'Yes, she did,' said Quin briefly. 'Look, I'm sorry but I'm not prepared to argue about this. I'm sure O'Malley will take her down in Tonbridge. He owes me a favour.'

'For God's sake, that's an hour on the train. She's saving for Heini's piano and –'

'Oh she is, is she? I mean, who the devil is Heini?'

'He's her boyfriend; he's on his way from Budapest and I don't mind telling you that I think he ought to get his own piano; she doesn't have any lunch because of him, and –'

'My God, Roger, don't tell me you've fallen for the girl.'

He had seriously hurt Felton's feelings. Roger's spectacle frames darkened, he scowled. 'I have *never* in my life got mixed up with a student and I never will; you ought to know that. Even if I wasn't married, I wouldn't. I have the lowest possible opinion of people who use their position to mess about with undergraduates.'

'Yes, I do know it; I'm sorry, I shouldn't have said that. But you see I knew the Bergers pretty well when I was in Vienna; I stayed with them one summer when Ruth was a child. It's entirely unsuitable that she should be in my class.'

Felton's brow cleared. 'Oh, if that's all . . . Good heavens, who cares about that?'

'I do.'

'I suppose you think you might mark her up in exams, but I shouldn't have thought there was much likelihood of that,' said Felton bitterly. 'You probably won't even be *here* when it's time to do the marking.'

'All right, you have a point. However —'

'She's *good* for us,' said Felton, speaking with more emotion than Quin had heard in him. 'She's so grateful to be allowed to study, she reminds the others of what a privilege it is to be at university. You know how cynical these youngsters can get, how they grumble. We too, I suppose, and suddenly here's someone who looks down a microscope as though God had just lowered a slide of paramecium down from heaven. And she's helping that poor little aspirin girl who always fails everything.'

'Exactly how long has Miss Berger been here?' asked Quin, whose ill temper seemed to be worsening with every minute.

'A week. But what has that to do with anything? You know perfectly well that one can tell the first time someone picks up a pipette whether they're going to be any good.'

'Nevertheless, she's leaving,' said Quin, tight-lipped.

'Then you tell her,' said Dr Felton, defying his superior for the first time in his life.

'I will,' said Quin, his face like thunder. At the door, he turned, remembering something he needed. 'Can you let me have the figures for last year's admissions as soon as possible? The VC wants them.'

196

Felton nodded. 'I've almost done them. They'll be ready for you this evening – I swear by Mozart's head.'

Quin spun round. '*What* did you say?'

Roger blushed. 'Nothing. Just a figure of speech.'

The room occupied by the Professor of Vertebrate Zoology was on the second floor and looked out over the walnut tree to the façade of the Vice Chancellor's Lodge and the arch with its glimpse of the river. The pieces of a partly assembled plesiosaur lay jumbled in a sand tray; the skull of an infant mastodon held down a pile of reprints. By the window, wearing a printed wool scarf left behind by his Aunt Frances, stood a life-sized model of Daphne, a female hominid from Java presented to Quin by the Oriental Exploration Society. The single, long-stemmed red rose in a vase on his desk had been placed there by his secretary, Hazel, an untroubling, middle-aged and happily married lady who could have run the department perfectly well without the interference of her superiors, and frequently did.

Ruth, summoned to the Professor's room, had come in still filled with the happiness his lecture had given her. Now she stood before him with bent head, trying to hold back her tears.

'But *why*? Why must I go? I don't understand.'

'Ruth, I've told you. In my old college in Cambridge members of staff weren't even allowed to *have* wives, let alone bring them into college. It's quite out of the question that I should teach someone I'm married to.'

'But you aren't married to me!' she said passionately.

'Not properly. You do nothing except send me pieces of paper about not being married. There is epilepsy and being your sister and a nun. And the thing about not consuming . . . or consummating or whatever it is.'

'It won't do, my dear, believe me. With the old VC we might have got away with it, but not with the Placketts. The scandal would be appalling. I'd have to resign which actually I don't mind in the least, but you'd be dragged into it and start your life under a cloud. Not to mention the delay to our freedom if we were known to have met daily.'

'All those things with C in them, you mean,' said Ruth. Fluent though her English was, the legal language was taking its toll. 'Collusion and . . . what is it . . . ? Connivance? Consent?'

'Yes, all those things. Look, leave this to me. I'm pretty sure I can get you on to the course down in Kent. They don't do Honours but –'

'I don't want to go away.' Her voice was low, intense. She had moved over to the window and one hand went out to rest on Daphne's arm as though seeking a sister in distress. 'I don't *want* to! Everyone is so kind here. There's Pilly who has to be a scientist because her father saw you striding about on a newsreel with yaks and that's *not* her fault, and I've promised Sam that I'd bring Paul Ziller to the Music Club and Dr Felton's classes are so interesting and he has such trouble with his wife wanting to have a baby and taking her temperature –'

'He told you that!' said Quin, unable to believe his ears.

'No, not exactly – but Mrs Felton came to fetch him and he was delayed and we began to talk. I'm not *reserved*, you know, like the British. Of course, when we said our marriage should be a secret, that was different. A secret is a secret, but otherwise . . . Even my goat-herding grandmother used to tell people things. She would roll down her stockings and say "Look!" and you had to examine her varicose veins. She didn't ask if you wanted to see her veins; she needed to show them. And, of course, the Jewish side of me doesn't like distance at all, but it's different with you because you are British and upper class and Verena Plackett is studying Palaeontology so that she can marry you when we have been put asunder.'

Quin made a gesture of impatience. 'Don't talk rubbish, Ruth. Now let's think how –'

'It isn't rubbish! She's bought a new dress for the dinner party tonight because you're coming. It's electric-blue taffeta with puffed sleeves. I know because the maid at the Lodge is the porter's niece and he told me. Of course she is very tall but you could wear your hair *en brosse* and –'

Quin took out his handkerchief and wiped his brow. 'Ruth, I'm sorry; I know you've settled in but –'

'Yes, I have!' she cried. 'There's so much here! Dr Elke showed me her bed bug eggs and they are absolutely beautiful with a little cap on one end and you

199

can see the eyes of the young ones through the shell. And there's the river and the walnut tree –'

'And the sheep,' said Quin bitterly.

'Yes, that too. But most of all your lecture this morning. It opened such doors. Though I don't agree with you absolutely about Hackenstreicher. I think he might have been perfectly sincere when he said that –'

'Oh, you do,' said Quin, not at all pleased. 'You think that a man who deliberately falsifies the evidence to fit a preconceived hypothesis is to be taken seriously.'

'If it *was* deliberate. But my father had a paper which said that the skull they showed Hackenstreicher could have been from much lower down in the sequence so that it wouldn't be unreasonable for him to have come to the conclusions he did.'

'Yes, I've read that paper, but don't you see –'

Tempted to pursue the argument, Quin forced himself back to the task that faced him. That Ruth would have been an interesting student was not in question.

'Look, there's no sense in postponing this. I shall ring O'Malley and get you transferred to Tonbridge and until then you'd better stay away.'

She had turned her back and was absently retying the scarf, with its motif of riding crops and bridles, round Daphne's neck. In the continuing silence, Quin's disquiet grew. He remembered suddenly the child on the Grundlsee reciting Keats . . . the way she had tried to make a home even in the museum. Now he was banishing her again.

But when she turned to face him, it was not the sad

200

handmaiden of his musings that he saw, not Ruth in tears amid the alien corn. Her chin was up, her expression obstinate and for a moment she resembled the primitive, pugnacious hominid beside whom she stood.

'I can't stop you sending me away because you are like God here; I saw that even before you came. But you can't make me go to Tonbridge. I didn't intend to go to university, I thought I should stay and work for my family. It was you who said I should go and when I thought you wanted me to come here I was so –' She broke off and blew her nose. 'But I won't start again somewhere else. I won't go to Tonbridge.'

'You will do exactly as you are told,' he said furiously. 'You will go to Tonbridge and get a decent degree and –'

'No, I won't. I shall go and get a job, the best paid one I can find. If you had let me stay I would have done everything you asked me; I would have been obedient and worked as hard as I knew how and I would have been *invisible* because you would have been my Professor and that would have been right. But now you can't bully me. Now I am free.'

Quin rose from his chair. 'Let me tell you that even if I am not your Professor I am still legally your husband and I can *order* you to go and –'

The sentence remained unfinished as Quin, aghast, heard the words of Basher Somerville come out of his own mouth.

Ruth put a last flourish to the bow round Daphne's neck.

'You have read Nietzsche, I see,' she said. '*When I go to a woman I take my whip*. How suitable that even the scarves your girlfriends leave behind have things on them for beating horses.'

But Quin had had enough. He went to the door, held it open.

'Now go,' he said. 'And quickly.'

The guest list for Lady Plackett's first dinner party was one of which any hostess could be proud. A renowned ichthyologist just back from an investigation of the bony fish in Lake Titicaca, an art historian who was the world expert on Russian icons, a philologist from the British Museum who spoke seven Chinese dialects and Simeon LeClerque who had won a literary prize for his biography of Bishop Berkeley. But, of course, the guest of honour, the person she had placed next to Verena, was Professor Somerville whom she had welcomed back to Thameside earlier in the day.

By six o'clock Lady Plackett had finished supervising the work of the maids and the cook, and went upstairs to speak to her daughter.

Verena had bathed earlier and now sat in her dressing-gown at her desk piled high with books.

'How are you getting on, dear?' asked Lady Plackett solicitously, for it always touched her, the way Verena prepared for her guests.

'I'm nearly ready, Mummy. I managed to get hold of Professor Somerville's first paper – the one on the dinosaur pits of Tendaguru, and I've read all his books, of course. But I feel I should just freshen up on ichthyology if I'm next to Sir Harold. He's just back from South America, I understand.'

'Yes . . . Lake Titicaca. Only remember, it's the *bony* fishes, dear.'

Sir Harold was married but really very eminent and it was quite right for Verena to prepare herself for him. 'I think we'll manage the Russian icons without trouble – Professor Frank is said to be very talkative. If you have the key names . . .'

'Oh, I have those,' said Verena calmly. 'Andrei Rublev . . . egg tempera . . .' She glanced briefly at the notes she had taken earlier. 'The effect of Mannerism becoming apparent in the seventeenth century . . .'

Lady Plackett, not a demonstrative woman, kissed her daughter on the cheek. 'I can always rely on you.' At the doorway she paused. 'With Professor Somerville it would be in order to ask a little about Bowmont . . . the new forestry act, perhaps: I shall, of course, mention that I was acquainted with his aunt. And don't trouble about Chinese phonetics, dear. Mr Fellowes was only a stop gap – he's that old man from the British Museum and he's right at the other end of the table.'

Left alone, Verena applied herself to the bony fishes before once again checking off Professor Somerville's published works. He would not find her wanting intellectually, that was for certain. Now it was time to attend to the other side of her personality: not the scholar but the woman. Removing her dressing-gown, she slipped

203

on the blue taffeta dress which Ruth had described with perfect accuracy and began to unwind the curlers from her hair.

'I found it fascinating,' said Verena, turning her powerful gaze on Professor Somerville. 'Your views on the value of lumbar curve measurements in recognizing hominids seem to me entirely convincing. In the footnote to chapter thirteen you put that so well.'

Quin, encountering that rare phenomenon, a person who read footnotes, was ready to be impressed. 'It's still speculative, but interestingly enough they've come up with some corroboration in Java. The American expedition . . .'

Verena's eyes flickered in a moment of unease. She had not had time to read up Java.

'I understand that you have just been honoured in Vienna,' she said, steering back to safer water. 'It must have been such an interesting time to be there. Hitler seems to have achieved miracles with the German economy.'

'Yes.' The crinkled smile which had so charmed her had gone. 'He has achieved other miracles too, such as the entire destruction of three hundred years of German culture.'

'Oh.' But this was a girl who only needed to look at a hound puppy for it to sink to its stomach and grovel – and she recovered her self-possession at once. 'Tell me, Professor Somerville, what made you decide to start a field course at Bowmont?'

'Well, the fauna on that coast is surprisingly diverse, with the North Sea being effectively enclosed. Then we're opposite the Farne Islands where the ornithologists have done some very interesting work on breeding colonies – it was an obvious place for people to get practical experience.'

'But you yourself? Your discipline? You will be there also?'

'Of course. I help Dr Felton with the Marine Biology but I also run trips up to the coal measures and down to Staithes in Yorkshire.'

'And the students stay separately – not in the house?'

'Yes. I've converted an old boathouse and some cottages on the beach into a dormitory and labs. My aunt is elderly; I wouldn't ask her to entertain my students and anyway they prefer to be independent.'

Verena frowned, for she could see problems ahead, but as the Professor looked as though he might turn to the left, where Mrs LeClerque, the unexpectedly pretty wife of Bishop Berkeley's biographer, was looking at him from under her lashes, she plunged into praise of the morning's lecture.

'I was so intrigued by your analysis of Dr Hackenstreicher's misconceptions. There seems no doubt that the man was seriously deluded.'

'I'm glad you think so,' said Quin, receiving boiled potatoes at the hands of a cold-looking parlourmaid. 'Miss Berger seemed to find my views unreasonable.'

'Ah. But she is leaving us, is she not?'

'Yes.'

'Mother was pleased to hear it,' said Verena, glancing at Lady Plackett who was talking to an unexpected last-minute arrival: a musicologist just returned from New York whose acceptance had got lost in the post. 'I think she feels that there are too many of them.'

'Them?' asked Quin with lifted eyebrows.

'Well, you know . . . foreigners . . . refugees. She feels that places should be kept for our own nationals.'

Lady Plackett, who had been watching benignly her daughter's success with the Professor, now abandoned protocol to speak across the table.

'Well, of course, it doesn't do to say so,' she said, 'but one can't help feeling that they've rather taken over. Of course one can't entirely approve of what Hitler is doing.'

'No,' said Quin. 'It would certainly be difficult to approve of that.'

'But she is rather a strange girl in any case,' said Verena. 'I mean, she talks to the sheep. There is something whimsical in that; something unscientific.'

'Jesus talked to them,' said the philologist from the museum. An old man with a white beard, he spoke with unexpected resolution.

'Well, yes, I suppose so.' Verena conceded the point. 'But she recites to it in German.'

'What does she recite?' asked the biographer of Bishop Berkeley.

'Goethe,' said Quin briefly. He was growing weary of the saga of the sheep. '"The Wanderer's Night Song"'.

206

The philologist approved. 'An excellent choice. Though perhaps one might have expected one of the eighteenth-century pastoralists. Matthias Claudius perhaps?'

There followed a surprisingly animated discussion on the kind of lyric verse which might, in the German language, be expected to appeal to the domestic ungulates, and though this was exactly the kind of scholarly banter which Lady Plackett believed in encouraging, she listened to it with a frown.

'Wasn't Goethe the man who kept falling in love with women called Charlotte?' asked the appealingly silly wife of the biographer.

Quin turned to her with relief. 'Yes, he was. He put it all in a novel called *Werther* where the hero is so in love with a Charlotte that he kills himself. Thackeray wrote a poem about it.'

'Was it a good poem?'

'Very good,' said Quin firmly. 'It starts:

Werther had a love for Charlotte
Such as words could never utter;
Would you know how first he met her?
She was cutting bread and butter.

And it ends with him being carried away on a shutter.'

Verena, watching this descent into frivolity with a puckered brow, now made a last attempt to bring Professor Somerville back to a subject dear to her heart.

'When is Miss Berger actually due to leave?' she asked.

'It isn't decided yet.'

He then turned resolutely back to Mrs LeClerque who began to tell him about a friend of hers who had become engaged to no fewer than three men called Henry, all of them unsuitable, and Verena decided to do her duty by her other neighbour.

'Tell me, do you intend to pursue your researches into the bony fishes here in England?' she enquired.

But for once her mother had let her down. The last minute arrival of the musicologist had necessitated a change in the seating arrangements. Blank-faced and astonished, the icon expert gazed at her.

It was Quin's habit to drive to Thameside in a large, midnight-blue Crossley tourer with brass lamps and a deep horn which recalled, faintly, the motoring activities of the redoubtable Mr Toad.

The day after the Placketts' dinner party, parking the car under the archway, he was confronted not by the usual throng shouting their 'Good mornings' but by two cold-looking students holding up a ragged banner inscribed with the words: *RUTH BERGER'S DIS-MISSAL IS UNFAIR.*

Safe in his room, he picked up the phone. 'Get me O'Malley down in Tonbridge, will you please, Hazel?'

'Yes, Professor Somerville. And Sir Lawrence Dempster phoned – he said would you ring him back as soon as possible.'

'All right; I'll deal with that first.'

By the time Quin had spoken to the director of the Geophysical Society, it was too late to phone O'Malley, who would be lecturing, and Quin applied himself to his correspondence till it was time to go to the Common Room where Elke, crunching a custard cream between her splendid teeth, brought up a subject he had declared to be closed.

'She wrote a first-class essay for me after less than a week. And in what is, of course, not her native language.'

'I'm not aware that Miss Berger has any trouble with English,' said Quin. 'She has after all been to an English school most of her life.'

His next attempt to phone Tonbridge was cut short by Hazel who announced that a deputation of students was waiting to see him.

'I can give them ten minutes, but no more,' he said curtly. 'I'm lecturing at eleven.'

The students filed in. He recognized Sam and the little frightened girl whose father made aspirins, and the huge Welshman with cauliflower ears – all third years whom he didn't know as well as he should have done because of his absence in India – but there were other students not in his department at all. It was Sam, wrapped in his muffler, who seemed to be their spokesman.

'We've come about Miss Berger, sir. We don't think she should be sent away.' It cost him to speak as he did, for Professor Somerville, hitherto, had been his god.

'We think it's victimization.' And as the Professor continued to look at him stonily: 'We think it's unfair in view of what the Jewish people –'

'Thank you; it is not necessary to remind me of the fate of Jewish people.'

'No.' Sam swallowed. 'But we can't see why she should go just because of a few technicalities.'

'Miss Berger is not being victimized. She is being transferred.'

'Yes. But so are the Jews and the gypsies and the Freemasons in Germany,' said Sam, scoring an unexpected point. 'And the Socialists. They're being transferred to camps in the East.'

'And she doesn't *want* to go,' said Pilly, stammering with nerves at addressing the man on whose account she was being put through so much. 'She likes it here and she *helps*. She can make you see things.'

'It's true, sir.' A tall, fair man whom Quin did not recognize spoke from the back. 'I'm from the German Department and . . . well, I don't mind telling you I got pretty discouraged studying the language when all you hear is Hitler braying on the radio. But I met her in the library and . . . well, if *she* can forget the Nazis . . .'

Quin was silent, his eyes travelling over the deputation.

'You seem to have forgotten one of Miss Berger's most fervent admirers,' he said. 'Why has nobody brought the sheep?'

*

210

It was as he was returning from lunch that Quin found a visitor in his room.

'You must forgive me for troubling you,' said Professor Berger, rising from his chair.

'It's no trouble – it's a pleasure to see you, sir.'

But Quin, as he shook hands, was shocked by the change in him. Berger had been a tall, upright figure, dignified in the manner of an Old Testament prophet. Now his face was gaunt and lined and there was a great weariness in his voice.

'Is it all right to talk German?'

'Of course.' Quin shut the door, ushered him to a better chair.

'I have come about my daughter. About Ruth. I understand there has been some trouble and I wondered if there was anything I could do to put it right.'

Quin picked up a ruler and began to turn it over and over in his hands.

'She will have told you that I'm arranging to have her transferred to the University of Tonbridge, down in Kent.'

'Ah. So that's it. I didn't know. She only told me that she had to leave.'

'It's hardly a secret. Everyone in the university here seems to make it their business.'

'Could I ask why she is being sent away?'

The old man's voice was dry and remote, but the distress behind the words was easy to hear and Quin, accustomed to thinking of himself as Berger's underling, found himself increasingly uncomfortable.

'I thought it was inadvisable that I should teach someone whose family I knew so well. It would lay your daughter open to charges that she was being favoured.'

The Professor smoothed his black hat. 'Really? I have to say that if I had refused to teach the children of men I knew well in Vienna, I would have had many empty seats at my lectures.'

'Perhaps. But British colleges are different. There is more gossip; they're smaller.'

'Professor Somerville, please tell me the truth,' said Berger, and it was not till he heard this man, thirty years his senior, address him by his rank, that Quin realized how hurt the old man was. 'Has Ruth done something wrong? Is she not equal to the course? We tried to teach her well, but –'

'No, absolutely not. Ruth is an excellent student.'

'Is it her manner then? Do you find her too forward? Reared among academics she perhaps appears lacking in respect?'

'Not at all. She has already made more friends than one would have believed possible, both among the students and the staff.'

'Then . . . can there have been . . . some kind of scandal? She is pretty, I know, but I would swear that she –'

Quin leant across his desk to speak with suitable emphasis. 'Please believe me, sir, when I tell you that I am sending her away only because I think that the connection with your family, the debt I owe you –'

'What debt?' the other man interrupted sternly.

'The symposium in Vienna, your hospitality. And the honorary degree.'

'Yes, the degree. We heard from colleagues that you went to the ceremony, but not to the dinner.'

'That's correct. When I heard that you were not there –' began Quin, and broke off. 'I should have thanked you for arranging it, but I went straight up to Bowmont.'

There was a pause. Then Professor Berger, speaking slowly, looking at the ground, said: 'My wife believes that it was you who helped Ruth in Vienna.'

Quin's silence lasted a fraction too long. 'Oh really? Why does she believe that?'

'You may well ask,' said the Professor, a trifle bitterly. 'Normal thought processes are entirely foreign to Leonie's nature. As far as I can gather it is because you dived into the Grundlsee to retrieve her sister-in-law's monograph on the Mi-Mi. Also because you danced twice with her god-daughter, Franzi, at the University Ball. Franzi had very bad acne and a squint and it was because you singled her out and were kind to her that she agreed to have her eye operated on, and the acne disappeared of itself, and now she is married and has two abominably behaved children and has fortunately settled in New York.'

'I'm afraid I don't entirely follow you,' said Quin apologetically.

'There were other reasons with which I won't bore you. Apparently you threw your hat over a *Herrenpilz* which Mishak was stalking, thereby preventing Frau

213

Pollack from getting it. We always regarded the mush-rooms near the house as ours and . . .' He shook his head. 'What a lost world that seems. But anyway, the gist of Leonie's argument is that people don't change; if you were kind then you would be kind now. If you found out that I was not at the university, you would look me up and find Ruth. That is what my wife thinks, not what I think, and I don't want you to say anything you would like to keep to yourself. But it is possible that if Leonie is correct you might feel worried about having Ruth here. You might feel that she would become too attached to you.'

'No, I don't feel that.'

'It would be natural, however. She has a very warm heart and she was always talking about you after you left us that summer. Not to mention the blue rabbit.' And as Quin frowned in puzzlement: 'The one you shot for her in the Prater. She went to bed with it for years and when its ear came off, we had to call in Dr Levy to perform surgery.'

'I'd forgotten.'

'You were young; the world was before you, it still is. Heaven forbid that you should cling to the past as we do. But what I wanted to say was that you need have no fears on that score . . . however fond Ruth is of you, however she might look up to you as . . .'

'An older man,' said Quin, raising his eyebrows.

Berger shrugged. 'She is totally committed to her young cousin, to Heini Radek. Everything she does in the end is for him. So you see you would be quite safe.

214

She will marry Radek and turn his music for him and choose the camellias for his buttonhole. It has been like that ever since he came to Vienna.'

'In that case does it matter so much where she gets a degree? Or even whether?'

'Perhaps I attach too much importance to learning: it is a characteristic of my race. Perhaps, too, I am one of those fathers who thinks no one is good enough for his daughter. Heini is a gifted boy, but I would have liked her to have a choice.' He changed tack. 'One thing is certain, Ruth won't go to Tonbridge. She spent the morning at the Employment Exchange and now she is writing letters of application and trying not to cry.'

'I'm sure she'll see reason.'

'Allow me to know my own daughter,' said Berger with dignity. He unhooked his walking stick, ready to leave. 'Well, you must do what you think right. I wouldn't have been pleased if someone had told me how to run my department. I'm going to Manchester for a few weeks and I'd hoped –'

'Ah yes!' Quin seized the change of subject with alacrity. 'You'll enjoy the Institute. Feldberg's a splendid fellow – but don't let that skinflint of an accountant do you out of the proper fee. There's a perfectly adequate endowment for classification work.'

'I was not aware that I had mentioned my appointment at the Institute,' said Professor Berger, looking at him sternly. 'Nor that I had been asked to classify the Howard Collection.'

Taken, so to speak, from the rear while defending his flank, Quin shuffled some papers on his desk.

'Things get about,' he murmured.

'So you arranged the job in Manchester? You asked them to get in touch with me? I should have guessed that.'

'Well, for heaven's sake, you've done nothing to help yourself since you came. A man of your eminence sitting in the public library next to a tramp! Why didn't you contact the people you've helped in your time? I only mentioned your name – Feldberg didn't even know you were in England!'

Berger had put on his hat, taken up his walking stick. When he spoke again, he was smiling. 'It is strange, I have so many degrees – so very many – and my wife failed even her diploma in flower arranging because she always put too many flowers in the vase, and yet you see she was right. People don't change.'

Only at the door did he turn, his voice grave once more, his face showing its utter fatigue. 'Let the child stay, Quinton,' he said, using the name he had used all those years ago. 'It's less than a year after all, and who knows what is in store for us.' And very quietly: 'She will not trouble you.'

But in the end it was not Berger's plea which secured a reprieve for Ruth, nor the intervention of the students. It was not even the obvious pleasure which Lady Plackett had shown in getting rid of a girl who did not fit into the general mould. It was a poster by the newspaper

216

kiosk Quin passed on the way home, announcing: *HITLER IN CZECHOSLOVAKIA. PICTURES.*

The pictures, when Quin bought the paper, showed the Führer grinning and garlanded with flowers, the swastika banners hanging from the buildings as they had done in Vienna. Austria in March, Czechoslovakia in October . . . could anyone believe it would stop there?

The average life of an infantry officer in 1918 had been six weeks. In the navy he might expect to last longer, but not much. When war came, as it surely must, would anyone mind who was married to whom and for how long?

'O'Malley says he's got no room,' was Quin's way of making his decision known to Dr Felton. 'Tell Miss Berger she can stay.'

And Roger nodded, and neither then nor later revealed what he had just read in the *University News*: that O'Malley was in hospital with concussion after a car crash and not in a position to say anything at all.

15

In the second week of October, Leonie's prayers on behalf of the nursery school teacher were answered. Miss Bates became engaged to be married – a triumph of camiknickers over personality – and went home to Kettering to prepare her trousseau. Her room on the ground floor back thus became vacant and Paul Ziller moved into it which made everybody happy. Ziller no longer had to practise in the cloakroom of the Day Centre but could stay at home; Leonie could get hold of his shirts to wash whenever it suited her and Uncle Mishak had direct access to the garden.

Mishak had not found it necessary to return the piece of land he had claimed at the time of the Munich crisis. They had told him to Keep Calm and Dig and he continued to do so. Since he couldn't afford to buy plants or fertilizer, his activities were limited, but not as limited as one might expect. The old lady two doors down still owned her house and, in exchange for help with the digging, she gave Mishak cuttings and seeds from her herbaceous border. Nor were Mishak's rambles through London's parks without reward, for he carried his Swiss army knife in his pocket, and a number of brown paper bags. No more than Dr Elke's tapeworms would have destroyed the host that nourished them would Mishak have caused harm to the plants he encountered, but a little discreet pruning often brought him back enriched by a cutting of philadelphus or a seedhead of clematis. And if there was no money for fertilizer, there was a plentiful supply of compost at Number 27 and the neighbouring houses, beginning with the remains of Fräulein Lutzenholler's soups.

Hilda, meanwhile, had made a breakthrough in the British Museum, braving the inner sanctum of the Keeper of the Anthropology Collection and confronting him with her views on the Mi-Mi drinking cup.

'It is not from the Mi-Mi,' said Hilda, peering earnestly through her spectacles, and gave chapter and verse.

The Keeper had not agreed, but he had not ejected her. That refugees were not allowed to work was a misapprehension. No one minded them working, what they were not allowed to do was get *paid*. Her credentials established, Hilda spent happy hours in the dusty basement of the museum, sorting the artefacts sent back by travellers in the previous century, for this woman who spelled death to the most hardened floor polisher, could handle the clay figurines and ankle bracelets she encountered in her profession with delicacy and skill.

A certain cautious hope thus pervaded Number 27

during October, the more so as Ruth, now re-established at college, was obviously loving her work. Even the gloomy Fräulein Lutzenholler had a new occupation, for Professor Freud had at last left Vienna and been installed in a house a few streets away. She did not expect to be noticed by Freud, (who was, in any case, extremely old and ill) because she had spoken well of Freud's great rival, Jung, at a meeting of the Psychoanalytical Society in 1921, but she liked just to stand in front of his house and *look*, as Cézanne had looked at Mont St Victoire.

With both Hilda and the psychoanalyst out of the way, and her husband busy preparing for his assignment in Manchester, Leonie could get through the housework unimpeded, but as the weather grew colder, she suffered a domestic sorrow which, though it caused her shame, she shared with Miss Violet and Miss Maud.

'I live with mice,' she said, her blue eyes clouding, for she felt the stigma keenly.

It was true. Mice, as the autumn advanced, were coming indoors in droves. They lived vibrant lives behind the skirting boards of Number 27, they squeaked in marital ecstasy behind the wainscot. Leonie covered everything edible, she scrubbed, she stalked and bashed with broomsticks, she bought poison out of her meagre allowance from the refugee committee – and they thrived on it.

'What about traps?' said Miss Maud. 'We could lend you some.'

But traps needed cheese, and cheese was expensive. 'That landlord,' said Leonie, stirring her coffee, 'I have said and said he must bring the rat-catching man, and he does nothing.'

Miss Maud then offered one of her kittens, but Leonie, with great politeness, refused.

'To live with mice, to live with cats – for me it is the same,' she said sadly.

Ruth too was troubled by the mice. She did not think that they could chew through the biscuit tin with the Princesses on the lid, but a great many documents of importance were collecting under the floorboards as Mr Proudfoot laboured on her behalf and it was disconcerting to feel that they provided a rallying point for nesting rodents.

But life in the university was totally absorbing. If there had been any anxiety about Heini's visa, she could not have given herself to her studies as she did, but Heini wrote with confidence: his father had now found exactly who to bribe and he expected to be with her by the beginning of November. If Heini had any worries they were about the piano, but here too all was going well. For Ruth still worked at the Willow three evenings a week and the café was beginning to attract people from up the hill. She would not have taken tips from the refugees even if they could have afforded them, but from wealthy film producers or young men with Jaguars in search of 'atmosphere', she took anything she could get and the jam jar was three-quarters full.

Ruth's response to news of her reprieve had been to ask Quin if she could see him privately for half an hour.

There was, she said, something she particularly wanted to tell him.

In trying to think of a place where they would meet no one of his acquaintance, Quin had hit on The Tea Pavilion in Leicester Square which no one in his family would have dreamt of frequenting, and was hardly a haunt of eminent palaeontologists. He had not, however, expected to score such a hit with Ruth who looked with delight at the Turkish Bath mosaics, the potted palms and black-skirted waitresses, obviously convinced that she was at the nerve centre of British social life.

The meeting began badly with what Quin regarded as an excessive outburst of gratitude. 'Ruth, will you please stop thanking me. And I don't take sugar.'

'I know that,' said Ruth, offended. 'I remember it from Vienna. Also that it is upper class to put the tea in first and then the milk because Miss Kenmore told me that that is what is done by the mother of the Queen. But to expect me not to thank you is unintelligent when you have probably saved my life and found a job for my father and now are letting me return to college.'

'Yes, well I hope you've thought that through properly. I don't know if the courts interest themselves in the details of how we spend our days but you know what Proudfoot said about collusion. If Heini comes back and finds that there are unnecessary delays to your marriage he won't be at all pleased. I think you should take that into consideration.'

'Yes, I have. But I'm sure it'll be all right and with

Heini it's more to do with being together, I told you. It would have happened before, but my father could never understand about the glass of water theory. One couldn't even discuss it in his presence.'

'What on earth is the glass of water theory?'

'Oh, you know, that love . . . physical love . . . is like drinking a glass of water when you are thirsty; it's nothing to make a fuss about.'

'I don't know if you could discuss it in my presence either,' said Quin meditatively. 'It sounds like arrant nonsense.'

'Do you think so?' Ruth looked surprised. 'But anyway, I don't think that he will mind about being married at once because of his career.'

'I wonder. It's my belief that the international situation will concentrate his thoughts wonderfully. I'll bet he'll want to claim you, and to do so legally, as soon as possible. However, I've made my point; if you're sure you know what you're doing, I'll say no more.'

The plate of cakes he had ordered for Ruth now arrived and was greeted by her with rapture.

'English patisserie is so . . . bright, isn't it?' she said, surveying the yellow rims of the jam tarts, the brilliant reds and greens of their fillings. She passed the plate to Quin who said he limited his consumption of bicarbonate of soda to medicinal purposes, and passed it back. 'Actually,' she went on, 'I wanted to say something important about the annulment. That's why I asked you to meet me. In case it goes wrong. I'm sure it won't, but in case. You see, I've been talking to Mrs

Burtt who is very intelligent and used to work for a lot of people who got divorced. Not annulled, but divorced. I didn't realize how different that was.'

'Who is Mrs Burtt?'

'She's the lady who washes up in the Willow Tea Rooms where I . . .' She broke off, suspecting that Quin, like her father, might make a fuss on hearing that she still had an evening job. 'It's a place where we all go to. Anyway, she told me exactly what you have to do to get divorced.'

'Oh, she did?'

'Yes.' Ruth bit into her jam tart. 'You go to a hotel somewhere on the South Coast. Brighton is best because it has a pier and slot machines and you book into a hotel with a special lady that you have hired. And then you and the lady sit up all night playing cards.' She looked up, her face a little troubled. 'Mrs Burtt didn't say what kind of card games – rummy, I expect, or perhaps *vingt-et-un*? Because for bridge you need more people, don't you, and poker is probably not suitable? And then when morning comes you get into bed with the lady and ring for the chambermaid to bring you breakfast, and she comes and then she remembers you and the detective who has followed you calls her to give evidence and you get divorced.'

She sat back, extremely pleased with herself.

'Mrs Burtt seems to be very well informed. And certainly if necessary I shall –'

'Ah, but *no*! That is what I wanted to say. You've been so incredibly good to me that I couldn't let you do that because I don't think you would enjoy it, so *I shall do it instead*! Only of course I won't hire a lady, I shall hire a gentleman which I shall be able to do by then because I shall have paid for Heini's piano and got a job. Except that I don't know any card games except Happy Families, but I shall learn and –'

'Ruth, will you please stop talking rubbish. As though I would involve you in any squalid nonsense like that.'

'It isn't nonsense. It's just as important for you to be free so that you can marry Verena Plackett.'

'I wouldn't marry Verena Plackett if she was the last –' began Quin, caught off his guard.

'Ah, but that is because you think she is too tall, but she could wear low heels or go barefoot which is healthy – and even if you don't marry her there are all the ladies who jump at you from behind pyramids and the ones who leave scarves in your rooms – and I want to *help*.'

'Well, you're not going to help by getting mixed up in that sort of rubbish,' said Quin. 'Now tell me about your parents – how are they getting on and how is life in Belsize Park?'

Though she was clearly offended by Quin's rejection of her plan, Ruth accepted the change of subject, nor did her hurt feelings prevent her from eating a second jam tart and a chocolate eclair, and by the time they left the restaurant, she was able to turn to Quin and make him a promise with her customary panache.

'I know you don't like to be thanked, but for tea

everybody gets thanked and I want to tell you that from now on I will never again try to be alone with you, I will be completely anonymous; I will,' said Ruth with fervour, 'be *nonexistent.*'

Quin stood looking down at her, an odd expression on his face. Ruth's eyes glowed with the ardour of those who swear mighty oaths, her tumbled hair glowed in the light of the chandeliers. A young man, passing with a friend, had turned to stare at her and bumped into the doorman.

'That would interest me,' he said thoughtfully. 'Yes, your nonexistence would interest me very much.'

Ruth was as good as her word. She sat at the back of the lecture theatre (though no longer in a raincoat); she flattened herself against the wall when the Professor passed; her voice was never heard in his seminars.

This did not mean that she failed to ask questions. As Quin's lectures opened more and more doors in her mind, she trained her friends to ask questions on her behalf, and to hear Pilly stumbling through sentences which had Ruth's hallmark in every phrase, gave Quin an exquisite pleasure.

Nevertheless, Nature had not shaped Ruth for nonexistence, a point made by Sam and Janet who said they thought she was overdoing it. 'Just because you knew him in Vienna, you don't have to fall over backwards to keep out of his way,' said Sam. 'Anyway it's a complete waste of time – one can see your hair halfway across the quad – I bet he knows exactly where you are.'

This, unfortunately, was true. Ruth leaning over the

parapet to feed the ducks was not nonexistent, nor encountered in the library behind a pile of books, a piece of grass between her teeth. She was not nonexistent as she sat under the walnut tree coaching Pilly, nor emerging, drunk with music, from rehearsals of the choir. In general, Quin, without conceit, would have said he was a man with excellent nerves, but a week of Ruth's anonymity was definitely taking its toll.

If Ruth was trying to keep out of the Professor's way, Verena Plackett was not. She emerged each morning from the Lodge, punctual as an alderman, bearing her crocodile skin briefcase and carrying over her arm a spotless white lab coat, one of three, which her mother's maids removed, laundered, starched and replaced each day. Verena continued to thank the staff on her parents' behalf at the end of every lecture; she accepted only the sycophantic Kenneth Easton as her partner in practicals; the liver fluke, seeing her coming, flattened itself obediently between glass slides. But it was in Professor Somerville's seminars that Verena shone particularly. She sat in the chair next to the Professor's, her legs neatly crossed at the ankle, and asked intelligent questions using complete sentences and making it clear that she had read not only the books he had recommended, but a great many others.

'I wonder what you think about Ashley-Cunningham's views on bone atrophy as expressed in chapter five of his *Palaeohistology*?' was the kind of thing the other students had to endure from Verena. 'It wasn't on our reading list, I know, but I happened to find it in the London Library.'

That Ruth might be a serious rival academically had not, at the beginning, occurred to Verena. A fey girl who conversed with sheep was hardly to be taken seriously. It was something of a shock, therefore, when the first essays were returned and she found that Ruth, like herself, was getting alphas and spoken of as someone likely to get a First. Verena set her jaw and decided to work even harder – and so did Ruth. Ruth, however, blamed herself, she felt *besmirched*, and at night when Hilda slept, she sat up in bed and spoke seriously to God.

'Please, God,' Ruth would pray, 'don't let me be competitive. Let me realize what a privilege it is to study. Let me remember that knowledge must be pursued for its own sake and please, *please* stop me wanting to beat Verena Plackett in the exams.'

She prayed hard and she meant what she said. But God was busy that autumn as the International Brigade came back, defeated, from Spain, Hitler's bestialities increased, and sparrows everywhere continued to fall. And Ruth, her prayers completed, would spoil everything and get out of bed and take her lecture notes to the bathroom, the only place at Number 27 where, late at night, one could study undisturbed.

As term advanced, the talk turned increasingly to the field course to be held at the end of the month. Of this break in the routine of lectures, the research students who had been to Bowmont spoke with extreme enthusiasm.

'You go out in boats and there are bonfires and cook-ups and on Sunday you go up to the Professor's house for a whopping lunch.'

Ruth was prepared to believe all this, but she was adamant about not going.

'I can't possibly afford the fare, let alone all those Wellington boots and oilskins,' she said. 'And anyway, I have to prepare for Heini. I don't mind, honestly.'

Pilly, however, did mind and said so at length, and so did Ruth's other friends.

And Dr Felton minded. He did more than mind. He was absolutely determined to get Ruth to Bowmont.

For there *was* a Hardship Fund. It existed to help students in difficulties and it was under the management of the Finance Committee on which Roger sat, as he sat on most of the committees that came the department's way since Quin had made it clear from the start that he was not prepared to waste his time in overheated rooms and repetitive babble.

The committee was due to meet on a Saturday morning just two weeks before the beginning of the course. Felton had already canvassed members from other departments and found only goodwill. The fund was healthily in credit, and everyone who knew Ruth Berger (and a surprising number of people did) thought it an excellent idea that it should be used to send her to Northumberland. It was thus with confidence and hope that Roger walked into the meeting.

He had reckoned without the new Vice Chancellor. Lord Charlefont had steered committees along at a spanking pace. Sir Desmond, whose degree was in Economics, thrived on detail: every test tube to be purchased, every box of chalk came under his scrutiny and at one o'clock, before the question of the Hardship Fund could be fully discussed, the committee was adjourned for lunch.

'Do you really have to go back?' asked Lady Plackett, who had hoped to persuade her husband to attend a private view.

'Yes, I do. Felton from the Zoology Department is trying to get one of the students on to Somerville's field course. He wants to use the Hardship Fund for that. It's a very moot point, it seems to me – there's a precedent involved. To what extent can *not* going on a field trip be classed as hardship? We shall have to debate this very carefully.'

'It's not the Austrian girl he wants the money for? Miss Berger?'

Sir Desmond reached for the agenda. 'It doesn't say so, but it seems possible. Why?'

'If so, I would regard it as most inadvisable. As you know, Professor Somerville wanted to send her away – there was some connection with her family in Vienna. He was obviously aware of the danger of favouritism. And Dr Felton has been paying her special attention ever since, so Verena tells me.'

'You mean –' Sir Desmond looked up sharply.

'No, no; nothing like that. Just bending the regulations to accommodate her. But if it got about that a fund intended strictly for cases of hardship was being used to give an unnecessary jaunt to a girl who is already here on sufferance, I think it could lead to all sorts of gossip and speculation. Better, surely, to keep the money for British students who are genuinely needy?'

'Well, it's a point,' said Sir Desmond. 'Certainly any kind of irregularity would be most unfortunate. She is a girl who has already attracted rather a lot of attention.'

'And not of a favourable kind,' said Lady Plackett.

'What is it?' asked Quin. He had just returned from the museum and was preparing to work late on an article for *Nature*.

'That creep, Plackett.' Roger's spectacle frames looked as though they had been dipped in pitch. 'He's blocked the Hardship Fund – we can't use it to get Ruth to Bowmont. It would set an unfortunate precedent if any student felt they could travel at the college's expense!'

'Ah. That's probably Lady Plackett's doing. She doesn't care for Ruth.' Quin, to his own surprise, found that he was very angry. He would have said that he did not want Ruth at Bowmont. Ruth being 'invisible' was bad enough here at Thameside – at Bowmont it would be more than he could stand, but the pettiness of the new regime was hard to accept.

'Does Ruth want to go?' he asked. 'Isn't the famous Heini due any day?'

'Not till the beginning of November; we'll be back by then,' said Roger. He stared gloomily into the tank of slugs. 'She wants to go right enough, whatever she says.'

'You're very keen to have her, you and Elke? Because she will benefit?'

'Yes . . . well, damn it, you run the course, you know it's the best in the country. But I wanted her to see the coast. I owe her . . .'

'You what?'

Roger shrugged. 'I know you think we make a pet of her – Elke and Humphrey and I . . . but she gives it all back and –'

'Gives what back?'

Roger shook his head. 'It's difficult to explain. You prepare a practical . . . good heavens, you know what it's like. You're here half the night trying to find decent specimens and then the technician's got flu and there aren't enough Petri dishes . . . And then she comes and stares down the microscope as though this is the first ever water flea, and suddenly you remember what it was all about – why you started in this game in the beginning. If her work was sloppy it would be different, but it isn't. She deserved more than you gave her for that last test.'

'I gave her eighty-two.'

'Yes. And Verena Plackett eighty-four. Not that it's my business. Well, I reckon nothing can be done, not with you falling over backwards not to favour her because she sat on your knee in nappies.'

'I do nothing of the sort, but you must see that I can't interfere – it would only do Ruth harm.' And as his deputy still stood there, looking disconsolate: 'How are things at home? How is Lillian?'

Roger sighed. 'No baby yet. And she won't adopt. If only I hadn't asked Humphrey to supper!' Dr Fitzsimmons had meant well when he had told Roger's wife about the drop in temperature a woman could expect before her fertile period, but he didn't have to watch Lillian come out of the bathroom bristling with thermometers and refusing him his marital rights until the crucial time. 'I shall be glad to go north for a while, I can tell you.'

'I shall be glad to have you there.'

Ruth was not disappointed in the findings of the Finance Committee because she did not know of Dr Felton's efforts on her behalf. But if she held firm over her decision to stay behind, she was perfectly ready to join in the speculations about Verena Plackett's pyjamas.

For Verena, of course, *was* going to Northumberland, and what she would wear in bed in the dormitory above the boathouse occupied much of her fellow students' thoughts. Janet thought she would turn into her wooden bunk in see-through black lace.

'In case the Professor comes up the ladder at midnight with a cranial cast.'

Pilly thought a pair of striped pyjamas was more likely, with a long cord which she would instruct

Kenneth Easton to tie into a double knot before retiring. Ruth, on the other hand, slightly obsessed by Verena's pristine lab coat which she deeply envied, suggested gathered calico, heavily starched.

'So you will hear her crackle in the night,' she said.

But in fact none of them were destined to see Verena's pyjamas, for the Vice Chancellor's daughter had other plans.

If Leonie each night looked eagerly to Ruth for her account of the day, and Mrs Weiss's dreaded 'Vell?' began her interrogation in the Willow Tea Rooms, Lady Plackett waited with more self-control, but no less avidity, for Verena's news.

Verena reported with restraint about the staff, but where the students were concerned, she permitted herself to speak freely. Thus Lady Plackett learnt about the unsuitable – not to say lewd – behaviour of Janet Carter in the back of motor cars, the dangerously radical views of Sam Marsh, and the ludicrous gaffes made by Priscilla Yarrowby who had confused the jaw bone of a mammoth with that of a mastodon.

'And Ruth Berger persists in helping her, of which one *cannot* approve,' said Verena. 'It is no kindness to inadequate students to push them on. They should be weeded out for their own sake and find their proper level.'

Lady Plackett agreed with this, as all thinking people must. 'She seems to be a very disruptive influence, the foreign girl,' she said.

She had not been pleased when Professor Somerville

234

had reinstated Ruth. There was something . . . excessive . . . about Ruth Berger. Even the way she smelled the roses in the quadrangle was . . . unnecessary, thought Lady Plackett, who had watched her out of the window. But on one point Verena was able to set her mother's mind at rest. Ruth was not liked by the Professor; he seemed to avoid her; she never spoke in seminars.

'And she is definitely not coming to Bowmont,' said Verena, who was unaware of her mother's interference in the matter of the Hardship Fund.

'Ah, yes, Bowmont,' said Lady Plackett thoughtfully. 'You know, Verena, I find that I cannot be happy about you cohabiting in a dormitory with girls who do . . . things . . . in the backs of motor cars.'

'I confess I have been worrying about that,' said Verena. 'Of course, one wants to be democratic.'

'One does,' agreed Lady Plackett. 'But there are limits.' She paused, then laid a soothing hand on her daughter's arm. 'Actually,' she said, 'I have had an idea.'

Verena lifted her head. 'I wonder,' she said, 'if it is the same as mine.'

16

'Look at him,' said Frances Somerville bitterly, handing her binoculars to her maid. 'Gloating. Rubbing his hands.'

Martha took the glasses and trained them on the middle-aged gentleman with the intellectual forehead, making his way along the cliff path towards the headland.

'He's writing in his book,' she said, as though the taking of notes was further proof of Mr Ferguson's iniquity.

'Well he needn't expect me to give him lunch,' said Miss Somerville. 'He can go to The Black Bull for that.'

Mr Ferguson had arrived soon after breakfast, sent by the National Trust at Quin's request to see if the Trust might interest itself in Bowmont. A man of impeccable tact, scholarly and mild-mannered, he had been received by Miss Somerville as though he had just crawled out of some particularly repellent sewer.

'Maybe it won't come to anything,' said Martha,

handing back the glasses. After forty years in Miss Somerville's service, she was allowed to speak to her as a friend. 'Maybe he won't fancy the place.'

'Ha!' said Miss Somerville.

Her scepticism was justified. Though Mr Ferguson would report officially to Quin in London, he had already indicated that three miles of superb coastline, not to mention the famous walled garden, would probably interest the Trust very much indeed.

So there it was, thought Frances wretchedly: there the men in peaked caps, the lavatory huts, the screeching trippers. Quin had made it clear that even if negotiations went forward, he would insist on a flat in the house set aside for her use, but if he thought she would cower there and watch over the defilement of the place she had guarded for twenty years, he was mistaken. The day the Trust moved in, she would move out.

Perhaps if the letter from Lady Plackett hadn't arrived just after Mr Ferguson took his leave, Miss Somerville would have reacted to it differently. But it came when she felt as old and discouraged as she had ever felt in her life and ready to clutch at any straw.

The Vice Chancellor's wife began by reminding Miss Somerville of their brief acquaintance in the finishing school in Paris.

You may find it difficult to remember the little shy girl so much your junior, wrote Lady Plackett, who was not famous for her tact, *but I shall always recall your kindness to me when I was homesick and perplexed.*

Miss Somerville did not remember either the home-sick junior or her own kindness, but when Lady Plackett went on to remind her that she had been Daphne Croft-Ellis and that she had been presented in the same year as Miss Somerville's second cousin, Lydia Barchester, the heel of whose shoe had come off as she left Their Majesties walking backwards, she read on with the attention one affords letters from those in one's own world.

I was so excited to find that your dear nephew was on our staff and he may perhaps have mentioned that Verena, our only daughter, is taking his course. She is quite enchanted with his scholarship and expertise and at dinner recently they had a most engrossing conversation which was, I fear, quite above my head. You will, however, be wondering what emboldens me to write to you after so many years away in India and I will be entirely frank. As you know, dear Quinton runs a field course for our students at Bowmont. To this course Verena, as one of his Honours students, will, of course, be required to go and indeed she is looking forward to it greatly. However her position here at Thameside is delicate, as I know you will understand. She herself insists on being treated like all the other students as regards examinations and academic standards and there is certainly no difficulty there, for she is very clever. But socially, of course, she leads a differ-

238

ent life, and we are careful not to encourage her classmates to take her presence at university functions for granted. Without some sense in which the Vice Chancellor and his family are different from ordinary academics, both staff and students, there could be no authority and no stability. This is something I need not explain to you.

So I am understandably anxious at the idea that Verena should share a dormitory with the other pupils. I gather that everyone 'mucks in' and sleeps in bunk beds and that there is no attempt to enforce any kind of discipline and though the students are, of course, the salt of the earth, some of them come from backgrounds which would, I think, make them uncomfortable if Verena was among them. Would it therefore be very impertinent of me to ask if my daughter could stay with you for the duration of the course? I understand that your nephew has his own rooms in the tower and that you are responsible for the domestic arrangements so that he would not need to concern himself with Verena unless he wished to do so. I myself shall be visiting the north at this time, and as Verena's twenty-fourth birthday happens to fall on the last Friday of the course, I might perhaps invite myself just for that day before going on to make contact with dear Lord Hartington and the many other friends and connections of my own family

239

which, after our long absence in India, I long to see again.

Do forgive me for being so blunt, but Verena is, understandably, so very dear to me and I cannot help wanting the best for her. And what could be better than to meet again the friend of my childhood, and protector?

With all good wishes,
Daphne Plackett

Miss Somerville read the letter through twice and sat for a while, pondering. Then she rang for Turton.

'Tell Harris I shall want the motor,' she said. 'I'm going to go over to Rothley.'

She was about to step into the old Buick, which she resolutely refused to let Quin replace, when a series of high-pitched yelps made her turn round and a shoe-sized puppy hurled itself at her legs, gathered itself up to leap onto the running board, missed, rolled over on to its back . . . and all the while its rat-like tail rotated in a frenzy and its unequal eyes gleamed with life affirmation and the prospect of togetherness.

'Take it away,' said Miss Somerville grimly. 'And tell whoever let it out that if they don't keep the door shut, I'll have it drowned.'

The chauffeur repressed a grin, for the passion of the mongrel puppy for Bowmont's mistress was a standing joke among the servants, but Miss Somerville, sitting stiffly in the back of the motor, could find no amusement in what had happened to her prize Labrador. The last of Comely's thoroughbred puppies had been weaned and sold to excellent homes when, sooner than expected, she had come on heat again and spent a night away. The result of this escapade was a litter the like of which Miss Somerville, in thirty years of breeding dogs, could not have imagined in her most fevered dreams. By bullying various underlings on the estate, she had managed to find homes for the older puppies – but to get anyone to take the runt of the litter, with its arbitrary collection of whiskers, piebald stomach and vestigial legs, she would have had to put the villagers into stocks. And somehow this canine disaster seemed to go with all the other threats to her ordered world: with cowmen who sang opera and strangers with notebooks tramping over Somerville land.

The road to Rothley led past Bamburgh, once Bowmont's rival to the north, and the causeway to Holy Island, before turning inland towards the Hall – a long, red sandstone building apparently kept aloft by fierce strands of ivy. The yapping of half a dozen Jack Russell terriers greeted her and presently she was in Lady Rothley's small drawing room while her friend perused the letter.

'One cannot really like the tone,' she said presently, 'but quite honestly, Frances, I do not see what you have to lose. At worst, Verena is a tiresome girl and you have her for a fortnight and at best . . .'

'Yes, that's what I thought. And she really does seem to be clever. She might interest him where sillier girls have failed.'

'I'll tell you one thing,' said Lady Rothley. 'If she's got Croft-Ellis blood in her, she'll soon scotch any nonsense about giving Bowmont to the National Trust! If Quin marries Verena Plackett, they won't get their hands on a square inch of midden. It's not for nothing that their motto is *What I have let no man covet*! If there's a meaner family in England, I've yet to hear of it.' And seeing her friend's face, 'No, I'm joking, it's not as bad as that – they're good landlords and go back to the Conqueror. If the girl manages to get Quin, she'll know how to behave.'

'You think I should invite her then?'

'Yes, I do. And more than that. I think we should put our shoulders to the wheel. I think we should rally round and really welcome the girl. If it's her birthday during the time she's here why don't you give a party for her, or a small dance? I know you don't care for all that, but we'll help you. Rollo's coming up next week with a friend from Sandhurst and Helen's girls are home. Nothing formal, of course, but it's years since Quin's seen his home *en fête* – and with the students here he can't run away like he sometimes does!'

Frances, quailing at the thought of so much sociability, now had another unpleasant thought. 'You don't think he'll expect the students to come? The ones down at the boathouse, I mean?'

'I shouldn't think so. Quin may be democratic, but he knows how things are done.' And coming over to lay her arm round Miss Somerville's shoulder in a rare ges-

ture of affection: 'This may be what we've been waiting for, Frances. Let's give the girl a chance.'

Miss Somerville returned to Bowmont as a woman with
a mission. The letter she wrote to Lady Plackett was
cordial in the extreme, and the instructions she gave to
Turton were explicit.

'We're having house guests next week – a Miss
Plackett, one of the Professor's students. I want the
Tapestry Room prepared for her, and the Blue Room
for her mother. And there'll be a small party on the 28th
which is Miss Plackett's birthday.'

Turton might be discreet, but the girls who prepared
the Tapestry Room for Verena were not and nor was
the cook, told to expect twenty or so young people for
supper and dancing. And soon it had spread to all the
servants' halls in North Northumberland that Quinton
Somerville was expecting a very special young lady and
that wedding bells were in the air at last.

And as below stairs, so above. Ann Rothley was as
good as her word. She telephoned Helen Stanton-
Derby, still suffering from the violin-playing chauffeur
that Quin had wished on her, and Christine Packham
over in Hexham and Bobo Bainbridge down in Newcastle – and all of them, even those with marriageable
daughters who would have done very well as mistress
of Bowmont, promised to welcome Verena Plackett
whose mother was a Croft-Ellis and who would, if she
married dear Quin, scotch once and for all this nonsense about giving his home away. Not only that, but

they unhesitatingly offered their offspring for Verena's party, for the knowledge that Quin had seen his duty at last made everyone extremely happy.

As for Lady Plackett, receiving a reply of such unexpected cordiality, she decided to accompany Verena herself and stay for a few days at Bowmont, returning for Verena's actual party.

'But I think, dear,' she said to her gratified daughter, 'that it might be best to say nothing about the invitation till just before we go. There could be jealousy and ill-feeling among the students – and you know how concerned dear Quinton is about any apparent favouritism.'

Verena thought this was sensible. 'We will leave Miss Somerville to acquaint him,' she said, and returned to her books.

And Frances did, of course, write to Quin and tell him what she had done, but the week before the students were due to leave, a Yorkshire quarryman turned up a leg bone whose size and weight caused pandemonium in the local Department of Antiquities. Answering a plea to authenticate the find and halt work in the gravel pit, Quin rearranged his lectures and drove north. Delayed by the importance of the discovery – for the bone turned out to be the femur of an unusually complete mammoth skeleton – and involved in a bloodthirsty battle with a rapacious contractor, Quin decided not to return to town, but make his way straight to Bowmont.

His aunt's letter thus remained unopened in his Chelsea flat.

It was the day after Quin left for Yorkshire that Ruth received the confirmation she had been longing for. Heini had booked his ticket, he was coming on 2 November and in an aeroplane!

'So no one will be able to take him off!' said Ruth with shining eyes.

'I can't believe I'm really going to see him,' said Pilly.

'Well you are – and you're going to hear him too!'

For now, of course, what mattered more than anything was to secure the piano. Ruth was only five shillings short of the sum she needed, and as though the gods knew there was no more time to waste, they sent, that very night, a young man named Martin Hoyle in to the Willow Tea Rooms.

Hoyle lived in a villa on Hampstead Hill with his mother and had independent means, but it was his ambition to be a journalist and he had already submitted a number of articles to newspapers and magazines, not all of which had been refused. Now he had had an idea which he was sure would further his career. He would extract from the refugees who had colonized the Willow, their recollections of Vienna; poignant anecdotes of the pomp and splendour of the Imperial City, or more recent ones of the Vienna of Wittgenstein and Freud. Not only that, but Mr Hoyle had an *angle*. He was going to contrast the rich stock of memories which they carried in their heads with the meagre contents of the actual luggage they had been allowed to bring. 'Suitcases of the Mind' was to be the title of the piece which he was sure he could sell to the *News Chronicle* or even to *The Times*.

He had come early. Though Ziller, Dr Levy and von Hofmann – all Viennese born and bred – were talking together by the window, it was Mrs Weiss, sitting alone by the hat stand, who accosted him.

'I buy you a cake?' she suggested.

To her surprise, the young man nodded.

'Thank you,' he said, 'but let me buy you one.'

Mrs Weiss did not object to this so long as he sat down and let her talk to him. Two slices of guggle were brought, and Mr Hoyle introduced himself.

'I was wondering if you would mind if we talked a little about your past? Your memories?' said Mr Hoyle. 'You see, I was once in Vienna; it was a city I loved so much.'

Mrs Weiss's eyes flickered. She had never actually been in Vienna, which was a long way from East Prussia and her native city of Prez, but if she admitted this, Mr Hoyle would go away and talk to the men by the window, whereas if she played her cards right, she could keep him at her table and when her daughter-in-law came to fetch her, she would see her in conversation with a good-looking young man.

'Vat is it you vant me to remember?' she enquired.

'Well, for example, did you ever see the Kaiser? Driving out of the gates of the Hofburg, perhaps?'

A somewhat frustrating quarter of an hour followed. In lieu of the Kaiser, Mr Hoyle received the old lady's low opinion of mutton chop whiskers; instead of famous premieres at the opera, he learnt of the laryngeal problems which had prevented her nephew, Zolly Federmann, from taking to the stage.

'But the Prater?' asked Mr Hoyle, growing a little desperate. 'Surely you must have bowled your hoop along the famous chestnut alley?'

Mrs Weiss had not, but described a rubber crocodile on a string, of which she had been very fond till some rough boys from an orphanage had punctured it.

'Well, what about the Giant Wheel, then?' Mr Hoyle wiped his brow. 'Surely you remember riding on that? Or the paddle boats on the Danube?'

It was at this point that Ruth entered, ready to begin the evening's work, and smiled at the old lady. To the men, Mrs Weiss would not have ceded the young journalist, but Ruth was different. Ruth was her friend. She became suddenly exasperated.

'I haf not been on the wheel in the Prater. I haf not been on the Danube in the paddling boat. I haf not seen Franz Josef coming from gates, and I do not remember Vienna because I haf never *been* in Vienna. I have been only in Prez and once to the fur sales in Berlin, but was cheated. So now please go away for I am only a poor old woman and my daughter-in-law makes me sleep in wet air and it should be better for everybody that I am dead.'

Needless to say, this outburst, clearly audible throughout the café, brought help from all sides. While

Ziller and Dr Levy consoled the shaken Mr Hoyle, Ruth comforted the old lady – and Miss Maud and Miss Violet agreed that under the circumstances (and because Mr Hoyle's article, if published, might be good for trade) two tables could be pushed together.

And soon Mr Hoyle's notebook began to fill up with useful anecdotes. Dr Levy told how he had assisted with the removal of an anchovy from the back of the Archduke Otto's throat; Paul Ziller described being hit by a tomato during the premiere of Schönberg's *Verklärte Nacht* and von Hofmann recounted the classic story of Tosca bouncing back from a too tightly stretched trampoline after her suicidal leap from the ramparts.

But it was at the Willow's waitress, as she too shared her memories, that Mr Hoyle looked most eagerly, for he knew now what was missing from his story. Love was what was missing. Love and youth and a central theme. A young girl waiting for her man, working for him. Who wanted suitcases when all was said and done? Love was what they wanted. Love in the Willow Tea Rooms . . . Love in Vienna and Belsize Park. If only she would talk to him, he would sell his story, he was sure of that.

And Ruth did talk to him; talking about Heini was her pleasure and delight. As she whisked between the tables with her tray, she told him of Heini's triumphs at the Conservatoire and how he had been inspired, in the meadow above the Grundlsee, to write an Alpine étude. He learnt of Heini's passion for *Maroni*, the sweet chestnuts roasted everywhere on street corners in the Inner City – and that at the age of twelve he had played a Mozart concerto based on the song of a starling which surprised Mr Hoyle who had thought of starlings as raucous despoilers on the roofs of railway stations.

'But you'll see, he'll play it here,' said Ruth, 'and you must absolutely *promise* to come!'

An hour later, Mr Hoyle closed his notebook and took his leave. Nor was he slow to show his gratitude. Coming to clear the tables at closing time, Ruth found, under his plate, a crisply folded note which she carried joyfully into the kitchen.

'Look!' she said. 'Just look! Can you believe it? A whole ten-shilling note!'

'You've got enough, then?' asked Mrs Burtt.

'I've got enough!'

The piano was expected in the middle of the morning, but Leonie had been up since six o'clock, cleaning the rooms, reblocking the mouseholes, polishing and dusting. By seven o'clock, she had begun to bake and here she was destined to run into trouble.

Leonie was relatively indifferent to the arrival of Heini's piano, but Ruth was bringing her friends to celebrate and that was important. Not Verena Plackett, who did not figure large in Ruth's accounts of her days, but Priscilla Yarrowby and Sam and Janet, and the Welshman who had discovered the piano in an obscure shop on the way back from the rugby field.

If her husband had been with her, Leonie would have

found it difficult to provide suitable refreshment, for the food budget was desperately tight, but the absence of the professor – much as she missed him – meant they had been able to eat potatoes and apple purée made from the windfalls Mishak collected on his rambles and *save*.

Leonie accordingly had saved, and bought two kilos of fine flour . . . had bought freshly ground almonds and icing sugar and unsalted butter and the very finest vanilla pods – and by nine o'clock was removing from the oven batch after batch of perfectly baked vanilla *Kipferl*.

At which point her plans for the morning began to go wrong. Leonie wanted Mishak to stay and meet Ruth's friends – she always wanted Mishak – but what she wanted Hilda to do was go to the British Museum and what she wanted Fräulein Lutzenholler to do was go up the hill and look at Freud.

She had reckoned without the power of the human nose to unlock emotion and recall the past. Hilda came first, stumbling out of the bedroom in her dressing-gown.

'It is true, then,' she said. 'I smelled them, but I thought it was a dream.' And she decided that as it was a Saturday, she would not go to the museum, but work at home.

Fräulein Lutzenholler, her fierce face tilted in disbelief, came next, carrying her sponge bag. 'Ah, yes: the piano,' she said and added the dreaded words, 'I will stay here and *help*.'

By the time the scent of freshly ground coffee came to blend with the warm, familiar scent of the thumb-sized crescents, it was clear that not only would no one voluntarily leave Number 27 that morning, but a great many others would come. Ziller, of course, had been invited, but presently Mrs Weiss arrived in a taxi and Mrs Burtt, whose day off it was, and then a lady from next door murmuring something ecstatic in Polish.

Thus Ruth, arriving with her friends, came to a house redolent of all the well-remembered smells and the sound of eager voices, and stopped for a moment, caught by the past, before she ran upstairs and threw her arms round Leonie.

'Oh, you shouldn't have baked, but how *marvellous*,' she said and rubbed her cheek against her mother's.

Anyone Ruth was fond of would have been welcomed with warmth by Leonie, but in Pilly she detected, beneath the expensive clothes and Harrods handbag, just the kind of poor little scrap she had protected in Vienna. As for Sam, he was so overawed at being in the same room as Paul Ziller, all of whose records he had collected, that he could hardly speak. Even without the arrival of the piano, the gathering had all the makings of a splendid party.

But punctually at 11.30, the piano did arrive.

'Easy does it,' said the removal man, as removal men have said throughout the ages, trundling the upright down the ramp and into the house – and 'steady there', as they fastened ropes and pulleys to raise it to the top floor.

Steadiness was difficult. Fräulein Lutzenholler had escaped from the sitting room and was giving advice; Hilda hovered . . . But at last the job was done and the keys handed, with a courtly bow, to Ruth.

'No, you unlock it, Huw,' she said – and everyone felt the rightness of the gesture, for it was the huge, monosyllabic Welshman, doggedly searching the music shops of London, who had found, in a distant suburb near the college rugby field, exactly the piano Heini wanted: A Bösendorfer, one of the last to come out of the old workshops and famous for its sweetness of tone.

'It makes it real now,' Ruth said softly, touching the keys. 'I can believe now that Heini is coming.'

'Come on, try it,' said Leonie, filling plates for the removal men, who thought they could leave now but found themselves mistaken.

Though one of the world's best violinists was in the room, Ruth sat down without embarrassment and played a Schubert waltz – and Ziller smiled for it always touched him, this passion for music which had been hers since infancy and transcended all limitations of technique.

'I suppose you wouldn't, sir . . . I mean . . . you wouldn't play?' Sam, nervous but entreating, had come to stand beside him.

'Of course.'

Ziller went to fetch his violin and played a Kreisler piece and a Beethoven bagatelle – and then he and Ruth

252

began fooling about, giving imitations of the customers in the Hungarian restaurant trying not to tip the gypsies who came to their table – and presently a quite extraordinary sound was heard: a rusty, wheezing noise which no one had heard before: Fräulein Lutzenholler's laughter.

It was Pilly who spoiled it all, poor Pilly who always got everything wrong.

'Oh, Mrs Berger,' she said impetuously, 'please, *please* won't you persuade Ruth to come on the field course with us? We want her to come so much!'

Leonie put down her coffee cup. 'What course is this?'

Silence fell as Ruth looked with deep reproach at her friend and Pilly blushed scarlet.

'It's at Professor Somerville's place,' she stammered. 'We're all going. In three days' time.'

'I have heard nothing about this,' said Leonie sternly.

'It doesn't matter, Mama,' said Ruth quickly. 'It's just some practical work that happens in the autumn term, but I don't need it.'

Leonie ignored her.

'Everyone is going except Ruth?'

Pilly nodded. Desolate at having upset her friend she moved towards Uncle Mishak, as those in trouble go to lean against the trunks of trees and her eyes filled with tears.

Sam now entered the lists. 'If Ruth hasn't mentioned it, it's because of the money. It costs quite a bit to go, but Pilly's father has offered to pay for Ruth – he's got more money than he knows what to do with and everyone knows how Ruth helps Pilly, but Ruth won't hear of it. She's as obstinate as a mule.'

'It is Professor Somerville who is giving this course?' Leonie asked.

'Yes. And it's the best in the country. We go to Bowmont and –'

Ruth now interrupted. 'Mama, I don't want to talk about it any more. I'm not taking money from Pilly and I'm not going and that's the end of it.'

Leonie nodded. 'You are quite right,' she said. 'To take money from friends is not good.' She smiled warmly at Pilly. 'Come, you will help me to make more coffee.'

Only when the students were leaving, did she take Sam aside.

'It is Dr Felton who makes the arrangements for this course?'

'That's right. He's a really nice man and he's very keen for Ruth to go.'

'And Professor Somerville? Is he also keen that she goes?'

Sam frowned. 'He must be, she's one of his best students. But he's odd – they both are. I've hardly heard him and Ruth exchange a word since she came.'

Leonie now had the information she wanted. On a practical level, her course was clear – but how to deal with her obstinate daughter?

'Mishak, you must help me,' she said that evening,

as the two of them sat alone in the sitting room which was in no way improved by the presence of the piano.

Mishak removed his long-stemmed pipe and examined the bowl to see if a few shreds of tobacco still adhered to it, but they did not.

'You are going to sell your brooch,' he stated.

'Yes. Only how to make her go?'

'Leave it to me,' said Mishak. And Leonie, who had intended to do just that, hugged him and went to bed.

17

Quin had never had any fault to find with the behaviour of the people who worked at Bowmont, but as he drove through the village and up the hill, it seemed to him that everyone was in an unusually genial and benevolent mood. In spite of the rain driving in from the sea, Mrs Carter who kept the post office, the blacksmith at the forge and old Sutherland at the lodge, came out to smile and wave and several times as he stopped, his hand was shaken with a cordiality which seemed to hint at some particular pleasure lying in store for him in which they shared.

'But you'll be wanting to get along today,' said Mrs Ridley at the farm when they had exchanged a few friendly words. 'You'll not be wanting to waste any more time, not today.'

Arriving at the house, he found Turton in a similar mood. The butler called him Master Quinton, a throwback to some twenty years ago and told him, beaming with good will, that drinks would be served in the drawing room in half an hour, giving him plenty of time to change.

This alone indicated more formality than Quin usually permitted, for he made it clear that when he came for the field course, he was here to work, but as he went inside he found further signs that all was not as usual. The hall at Bowmont, with its arbitrary collection of broadswords, incomprehensible tapestries and a weasel which the Basher had stuffed, but without success, was not a place in which anybody lingered. Today, though, in spite of his aunt's conviction that warmth inside the house spelled softness and decay, the ancient deposit of pine cones in the grate had been replaced by a fire of brightly burning logs, and though flowers were seldom cut and brought indoors, Frances preferring to let her plants grow unmolested, the Chinese vase on the oak chest was filled with dahlias and chrysanthemums.

But it was his aunt's attire as she came forward to welcome him, that confirmed his fears. Frances always changed for dinner, which meant that she replaced her lumpy tweed skirt by a slightly longer one of rusty silk – but there was one outfit which for decades had signalled a special occasion: a black chenille dress whose not noticeably plunging neckline was covered with an oriental shawl. It was this that she was wearing now, and Quin's last hope of a quiet evening to prepare for his students vanished.

'You look very splendid,' he said, smiling at her. 'Do we have visitors?'

'You know we do,' said Aunt Frances, coming

257

forward to give him her customary peck on the cheek. 'I wrote to you. They'll be down in a minute – you just have time to change.'

'Actually, I *don't* know, Aunt Frances! I've come straight from Yorkshire. What did you write?'

Aunt Frances frowned. She had hoped that Quin would come prepared and joyful. 'That I've invited the Placketts. Verena and her mother.' And as Quin remained silent: 'I knew Lady Plackett as a girl – surely she told you? We were together at finishing school.'

She looked at Quin and felt a deep unease. The signs of displeasure were only too familiar to her after twenty years of guardianship: Quin's nose was looking particularly broken, his forehead had crumpled into craters of the kind seen on pictures of the moon.

'Verena's one of my students, Aunt Frances. It would be very wrong for me to treat her in a way that is different from the rest.'

Relief coursed through Aunt Frances. It was fear of seeming to single Verena out that was holding him back, nothing more.

'Well, of course I see that, and so does she. In fact she's said already that she expects no special treatment while you are working out of doors, but Lady Plackett is a friend – it would be very strange for me to refuse to entertain her daughter.'

Quin nodded, smiled – and the devastated features recomposed themselves into that of a personable man. Already he felt compunction: Aunt Frances must have been lonelier than he realized if she could contemplate entertaining the Placketts. Perhaps it had all been a mask, her unsociability, her stated desire to be alone – and he wondered, as he had not done for a long time, just how hurt she had been over her rejection on the Border all those years ago.

'That's all right, I'm sure it'll all work out splendidly. I'd better go and change.'

But before he could make his way to the tower, he heard, somewhere above him, a cough. It was not a shy tentative cough, it was a clarion cough signalling an intention – and Quin, searching for its source, now saw a figure standing on the upstairs landing.

Verena, who had read so much, had also read that no man can resist the sight of a beautiful woman descending a noble staircase. She had watched Quin's arrival out of her bedroom window and now, gowned simply but becomingly in bottle-green Celanese, she placed one hand on the carved banister, gathered up her skirt, and while her mother waited unselfishly in the shadows, began to make her way downstairs.

The descent began splendidly. Not only the long back, the long legs of the Croft-Ellises came to her aid, but the training she had received before her presentation at court. Verena, who had kicked her diamanté-encrusted train backwards with unerring aim as she retreated from Their Majesties, could hardly fail to walk with poise and dignity towards her host.

The first flight was accomplished and Quin stood as she had expected, his head thrown back, watching. She was not quite ready yet to utter the words she had prepared, but almost. 'You cannot imagine what a pleasure it is to be in Bowmont after all we have heard of it,' was what she planned to say.

But she didn't say it. She didn't, in fact, say anything coherent. For someone – and Aunt Frances was beginning to suspect the second housemaid whose father was a Socialist – had once more opened a door.

The puppy was not primarily interested in Verena, it was Aunt Frances that he desired, but as he passed the staircase, the mountaineering thirst which had sent him dashing at the running board of the Buick reasserted itself. With a growl of aspiration, he gathered himself together and leapt, managing to reach the bottom step at the same time as Verena completed her descent.

Verena did not tread the puppy underfoot, nor did she fall flat on her face. Anyone else would have done so, but not Verena. She did, however, stumble badly, throw out an arm, stagger – and land in disarray on her knees.

Quin, of course, was beside her in an instant to help her up – and to lead her to a chair where, being a Croft-Ellis, she at once made light of her mishap.

'It is nothing,' she said, as brave British girls in school stories have said for generations, spraining their ankles, biting their lips as they are carried away on gates.

But about the puppy it was more difficult to be charitable, especially as she had torn the lining of her dress, and Lady Plackett, hurrying down to aid her daughter, did not even make the attempt.

'What an extraordinary creature!' she said. 'Does it belong to one of the servants?'

Miss Somerville, mortified, said the puppy was going to the village carpenter on the following day and tried to catch it, but it was Quin who seized the little dog, upended it, and examined it with the intensity which zoologists devote to a hitherto undescribed species.

'Amazing!' he said, grinning at his aunt. 'Those abdominal whiskers must be unique surely? Does Barker know that he is to be the most fortunate of men?

Miss Somerville, not amused by his levity, said Barker was behind with repairs to the pews in the church and would presumably know his duty, and carried the dog from the room.

In spite of this inauspicious beginning, dinner went off well and Miss Somerville, reviewing the evening in the privacy of her bedroom, had every reason to be satisfied. Perhaps Quin's chivalry had been aroused by Verena's unfortunate descent; at any rate he was attentive and charming and Verena said everything that was proper. She admired the portrait of the Somervilles, even declaring that the Basher's face was full of character; she was able to be intelligent about farming, for her uncle in Rutland not only bred Border Leicesters but had a prize herd of Charolais cattle. And when Miss Somerville mentioned – trying to make a joke of it – Quin's intention of making the house over to the Trust, the Placketts had been as incredulous and aghast as she had hoped.

'You cannot be serious, Professor!' Lady Plackett had exclaimed. And Verena, risking a somewhat outspoken remark said: 'Forgive me, but I would feel as though I was betraying my unborn children.'

In fact Verena, throughout the evening, said all the things that Frances had been thinking. Verena was sound on the subject of refugees and had, when Quin was out of the room, expressed satisfaction that an Austrian girl in her year would not be coming up with the others later that night. She was able to trace a connection between the Croft-Ellises and the Somervilles, distant but reassuring, and what she said about the puppy was exactly what Miss Somerville herself had been thinking – it really *was* kinder in cases of this sort to drown the little things at birth.

'A very pleasant girl,' said Miss Somerville, as Martha came to bring her her bedtime cocoa.

A medieval monk bent on poverty, chastity and the subjugation of the flesh would have been entirely at home in Miss Somerville's bedroom. The window was open, letting in gusts of the damp night air, the rugs on the bare floorboards were worn, the mattress on the four-poster had been lumpy when Frances came to Bowmont and was lumpy still.

Martha agreed. 'She's made a good impression below stairs,' she said, not thinking it necessary to add that a Hottentot with smallpox would have done the same if it ensured that Bowmont remained in private hands and that the servants' jobs were safe.

It was Martha who had gone with Frances to the

house of her fiancé on the Border, Martha who had come back after twenty-four hours and kept her peace for forty years about what had happened there – but even Martha could go too far.

'Why don't you let me get you a hot-water bottle?' she asked now, for her mistress, in spite of the success of the evening, was looking tired and drawn and the cold did nothing for her arthritis.

'Certainly not!' snapped Frances. 'On December the 1st I have a bottle and not a day earlier – you know that perfectly well.' But she allowed Martha to pick up the battered silver hair brush and brush out her sparse grey hair. 'I take it it was Elsie who let the puppy out?' she said presently.

Martha nodded. 'She's soft, that girl. It's with Comely not having anything to do with it. She hears it crying.'

'Well, see that it's taken down to Barker first thing in the morning; it nearly caused a nasty accident.'

'It'll have to be the day after. He's away over at Amble tomorrow. They're breaking up a ship and he's got some wood ordered.'

Lying in bed, her icy feet curled under her, Frances again thought how well the evening had gone – and in any case she meant to go and live in the village once Quin was married. True, Quin had not shown any particular interest in Verena, but that would come – and glad of an excuse, she picked *Pride and Prejudice* off the bedside table. '*She is tolerable; but not handsome enough to tempt* me,' Mr Darcy had said when he first saw Elizabeth Bennet. Oh yes, there was plenty of time.

Unaware of his aunt's hopes, and deeply unconcerned with the fate of Verena Plackett, Quin stood by the window of his tower room and looked out at the ocean and the moon, continually obscured by fierce black clouds. It was still raining but the barometer was rising. It had been a risk bringing the students up so late in the year, but if Northumberland did choose to lay on an Indian summer, they would find themselves most richly rewarded. The autumn could be breathtakingly lovely here.

Quin had slept in the room at the top of the tower since his grandfather had led him there at the age of eight, a bewildered orphan in foreign clothes and a pair of outsize spectacles supposed to strengthen his eyes after an attack of measles. Separated by three flights of stairs from his nurse, laid to rest each night under the pelt of a polar bear which the Basher had shot in Alaska, Quin had gone to bed in terror – yet even then he would not have changed his eyrie for the world.

The students were due any moment now: the bus hired to fetch them from Newcastle could bump its way right down to Anchorage Bay. He'd been down earlier to check that the arrangements were in order: the stove lit in the little common room, the Bunsen burners connected to the Calor gas, the blankets in the dormitories above the lab properly aired. Everything was in hand yet he felt restless, and hardly aware of what he was doing, he picked up the guitar in the corner of the room and began to tune the strings.

Quin's guitar studies had not progressed very far. He had in fact stayed stuck on Book Two of the manual and his friends at Cambridge had always been unpleasant about his performance, putting their fingers in their ears or leaving the room. But though he could play only a few of the pieces in the book, they covered the normal range of human emotion: 'Tiptoe Through the Tulips' was cheerful and outgoing; 'Evening Elegy' was lyrical and romantic – and the 'Mississippi Moan' was – well, a moan.

It was this piece which had particularly emptied the room when he played it at college, but Quin was much attached to it. Now, as the plaintive lament from the Deep South stole through the room, Quin realized that he had not chosen the 'Moan' at random. He did in fact feel a sense of disquiet . . . of unease . . . and a few broken chords later, he realized why.

For it had to be admitted that he had not behaved well over Felton's efforts to bring Ruth to Bowmont. Roger worked ceaselessly for the students and deputized willingly for him, enduring all the boredom of committees. If he had set his heart on bringing the girl to Northumberland, Quin should have helped him. It would have been perfectly simple to work something out, nor was he in the least troubled by the disapproval of the Placketts. The truth was, he had acted selfishly, not wanting to be involved in the girl's emotionalism, her endless ability to live deep.

Well, it was done now, and the 'Moan' – as it so often did – had cleared the air. Putting regret behind him, Quin moved to his desk and picked up Hackenstreicher's latest letter to *Nature*. Time to put this idiot out of his misery once and for all. Pulling the typewriter towards him, he inserted a clean sheet of paper.

Dear Sir, he wrote, *It is perhaps worth pointing out in connection with Professor Hackenstreicher's communication* (Nature, *August 6th 1938) that his examination of a single cranial cast of Ceratopsian* Styracosaurus *scarcely warrants a rejection of Broom's reconstruction of evolution from a common stock. Not only was the cast incomplete, but its provenance is disputed by . . .*

He was still writing as the bus passed the gates behind the house and bumped its way towards the beach.

Ruth woke very early in the dormitory above the boathouse. Everyone else still slept; Pilly, beside her, was curled up against the expected disasters of the coming day – only a few tufts of hair showed above the grey blanket. At the end of the row of bunks, Dr Elke's slumbering bulk beside the door protected her charges.

Of the previous night, Ruth remembered only the driving rain, the sudden chill as they scuttled indoors from the stuffy bus . . . that and the monotonous slap of the waves on the beach.

But now something had happened – and at first it seemed to her that that something was simply . . . light.

She dressed quickly, crept past her sleeping friends, past Dr Elke, twitching as she rode through Valhalla in her dreams, climbed down the ladder and opened the door.

'Oh!' said Ruth, and walked forward, unbelieving, bewildered . . . dazzled. How could this have happened overnight, this miracle? How could there be so much light, so much movement; how could everything be so terribly *there*?

The sun was rising out of a silver sea – a sea which shimmered, which changed almost moment by moment. And the sky changed too as she watched it; first it was rose and amethyst, then turquoise . . . yet already a handful of newly fledged cotton-wool clouds waited their turn . . .

And the air moved too – how it moved! You didn't need to breathe, it breathed itself. It wasn't wind now, not yet, just this newly created, newly washed air which smelled of salt and seaweed and the beginning of the world.

There was too much. Too much beauty, too much air to breathe, too much sky to turn one's face to . . . and unbelievably too much sea. She had imagined it so often: the flat, grey, rather sad expanse of the North Sea, but this . . .

A shaft of brilliant light pierced the surface and

267

caught the needle of a lighthouse on a distant island . . . There were fields on this ocean: patches of shining brightness, others like gunmetal and calm oases like lagoons. It never stopped *being*, the sea, she had not been prepared for that.

The tide was out. Taking off her shoes and stockings, she felt the cool, ribbed sand massaging her bare feet. There were acres of it; golden, unsullied . . . Moving drunkenly towards the edge of the water, she began to calm down enough to notice the inhabitants of this light-dappled world . . . Three heavy, ecclesiastical-looking birds diving from a rock – cormorants she thought – but could not name the narrow-winged flock whose white-ness was so intense that they seemed to be lit up from within.

Now she came to the first rock pool and here was a simpler, more containable, delight. Dr Felton had taught her well; she knew the Latin names of the anemones and brittle stars, the little darting shrimps, but this was the world of fairy tale. Here were sub-merged forests, miniature bays of sand, pebbles like jewels . . .

By the rim of the ocean, she paused and put a foot into the water, and gasped. It was like being electro-cuted, so cold. Even the foam carried a charge . . . and then almost at once she became accustomed to it. No, that was wrong; you couldn't become accustomed to this invigorating, fierce stab of cold and cleanness, but you could want more of it and more.

I didn't know, she thought. I didn't imagine that anything could be like this, could make one feel so . . . purged . . . so clean . . . so alone and unimportant and yet so totally oneself. For a moment, she wanted everyone she loved to be there – her parents and Mishak and Mishak's beloved Marianne risen from the dead, to come and stand here beside the sea. But then the sky performed one of its conjuring tricks, sending in a fleet of purple clouds which moved over the newly risen sun, so that for a moment everything changed again – became swirling and dark and turbulent . . . and then out came the sun once more, strengthened . . . higher in the sky . . . and she thought, no, here I can be alone because there isn't any alone or not alone; there's only light and air and water and I am part of it and everyone I love is part of it, but it's outside time, it's outside needing and wanting.

It was at this point of exaltation that she noticed a small white sail and a boat coming round the point and making for the bay.

Quin too had woken at dawn and made his way to the sheltered cove by Bowmont Mill where he kept the dinghy when it was not in use. He'd been glad of an excuse to get away from the house and bring the boat round for the students; glad that the weather had lifted: the golden day was an unexpected bonus. For the rest he was without thought, feeling the wind, tending his sail . . .

He saw the lone figure as soon as he rounded the point and even from a distance realized that the girl, whoever she was, was in a state of bliss. The breeze whipped her hair, one hand held the folds of her skirt as she moved backwards and forwards, playing with the waves.

The obvious images were soon abandoned. This was not Botticelli's Venus risen from the foam, not Undine welcoming the dawn, but something simpler and, under the circumstances, more surprising. This was Ruth.

She stood quietly watching as he dropped his sail and allowed the dinghy to run onto the sand. It was not until she waded out to help him, pulling the boat up with each lift of the waves, that he spoke.

'An unexpected pleasure,' he said idiotically – but for Ruth the creased, familiar smile threatened for a moment the impersonality of this scoured and ravishing world. 'I didn't think you were coming.'

'My mother bullied me and Uncle Mishak. Oh, but imagine; if they hadn't. Imagine if I'd missed all this!'

'You like it?' asked Quin, who found it advisable to confine himself to banalities, for it had been disconcerting how well she had fitted the dream of those who come in from the sea: the long-haired woman waiting by the shore.

She shook her head wonderingly. 'I didn't think there could be anything like this. You lose yourself in music, but in the end music is about how to live; it comes back to you. But this . . . I suppose one *can* have petty thoughts here, but I don't see how.'

The dingy was beached now. Quin took a rope from the bows and tied it round a jagged rock – and together they made their way towards the boathouse. Since she had walked in a trance towards the rim of the sea, Ruth had never once looked backwards to the land. Now she stopped dead and said: 'Oh, what is that? What is that place?'

'What do you mean?' Quin, at first, didn't understand the question.

'Up there. On the cliff. That building.'

'That? Why, surely you know? That's Bowmont.'

Ruth was unlucky. She could have seen it in driving rain or in winter when the wind blew so hard that no one had time to look upwards. She could have seen it, as many had, when a shipwreck brought weeping women to the shore, or on a day when the notorious 'fret' made it no more than a threatening, looming shape. But she saw it on a halcyon morning and she saw it, almost, from the sea. She saw it – half home, half fortress – with the pale limestone of its walls turned to gold and the white horses licking softly against the cliffs it guarded. Gulls wheeled over the tower, and the long windows threw back the dazzle of the sun.

'You said it was a cold house on a cliff,' said Ruth when she could speak again.

'So it is. You'll see when you come to lunch on Sunday.'

Ruth shook her head. 'No,' she said quietly, 'I shan't be coming to lunch on Sunday. Nor on any other day.'

It was Kenneth Easton who had told the students that Verena would not be coming to the boathouse.

271

'She's staying up at Bowmont,' he said as the train steamed out of King's Cross Station. 'The Somervilles have invited her.' And as they stared at him: 'It's only natural – her family and the Professor's belong to the same world. It's what you'd expect.'

'Well, I wouldn't,' Sam had said staunchly. 'It's not like the Professor to single one student out.'

'Lady Plackett's going to be there as well. She and the Professor's aunt are old friends. And there's going to be a dance for Verena's birthday. The Somervilles insisted,' said Kenneth, well briefed in Verena's version of events.

For Pilly and Janet, the thought that they wouldn't have to share a dormitory with Verena came as a welcome relief, but Ruth had been silent for a while, staring out at the flat, rain-sodden fields. Quin's story and hers was over – yet it had hurt a little that in spite of what he had said about Verena, he cared for her after all.

It had not taken her long to school her thoughts and tell herself how little this concerned her, but she meant what she said about not coming to lunch. Exaltation was one thing, but seeing Verena Plackett lording it in the house which, if this had been a proper marriage, would have been her home, was quite another.

One could expect only so much uplift, even from the sea.

Pilly had come closest in the speculations about Verena's pyjamas. They were blue and mannish, but elasticated at the ankle for she wore them to do her exercises.

Verena always exercised with vigour, but this morning her press-ups had a particular élan and her thighs scissored the air with a special purpose, for she had decided, if all went as she hoped and she became Mrs Somerville, to accompany Quin on his expeditions, and fitness now was imperative.

Her window took in a view of the bay and the boathouse where the other students still slept. Verena had no objection to the laboratory; as Quinton's helpmeet and fellow researcher, she approved of a field station so close to the house, but the bringing up of students would not be encouraged. Quin's future, it seemed to her, lay more in some role like President of the Royal Society or head of an institute – it was surely a waste of time for such a man to spend time in teaching.

Next door, Lady Plackett heard the familiar bumps and thumps with satisfaction. Her daughter had made an excellent impression the night before and she herself, encouraged by the warmth of her welcome, had decided to stay for the duration of the field course so as to help in the preparations for Verena's dance. As for Miss Somerville – whom she had heard spoken of as unsociable to a degree – her friendliness was now explained. If her nephew really was contemplating giving his home away, it would be very much in her interest to see him married, and to a girl who would not permit such folly.

At a quarter to eight precisely, Verena and Lady Plackett descended and were greeted with relief by their hostess. Neither of them wore fur coats or asked about central heating, and though Miss Somerville made a suitable enquiry about the night they had passed, she realized at once that it was superfluous.

'Verena always sleeps well,' said Lady Plackett, and Verena, with a calm smile, agreed.

Comely now arrived, and the old Labrador with a white muzzle, and they were permitted by Verena to wag their tails at least half a dozen times before being requested to 'Sit!' which they instantly did. Her credentials as a dog lover established, she moved over to the sideboard where she helped herself to bacon, sausages and scrambled eggs.

'Verena never puts on weight,' commented Lady Plackett fondly, and Miss Somerville saw that this might be so. 'All the Croft-Ellises can eat as much as they wish without putting on an ounce.'

But as they progressed to toast and marmalade, it was natural to enquire about the Professor. 'Has he breakfasted already?' Verena asked.

'Quin just has coffee over in his rooms. He's gone to Bowmont Cove to fetch the dinghy.'

The Placketts exchanged glances. If Quin was going to keep himself to himself in the tower and creep off to the boathouse at dawn, it might be necessary for Verena to change her routine.

Since work on the first day was not due to begin until 9.30, the Placketts accepted an invitation to look round the rest of the house which, arriving late the previous afternoon, they had not yet explored. Politely

274

admiring everything they saw, they had the added satisfaction of being able to make comparisons. In the
library, Verena was able to point out that her Croft-Ellis
uncle also owned a set of Bewick woodcuts which were,
perhaps, a little more extensive, and in the morning
room Lady Plackett was reminded of the petit-point
stool covers which her grandmother had stitched when
she first came to Rutland as a bride.

'In no way better than these, dear Miss Somerville,
though the Duchess asked if she could copy them.'

A tour of the grounds followed. Crossing the lawn
and the bridge over the ha-ha, they passed the door of
the walled garden and Miss Somerville asked if they
would like to see it.

'Ah yes,' said Lady Plackett. 'It's well known, isn't
it? Of course we have a famous walled garden in Rutland too, as you probably know.'

Miss Somerville resisted the impulse to say that there
was nowhere like her walled garden, and opened the
door. She always wanted to put her finger to her lips
when she did this, but Verena and Lady Plackett had
already begun to admire, in loud, clear voices, the
garden's lay-out, though Verena was able to point out
a spot of canker on the stem of a viburnum which she
thought might interest Elke Sonderstrom.

But though she endeavoured to conceal it, Verena
was growing restive.

'I mustn't be late for work,' she said laughingly. The
idea of Professor Somerville already mingling with the
students was not attractive; she had particularly wanted

to arrive in his company and make clear her special status as a house guest. 'I'll have to go and get my things.'

'We'll go in round the front,' said Miss Somerville, never able to resist a little early-morning viewing through her binoculars.

Lady Plackett's praise of the view from the sea terrace was warm enough to satisfy even Miss Somerville, but Verena, as she requested for a moment the loan of Miss Somerville's binoculars, seemed for some reason to be displeased.

'How extraordinary,' she said, fixing her eyes on two people standing together by the edge of the sea. One was Professor Somerville, looking unfamiliar in a navy sweater and rubber boots. The other was a girl, barefooted, with wind-blown, tossing hair. And to her mother: 'Unless I'm mistaken, Miss Berger has managed to get herself up here after all. I wonder what strings she pulled to achieve *that*?'

Lady Plackett took the binoculars. Her sight was less keen than her daughter's but she too agreed that the girl was Ruth. She turned to Miss Somerville. 'This is unfortunate,' she said. 'And quite irregular. The girl is a Jewish refugee who seems to think that she is entitled to every sort of privilege.'

'One must not belittle her, of course,' said Verena, anxious to be fair. 'She works extremely hard. She is a waitress in a café in the north of London.'

'They say she brings in all sorts of trade,' said Lady Plackett meaningfully.

Miss Somerville sighed. She took back her binoculars, but she did not put them to her eyes. If there was one thing she did not wish to examine so early in the morning, it was a Jewish waitress on Bowmont beach.

18

The first day of the field course was, by tradition, spent close to Bowmont's shores. Though everyone worked hard, learning the sampling techniques they would need to make proper observations, there was a festive air among the students – for if this was science it was also a marvellous seaside holiday and the experienced staff made no attempt to curb their pleasure. Indeed Dr Felton himself, his hornrims turning to russet or amber to match the creatures he fished from the pools, looked like a boy let out of school – and Dr Elke, pacing the littoral in shorts and a straining, reindeer-covered sweater was a sight to make the gods themselves rejoice.

Which was as well, for the coast of North Northumberland was continuing to drive Ruth a little mad. She knew it was not really British to feel like this, but her state of ecstasy, though she tried to control it, continued to get the better of her. It got her by the throat when she saw a wave lift itself against the light so as to make a window for the sky; it came at her with the dazzle of a gull's wing; it was transmitted through her bare feet as she followed the wave ripples in the sand. She filled her pockets with shells and when her pockets were full, she fetched her sponge bag and filled that. She bit into the bladders of seaweed, choked on the salty liquid, and did it again.

And she beachcombed . . .

'Look, oh *look*!' cried Ruth every ten minutes – and then whoever was closest had to go and examine what was undoubtedly a plank from the treasure chest of a Spanish galleon, or a coconut from the distant Indies. Dr Felton might point out, gently, the words 'Bentham and Son, Sanitary Engineers' on the back of the plank, making the galleon theory unlikely; Janet might turn the coconut round so as to reveal the stamp of a Newcastle grocer – but it made no difference to Ruth whose next find was as mysterious and magical as the one before.

Verena's approach to the delights of the seashore was different. She had appeared after breakfast in a white cable-knit sweater as pristine as her lab coat and now, followed by Kenneth Easton who received the contents of her net as once he had received the contents of her stomach, she moved unerringly over banks of seaweed and through rocky pools.

'Not, I think, a *bearded* horse mussel?' said Verena, addressing Dr Felton, but throwing a sidelong glance at the Professor who was showing Huw and Sam how to sink a box quadrant into a patch of sand. 'A horse mussel, but not, I would hazard, bearded?'

Dr Felton, examining the creature she had prised from the rock, agreed with her, and Kenneth, moved to spontaneous admiration, said: 'Really, Verena, you are quite brilliant with bivalves!'

But it was not only bivalves with which Verena was brilliant. The other students might be glad to recognize a limpet, but Verena could tell a slit limpet from a key-hole limpet; she knew of a whole armoury of limpets; tortoiseshell limpets and slipper limpets and blue-rayed limpets, and was aware that the brave periwinkle, fighting dessication on the higher rocks, might be smooth or edible or rough.

But Ruth, here in this world which washed one free of pettiness, did not, as she would have done in London, go to the reference books in the laboratory to search for mussels that were yet more bearded, or a bristlier bristle worm than the one turned up by Verena's spade. She did not want to read about mussels, she wanted to hold one and marvel at the blue and black striations of its shell. She was free of the urge to excel and succeed; she even gave up her complicated manoeuvres to keep out of the Professor's way – and when she found her most valuable treasure of the morning, it was to him she came.

'Look!' said Ruth for the hundredth time. 'Oh, look! *Emeralds*!' He held out his hands and she tipped the smooth green stones into his palms.

'Could they be?' she said. 'My great aunt had a bracelet and the stones looked just like that!'

He didn't laugh at her. There were gem stones on this

coast: carnelians and agates and amethysts – and leading her gently away from her dream, he said: 'Only the sea does that – makes stones so perfect and so smooth. You could hire the best jeweller in the world and set him to work for a year and a day and he wouldn't get anywhere near.'

He took one and held it to the light and as she came closer to look, he thought how wonderfully emeralds would have become her with her dark eyes and lion-coloured hair.

But Verena, never far from the Professor, now appeared by their side. 'Good heavens, girl,' she said, peering at the stones. 'They're just bits of bottle glass – surely you knew that? Even in Vienna they must have bottles.'

She looked at Quin, ready to share the joke of Ruth's idiocy – but he had turned away and was putting the stones back into Ruth's cupped hands as carefully as if they really were precious jewels.

'Bottles can be extremely important,' he said, holding her eyes. 'It isn't necessary for me to tell you that.'

And she flushed and smiled and moved away, feeling a glow of warmth, for whether they were emeralds or not mattered very little, but that he remembered what she had told him, there by the Danube – that mattered a lot!

At lunchtime Verena, approaching the Professor, said: 'Isn't it time we went to the house? Luncheon is at one o'clock, I understand?'

But here she suffered a reverse.

'Yes, you go; my aunt's a stickler for punctuality. I'll stay down here – I don't usually bother much with lunch.'

This remark caused considerable amusement to Dr Elke who had past experience of Quin's conviction that he did not eat in the middle of the day, and gathering two of the girls to help, she made her way to the boathouse where she unwound an extra coil of sausages which Pilly proceeded to fry with an expertise which amazed her friends.

'Why aren't you afraid of sausages?' asked Janet, as Pilly deftly turned the sizzling, ferociously spitting objects. 'They're much more dangerous than the experiments we do.'

'I don't have to *learn* sausages,' said Pilly.

But in the afternoon Verena came into her own again, for the Professor took boatloads of students out into the bay to show them how to sweep for plankton and Verena, who had sailed in India and crewed for her cousin at Cowes, was in her element. She had only to twitch once at its toggle, and the outboard motor roared into life; she knew exactly what to do with sails, she rowed like an Amazon, so that it was natural that as the students changed places, Verena should remain by the Professor and help.

Secure in her position, she was extremely gracious to her inexperienced classmates, helping them into the dinghy and giving them instructions on seamanship so as to leave the Professor free to show them how to work the nets. Only when Ruth came aboard in her turn and offered to take one of the oars, did Verena's graciousness desert her.

'Can you row?' she said snubbingly. 'I didn't think anyone had boats in Vienna.'

But Ruth, though she set a murderous pace, said nothing. She was in the grip of a new and noble resolution which, late that night, she proceeded to share with her friends.

'I have decided,' she announced, 'to love Verena Plackett!'

The students were sitting round a bonfire of driftwood, roasting potatoes in the light of the moon – a dramatic setting in keeping with Ruth's uplifted state. Only Kenneth Easton was absent. He had wandered away by himself for it had been hard for him seeing Verena go up to the house to dine with the Professor. Kenneth had examined his face carefully in the scrap of mirror which was all the students had to shave by and couldn't help noticing how much more regular his features were than the Professor's, how much less broken-looking his nose, and if he smoked a pipe he was certain he would have been able to keep it alight for reasonable stretches of time. Yet it was clear that it was the Professor Verena preferred and now, alone and melancholy, he gazed up at the lighted windows of Bowmont and sighed.

'I mean it,' persisted Ruth as her friends stared at her. 'I'm entirely serious.'

'You're mad,' said Janet, spearing another potato. 'Raving mad. Verena is entirely and utterly awful.'

'Yes, I know,' said Ruth. 'So there is no point at all in trying to *like* her. Liking Verena would be to attempt the impossible. But there was an old philosopher who used to come and see us in Vienna – he had a long white beard and he used to meditate every day on a bench outside the Stock Exchange – and what he said was: "You must love what you cannot like." He said it quite often.'

'I don't know what that means,' said Pilly sadly – and a thin bespectacled youth called Simon said he didn't either.

'It sounds better in German,' Ruth admitted, 'but what it means is that though you can't like everybody, you can love them deep down – in fact the more you don't like them, the more important it is that you should. You have to love them as though they were your brother or sister . . . as part of the created world. As a fellow sinner,' said Ruth, getting excited and dropping her potato in the sand.

Sam, though he knew it was not a Lancelot-like remark, said she was talking nonsense, and Janet pointed out that sinners were a doddle compared to Verena.

'Sinners are *human*,' she said.

But nothing could deflect Ruth from the noble path she had chosen and she quoted yet another European sage, the great Sigmund Freud, who had said that a thing cannot become lovable until it is loved.

'Like Beauty and the Beast. You have to kiss it before it becomes a prince.'

As was inevitable the conversation now became

ribald, but as she accepted the less burnt half of Sam's potato, Ruth's eyes were shining with moral virtue and the consciousness of right.

'You'll see. I'll begin tomorrow when we go to Howcroft. I shall love her *all day*.'

'Barker's taken him then?' asked Miss Somerville encountering Martha the following morning as she returned from the village. 'He's agreed?'

The puppy had been conveyed to the carpenter's house before breakfast, but Martha's kind, round face looked unaccustomedly shifty. 'No, he hasn't. He won't have him.'

'Won't *have* him?' Miss Somerville was incredulous. 'Did you point out that the work on the pews is two months overdue?'

'Yes, I did. He says his wife's got asthma and she's expecting and the doctor said she wasn't to go near anything with hair.'

'I must say I find that extraordinary. People like that wouldn't have *heard* of asthma in the old days. It makes you wonder whether education is such a good thing.' She bent to pick up her gardening trug. 'Where is it, then?'

'He offered to shoot it for me,' said Martha. 'He said it wouldn't feel a thing – well, that's true enough; he's done enough poaching in his time, Barker has – he could knock down a hare at fifty yards and no trouble.'

Miss Somerville straightened her back. Her face was expressionless.

'So you agreed? It's been shot?'

'No, I didn't,' said Martha shortly, and watched her employer's hands relax on the handle of the trug. 'Drowning the things at birth before their eyes are open is one thing, but shooting them in cold blood is another. If you want it shot, you can give the instructions yourself.'

'Where is it, then?'

'One of the students took it. I met her coming up for the milk. She says she'll keep it; they're off to Howcroft Point, I thought she might as well with Lady Plackett not being too fond of it and company coming.'

Miss Somerville nodded. The Rothleys were coming for drinks and the Stanton-Derbys, to welcome Verena and talk about the dance, and she didn't really want any more jokes about the little dog. She was setting off across the lawn when Martha said: 'Who's this Richard Wagner, then? Some kind of musician fellow?'

'He was a composer. An extremely noisy one, with a reprehensible private life. Why?'

'This girl . . . the one who's taken the puppy . . . she said he had a step-daughter with eyes like that – Wagner did. One blue and one brown, same as the puppy. Daniella she was called.'

'The student?'

'No, the stepdaughter.'

Deciding not to pursue the matter, Miss Somerville made her way to the garden. She thought she would postpone talking to Lady Plackett about the extraordinary behaviour of the carpenter. After all, it was none of her business.

Ruth, meanwhile, had reached the boathouse.

'What is it?' enquired Dr Elke, looking at Comely's love child which was climbing with passionate enthusiasm over her feet.

'It's a mixture,' admitted Ruth.

Dr Elke said she could see that and removed her shoe from the puppy's grasp.

'But full of personality?' suggested Ruth. 'Though not perhaps strictly beautiful.'

'No, not strictly.'

'Voltaire wasn't beautiful either,' said Ruth, 'but he used to say that if he had half an hour to explain away his face, he could seduce the Queen of France.'

'More than half an hour would be necessary in this case,' said Dr Elke, and told Ruth to pass the hammers, for she was checking supplies for the day's fossil hunting on the cliffs off Howcroft Point.

Ruth did so. There was a pause. Then: 'I thought he might come with us on the bus? Martha said he was very fond of transportation and he's never sick.'

'Ask the Professor,' said Elke and went into the lab.

Since Quin at that moment came down the path, Ruth repeated her request.

'I thought he might be useful,' she said.

'Really?' Quin's eyebrows were raised in enquiry. 'What sort of usefulness had you in mind?'

'Well, dogs are always digging up bones. Suppose he

found something interesting? The femur of a torosaurus, perhaps?'

'That would certainly be interesting on the coal measures,' said Quin drily. But seeing Ruth's face, he relented. 'Keep him out of the way; I suppose he can't do much harm on the moors.'

By the time the bus deposited them at Howcroft Point, the puppy had acquired the kind of following that Voltaire himself would have envied. Pilly had held him on her knees throughout the journey, Janet spoke to him in a voice which made Ruth understand what happened in the backs of motor cars, and Huw was on hand to lift him over boulders which defeated even his intrepid scramblings.

It was another perfect day. The cliffs here were topped by heather and gorse, the curlews called – but the work now was hard. For here, in the carboniferous outcrop which ran from the moors out onto the shore, were embedded those creatures that determined all subsequent life on earth. Fragments of ancient corals, whorled molluscs, each characteristic of the layered zones, had to be prised from the rock, labelled, wrapped and carried back to the laboratory. And since no day is complete without the chance for self-improvement, Ruth was fortunate, for the opportunities for loving Verena Plackett on Howcroft Point were endless. Always at the Professor's heels, she tapped unerringly with her brand-new hammer, finding not only an undoubted specimen of *caninia*, but also a crinoid complete with tentacles – and laughed merrily whenever Pilly mispronounced a word.

Since the tide was high, they had lunch above the strand on a patch of heather while the puppy consumed sandwiches, fell in and out of rabbit holes and fell suddenly and utterly asleep on Huw's collecting bag. Most of the students too were glad to be lazy, but Ruth, accustomed to the ascent of high places from which to say '*Wunderbar!*' scrambled to the top of the hill which commanded a view of the coast for miles, and the moors inland, still showing glimmers of purple. It was not till she caught the whiff of tobacco from behind a boulder that she realized she was not alone.

'It's quite something, isn't it?' said Quin, gesturing with his pipe at the low line of Holy Island to the south, and the dramatic pinnacle of Howcroft Rock. 'I'm glad you've seen it like this – autumn and winter are best for the colours.'

She nodded. 'People always say that views are breathtaking, don't they? But they should be breath-giving, surely?' She turned to smile at him. 'And I don't just mean the wind.'

For a few minutes they stood side by side in silence, watching the dazzle of spray over the rocks, the unbelievable dark blue of the water. A curlew called above them, the scent of vanilla drifted from a late flowering bush of gorse.

'I came here for the first time when I was ten,' said Quin. 'I bicycled from Bowmont with my hammer and my *Boy's Own Book of Fossils*. I started to chip at the rock – and suddenly there it was. An absolutely perfect cycad, as clear and unmistakable as truth itself. That was when I knew I was immortal – that I personally without the slightest doubt would solve the riddle of the universe.'

'Yes, I know that one. Things that are for you. No doubts, no hesitation.'

'Music in your case, I suppose,' he said resignedly, waiting for the ubiquitous Mozart to appear on the horizon, towing Heini in his wake.

'Yes. The first time I heard the Zillers play. But . . .' She shook her head, 'I loved the Grundlsee. I really loved it, the lake and the berries and the flowers, but when we went there it was still part of the way I'd always lived . . . with the university and people talking about psychoanalysis and all that. But here . . . the first morning by the sea . . . and now, still . . . I don't understand what's happened.' She looked up at him and he saw the bewilderment on her face. 'I feel as though I shall be homesick for this place all my life . . . for the sea . . . but how can I be? What has it to do with me? It's Vienna I'm homesick for. I *must* be.'

His silence lasted so long that she turned her head. It seemed to her that his face had changed – he looked younger, more vulnerable, and when he spoke it was without his usual ease.

'Ruth, if you wanted it to be different . . . If –'

He broke off. A shadow had fallen between them and the sun. Tall and looming, Verena Plackett stood there, holding out a piece of rock.

290

'I wonder if you could clear up a point for me, Professor,' she said. 'I think this must be one of the brachiopods, but I'm not entirely sure.'

Quin did not speak to Ruth again till after their return. He was making his way up the cliff path when he heard footsteps and turned to find her hurrying after him, the puppy in her arms.

'I'm sorry to bother you, but could you be so kind as to take him up to the house? Pilly would, but she's busy cooking and I promised Martha I'd see that he got back safely.'

'Why don't you take him yourself? You've obviously made friends with Martha.'

'No.'

He remembered her refusal to come to lunch, and meaning to tease her, said: 'You'll have to look at the place sometime, you know. After all, if I'm killed before Mr Proudfoot can put us asunder, Bowmont will be yours.'

Her reaction amazed him. She was furious; her face distorted – he almost expected her to stamp her feet.

'How *dare* you talk like that! How dare you? Mr Chamberlain said there would be no war, he promised . . . and even if there is you don't have to fight in it. It was absolutely unnecessary you going off to the navy like that, everyone said so. You could do much more good doing scientific work. It was ostentatious and stupid and *wrong*.'

'Come, I was only joking.'

291

'Exactly the sort of jokes one would expect from an Englishman. Jokes about people being dead.'

She thrust the puppy in his arms and stamped away down the hill.

'As a woman I was unfortunately not able to follow the sport,' said Verena, who was engaging Lord Rothley in a conversation about pigsticking. 'But I watched it in India and found it quite fascinating.'

Lord Rothley mumbled something and held out his glass to Turton who, detecting a certain glassiness in his lordship's eye, filled it to the brim with whisky.

The party was a small one: The Rothleys, the Stanton-Derbys and the widowed Bobo Bainbridge, come to welcome the Placketts and discuss the arrangements for Verena's dance. Needless to say Verena, who had prepared so assiduously for Sir Harold in the matter of the bony fishes, had gone through the *Northumberland Gazette* to ascertain the interests of the guests, though in the case of Lord Rothley she had been deceived a little by the small print. It was pig *breeding* rather than pig *sticking* that interested his lordship.

Her duty to him completed, Verena moved over to Hugo Stanton-Derby standing with Lady Plackett by the fireplace. The excellent relationship which Verena enjoyed with her mother had enabled them to divide their labours: Verena had repaired to the *Encyclopaedia Britannica* in the library to read up about Georgian snuff boxes which Stanton-Derby collected, while Lady

Plackett immersed herself in the *Financial Times* for it was as a stockbroker that he earned his living.

The resulting conversation was as informed and intelligent as might have been expected, and when Verena turned to the women, they found her most understanding and sympathetic about their complaints. For as might have been expected, the refugees that Quin had wished on them were continuing to be ungrateful and difficult. Ann Rothley's dismissed cowman had been taken on by the Northern Opera Company and caused havoc among the servants.

'They're all asking for time off to go to Newcastle and hear him sing in that ridiculous opera – the one where they burn a manuscript to keep warm. Something about Bohemians.'

And Helen's chauffeur too was giving trouble: he was threatening to leave and go to London to try and join a string quartet.

'Well if he does at least you won't have to listen to all that chamber music,' said Frances.

But, of course, it wasn't so simple – it never is.

'Actually, he's rather good at his job,' said Helen, 'and much cheaper than an Englishman would be.'

Only with Bobo Bainbridge did Verena not attempt to converse. Bobo, whose adored husband had dropped dead nine months ago and whose mother-in-law did not approve of displays of grief, now navigated through her social engagements by means of liberal doses of Amontillado, and for women who let themselves go in this way, Verena had nothing but contempt.

At nine o'clock, Quin took the men to smoke and play billiards in the library and the women were left to discuss Verena's party.

This, somewhat to Frances' dismay, soon grew into a much larger affair than she had intended. Her suggestion of a buffet supper and dancing to the gramophone caused Lady Plackett considerable surprise.

'The *gramophone?*' she said in offended tones. 'If it is a matter of expense . . .'

'No, of course it isn't,' interrupted Ann Rothley, rather put out by this gaffe, 'but actually, Frances, there's a very good little three-piece band just starting up in Rothley – it would be a kindness to give them work.'

So the three-piece band was agreed on, and Helen Stanton-Derby (over-ruling Lady Plackett's suggestion of lilies and stephanotis from the florist in Alnwick) said she would do the flowers. 'There's such lovely stuff in the hedges now – traveller's joy and rosehips . . . with only a little help from the gardens one can make a marvellous show.'

'And I thought mulled wine,' said Frances. 'Cook has an excellent recipe.'

Mulled wine, however, affected Lady Plackett as adversely as the gramophone had done and she asked if she could contribute to a case of champagne, an offer which Miss Somerville refused. 'I'll speak to Quin,' she said firmly; 'he's in charge of the cellar,' and they went on to discuss the menu and the list of guests.

Comments on Verena, as the County drove home, were entirely favourable.

'A very sensible girl,' said Ann Rothley and her husband grunted assent, but said he was surprised that Quin, who'd had such beautiful girlfriends, was willing to marry somebody who, when all was said and done, looked like a Roman senator.

His wife disagreed. 'She has great presence. All she needs is a really pretty dress for the dance and she'll be as attractive as anyone could wish.'

An unexpected voice now spoke from the back of the motor where Bobo Bainbridge had been supposed to be asleep.

'It will have to be a *very* pretty dress,' said Bobo – and closed her eyes once more.

Frances, meanwhile, had followed Quin into the tower – a thing she did seldom – to ask his advice about the drinks.

'Ah yes, Verena's dance.' Quin had taken so little notice of discussions about this event that it took an effort to recall it. 'It's on Friday week, isn't it? Does Verena want me to look in or would she prefer to entertain her friends on her own?'

Frances looked at him in dismay. 'But of course she wants you to be there. It would look very odd if you weren't.' And then: 'You do like Verena, don't you?'

'She's an excellent girl,' said Quin absently. And then: 'Who have you invited?'

'Rollo's coming up from Sandhurst – he won the

Sword of Honour, did Ann tell you? And he's bringing a friend of his who's going to join the same regiment. And the Bainbridge twins have got leave from the air force so –'

'From the *air force*? Mick and Leo? But they can't be more than sixteen!'

'They're eighteen, actually – they went in as cadets. Bobo was hoping one of them would stay on the ground, but they've always done things together; they're both fully fledged pilots now.'

'My God!' Bobo's adored twins had kept her alive after her husband's death. When they came home, she sobered up, became the friendly, funny person she had been throughout his childhood.

'And both Helen's girls are coming up from London. Caroline's going to marry that nice red-haired boy in the Marines – Dick Alleson.' Caroline had carried a torch for Quin for many years and everyone had rejoiced when she became so suitably engaged.

She went on counting off the guests and Quin looked out over the silvered sea. It might not come – the war – but if it did, there was not one of those gilded youths but would be in the thick of the slaughter.

'I know what we'll drink, Aunt Frances!' he said, taking her hands. 'The Veuve Clicquot '29! I've got two cases of it and I've been saving it for something special.'

Frances stared at him. She was no connoisseur of wine but she knew how Quin prized his fabulous champagne. 'Are you sure?'

'Why not? Let's make it a night to remember!'

Frances went to bed a happy woman, for what could this open-handed gesture mean except that he wished to honour Verena? But the next morning came the remark she had been dreading.

'If there's a party of young people, we must ask the students if they'd like to come along.'

Gloom descended on Aunt Frances. Jewish waitresses, girls who did things in the backs of motor cars, to mingle with the decently brought up children of her friends.

'They're coming to lunch on Sunday. Surely that's enough?'

Quin, however, was adamant. 'I can't single Verena out to that degree, Aunt Frances, you must see that.'

But to Frances' great surprise, Verena entirely agreed with Quin and offered herself to invite the students.

She was as good as her word. Arriving at the boathouse while everyone was still at breakfast, she said: 'There's going to be a dance up at Bowmont for my birthday. Anyone who wouldn't feel uncomfortable without the proper evening clothes would be entirely welcome.'

By the time Quin appeared to begin the morning's work, she was able to tell him with perfect truth that the students had refused to a man.

19

'But why? Why won't you come? Everyone is invited – all the students go to Sunday lunch at Bowmont. It's a ritual.'

'Well, it'll be just as much of a ritual without me. I'm waiting for a message from Heini and –'

'Not on a Sunday. The post office is shut.'

The other students joined in, even Dr Elke – but Ruth was adamant. She didn't feel like a big lunch, she was going for a walk; she thought the weather might be breaking.

'Then I'll stay with you,' said Pilly, but this Ruth would not hear of and Pilly was not too hard to persuade, for the thought of sitting in a well-upholstered chair and eating a substantial Sunday lunch was very attractive.

It was very quiet when the others had gone. For a while, Ruth wandered along the shore, watching the seals out in the bay. Then suddenly she turned inland, taking not the steep cliff path that led up to the terrace, but the lane that meandered between copses of hazel and alder, to join, at last, the drive behind the house.

She had been along here before on the way to the farm and now she savoured again the rich, moist smells as the earth took over from the sea. She could still hear the ocean, but here in the shelter were hedgerows tangled with rosehips and wild clematis; sloes hung from the bushes; and the crimson berries of whitebeam glinted among the trees.

After a while the lane looped back, passing between open farmland where freshly laundered sheep grazed in the meadows and she leant over the fence to speak to them, but these were not melancholy captives in basements, but free spirits who only looked up briefly before they resumed their munching.

She was close to the house now, but hidden from it by a coppice of larches. If she turned into the drive she would reach the lawns and the shrubberies on the landward side. The students had been told they could go where they wanted, and Ruth, who could not face Verena lording it over Quin's dining table, still found that she was curious about his home.

Crossing the bridge over the ha-ha, she came to a lichen-covered wall running beside a gravel path – and in it, a faded blue door framed in the branches of a guelder-rose. For a moment, she hesitated – but the grounds were deserted, no sound came to break the Sunday silence – and boldly she pushed open the door and went inside.

'I expect it's the dietary laws,' said Verena reassuringly to Aunt Frances. 'She is a Jew, you know, from Vienna. Perhaps she expects that we shall be eating pork!' And she laughed merrily at the oddness of foreigners.

Pilly and Sam, sipping sherry in the drawing room, looked angrily at Verena.

'Ruth doesn't fuss at all about what she eats, you know that – and anyway she was brought up as a Catholic.'

But this was not a very promising defence for no one knew now what excuse to make for Ruth. Aunt Frances, however, accepted the kosher version of events, remarking that it had been the same with the cowman Lady Rothley had employed in the dairy. 'We could have given her something else, I suppose. An omelette. But there is always the problem of the utensils.'

Lady Plackett was spending the day with relatives in Cumberland, but Verena had accompanied the Somervilles to church and heard Quin read the lesson, and now, dressed in a cashmere twin set and pearls, she set about trying to put her classmates at ease. She had already prevented Sam and Huw from trying to dispose of their own coats, explaining that there was a butler there for the purpose and as they took their places at table, she kept a watchful eye on those who might have trouble with their knives and forks. Though Bowmont now was run with a minimum of servants, Verena was aware that the man serving at the sideboard, the maid with her cap and apron, might overwhelm those from simple homes, and since Dr Felton was conversing with Miss Somerville, and Dr Elke was giving Quin an account of a recent journey to Lapland, Verena applied herself to the burden of making small talk, asking Pilly about the average consumption of aspirin per head of the population and enquiring whether Janet's father managed his parish with one curate or two. She also found time to check up on her protégé, Kenneth Easton. There was no question as yet of inviting Kenneth to the Lodge and she would, for example, have been far from happy to see him tackle an artichoke in melted butter, but considering his origins in Edgware Green, Kenneth was doing rather well.

They took coffee in the drawing room and then Quin rose and offered croquet on the lawn or the use of a rather bumpy tennis court, and bore Roger and Elke off to billiards in the library.

'Would anyone like to look round the house?' asked Miss Somerville.

Several students said they would, but before the party could set off, Verena said with proper deference: 'Would you like *me* to show them round, Miss Somerville? I'm sure you must want to rest.'

For a moment, Frances' eyebrows drew together in a frown. But she herself had bidden Verena make herself at home; the girl was only trying to be helpful.

'Very well – only not the tower, of course.'

Leaving behind a very disgruntled group of students, she left the room. But she did not go upstairs to rest. Instead, she went to the lumber room to fetch a bag of bonemeal and the bulbs that had come the previous day from Marshalls, and made her way to the garden.

Opening the door in the high wall, Aunt Frances saw with displeasure that she was not alone.

A girl was standing with her back to her, one arm raised to a spray of *Autumnalis* where it climbed, loaded with blossom, up the southern wall. Moving forward angrily to remonstrate, Frances found that the girl was not in fact stealing a rose, but was rather, with some skill, tucking a stray tendril back behind the wire before burying her nose once more in the fragrance of the voluptuous deep-pink flowers.

'You're trespassing,' she said, in no way placated by this appreciation of one of her favourite plants.

The girl spun round, startled, but not, in Miss Somerville's opinion, suitably cowed. 'I'm sorry. Professor Somerville said we could go into the grounds, but I can see this would be different. It's almost like a room, isn't it? – a *hortus conclusus*. All it needs is a unicorn.'

'Well, it's not going to get a unicorn,' said Aunt Frances irritably. 'The sheep are bad enough when they get in.'

She put down her trug and glared at the intruder.

'I will go,' promised Ruth. 'Only it's so unbelievable, this garden. The shelter . . . and the way it's so contained and so rich . . . and the roses still going on as though it's summer, and all those tousled, tangly things. And those silver ones like feathers; I don't know what they're called.

'Artemesia,' said Aunt Frances, still scowling.

'It's magic. To have that and the sea, the two worlds . . . And your scarf!'

'What on earth are you talking about?' said Aunt Frances, wondering if the intruder was unhinged, for she was looking at the scarf round her neck as she had looked at the white stars of a lingering clematis.

'It's beautiful!' said Ruth, feeling suddenly remarkably happy. 'I saw it on the hominid in Professor Somerville's room, but it looks *much* better on you!'

'Don't be silly, it's just an old woollen thing. I'm surprised Quin remembered to bring it up.'

But she now had to face the fact that she was in the presence of the missing student, the one who had refused to come to lunch. Like many of the girls of her generation, Frances had spent six months being 'finished' in Florence where she had found it difficult to distinguish between Titian and Tintoretto and been unpleasantly affected by the climate. Still, she had retained enough to be aware that the intruder, in spite of her dark eyes, belonged to the tradition of all those Primaveras and garlanded goddesses accustomed to frolicking in verdant meadows. If she had indeed been about to pluck a flower for her hair it would not have been unreasonable. As a Jewish waitress for whom special food had to be prepared, however, she was not satisfactory.

'You're the Austrian girl, then? The one with dietary problems?'

'I don't *think* I have dietary problems,' said Ruth,

puzzled. 'Though I'm not very fond of the insides of stomachs. Tripe is it?'

'Miss Plackett informed us that you didn't eat pork. It is very foolish to suppose that anyone would make you eat what you don't want. And anyway you could have had an omelette.'

She knelt down and began to clear a patch of earth for her bulbs, and Ruth knelt down beside her to help.

'But I like pork very much. We often had it in Vienna – my mother does it with caraway seeds and redcurrant jelly; it's one of her best dishes.'

Miss Somerville tugged at a tuft of couch grass. 'I thought you were a Jewish refugee,' she said, a touch of weariness in her voice, for she could see again that life was not going to be simple; that it was the blond cowman all over again.

'Yes, I suppose I am. Well, I'm five-eighths Jewish or perhaps three-quarters – we don't know for certain because of Esther Olivares who may have been Jewish but may have been Spanish because she came from Valencia and was always painted in a shawl which could have been a prayer shawl but it could have been one that she wore to bull fights. But my mother was a Catholic and we've never been kosher.' She pulled up a mare's-tail and threw it onto the pile of weeds. 'It's a bit of a muddle, I'm afraid – the poor rabbi in Belsize Park gets quite cross: all these people being persecuted who don't even know when Yom Kippur is or how to say kaddish. He doesn't think we *deserve* to be persecuted.' She turned to Aunt Frances: 'Would you like me to stop talking? Because I can. I have to concentrate, but it's possible.'

Miss Somerville said she didn't mind one way or another and passed her the bag of bonemeal.

'I just can't believe this garden! I used to think that when I went to heaven I'd want to find a great orchestra like you see it from the Grand Circle of a concert hall – all the russet-coloured violins and the silver flutes and a beautiful lady harpist plucking the strings. But then when I came here I thought it had to be the sea. Only now I don't know . . . there can't be anything better than this garden. Whoever made it must have been so *good*!'

'Yes. She was a Quaker.'

'Gardeners are never wicked, are they?' said Ruth. 'Obstinate and grumpy and wanting to be alone, but not wicked. Oh, look at that creeper! I've always loved October so much, haven't you? I can see why it's called the Month of the Angels. Shall I go and fetch a wheelbarrow?'

'Yes, it's over there behind the summerhouse. And bring a watering can.'

Ruth disappeared. Minutes passed; then there was a cry. Displeased, and for a moment fearful, Miss Somerville rose.

Ruth was kneeling down by a patch of mauve flowers which had gone wild in the grass behind the shed. Flowers like slender goblets growing without leaves so that their uncluttered petals opened to the sky and their golden centres mirrored the sun. She was kneeling and she was worshipping – and Miss Somerville, made nervous by what was obviously going to be more emotion, said sharply: 'What's the matter? They're just autumn crocus. I put some in a few years ago and they've spread.'

'Yes, I know. I know they're autumn crocus.' She looked up, pushing her hair off her forehead, and it was as Miss Somerville had feared; there were tears in her eyes. 'We used to wait for them every year before we left the mountains. There were meadows of them above the Grundlsee and it meant . . . the marvellousness of summer but also that it was time to leave. Things that flower without their leaves . . . they come out so pure. I never thought I'd find them here by the sea. Oh, if only Uncle Mishak was here. If only he could see them.'

She rose, but it was hard for her to pick up the handle of the barrow, to turn her back on the flowers.

'Who's Uncle Mishak?'

'He's my great-uncle . . . he loves gardening. He's managed to make a garden even in Belsize Park and that isn't easy.'

'No, I imagine not. A dreadful place.'

'Yes, but it's friendly. He's cleared quite a patch, and now he's trying to grow vegetables for my mother . . . We can't get fertilizer but –'

'Why on earth not? Surely they sell it there?'

'Yes, but we can't afford it. Only it doesn't matter – we use washing-up water and things like that. But oh, if he saw these! They were Marianne's favourite flowers. It was the wild flowers she loved. She died

306

when I was six but I can remember her standing on the alp and just looking. Most of us ran about and shrieked about how lovely they were, but Marianne and Mishak – they just looked.'

'She was his wife?' asked Aunt Frances, realizing she would be informed whether she wished it or not.

'Yes. He loved her – oh, my goodness those two! She was very tall and as thin as a rake, with a big nose, and she had a stammer, but for him she was the whole world. It was very hard for him to leave Vienna because her grave is there. He's old now, but it doesn't help.'

'Why should it?' said Miss Somerville tartly. And in spite of herself: 'How old?'

'Sixty-four,' said Ruth, and Miss Somerville frowned, for sixty-four is not old to a woman of sixty.

Ruth, working in the compost, looked up at the formidable lady and made a decision. You had to be worthy to hear the story of Mishak's romance, but oddly this sharp-tempered spinster who had left Quin alone *was* worthy.

'Would you like to hear how they met – Uncle Mishak and Marianne?'

'I don't mind, I suppose,' said Aunt Frances, 'as long as you go on with what you're doing.'

'Well, it was like this,' said Ruth. 'One day, oh, many, many years ago when the Kaiser was still on his throne, my Uncle Mishak went fishing in the Danube. Only on that particular day, he didn't catch a fish, he caught a bottle.'

She paused to judge whether she had been right, whether Miss Somerville was worthy, and she had been.

'Go on then,' said the old lady.

'It was a lemonade bottle,' said Ruth, pushing back her hair and getting into her stride. 'And inside it was a message . . .'

Late that night, Aunt Frances stood by her bedroom window and looked out at the sea. It had rained earlier, raindrops as big as daisies had hung on the trees, but now the sky was clear again, and the moon was full over the quiet water.

But the beauty of the view did little for Miss Somerville. She felt unsettled and confused. It was all to be so simple: Verena Plackett, so obviously suitable, would marry Quin, Bowmont would be saved and she, as she had intended all along, would move to the Old Vicarage in Bowmont village and live in peace with Martha and her dogs.

Instead, she found herself thinking of a woman she had never known, a plain girl standing terrified before a class of taunting children in an Austrian village years and years ago. '*She was as thin as a rake,*' the girl in the garden had said, '*with a big nose, and she had a stammer. But for him she was the whole world.*'

Frances had been just twenty years old when she went to the house on the Scottish Border, believing that she had been chosen freely as a bride. She knew she was plain, but she thought her figure was good, and she was a Somerville – she believed that that counted. The house was beautiful, in a fold of the Tweedsmuir Hills. She had liked the young man; as she dressed for dinner that first night, she imagined her future: being a bride, a wife, a mother . . .

It was late when she returned to her room where Martha waited to help her to bed. She must have left the door open, for she could hear voices outside in the corridor.

'Good God, Harry, you aren't really going to marry that anteater?' A young voice, drawling, mocking. A silly youth, a friend of her fiancé's who'd been at dinner.

'You'll have to feed her on oats – did you see those *teeth*!' A second voice, another friend.

'She's like a hacksaw; she'll tear you to pieces!'

And then the voice of her young man – her fiancé – joining in the fun. 'Don't worry, I've got it all worked out. I'll go to her room once a month in my fencing kit, that's padding enough. Then as soon as she's pregnant I'm off to town to get myself a whizzer!'

It was Martha who shut the door, Martha who helped her to undress. Martha who kept silence when, the next morning, Frances left the house and said nothing, enduring the anger of her parents, the puzzlement of the family on the Border. That had been forty years ago and nothing had happened since. No door had opened for Frances Somerville as it had opened for that other girl in an Austrian village. No black-suited figure with a briefcase had stood on the threshold and asked her name.

Irritated, troubled, Frances turned from the window,

and at that moment Martha came in with her evening cocoa – and the puppy at her heels.

'*Now* what?' she said, relieved to have found something to be angry about. 'I thought you were taking him down to The Black Bull after tea.'

'Mrs Harper sent word she couldn't have him,' said Martha. 'Her mother-in-law's coming to live and she hates dogs.' She looked down at the puppy who was winding himself round Miss Somerville's legs like a pilgrim reaching Lourdes. 'He's a bit unsettled, not having been down with the students today.'

Frances said she could see that and picked him up. Nothing had improved: not his piebald stomach, not his conviction that he was deeply loved.

That was what things were coming to, she thought. Twenty years ago, the wife of a publican would have been honoured to have a dog from the big house. Any dog. It was all of a piece, this idiot mongrel . . . all of a piece with waitresses who wept over the autumn crocus, with cowmen who sang and Wagner's stepdaughter with her unequal eyes. Comely slept in her kennel; she would not have dreamt of coming upstairs. And it wasn't any good rereading *Pride and Prejudice* yet again. Mr Darcy might have been disappointed in Elizabeth Bennet in chapter three, but by chapter six he was praising her fine dark eyes.

'I'll take him down,' said Martha, reaching for the dog.

'Oh, leave him for a bit,' said Frances wearily. Still

holding the puppy in her arms, she sat down in the chair beside her bed.

'*I have come to fetch you,*' *the little man had said, opening his briefcase, removing his hat . . .*

It began so well, the trip to the Farnes. The weather had been unsettled for the past two days, but now the sun shone again and as the *Peggoty* chugged out of Seahouses harbour, they felt that lift of the heart that comes to everyone who sails over a blue sea towards islands.

The puppy felt it too, that was clear. Its rejection by the innkeeper had left it emotionally unscarred and its position as student mascot was now established. Quin would not allow it in the dinghy, but the *Peggoty* was a sturdy fishing boat which he rented each year and there was a cabin of a sort where the owner stored his lobster pots and tackle – the dog could be shut in there when they landed.

Dr Felton had stayed behind to sort out the previous day's samples; Quin was at the wheel, steering for one of the smaller islands where the warden was waiting to show them the work in progress. They had missed the spectacular breeding colonies of the spring when the cliffs were white with nesting guillemots and razorbills and the puffin burrows honeycombed the turf, but there were other visitors now: the migrant goldcrests and fieldfares and buntings – and the seals, hundreds of them, returning to have their pups.

They passed Longstone lighthouse and the Keeper,

digging his vegetable patch, straightened himself to wave.

'That's where Grace Darling came from, isn't it?' asked Sam, thinking how like the Victorian heroine in the paintings Ruth looked with her wind-whipped hair.

Quin nodded. 'The Harcar rocks are to the south, where the *Forfarshire* broke up. We'll see them on the way back.'

'It's amazing that Mrs Ridley's grandmother knew her, isn't it?' said Ruth. 'Well, the family . . . someone in a legend. She said it wasn't the tuberculosis so much that killed her, but the fuss they made of her afterwards making her a heroine. I wouldn't mind being a heroine – it wouldn't kill me!'

Quin didn't doubt this. 'How did you meet Mrs Ridley's grandmother?' he asked curiously. 'She usually keeps herself to herself.'

'I went to fetch some eggs and we got talking.'

They were very close to the shore when it happened. Dr Elke had gone into the cabin to hand out their belongings, Quin was watching the point, steering for the jetty on the far side.

And what did happen at first was simply funny. A large bull seal bobbed up unexpectedly not four feet from the boat on the island side. A benevolent, comical seal with long grey whiskers, making himself known.

The puppy had been asleep on a pile of canvas. Now he woke, lifted his head.

The seal sneezed.

The effect was electric. The puppy let out a sharp

bark of excitement and clambered onto the gunwale. What he was seeing was unheard of . . . an ancestor? A monster? His barks became frenzied; he scrabbled with his feet against the wood.

The boat tilted.

It took only a second . . . one of those seconds that no one can believe are irreversible.

'He's gone! Oh God, the puppy's gone!'

Quin looked round, assessed the creature's chances. The sea was calm, but the tide here ran at five knots. To be dashed against the rocks or swept past them out to sea were the alternatives – yet he began to turn the boat, heading her into the wind.

No one dreamt that this was only the beginning. Ruth was impetuous, but she was not mad. Dr Elke was just emerging from the cabin, she was too far away to see; the others were leaning over the side, trying to chart the progress of the little dog as he bobbed up, paddling frantically, and vanished into the trough of a wave. Only when Pilly began to scream – then they saw. Saw Ruth's bewildered face as the current took her, saw her head turn . . . not to search for the dog now . . . to measure her terrifying speed.

The next seconds were the stuff of Quin's nightmare for years to come: those seconds in which he forced himself to remain where he was till he had turned the boat fully into the wind and shut down the engine. Not letting himself move till he could rely on the *Peggoty* to hold steady.

'Keep her exactly like this,' he said to Verena. '*Do nothing else*,' and she nodded and took the wheel.

Now there could be speed, but as he took the rope Elke was holding out to him there were more moments lost for Sam had climbed onto the gunwale, was taking off his jacket, and Quin lunged out to pull him back onto the deck with such force that the boy lay there stunned. And then the rope was round his waist, the knot secure.

'Now let me down,' said Quin – and at last was in the sea.

The rocks were his only chance . . . if she could cling on long enough for him to reach her, but they loomed out of the water, barnacle encrusted and sheer. He saw her struggling for a hold . . . begin to pull herself out . . . then lose her grip and try to swim back towards him, but that was hopeless. No one could swim against that tide.

In the *Peggoty*, Huw turned his head and retched suddenly, the rope unmoving in his huge hands.

Quin was closer now . . . close enough for her to put out an arm to reach him – and then a wave broke over her head, and she was gone. Twice he found her . . . and lost her. And then, when hope was almost gone, he found something that he could grasp and hold and wind round his hand . . . Something that did not escape him; her hair.

'No!' said Dr Elke. 'Leave her. You can talk to her later.'

Quin shook her off. Refusing to strip his soaking

clothes, his teeth chattering, he had waited to turn the boat and set her on course for the harbour, but he would wait no longer. His anger was like nothing he had ever known: it came from the gods – a visitation abolishing cold, propriety, compassion.

Ruth lay where they had dragged her, naked but for a rough grey blanket, in the stuffy cubby hole beneath the deck. Her hair was coiled in an unappealing tangle among the lobster pots; there was a smell of fish, and tar. It was almost dark, but not so dark that she couldn't see Quin's face.

'Well, I hope you're satisfied. You're a heroine now, aren't you – you and Grace Darling! You've put the life of half your friends at risk – that besotted youth who gawps at you tried to jump in after you, but that doesn't matter, of course. Nothing matters as long as you can be in the limelight, you attention-seeking spoilt little brat. Well, let me tell you, Ruth, no one will ever take you on any field trip again, I'll see to that. You're a danger to everyone, you're incapable of the two things that are needed – unselfishness and common sense. Dear God, Verena Plackett is worth ten of you. As soon as the doctor's seen you, I'm packing you off home.'

She had closed her eyes, but there was no escaping his voice.

'Is he dead?' she managed to say.

'Who?'

'The puppy.'

'Almost certainly, I should think. You can be glad he's the only casualty. This isn't some amusing Austrian

315

lake, you know. This is the North Sea.' And as she turned her head, trying to hide the tears under her lashes, his rage mounted again. 'Are you even listening to what I'm saying? Are you capable of understanding just what you've done?'

Her voice, when it came, was almost inaudible. 'Could I . . . please . . . have a bucket? I'm going to be sick.'

Late that evening there was a kind of miracle. A message from the coastguard carried to the boathouse to say that the puppy had been washed onto the shingle further down the island and was alive. But Ruth was not there to share in the rejoicing.

'We have to tell her,' said Pilly. 'We have to find some way of getting a message to the house.'

'The Professor will tell her,' said Dr Elke.

'No, he won't.' Pilly's round blue eyes were desperate. 'He'll go on punishing her. He hates her.'

Dr Elke was silent. Existing in extreme content without the company of men, she sometimes saw further than she wished to.

'No, Pilly,' she said sadly. 'He doesn't hate her. It's not like that.'

20

Ruth woke, bewildered, from a drugged sleep. The clock beside the bed said three o'clock – the pre-dawn hour in which demons gibber and people die. At first she didn't know where she was . . . she seemed to be in a large bed covered by some kind of animal skin: the pelt of a bear or something even more exotic. Then, as she touched it, she remembered.

She was in Quin's tower. He had given instructions to have her carried there after the boat landed – still furious, taking no notice when she said that she was perfectly well, that she wanted to go back to the boat-house with the others. He'd told the students to keep away and sent for two men from the farm to carry her.

'No one is to go near her till she's seen a doctor,' he'd said.

This wasn't help; it wasn't concern; it was punishment.

The doctor had come earlier, an old man, sounding her chest, feeling her pulse.

'I'm all right,' she'd kept saying, and he said, 'Yes, yes,' and left her something in a bottle to make her sleep.

But she wasn't all right. Even the news brought in by Martha – that the dog was safe – couldn't make her all right. It wasn't the waves breaking over her head that had troubled her half-sleep. It was what Quin had said: his rejection, his cruelty. She was in disgrace, she was to be sent home.

She got up, her bare feet feeling the wooden boards. This was the most masculine room she had ever seen; almost without furniture, the uncurtained windows letting in pools of moonlight, the bear skin thrown carelessly over the bed with its single pillow. To sleep thus was to get as close as one could get to sleeping out of doors.

The nightdress she was wearing must have belonged to Aunt Frances; made of thick white flannel, it billowed out over her feet; the ruffles on the neck half buried her chin. Turning on the lamp, she saw, on a small desk pushed against the wall, the photograph of a young woman whose dark, narrow face above the collar of the old-fashioned dress was startlingly familiar. Picking it up, she carried it to the window and examined it.

'What are you doing?'

She turned abruptly, caught out again, once more in the wrong.

'I'm sorry; I woke.'

Quin's face was still drawn and closed, but now he

made an effort. 'There's nothing wrong with her physically,' the doctor had said to him, 'but she looks as though she's had some kind of shock.'

'Well, obviously,' Quin had replied. 'Nearly drowning would be a shock.'

But old Dr Williams had looked at him and shaken his head and said he didn't think it was that; she was young and strong and hadn't been in the water long. 'Go easy,' he'd said, 'treat her gently.'

So he came over, took the picture from her hand. 'Are you feeling better?'

'Yes, I'm perfectly all right. I wish I could go.'

'But you can't, my poor Rapunzel; not till the morning. Even your pretty hair wouldn't be long enough to pull up a prince to rescue you.'

'And there's a shortage of princes,' she said, trying to speak lightly for the edge was still there in his voice.

Quin said nothing. Earlier he had found Sam on the terrace, looking up at Ruth's window, and sent him away.

'It's your mother, isn't it?' she asked, looking down at the portrait.

'Are we so alike?'

'Yes. She looks intelligent. And so . . . alive.'

'Yes, she was, I believe. Until I killed her.'

It was Ruth now who was angry. 'What rubbish! What absolute poppycock. *Schmarrn!*' she said, spitting out the Viennese word, so much more derogatory than anything in English. 'You talk like a kitchen maid.'

'I beg your pardon?' he said, startled.

But his attack on the boat had freed Ruth. Born to please, trained to put herself at the service of others, she now abandoned the handmaiden role.

'I shouldn't have said that. Kitchen maids are often highly intelligent, like your Elsie who told me the names of all the plants on the cliff. But you talk like someone in a third-rate romantic novel – you killed her, indeed! Well, what does one expect from a man who sleeps under dead animals . . . a man who owns the sea!'

She had succeeded better than she'd hoped in riling him. 'Nobody owns the sea,' he said. 'And if it interests you, I'm giving away what I do own. The year after next, Bowmont goes to the National Trust.'

She took a deep breath. She was, in fact, totally confounded and worse than that, utterly dismayed; she felt as though she had been kicked in the stomach.

'All of it?' she stammered. 'The house and the gardens and the farm?'

'Yes.' He had recovered his equanimity. 'As a good Social Democrat I'm sure you'll be pleased.'

She nodded. 'Yes . . .' she struggled to say. 'It's the right thing to do. It's just . . .'

But what it was was something she could not put into words. That she was devastated by the loss of a place which had nothing to do with her, which she would never see again. That she had been storing Bowmont in her mind: its cliffs and flowers, its scents and golden strands . . . There would be a lot of waiting in her life with Heini: sitting in stuffy green-rooms, accompanying him in crowded trains. Like the coifed girls in medieval cloisters who wove mysterious trees and crystal rivers into their tapestries, she had spun for herself a dream of Bowmont: of paths where she could wander, of a faded blue door in a high wall. And the dream meant Bowmont as it was – as Quin's demesne, as a place where an irascible old woman bullied the flowers out of the ground.

'Is it because you will benefit the people?' she asked, sounding priggish but not knowing how to say it otherwise.

Quin shrugged. 'I doubt if the people – whoever they are – are all that interested in Bowmont; the house is nothing much. What they want, I imagine, is access to the sea and that could be arranged with a few more rights of way. I'm afraid I don't share your passion for "the people" in the abstract. One never knows quite who they are.'

'Well, why then?'

Quin took the portrait of his mother from her hands. 'You chose to sneer when I said I killed her. Yet it is not untrue. My father knew that she was not supposed to have children. She'd been very ill – they met in Switzerland when he was there in the Diplomatic Service. She was in a sanatorium, recovering from TB. He wanted a child because of Bowmont. He wanted an heir and he didn't mind what it cost. An heir for Bowmont.'

'And if he did?' Ruth shrugged. She seemed to him relentless, suddenly; grown up, no longer his student, his protegée. 'Men have always wanted that. A tobacconist will want an heir for his kiosk . . . the poorest rabbi

321

wants a son to say kaddish for him when he's dead. Why do you make such a thing of it?'

'If a man forces a woman to bear a child . . . if he risks her life so that he can come to his own father – the father he quarrelled with and loathed – and say: "Here is an heir" – then he is committing a sin.'

But she wouldn't heed him. 'And what of her? Do you think she was so feeble? Do you think she didn't want it? She was brave – look at her face. She wanted a child. Not for Bowmont, not for your father. She wanted one because a child is a marvellous thing to have. Why do you patronize women so? Why can't they risk their lives as men do? They have a right, as much as any man.'

'To jump into the sea for a half-grown mongrel?' he jeered.

'Yes. For anything they choose.' But she bent her head, for she knew she had risked not only her own life, but his and perhaps Sam's – that his cruelty down there on the boat had had a cause. 'I'm a mongrel too,' she said very quietly. 'And anyway your aunt loves it.'

'Loves the puppy? Are you *mad*? She's done nothing but try to give it away.'

Again that shrug, so characteristic of the Viennese. 'My father always says, "Don't look at what people *say* look at what they *do*." Why did your aunt choose the carpenter – everyone knew his wife had asthma and she wasn't allowed to have pets? Why the publican when his mother was attacked by an Alsatian when she was little and she was terrified of dogs?'

'How do you know all this?' he said irritably. How did she know, in a week at Bowmont, that Elsie was interested in herbalism, that Mrs Ridley's grandmother knew the Darlings? It was infuriating, this foible of hers: this embarrassing ability to go in deep. Whoever married her would be driven mad by it. Heini would be driven mad by it. 'Anyway, my father never recovered. He carried the guilt and wretchedness for the rest of his life. It probably killed him too – he volunteered in 1916 when there was no need to do so.'

'There you go again. The English are so melodramatic! A bullet killed him.'

'What's the matter with you?' asked Quin, not accustomed to being deflated by a girl whose emotionalism was a byword. And amazed by what he was about to do, he went over to the desk, unlocked a drawer, and took out a faded exercise book with a blue marbled cover.

'Read it,' he said. 'It's my father's diary.'

The book fell open at the page he had read a hundred times and not shown to a living soul, and Ruth took it and moved closer to the lamp.

'I came back from Claire's funeral, she read, *and Marie brought me the baby, as though the sight of it could console me, that puce, wrinkled creature with its insatiable greed for life. The baby killed her – no, I killed her. I was cleverer than the doctors who told me she musn't bear a child. I knew better, I wanted a son. I wanted to bring*

*the boy back to Bowmont and show my father
that I had produced an heir – that he need despise
me no longer. Yes, I who hated him, who fled
Bowmont and turned my back on the iniquities
of inheritance and wealth, was as tainted as he
was by the desire for power. Claire wanted a
baby; I try not to forget that, but it was my job
to be wiser than she.*

*Now I have to try and love the child; he is not
to blame, but I have no desire to live without her
and no love left to give. If I have a wish it is that
he at least will relinquish his inheritance and go
forth as a free man among his equals.*

Ruth shut the diary. 'Poor man,' she said quietly. 'But
why do you embalm him? You should grow radishes,
like Mishak.'

'What?' For a moment he wondered whether her
brain had been affected by the accident.

'Marianne didn't like radishes. His wife. He never
grew them when she was alive. When she died, he said,
"Now I must grow radishes or she will remain under
the ground." He meant that the dead must be allowed
to move about freely inside us, they musn't be encap-
sulated, made finite by their prejudices.' She paused,
moving her hair out of her eyes in a gesture with which
he was utterly familiar. 'He grows a lot of radishes and
I don't like them very much as it happens, but I eat
them. All of us eat them.' She paused. 'Perhaps it's right
to give Bowmont away; I don't know about that, and

324

it's none of my business – but surely it must be because you want to, not because of what you think he might have wanted? He would have grown and changed and seen things differently perhaps. Look how you hated me this afternoon – but you have not always done so and perhaps one day you will do so no longer.'

Quin looked at her, started to speak. Then he took the diary and locked it up again in the bureau. 'Come,' he said, 'I think it's time you met the Basher.'

He took his old tweed jacket off the peg behind the door and put it round her shoulders. As he led her downstairs, he made no attempt to be unheard, switching on lights as he came to them, walking with a firm tread. He knew exactly what he would do if they were discovered and that it would cause him no moment of unease.

They made their way down the corridor that connected the tower with the body of the house and as he steered her, one hand on her back, through the rooms, she touched, here and there, the black shabby leather chair, the surface of a worn, much-polished table, learning Quin's house, and liking what she learnt. Inside the fortress was an unpretentious home, and the hallmark of the woman who had been its curator was everywhere. Aunt Frances, who had left Quin alone, had left his house alone also. There was none of the forbidding grandeur Ruth had imagined; only a place waiting quietly for those who wished to come.

But this was a journey with a particular end, and by the far wall of the library, Quin stopped. In Aunt

Frances's flannel nightgown, Quin's jacket hanging loose from her shoulders, Ruth stared at the portrait of Rear Admiral Quinton Henry Somerville in his heavy golden frame.

The Basher had been seventy when the portrait was commissioned by his parishioners and the artist, a local worthy, had clearly done his best to flatter his sitter, but his success had been moderate. The Basher's cheeks, for which a great deal of rose madder had been required, showed the broken veins caused by the whisky and the weather; his short, surprisingly snub nose was touched at the tip with purple. In spite of his grand dress uniform and the bull neck rising from its braided collar, Quin's grandfather, with his small mouth, bald pate and obstinate blue eyes, resembled nothing so much as an ill-tempered baby.

'And yet,' said Ruth, 'there is *something* . . .'

'There's something all right. Pig-headedness, ferocity . . . in the navy he bullied his officers; he thought flogging was good for the ratings. He married for money – a lot of money – and treated his wife abominably. And when he died, every single soul in North Northumberland came to the funeral and shook their heads and said that the good times were past and England would never be the same again.'

'Yes, I can see that it might be so.'

'He despised my father because he liked poetry – because he liked to be with his mother in the garden. He was terrified that he'd bred a coward. Cowardice frightened him; it was the only thing that did – to have a son who was a weakling. My father was wretched at school – he went when he was seven and he cried himself to sleep every night for years. He hated sailing, hated the sea. He was a gentle soul and the Basher despised him from the bottom of his heart. He was determined that my father should go into the navy, but my father wouldn't. He stood up to him over that. Then at fifteen he ran away to one of his mother's relatives. She took him abroad and he joined the Diplomatic Service and did very well – but he never went back to Bowmont. He loathed everything it stood for – power, privilege, Philistinism – the contempt for the things he valued. Yet you see when it came to the point, he risked my mother's life so that it could all go on.'

Ruth was silent, looking at the portrait, wondering why this ferocious Englishman should have a nose like Beethoven's, wondering why she did not dislike that hard old face.

'But you liked him?'

'No.' Quin hesitated. 'I was eight when I came to Bowmont. I'd heard only awful stories about him and he was all that I had heard. He put me into the tower to sleep under the bear he'd shot, teeth and all. I was there alone, a child with a father blown to pieces in the war. I was terrified of the dark – I'd come straight from Switzerland and heard the servants talk about my mother's death – the screams, the blood when I was born. Going to bed was purgatory. I liked the tower but I wanted a night light – I begged for one, but he said no. I wasn't afraid of anything out of doors . . .

climbing, sailing . . . I loved the sea as he did. He saw that, but he was obstinate. One day I said: "If I sail alone to Harcar Rock and back, can I have a night light?" He said: "If you sail alone to Harcar Rock, I'll beat you within an inch of your life." He used to talk like that, like a boy's adventure story.'

'Harcar? That's where the *Forfarshire* went down? Where Grace Darling rowed to?'

'Yes. Anyway, I did it. I got the dinghy out at dawn – I was small but I was strong; sailing's a knack, nothing more. Even so, I don't know why I wasn't killed; the currents are terrible there. When I came back he was standing on the shore. He didn't say anything. He just frogmarched me up to the house and beat me so hard that I couldn't sit down for a week. But that night when I went to bed, there it was – my night light.'

'Yes,' said Ruth, after a pause. 'I see.'

'I could do it, Ruth. It's no trouble to me to be Master of Bowmont. Physical things don't bother me. I can find a wife –' He checked himself, 'a new wife – I can breed sons. But I don't forget what it did to my father. I don't forget that my mother died for his dynastic pride. So let someone else have it. I shall be off on my travels again soon in any case. Unless –' But there was no need to speak to her of the war he was sure would come.

Back in the tower, he took the jacket from her shoulders, turned back the covers.

'Tomorrow you shall go back to your friends, Rapunzel,' he said. 'Now get some sleep.'

The sudden gentleness almost overset her.

'Can I stay, then?' she managed to say.

'Yes, you can stay.'

'Oh, my *dear*!' said Lady Plackett as her daughter turned from the mirror on the evening of the dance. 'He will be *overcome*!' – and Verena smiled for she could not help thinking that her mother spoke the truth.

Miss Somerville's letter suggesting a party for her birthday had sent Verena to Fortnum's in search of a suitable dress, where their chief *vendeuse* had suggested a simple Greek tunic of white georgette for, as she pointed out, Verena's beauty was in the classical style.

Verena had refused. She wanted, on the night that she hoped would seal her fate, to be thoroughly and unexpectedly feminine and ignoring the ill-concealed disapproval of the saleswoman, she had decided on a gown of strawberry-pink taffeta with a tiered skirt, each tier edged with a double layer of ruffles. The big leg-o'-mutton sleeves too were lined with ruffles, as was the heart-shaped neckline, and wishing to emphasize the youthful freshness which (she was aware) her high intelligence sometimes concealed, she wore a wreath of rosebuds in her hair.

Had this been the informal dance originally planned, her toilette might have been too sumptuous, but the party, as the Placketts hoped, had snowballed to the point where the word 'informal' hardly applied. As Verena stepped into her satin sandal – carefully low-heeled since Quin, now past his thirty-first birthday, could not really be expected to grow any more – other girls all over Northumberland were bathing, young men were tying their black ties or putting on dress uniforms, ready to make their way to Bowmont. For after all, it had always been rather special, this sea-girt tower with its absent owner, its fierce chatelaine – and perhaps they knew what Quin knew; that Fate was knocking on the door and pleasure, now, a kind of duty.

Ann Rothley and Helen Stanton-Derby had come over early to help Frances. Helen had brought armfuls of bronze and gold chrysanthemums, of rosehips and traveller's joy, and disappeared with rolls of chicken wire to transform the drawing room into a glowing autumnal bower while Ann had slipped upstairs to supervise Frances' toilette. Had Miss Somerville worn anything other than her black chenille and oriental shawl, the County would have been seriously upset, but Ann could sometimes succeed where Martha failed in coaxing her friend's hair into a less rigorous style and persuading her that a dab of snow-white powder in the middle of her nose did not constitute suitable make-up.

Now the three women sat in the hall, drinking a well-earned glass of sherry before the arrival of the guests.

'Doesn't everything look lovely!' said Ann. 'You can just see the place preening itself! You'll see, it's going to be a tremendous success.'

'I hope so.' Frances was looking tired.

'And Verena being such a heroine, too!' said Helen,

a little blood-stained round the fingers from the chicken wire. 'We're all so impressed.'

For Verena's version of what had happened on the Farnes had gained general currency. Everyone knew that a foreign girl had lost her head and jumped into the sea, putting everyone's life into jeopardy, that Quin had been furious, and that Verena, by keeping calm and holding the boat steady, had been able to avert a tragedy.

'I'm not quite sure why the girl jumped in the first place?' asked Helen. 'Someone said it was to save that mongrel puppy of yours, but that can't be right surely?'

'Yes, that seems to have been the reason,' said Frances.

Though they could see that Frances didn't really want to discuss the accident, her friends' curiosity was thoroughly aroused.

'It seems such an extraordinary thing to do,' said Ann. 'And for a foreigner! I thought they didn't like animals. Though I must say the cowman was the same – when a calf died you had to drag him away or he'd have spent all night weeping over the cow.'

'How is he getting on?'

'He's gone down to London – they've taken him on in the chorus at Covent Garden and the dairymaid's distraught. Silly creature – he never gave her the least encouragement.' But the change of subject had not, as Frances hoped, diverted her. 'What's she like, this girl? The one who jumped?'

'She's blonde too,' said Frances wearily.

Helen Stanton-Derby sighed. 'Well, it's all very unsatisfactory,' she said. 'Let's just hope something can be done about Hitler before the place is flooded out.'

But Ann now was looking upwards – and there stood Verena ready to descend!

Just for a moment, the faces of all three ladies showed the same flicker of unease – a flicker which was almost at once extinguished. It was touching that Verena had taken so much trouble, and in the softer light of the drawing room or beneath the Chinese lanterns on the terrace, the colour of the dress would be toned down. And anyway, it wasn't what they thought of her dress that mattered – it was how she looked to Quin.

They turned their heads and relief coursed through them. Quin had entered the hall and moved over to the staircase. He meant to welcome her, to tell her how nice she looked.

And up to a point, this was true. Reminded of Verena's unfortunate tumble on the night she came, touched by his aunt's mysterious but undoubted affection for the Placketts he smiled at the birthday girl and though Lady Plackett was standing by to pay the necessary compliments, it was he who said: 'You look charming, Verena. Without doubt, you'll be the belle of the ball.'

As he led her through to the drawing room, a distant telephone began to ring.

Down on the beach, Ruth was gathering driftwood. It

was a job she loved; a kind of useful beachcombing. The puppy was with her; 'helping', but cured of the sea. When she went too near the water, he dropped the sticks he had been corralling, and sat on his haunches and howled.

'It's going to be a lovely bonfire; the best ever,' said Pilly, and Ruth nodded, wrinkling her nose with delight at the smell of wood smoke and tar and seaweed, and that other smell . . . the tangy, mysterious smell that might be ozone but might just be the sea itself. The happiness that Quin had shattered on the boat had returned. She felt that she wanted to stay here for ever, living and learning with her friends.

Looking up, she saw a man come down the cliff path and go into the boathouse, and presently Dr Felton came out and made his way towards them.

'Your mother telephoned, Ruth. She wants you to ring her back at once. She's waiting by the phone.' And seeing her face: 'I'm sure it's nothing to worry about. I expect Heini's come early.'

'Yes.' But Ruth's face was drained of all colour. No one telephoned lightly at Number 27. The phone was in the hall, overheard, rickety. The coins collected for it always came out of a jam jar as important as hers for Heini, one spoke over a buzz of interference. Her mother would not have phoned without a strong reason when she was due home so soon in any case. It could, of course, be marvellous news . . . Heini on an earlier plane . . . it could be that.

'I'll come with you,' said Pilly.

'No, Pilly, I'd rather go alone. You keep the dog.'

The servant was waiting, ready to escort her.

'If you come with me, miss, I'll take you to Mr Turton. There's a bit of a row going on at the house with the guests arriving, but Mr Turton's got a phone in his pantry. You'll be private there.'

'Yes,' said Ruth. 'Thank you.' And swallowed hard because her mouth was very dry, and dredged up a smile, and followed him up the path towards the house.

She had managed the bonfire; she had said nothing to the others. She had joined in the singing and helped with the clearing up. But now, lying beside Pilly in the dormitory, she knew she could endure it no longer, being here in this untouched place which washed one clear of anguish, which deceived one into thinking that the world was beautiful.

She had to get back; she had to get back at once. Three more days here were unendurable now that she knew what she knew – and her mother's incoherent voice, scarcely audible, came back to her yet again – her desperate efforts to tell all she had to tell against the interruptions and the noise.

It was well past midnight; everyone was asleep. Ruth rose, dressed, scribbled a note by torchlight. She would take only the small canvas bag she used on her collecting trips – Pilly would bring the rest. She'd get a lift to Alnwick and wait for the milk train which connected with the express at Newcastle. It didn't really matter how long she took, only that she was on her way. Every half-hour she spent here was a betrayal.

She crept down the ladder, let herself out. The beauty of the moonlit sea, even in her wretchedness, took her breath away, but she would not let herself be seduced again, not ever – and she began to walk quickly up the lane between the alders and the hazel bushes.

Then, as she came up behind the house, she heard music. Cole Porter's 'Night and Day', a wonderful tune, dreamy . . . and saw light streaming out onto the terrace.

Of course. Verena's dance. She had entirely forgotten – inhabiting, since her mother's phone call, a different world. As she crossed the gravel, meaning to take a short cut to the road, she saw that the drive was full of cars: two-seaters mostly, the colour bleached out of them by moonlight, but the shape – predatory, privileged – perfectly clear. Cars for laughing young men with scarves blowing behind them, young men with goggles and one arm round their giggling girls, driving too fast.

There had been a shower earlier. As she made her way across the lawn, her shoes were soaked. The Chinese lanterns swayed in the breeze, but the long windows were uncurtained and open at the top. She could see as clearly as on a stage the couples revolving. The melody had changed; it was a tango now. She knew the words: *It was all 'cos of my jealousy*. Some of the guests were dancing cheek to cheek, most were hamming it up, because it was impossible for the British to

335

take anything seriously; certainly not jealousy, certainly not love.

The room, now that the double doors were open, seemed vast; the banks of flowers, the silver champagne buckets belied the informality of Verena's dance. A few older women sat round the edge, watching the girls in their perms and pastels, the arrogant young men.

And how arrogant they were; how they brayed and shrieked as the music stopped, tossing their heads, pulling their girls to the array of glasses, pouring out more drinks. How they laughed, and slapped each other on the back, while in Vienna people were being piled into cattle trucks and taken to the East, and Heini –

But her mind drew back. It would not follow Heini.

Now she could see Quin. He had come into the room and he was carrying something in a tall glass – carrying it to Verena, to where she sat in a high-backed chair. He didn't look like the braying young men, even in her anger she had to admit that. He looked older and more intelligent, but he was part of all this. He belonged.

Verena was simpering and he bent his head attentively, squiring her, while the dowagers smirked and nodded. It seemed to be true, what everyone said – that he would marry Verena. She was pointing to something on the floor and he bent to pick it up and handed it to her, gallantly, with a bow. A rose from her extraordinary headdress! Quin as a *Rosenkavalier* – that was rich! A man who'd rushed out of the Stadtpark as though the music of her city was a plague . . .

And as if they read her thoughts, the three serious dark-suited men on the dais launched into a waltz! Not Strauss, but Lanner whom she loved as much. She knew it well, she had danced to it with Heini in the Vienna Woods.

'Oh no! Not that old stuff!' She could hear the braying, blond young man with the slicked-back hair. 'Give us something decent!' A second youth, almost identical, staggered up to the band, shaking his head.

But the band went doggedly on: playing not well, perhaps, but carefully, and the young men gave in and pulled the girls out and began to lurch about, parodying the sweetness of the waltz, exaggerating the steps. Most of them were drunk now, they enjoyed colliding with each other, enjoyed deriding the music of another land. Now one of them stumbled and almost fell – a tall youth with black curls and that was *really* funny. His partner tried to pull him up and then a red-haired boy with freckles flicked champagne into his face. It was all so hilarious. All such a scream . . .

The stone was in her hand before she knew that she had picked it up. She must have seen it earlier, for it was the right size, heavy enough to make an impact, small enough for her to propel it with force. The act of throwing it was wonderful: a catharsis – and the crash of the splintered glass. It seemed that she waited for seconds, minutes almost, yet it was not so, for by the time Quin came out on to the terrace, followed by an excited, angry group of revellers, she was already running back

337

out of the light, across the grass . . . was down in the lane which would lead her to the road.

'There she is!'

'It's a girl! Come on, let's get her!'

Then Quin's voice, quiet, yet a whiplash. 'No. You will all go back inside. I know the girl, she comes from the village and I will deal with her.'

They obeyed him. He had seen where she went, but there was a danger she would turn from the lane into the copse for shelter, and though he knew she could not escape, for the wood ended in a high fence and a stream, there were sometimes gin traps there, set by poachers. Even so, he schooled himself not to run till he was out of sight of the house.

He caught up with her easily. She had done exactly as he had expected.

'Wait!' he shouted. 'There may be traps! Take care!' He spoke in German, using all the means to calm her, approaching slowly. 'Don't move.'

But she had already stopped. When he came up to her she was leaning against a spruce sapling, her posture, in the fleeting moonlight, that of a young St Sebastian waiting for arrows.

His words, when they came, punctured her martyred pose in an instant.

'I don't like bad manners,' said Quin quietly. 'These people are my guests.'

Her head went up. 'Yes. The kind of guests one would expect you to have – a man who owns the sea. Braying, mindless idiots who mock at music. Don't they know what is going on? Can't they even read? Have they seen the papers? No, of course they only read the sporting pages; which horse has gone faster than another and the report of who curtseyed to the King in a headdress of dead ostriches.' She was shaking so much that her words came in bursts between the chattering of her teeth. 'Today . . . now . . . while they get drunk and scream in their ridiculous clothes, my people are gathered up and put into cattle trucks and sent away. While they pour wine onto the floor and fall over, young boys who believed in the brotherhood of man are beaten senseless in the street.'

Quin made no move to comfort her. He was as angry as she was, but his voice was entirely controlled. 'I will not point out to you that your people – using the word in a different sense – stood in the Heldenplatz and yelled in their thousands for Hitler. But I will tell you this. In mocking at the people you saw here, you commit more than ill manners; you commit an injustice over which you will burn with shame – and very soon. For it is these braying boys who the moment war comes will flock to fight. It is they who will confront the evil that is Hitler even though they do it for a jape and a lark. The boy who drank too much and fell over has just passed out of Sandhurst. He's Ann Rothley's only son and if war breaks out I wouldn't give him six months. His friend – the one who poured champagne over him – is a lieutenant in the Marines. He's engaged to that girl in the blue dress and they've put their wedding forward because he's being posted overseas. The Bainbridge

339

twins – the ones who don't like waltzes – are in the air force. Both of them. I suppose they might last a year because they're excellent pilots, but I doubt it. You will be able to look into that room this year or next year or the year after and see a roomful of ghosts – of dead men and weeping women. While your Heini, I wouldn't be surprised, will still be playing his arpeggios.'

'No!' Her voice was scarcely audible. She could not turn from the shelter of the tree. 'I had a phone call this evening. They've caught him. Heini is in a camp.'

21

'I can't,' said Heini in a choking voice. 'I can't do it.'

The red face of the camp commandant with its brutal jaw, its small blue eyes, thrust itself into Heini's.

'Oh, I think you can. I think you'll find you can.'

Heini saw the flash of the knife in the commandant's hand, and realized that he was defeated. There was not even a potato peeler – he was expected to peel three buckets of potatoes under a cold water tap. He had explained that he was a pianist, that his hands were not like other people's, that they were his livelihood, and no one had listened, no one cared. One slip of the blade and he would not be able to practise, perhaps for weeks.

Beside him, Meierwitz had already started, neatly slicing off the discoloured eyes, dropping the naked potatoes into the water. But Meierwitz was different, he came from a working-class district in the Ruhr; Meierwitz was used to hardship; he whistled as he worked, he pointed out a robin on the fence post, watching them.

For Heini, the grey fields, the grey sky, the murmur of the sea on the shingle beach a mile away, were a featureless, nightmare world. The somnolent black and white cows grazing behind the barbed-wire perimeter of the camp might have been creatures from Hades. It was his third day in captivity and already he knew that he would crack up under the strain. The men slept six to a hut, they rose at seven to do PE in the freezing cold, breakfast was porridge which he had read about and never seen, and bread and dripping – and always tea, tea, tea – never once a cup of coffee. Then came these frightful chores – potato peeling, vegetable slicing, any of which could damage his hands, and in the evening the raucous noise of mouth organs or the wireless or people playing poker for matchsticks. And now lectures were being organized, compulsory ones, and the previous night there had been a film show where a mindless comic had run about playing the ukelele and losing his trousers. If this was what passed for culture among the British, he was going to be very unhappy here.

Meierwitz had chopped off a piece of potato and thrown it at the robin who considered it, his head on one side, and decided it was unworthy as an offering, and the brutal commandant, an ironmonger from Graz who was determined to lick this miscellaneous gaggle of refugees into a worthy task force, came by and told him not to bother. 'He only eats worms,' he said, already rather proud of the picky attitude of this most British of birds, and threw a contemptuous glance at

342

Heini Radek. You'd think he'd be glad to get out of Europe instead of whinging on about his hands.

For Heini, the discovery that his visa was a forgery had come out of the blue. The hours spent in the immigration huts at the airport were a nightmare that he would remember to his dying day. Along with the others whose papers were not in order or those who had come over on block visas, he'd been taken to this transit camp and treated – he considered – like an animal; herded, rubber-stamped, pushed about. At first he had thought he might be sent back but public opinion in Britain had at last woken up to the plight of the refugees and after the first day, everyone at Dovercamp had learnt that they could remain. Those who volunteered for agricultural work or were willing to join the Pioneer Corps could be released quickly; the rest had to be processed, sorted, above all a sponsor had to be found to guarantee that they would not become a burden on the taxpayer.

The euphoria this had produced in the other inmates had passed Heini by. There was certainly no question of his volunteering for agricultural work or becoming a Pioneer. No one seemed to understand that music wasn't some selfish pursuit; it was his mission. The volunteer ladies who took down his particulars in appallingly slow handwriting seemed to find this impossible to grasp. One had spelled 'Conservatoire' as 'conservatory' and thought he was a horticulturist, and another had said that there seemed to be an awful lot of music 'over there'. It was two days before he had been allowed to phone Frau Berger, but the line was so bad that he could hardly hear her and it was difficult to remember that this family, who had once been able to open doors to every chancellory in Vienna, were now as penniless and stateless as he was himself. The Bergers could not guarantee him financially; their name, with the bullying ladies in the office, carried no weight. Yet they would find someone to sponsor him; they would help him. And Ruth would come. All his hope centred on her as he plunged his hands into the bucket and took out another spud.

More persecution followed in the long day. The commandant had decided to dig a vegetable patch on the perimeter of the camp and all the able-bodied men were marshalled to dig. The soggy earth, the blunt and heavy spade, made the task appallingly heavy and he could actually feel the callouses come up on his palms. Yet when he gave up after half an hour, there were nudges and glances and someone pointed out that if Professor Lipchitz, an elderly musicologist from Dresden, could work in the fields, then so could he.

It was as they sat drinking tea from enamel mugs and eating the dry biscuits they were issued in the afternoon, that a boy from the office poked his head round the door of the hut.

'Mr Radek?' he called.

Heini rose, his heart pounding.

'There's someone to see you in the office.'

'Who . . . ?' stammered Heini.

'A girl,' said the messenger. 'A stunner,' and looked with new respect at Heini.

Ruth stood quietly, waiting for him to come. She had travelled since the previous night and had scarcely eaten, but she needed nothing, transfigured as she was by joy.

All the way down from Northumberland, in terror and despair, she had prayed, dedicating her life afresh to Heini, offering everything that she held dear if only he was safe. And then the thing had happened that never happened: the second chance. Leonie explaining that Heini was here, that she had misheard, that the camp was in England and she could go to him.

Then Heini entered and she could not speak for this was not the *Wunderkind* she had known, this was a frightened, shabby boy with stubble on his chin and a beaten look in his eyes – and overwhelmed by love and pity, she opened her arms and made the gesture that had always spelled sanctuary for him, shaking forward her hair so that it sheltered them both.

'Thank God, Ruth! I thought you'd never come.'

'Oh, darling; you're really here. It's you.' Her voice broke 'I thought you were in a proper camp, you see. I thought they'd got you.'

'This is a proper camp. It's awful, Ruth.'

'Yes . . . yes . . . but you see I thought you were in Dachau or Oranienburg. My mother phoned and I couldn't hear her properly. Then when I learnt you were safe . . . I'll never forget it as long as I live.'

And she would never forget what she had vowed: to serve Heini for all her days and expiate for ever that time of betrayal she had spent Lotus-eating by the sea.

'You're going to take me home, aren't you, darling? Now?'

'Heini, I can't this minute. I have to get hold of Dr Friedlander – I'm sure he'll sponsor you, but he's away for the weekend. I'll be on his doorstep first thing tomorrow and then it'll just be a very few days.'

'A few days!' Heini lifted his head. 'Ruth, I can't stay here that long. I can't!'

'Oh, please, darling! We'll all be working for you – and they're friendly here, aren't they? I spoke to the secretary.'

'Friendly!' But there was such comfort in her presence that he decided to be brave and managing to change the subject, he said: 'Did you get a piano?'

'Yes. A Bösendorfer!'

'A grand?'

'No, love; we've only got a very small sitting room. But it's a beauty!'

He was disappointed, but he would not reproach her. She was his lifeline; his saviour.

They were still clasped in each other's arms when the secretary returned.

'It's time for your bus, dear,' she said. 'You mustn't miss it: it's the last one.'

It was as Ruth picked up her cloak that she saw a bird, untroubled by barbed wire, sitting on a fence post outside the window.

'Oh, look Heini! It's a starling! That's an omen for us, isn't it? It must mean good luck.'

She drew him to the window. The bird cocked its head, bright-eyed, but not looking quite right at the nether end.

'He's lost some tail feathers,' said the secretary. 'Been overdoing it.'

'Yes.' Ruth could see that, but it was of no consequence. An omen was an omen. Tail feathers did not come into a thing like that.

22

At the beginning of December, Leonie decided to celebrate Hanukkah, the Jewish Festival of Light.

One way or another, she felt that light would be a good idea. Kurt was still in Manchester and she missed him; the news from Europe grew increasingly grim and the weather – foggy and dank and not at all like the crisp, snowy weather she remembered in Vienna – did little to lift the spirits.

There was also the problem of Heini. Heini had been sleeping on the sofa for a month and practising for eight hours a day in her sitting room, and though Leonie accepted the need for this, she found herself wondering, as she crept round him with her duster, about the friends and relatives of earlier piano virtuosos. Was there, somewhere in an attic in Budapest, an old lady whose mother had run screaming into the street to escape yet another of Liszt's brilliant arpeggios? Did the sale of cotton ear plugs soar in some French pharmacy as the inhabitants of the rue de Rivoli adjusted to

Chopin's practice hours? What did those Viennese land-ladies *really* feel when Beethoven left another piano for dead?

There was also the question of food. Heini had brought some money from Hungary, but he needed it to insure his hands; she saw that, and the rest went on fares as he sought out agents and impresarios who could help him.

'It's for Ruth,' Heini would say with his sweet smile. 'Everything I do is for Ruth.'

Everyone accepted this; Heini had declared his intention of marrying Ruth as soon as he was established and keeping her in comfort, so there could be no question of criticizing anything he did. If he stayed an hour in the bathroom it was because he had to look nice at interviews; if he left his clothes on the floor for Leonie to pick up it was because he was working so hard at his music that there was no time for anything else, and without complaint the inhabitants of Number 27 adapted to his presence.

Mishak was not musical. Silence was his metier; he navigated through the day by gentle sounds: a thrush outside the window, the fall of rain, the whirr of a lawn-mower. Now, as Heini pounded his piano, he was cut off from all these. He got up even earlier and worked in the garden till Heini rose; then walked. But the days were drawing in, Mishak was sixty-four – and increasingly, for he was not convivial by nature, he too was driven to the Willow.

Paul Ziller, when Heini came, had hoped that they

would play duets, for the repertoire for violin and piano is varied and very beautiful. But Heini, understandably, wanted to concentrate on a solo career and since the house was not sufficiently soundproof to accommodate two practice sessions, the sight of Ziller carrying his Guarneri to the cloakroom of the Day Centre once more became familiar in Belsize Park.

Hilda too altered her routine. The Keeper of the Anthropology Department now trusted her with a key. She took sandwiches and stayed in the museum till late, timing her arrival at Number 27 to coincide with the ascent of Fräulein Lutzenholler onto her bedroom chair.

That they could grow to be grateful to the gloomy psychoanalyst was something none of them could have foreseen, but it was so. For at 9.30, come rain or shine, she climbed on to her chair with a long-handled broom and pounded on the floor of the Bergers' sitting room as a sign that she was now going to bed and the music must stop.

Only, of course, that meant Leonie could not complain about the state of the cooker so all in all, a Festival of Light was badly needed and since she herself was vague as to how it was performed, she took her problem to the Willow.

'I buy you a cake?' said Mrs Weiss.

Leonie accepted and asked the old lady for instructions.

'There are candles,' said Mrs Weiss positively. 'That

I know. One lights one each day for eight days and they are put in a menorah.'

'How can that be?' asked Dr Levy. 'If there are eight days there are eight candles and a menorah only has seven branches. And there are certainly prayers. My grandmother prayed.'

'But what did she pray?' asked Leonie, tilting her blonde head in resolute pursuit of Jewishness.

Dr Levy shrugged and Ziller said that von Hofmann would know. 'He'll be here in a minute.'

'Why should he know? He has no Jewish blood at all,' said Mrs Weiss dismissively.

'But he was in that Isaac Bashevis Singer play, don't you remember? *The Nebbich*. That's a very Jewish play,' said Ziller.

But von Hofmann, when he came, was hazy. 'I wasn't on in that act,' he said, 'but it's a very beautiful ceremony. All the actors were very much moved and Steffi bought a menorah afterwards in the flea market. I could ask her – she's selling stockings in Harrods.'

No one, however, wanted to trouble Steffi who was an exceedingly tiresome woman though a good actress, and Miss Violet and Miss Maud, who had been listening to this exchange, now said that they'd soon have to start thinking about getting their Christmas decorations up.

Leonie brightened, approaching familiar ground.

'What do you do for Christmas?' she asked the ladies.

'Well, we go to evensong,' said Miss Maud. 'And we

351

decorate the tea rooms with paper chains and put a sprig of holly on each of the tables.'

'And the advent rings?' asked Leonie.

'We don't have those,' said Miss Maud firmly, scenting a whiff of popery.

'But a little tree with red apples and a sliver star?'

The ladies shook their heads and said they didn't believe in making a fuss.

'But this is not a fuss,' said Leonie. 'It's beautiful.' And shyly: 'I could make some *Lebkuchen* . . . gingerbread, you know . . . hearts with icing and red ribbon?'

'Georg has a big fir tree in his garden,' said Mrs Weiss. 'I can cut pieces from it in the night when Moira sleeps.'

'My wife brought her little glockenspiel,' said the banker unexpectedly. 'I said to her she is stupid, but she had it from a child.'

Back in the kitchen, Miss Maud and Miss Violet looked at each other.

'I suppose it won't hurt,' said Miss Maud, 'though I don't want pine needles all over the place.'

'Still it's better than that Hanukkah thing of theirs. I mean, they won't get very far if they can't remember how to do it,' said Miss Violet.

Mrs Burtt wrung out her cloth and hung it over the sink, above which Ruth had pinned a diagram showing *The Life History of the Pololo Worm.*

'And it'll cheer Ruth up to see the place look pretty,' she said.

Miss Maud frowned, wondering why their waitress

should need cheering. 'She's very happy since Heini came. She's always saying so.'

'But tired,' said Mrs Burtt.

Three days after Leonie's failure over the Festival of Light, Ruth called at the post office on her way to college and drew out of her private box a small packet with a red seal which she opened with a fast-beating heart.

Minutes later, she stood in the middle of a crowd of hurrying people, staring down at the dark blue passport with its golden lion, its prancing unicorn and the careless motto: *Dieu et Mon Droit.*

'I am a British subject,' said Ruth aloud, standing on the pavement opposite a greengrocer's shop and seeing the Secretary of State in a top hat wafting her through foreign lands.

If only she could have shown it to everyone: the naturalization certificate which confirmed her status; the passport she held in her own right! If only she could have marched into the Willow holding it aloft and danced with Mrs Burtt and hugged her parents. People in Europe would have killed for what she held in her hand – yet no one would have grudged her her luck, she knew that.

But, of course, she could show it to no one. It was Ruth Somerville, not Ruth Berger, that His Britannic Majesty wished to pass without let or hindrance anywhere in the world, and the passport would have to go with the rest of her documents to be scuttled over by the recalcitrant mice.

She was early for college. Since Heini came, Ruth had slept with the alarm under her pillow set for 5.30 so that she could do two hours of work while it was still quiet, Now, as she sat in the Underground, she wanted to mark this day; pay some kind of tribute – and on an impulse she left the train three stops before her destination and climbed the steps of the National Gallery to look down at Trafalgar Square.

She was right, this *was* the heart of her adopted city. The fountains sparkled, the lions smiled . . . Through the Admiralty Arch opposite she could see the end of The Mall leading to Buckingham Palace where the shy King lived who was being so good about his stammer, and the soft-voiced Queen looked after the princesses on her biscuit tin.

She tilted her head up at Nelson on his column; the little man who was the favourite hero of the British and who had said, 'Kiss me, Hardy,' or perhaps, 'Kismet, Hardy,' – talking about fate – and then died. He had been so brave . . . but then they were brave, the British. Their girls felled each other with hockey sticks and never cried; their women, in earlier times, had stridden through jungles in woollen skirts to turn the heathen to the word of God.

And she too would be strong and brave. She would do well in the Christmas exams *and* stay awake for Heini when he needed to talk late at night. It was ridiculous to think that anyone needed more than four hours' sleep. She could do it all: her essays, her revision, her

work at the Willow and still help Heini with his inter-
pretations.

*The Will Has Only To Be Born In Order To Tri-
umph* quoted Ruth who had read this motto on a
calendar and been much impressed.

It was only now that she gave her mind to the letter
which Mr Proudfoot had enclosed and saw that she was
bidden to attend his office on the following afternoon.

Proudfoot had thought it simplest to see Ruth personally and had said so to Quin. 'It would make sense if
you came together, but I suppose we can't be too careful.'

For after naturalization came the next stage – annulment. To facilitate this, a massive document had been
prepared, requiring to be signed by both parties in the
presence of a Commissioner for Oaths – and involving
Dick Proudfoot's articled clerk in several hours of work.
This affidavit was to be submitted to the courts in the
hope that it would come before a judge who would
accept it as evidence of nullity without demanding further proof. Whether this would in fact happen was
anyone's guess since the procedure involving annulment
in foreign-born nationals was under review and things
that were under review never, in Mr Proudfoot's experience, became simpler.

It so happened that Ruth was waiting in the outer
office and that he saw her first with her back turned,
looking at a small watercolour on the far wall. The sun
came at a slant through the window and touched her

hair so that it was the golden tresses, the straight back, he saw first – and immediately he steeled himself, waiting for her to turn. Mr Proudfoot was deeply susceptible to women and had once driven his car into a telephone kiosk on the pavement of Great Portland Street because he was watching a girl come out of her dentist and he knew that when girls with rich blonde hair turn round there is disappointment. At best mediocrity, at worst a sharp, discontented nose, a petulant mouth, for God sensibly preserves his bounty.

'Miss Berger?'

Ruth turned – and Mr Proudfoot felt a surge of gratitude to his Creator. At the same time, his view of Quin as a chivalrous rescuer of unfortunates receded. What surprised him now was Quin's haste to get rid of a girl most people would have latched on to with a bulldog bite.

'This is such a nice picture,' she said when they had shaken hands. 'It's so friendly . . . the way the tree roots curve right down into the water. It was like that where we used to go in the summer, on the Grundlsee.'

'Yes. It was done in the Lake District; I suppose it's the same sort of landscape.'

'Who painted it?'

'Actually, I did. When I was a student. I used to dabble in watercolours a bit,' he said, retreating into British modesty.

Ruth did not care for this. 'It has nothing to do with dabbling,' she said reproachfully. 'It's beautiful. But I suppose now you paint the river and the places round here?'

'No. As a matter of fact, I haven't put a brush to paper for years.'

'Why is that? Because there is so much to do here?' she said, following him into the office.

'Well, yes . . . but I suppose I could find time. One gets discouraged, you know, being an amateur.'

Ruth frowned. 'I don't want to be impertinent when you've been so helpful about getting me naturalized and now annulled – but I think that's very wrong. An amateur is someone who loves something. In all the Haydn Quartets there is a part for an amateur – the second violin, usually, or the cello – but it's just as beautiful.'

But the sight of the document Mr Proudfoot had prepared for her now silenced Ruth as she waded, biting her lip, through its several pages of parchment, its red seal, its Gothic script and the strange words in which she wished the law to know that she had never been laid hands on, or laid hands herself, on Quinton Alexander St John Somerville.

'I don't know if this will work, Miss Berger – some judges won't accept an affidavit without medical evidence and Quin is determined not to put you through anything like that.' He flushed, unable to pursue the subject.

'Yes. He is being so kind – so very kind – which is why I must get this annulment through quickly so that he can marry someone else.'

Proudfoot, who had been led to believe that it was Ruth who was in a hurry, looked surprised.

'Does he want to marry anyone else?'

'Perhaps not he, but other people. Verena Plackett, for example.'

'I don't know who Verena Plackett is, but I assure you that Quinton can look after himself. People have been trying to marry him since he was knee-high to a goat.' He pulled the formidable paper closer. 'Now listen, my dear, because this document is unique and it's complicated and you have to get it right. You must sign it exactly where I've pencilled it – there and there and again over the page – with your full name and in the presence of a Commissioner for Oaths. He'll make a charge and Quin has asked me to give you a five-pound note to cover the cost. Any commissioner will do, there's sure to be one in Hampstead. When you've done it, bring it back to me – I wouldn't trust the post; if it's lost we'll miss the next sitting of the courts and then we're in trouble. And if there's anything you don't understand, just let me know.'

'I think I understand it,' said Ruth. 'Only perhaps you could wrap it in something for me?' For her straw basket contained, in addition to her dissecting kit and lecture notes, the remains of Pilly's sandwiches which, now that Heini was eating with them, she took back to Belsize Park rather than feeding to the ducks.

'Don't worry – there's a cardboard tube – it gets rolled up and put inside. I'll expect you in a few days, then. Take care!'

'What do you think?' said Milner, looking at Quin with his head on one side and an ill-concealed glint of excitement in his eyes.

Quin stood looking down at the drawer of fossil-bearing rocks which Milner had pulled open, first unlocking the storage room with rather more formality than usually went on in the Natural History Museum.

'You're right, of course. It's part of a pterosaur. And I'd have sworn it was from Tendaguru. The Germans have got two casts like that in Berlin from the 1908 expedition. I've seen them.'

'Well, it isn't. Do you know where this was found?'

Quin, tracing out the beaked skull, still partly embedded in the matrix, shook his head. A wing-lizard, immemorially old and very rare.

'On the other side of the Kulamali Gorge – eight hundred miles away. He showed me the place on the map. Farquarson may be no more than a white hunter, but he's no liar and he knows Africa like the back of his hand. I've written down the exact location.'

Quin laid the bone back in the tray. 'Are you serious? South of the Rift?'

'That's right. He didn't know how important it was and I didn't tell him. It's a bit of luck, him not being a palaeontologist, otherwise we'd have everyone down on us like a ton of bricks. Whereas as it is . . .'

Quin held up a restraining hand. Milner had been six months in England, caught in the administration of the civil service which ran the museum, sorting, annotating, preparing exhibitions he regarded as a waste of time. That he wanted to be off again was clear enough.

'I can't follow this through now. I spent most of last year away; it isn't fair on my colleagues.' He pushed the steel cabinet shut, turned away. 'Still, I'd like to see Farquarson's report. You do get those sandstone plateaus there . . . it's not impossible. Oh, damn you, Jack – I've got to go and set the end of term exams; I'm a staid academic now!'

Milner said nothing more, content to have sown a seed. Sooner or later Quin would crack. Milner had other chances to travel, but he would wait. Journeys weren't the same without Somerville – and it would do the Professor good to get away. He hadn't been quite himself the last few weeks.

Verena had returned well satisfied with her time at Bowmont. True Quin had not declared himself, but he had been extremely attentive at the dance, and if it hadn't been for that madwoman throwing a stone, they might have got much further. Quin had come back from dealing with her in a different mood: sombre and absentminded, and who could blame him? Having an insane person on one's estate could hardly be a pleasure.

Meanwhile back at the Lodge, she settled down to work. For one of the best ways to approach Quinton was through his subject and Verena, as the Christmas exams approached, worked harder than she had ever worked before.

Needless to say the Placketts did everything they could to help. No one was allowed to talk outside the study door, the maids knew better than to hoover when Verena was writing her essay; a special consignment of textbooks was brought over from the library, including reference books which were needed by the other students.

Not only did Verena work, she also exercised with even greater vigour for she had never lost sight of her ideal: that of accompanying Quin to foreign parts. There was only one point on which she had been doubtful and Quin himself now provided the assurance that she sought.

It happened at a dinner party to which her mother had invited Colonel Hillborough of the Royal Geographical Society. Hillborough was a celebrated traveller and a modest man who worked selflessly for the Society, and he had expressed the hope that Professor Somerville, whom he knew well, would be present.

Whatever Quin's views on the Placketts' dinners, there could be no question of refusing, and three days after he had talked to Milner in the museum, he found himself once more sitting at Verena's right hand.

It was a good evening. Hillborough had just come back from the Antarctic and seen Shackleton's hut exactly as he had left it: a frozen ham, still edible, hanging from the ceiling, his felt boots lying on a bunk. As he and Quin talked of the great journeys of the past, most of the other guests fell silent, content to listen.

'And you?' asked Hillborough as the ladies prepared to leave the room. 'Are you off again soon?'

Quin, smiling, put up a hand. 'Don't tempt me, sir!'

It was then that Verena asked the question that had long been on her mind. 'Tell me, Professor Somerville,' she said, giving him his title, though in private, now that she had waltzed in his arms, she always used his Christian name. 'Is there any reason why women should not go on the kind of expeditions that you organize?'

Quin turned to her. 'No reason at all,' he said firmly. 'Absolutely none. It's a subject I feel strongly about, as it happens – giving women a chance.'

Verena, that night, was a happy woman. It could not mean nothing, the vehemence of his assurance, the warmth in his eyes – and she now decided that exercising in her rooms was not enough. If she wanted to be sufficiently fleet of foot she would need something more challenging – and the obvious game for that was squash. Squash, however, needs a partner and fighting down her hesitation (for she did not want to elevate him too markedly) she invited Kenneth Easton to accompany her to the Athletic Club.

She could not have known the effect of this summons on poor Kenneth, living with his widowed mother in the quiet suburb of Edgware Green. Piggy banks were emptied, post office accounts raided, to equip Kenneth with a racket and a pair of crisp white shorts to brush his even whiter knees.

And the very next Tuesday, he had the happiness of

leaving Thameside with the Vice Chancellor's daughter, bound for health and fitness on the courts.

'I feel so *guilty*,' said Ruth to the sheep. 'So ashamed.' Since her naturalization she had taken to talking to it in English. 'I don't know how I came to *do* such a thing.'

The sheep shifted a hoof and butted its head against the side of the pen. It had consumed the stem of a Brussels sprout which Mishak had dug out of the cold ground of Belsize Park, and seemed to be offering sympathy.

'I know it's wrong to complain to you when you have such a hard life,' she went on – and indeed the future of the sheep, rejected by the meat trade due to its contamination by science, and by science due to its solitary state, was bleak. 'I would give anything to be able to help you and I know exactly where you should be . . . it's a Paradise, I promise you. There are green, green fields and the air smells of the sea and every now and then a tractor comes and tips mangelwurzels onto the grass.'

But it was better not to talk about Bowmont even to the sheep. She still dreamt about it almost nightly, but that would pass. Everything passed – that was something all the experts were agreed about.

'I just hope he's in a good mood,' she said, picking up her basket.

But this was unlikely. Quin, since Heini came, had scarcely thrown her a word. Well, why should he? The shame of that moment when she had thrown the stone would be with her for always. There were other

363

rumours about the Professor: that he was living hard, burning the midnight oil.

She made her way to the lecture theatre, and as he entered her worst fears were confirmed.

'He looks as though he's had a night on the tiles,' said Sam.

Ruth nodded. The thin face was pale, the forehead exceedingly volcanic, and someone seemed to have sat on his gown.

Yet when he began to lecture the magic was still there. Only one thing had changed – his exit. Moving with deceptive casualness towards the door, Quin delivered his last sentence – and was gone. Alone among the staff, Professor Somerville did not get thanked by Verena Plackett.

She had been told to come at two, but he was late and she had time to examine the hominid, looking a little naked without Aunt Frances' scarf, and wander over to the sand tray where the jumbled reptile bones were slowly becoming recognizable.

Quin, coming into the room, saw her bending over the tray as she had done in Vienna. It seemed to him that she looked as she had looked then; lost and disconsolate, but he was in no mood for pity. His own evening with Claudine Fleury had been an unexpected failure. Their relationship was of long standing, well understood. A Parisienne whose first two husbands had not amused her, she lived in the luxurious Mayfair house of her father, a concert impresario frequently absent in America, and was the kind of Frenchwoman every full-blooded male dreams up: petite and dark-eyed with a fastidious elegance which transformed everything she touched.

Last night, the evening had fallen into its accustomed pattern: dinner at Rules, dancing at the Domino and then home to the comforts of her intimately curtained bed.

If there had been a fault, it had been his, he knew that, and he could only hope that Claudine had noticed nothing. The truth was that everything which had drawn him to her: her expertise, her detachment, the knowledge that she took love lightly, now failed in its charm. He had experienced that most lonely of sensations, lovemaking from which the soul is absent – and Ruth, seeing his closed face, laced her hands together and prepared for the worst.

'What can I do for you?'

Ruth took a deep breath. 'You can forgive me,' she said.

Quin's eyebrows rose. 'Good God! Is it as bad as that? What do you want me to forgive you for?'

'I'll tell you . . . only please will you *promise* me not to mention Freud because it makes me very angry?'

'I shall probably find that quite easy,' he said. 'I frequently go for months at a time without mentioning him. But what has he done to upset you?'

'It isn't him, exactly,' said Ruth. 'It's Fräulein Lutzenholler.' And as Quin looked blank, 'She's a psychoanalyst: she comes from Breslau and she's been nothing but trouble! She burns everything – even boiled eggs and it's difficult to burn those – and her soup gets all over the stove and my mother is sure that it's because of her we have mice. And every night at half-past nine she gets on a chair and thumps on the ceiling to stop Heini practising. And then she *dares* . . .' Ruth's indignation was such that she had to stop.

'Dares what?'

'She dares to talk to me about Freud and what he said about losing things.'

'What did he say?'

'That we lose what we want to lose . . . and forget what we want to forget. It's all in *The Interpretation of Dreams* or something. I would never have told her that I'd left the papers on the bus, but there was no one else in and I'd been up and down to the depot and the Lost Property Office and I was absolutely frantic. I didn't tell her *what* I'd left on the bus, of course, only that it was important – and then she dares to talk about my unconscious – a woman who leaves black hair all over the bathtub and tortures carrots to death at ninety degrees centigrade!'

Quin leant across the desk. 'Ruth, would you just tell me very quietly what this is about? What did you leave on the bus?'

She pushed back her hair. 'The annulment papers. All those documents that Mr Proudfoot gave me. They were in a big cardboard tube and he took such trouble!'

Quin had risen, walked over to the window. His back was turned towards her and his shoulders were shaking. He was really angry, then.

366

'I'm so sorry. I'm terribly sorry.'

Quin turned and she saw that he had been trying not to laugh.

'You think it's *funny*,' she said, amazed.

'Well, yes, I'm afraid I do,' he said apologetically. He came over to stand beside her. 'Now tell me exactly how it happened. In sequence, if possible.'

'Well, I'd been to Mr Proudfoot and I had my straw basket and this huge scroll and I thought I would go straight to Hampstead on a bus to get it signed by the Commissioner for Oaths because I knew there was one in the High Street. And I got one of those old-fashioned buses which are open on top, you know, and of course there aren't any double-deckers in Vienna, so I went upstairs and I got the front seat too! And I was just looking at everything because being so high and so open is so lovely and when we came to the edge of the Heath I looked down and there was a patch of *Herrenpilze*; you know – those big mushrooms we found on the Grundlsee? They were behind the ladies lavatory and I knew they wouldn't be there long because you some-times get bloodshed up there with the refugees fighting each other for them, so I rushed down to get off at the next stop and pick them because food is a bit tight since Heini – I mean my mother is always glad of something extra. And when I turned into the park I realized that I'd forgotten the papers, but I wasn't in too much of a panic because I was sure they'd be at the depot, but they weren't and they weren't in the Lost Property Office either and I've been back and forward the last two days and it's just hopeless. And I don't know how to explain to Mr Proudfoot who's been so kind and taken so much trouble.'

'Don't worry, I'll tell him. Only, Ruth, don't you think there's a case now for telling Heini and your parents about our marriage? We haven't after all done anything we need be ashamed of. I'm sure they'd be –'

'Oh, no, please, please!' Ruth had seized his arm and was looking entreatingly into his face. 'I beg of you . . . My mother's very good, she does all Heini's washing and she feeds him and she doesn't complain when he's in the bath for a long time . . . but being a concert pianist is something she doesn't altogether understand. You see, when Paul Ziller found a job for Heini two evenings a week playing at Lyons Corner House, she really wanted him to take it.'

'But he didn't?'

'No. He said once you go down that road you never get back to being taken seriously as a musician, but, of course, Paul Ziller does it and my mother . . . She's already so grateful to you for getting work for my father and she'd come to see you and you'd *hate* it.'

'Would I?' said Quin, in a voice she hadn't heard him use before. 'Well, perhaps. Anyway, I'll phone Dick and he'll get some new papers drawn up. Don't worry, we've probably only lost a month or two.'

She smiled. 'Thank you. It's such a relief. I can face my essay on "Parasitism in the Hermit Crab" now. It was just a blur before.'

It was not till the end of the day that Quin, mysteriously restored to good humour, could ring his lawyer.

'She has done *what*?' said Proudfoot incredulously.

'I've told you. Left the annulment papers on the bus.'

'I don't believe it! They were in a damn great roll as long as an arm and tied up with red tape.'

'Well, she has,' said Quin, outlining the saga of the edible boletus. 'So it's back to the drawing board, I'm afraid. Can you get another lot drawn up?'

'I can, but not this week – my clerk's off ill. And after that I'm going to Madeira for a fortnight so you can forget the next sitting of the courts.'

'Well, it can't be helped,' said Quin – and it seemed to Dick that if he wanted to marry Verena Plackett, he did not do so badly. 'What are you going to do in Madeira?'

'Have a holiday,' said Proudfoot. 'And paint. Your wife thought I should take it up again.'

'My –' Quin broke off, aware that he had never used those words about Ruth.

'Well, she is your wife, isn't she? God knows why you want to get rid of her – you must be mad. However, it's none of my business.'

'No, it isn't,' said Quin pleasantly. 'And I warn you, when she comes to see you again don't mention Professor Freud or you'll get your head bitten off.'

'Why the devil should I mention him? I don't understand the first thing about all that stuff.'

'That's all right then. I'm only warning you.'

23

It was Paul Ziller who introduced Heini to Mantella.

'He's a very good agent. A bit of a thruster, but they have to be. Why don't you go and see him?'

'Do you use him?'

Ziller shook his head. 'He's only interested in soloists and celebrities.'

'Well, you could be a soloist.'

'No. I'm an ensemble player.' Ziller was silent, pursuing his thoughts. Returning to the Day Centre to re-establish his claim, he had found, among the wash basins, an emaciated and exceedingly shabby man playing the cello – and playing it well. This had turned out to be Milan Karvitz from the Prague Chamber Orchestra, just returned from the International Brigade in Spain . . . and Karvitz, in turn, had brought along the viola player from the disbanded Berliner Ensemble. The three of them played well together though it was a tight fit in the cloakroom, but the repertoire for string trio was limited and now a man had written from Northumberland where he was working as a chauffeur. Ziller knew him by reputation – a fine violinist, an unselfish player – but it was out of the question. He could never replace Biberstein; never. 'Anyway,' he went on, pulling himself out of his reverie, 'I've spoken to him about you. Why don't you go along?'

Mantella, though brought up in Hamburg, was a South American by birth, with an olive skin, a pointed black beard and a legendary nose for sniffing out talent. In Heini, presenting himself the following day in the elegant Bond Street office, he at once saw possibilities. The musical gift could not be in doubt – all those medals from the Conservatoire and a debut with the Philharmonic promised in Vienna – but more importantly, the boy had instant emotional appeal. Even Mantella, however, could not get a concert for a pianist unknown in England and not yet established on the continent.

He had, however, a suggestion to make.

'There's an important piano competition here at the end of May. It's sponsored by Boothebys – the music publishers. They're big in the States and here too. No, don't look like that; it may be commercially sponsored, but the judges are absolutely first class. They've got Kousselovsky and Arthur Hanneman and the Director of the Amsterdam Conservatoire. The Russians are sending two candidates and Leblanc's entered from Paris.'

'He's good,' said Heini.

'I tell you, it's big. After all, Glyndebourne is run by auctioneers! The commercial sponsorship means that

371

the prizes are substantial and the press is getting interested. The finals are held in the Albert Hall – they've got the BBC Symphonia to accompany the concertos – and that isn't all!' He paused for dramatic effect. 'Jacques Fleury is coming over from the States!'

That settled it. Fleury was one of the most influential concert impresarios in the world with houses in Paris and London and New York. 'What are the concertos? I could learn a new one, but I've only got a rotten little piano and I'd rather play something I've studied.'

Mantella pulled out the brochure. 'Beethoven's Number 3, the Tchaikovsky Number 1 . . . Rachmaninoff 2 . . . and Mozart Number 17.'

Heini smiled. 'Really? Number 17? The Starling Concerto? Well, well!'

Mantella's glance was sharp. 'What do you mean, the Starling Concerto?'

'The last movement is supposed to be based on the song of a starling Mozart had. My girlfriend would want me to play that – I used to call her that . . . my starling – but it isn't showy enough. I'll play the Tchaikovsky.'

'Wait a minute – didn't I see something in the papers? Did she ever work as a waitress?'

'Yes, she did. She still does in the evening, but she won't for long; I'll see to that.'

'I remember . . . some article by a chap who went into a refugee café. There was a picture . . . lots of hair and a snub nose.' Mantella twiddled his silver pencil.

The girl had been very pretty – girls with short noses always photographed well. 'I think you should play the Mozart.'

Heini shook his head. 'It's too easy. Mozart wrote it for one of his pupils. I'd rather play the Tchaikovsky.'

'You can give them the pyrotechnics in the preliminary rounds. You get the chance to play six pieces and only two of them are obligatory: a Handel suite and Beethoven's *Hammerklavier*. You can dazzle them with Liszt, Chopin, Busoni . . . show them nothing's too difficult. Then when you're through to the finals come on quietly and play the Mozart.'

'But surely –'

'Heini, believe me; I know what I'm talking about. The Russians will go for Tchaikovsky and Rachmaninoff and you can't beat them. And we can use the story – you and the girl. Your starling. After all, we're not just trying to win, we're trying to get you engagements. America's not out of the question – I have an office there.'

'America!' Heini's eyes widened. 'It's what I've dreamt of. You mean you'd be able to get me a visa?'

'If there's enough interest in you. Fleury could fix it if he wished. Now here are the conditions of entry and the dates. There's a registration fee, but I expect you can manage that.'

'Yes.' The Bergers were funny about Dr Friedlander – they wouldn't take anything from him, but that was silly. The dentist was musical; he'd be glad to help.

'Good.' Mantella rose as a sign that the interview

was over. 'Come back next week with the completed form – and bring the girl!'

Heini left the office in a daze. Passing Hart and Sylvesters in Bruton Street, he stopped to stare at a pair of hand-stitched gloves in the window. Liszt had always come onto the platform in doeskin gloves and dropped them onto the floor before he went to the instrument. He was glad Mantella had mentioned Liszt – he'd play the Dante Sonata; it was hellishly difficult but that was all to the good. It was time virtuoso playing came back into fashion. People like Ziller were all very well, but even the greatest musicians had not been averse to an element of showmanship.

How pleased Ruth would be that he had decided to play the Mozart! Well, Mantella had decided, but there was no need to mention that; no point in depriving her of the happiness she would feel. And if it meant America! They would be married over there – he'd rather dreaded a scrappy wedding in the squalor of Belsize Park.

Abandoning the hand-stitched gloves, dreaming his dreams, Heini made his way to Dr Friedlander's surgery in Harley Street.

'She's done it!' said Dr Felton gleefully, pushing away the pile of exam papers he had been marking. He'd checked and double checked to make sure he'd been completely fair, and he had. Ruth had beaten Verena Plackett by two marks in the Marine Zoology paper, and by three in the Parasitology.

'Which, considering what she's been up against, is quite an achievement,' said Dr Elke, inviting her fellow members of staff to a celebratory glass of sherry in her room.

They had all been worried about Ruth who had been found asleep in various unexpected places in the college and had ended up in the Underground terminus of the Northern Line after a longer night than usual discussing the fingering of Beethoven's *Hammerklavier*.

'And Moira's decided to adopt!' said Dr Felton, in the grip of end-of-term euphoria. 'So no more thermometers!'

The marks, when they went up on the board, gave general satisfaction. Verena was top in the other two theory papers and since one of these was Palaeontology, she was content. Sam had done unexpectedly well, and both Huw and Janet were comfortably through.

But it was Pilly's results that were the most surprising. She had failed only the Physiology practical in which she had fainted while pricking her finger to get a sample of blood, and was to be allowed to take her Finals without a resit.

'And it's all because of you, Ruth,' said Pilly, hugging her friend.

The party on the last day of term was thus a cheerful affair. Heini came, and even those of Ruth's friends who had been critical of his demands were charmed by his broken accent and wistful smile. Since his meeting with Mantella, he had been in excellent spirits and when Sam produced a pile of music from the piano stool and begged him to play, he did so without demur.

Quin, on the same evening, had been bidden to a pre-Christmas gathering of eminent academics at the Vice Chancellor's Lodge. Arriving purposely late, he paused for a few moments outside the lighted windows of the Union Hall.

Heini was at the piano and Ruth sat by his side. She wore the velvet dress she had worn on the Orient Express and her head was bent in total concentration as she followed the score. Then she rose, one arm curved over the boy's head . . . her fingers, in one deft movement, flicked the page.

'You have to be like a wave when you turn over,' she had told him on the train. 'You have to be completely anonymous.'

Quin walked on across the darkened quadrangle. It seemed to him that he had never seen an action express such dedication, such gracefully given service – or such love!

Christmas Eve in the Willow would have surprised passers-by who were given to understand that it was a refugee café largely frequented by displaced persons and run by austere and frugal spinsters.

The tables had been pushed to the edge of the floor and in the centre stood the tree in all its festive glory. This tree had not been dug out of the garden of Mrs Weiss's son, Georg, while her daughter-in-law slept, though the old lady had been perfectly willing to attempt this foul deed. It had been bought in a shop, yet it was Mrs Weiss who was its source. A week before Christmas the hard-pressed Moira had paid a secret visit to Leonie and struck a bargain. A liberal sum of money which Moira could well spare if Leonie could guarantee that her mother-in-law was out of the house for the whole of Christmas Eve.

'I've got some people coming in – clients of George's; important ones. You understand?'

Leonie, at first, had been inclined to refuse, but on reflection it seemed to be a fair bargain. She herself, while still prosperous and in her native land, would have paid twice what Moira was offering to be sure of Christmas Eve without Mrs Weiss. She took the money and went shopping with the old lady for the tree, the silver tinsel, the candles, the spices, the rum . . .

Now the café was a bower of green, the glockenspiel of the banker's wife set up a sweet tinkling over the hubbub of voices . . . Voices which were stilled as Miss Maud, now primed in the mysteries of an Austrian Holy Night, handed the matches to Ruth.

'Careful!' said Professor Berger, as he had said every year since Ruth was old enough to light the candles on the tree.

He had travelled overnight on the bus from Manchester and would greatly have preferred to be at home with his family, but now as he looked at the circle of faces and touched his daughter's head, he was glad they had come together with their friends.

'I never seen it like that,' said Mrs Burtt. 'Not with real candles.'

And Miss Violet and Miss Maud forgot the needles dropping on the floor and the wax dripping on to the tablecloths and even the appalling risk of fire, for it was beyond race or belief or nationality, this incandescent symbol of joy and peace.

Then came the presents. How these people, some of whom could scarcely afford to eat, had found gifts remained a mystery, but no one was forgotten. Dr Levy had discovered a postcard of the bench where Leonie had been overcome by pigeons and made for it a wooden frame. Mrs Burtt received a scroll in which Ruth, in blank verse, proclaimed her as Queen of the Willow. Even the poodle had a present: a bone marrow pudding baked on the disputed cooker at Number 27.

But Heini's presents were the best. It had occurred to Heini that while he was borrowing money from Dr Friedlander for the competition, he might as well borrow a little extra for Christmas, and the dentist had been perfectly happy to lend it to him. So Heini had bought silk stockings for Leonie and chocolates for Aunt Hilda and a copy of *The Meditations of Marcus Aurelius* for the Professor who was fond of the Roman Stoic. This had used up more money than he expected and when he went into a flower shop to buy red roses for Ruth, he found the cost of a bunch to be exorbitant. It was the assistant who had suggested a different kind of rose – a Christmas rose, pale-petalled and golden-hearted, and put a single bloom, cradled in moss, into

378

a cellophane box – and now, as he saw Ruth's face, he knew that nothing could have pleased her more.

After the presents came the food – and here the horsehair purse of Mrs Weiss had turned into a horn of plenty, emitting plates of salami and wafer-thin smoked ham . . . of almonds and apricots, and a wild white wine from the Wachau for which Leonie had scoured the shops of Soho.

But at eleven, Ruth and Heini slipped out together and walked hand in hand through the damp, misty streets.

'It was lovely, wasn't it?' said Ruth. 'And you look so elegant!' On the first day of the holidays, she had returned to the progressively educated children of the lady weaver and used the money she had earned to buy Heini a silk scarf to wear with his evening clothes. 'But, oh if only it would snow! I miss snow so much – the quietness and the glitter. Do you remember the icicles hanging from the wall lamps in the Hofburg? And the C Minor Mass coming out of the Augustiner chapel, and the bells?'

They had reached the door of Number 27. 'I'll play it for you,' said Heini pulling her into the house. 'Come on! I'll play the snow and the choirboys and the bells. I'll play Christmas in Vienna.'

And he did. He sat down at the Bösendorfer and he made it for her in music as he had promised. He played Leopold Mozart's 'Sleigh Ride' and wove in the carols that the Vienna Choirboys sang: 'Puer Nobis' and the rocking lullaby which Mary had sung to her babe . . .

He played the tune the old man had wheezed out on his hurdy-gurdy in the market where the Bergers bought their tree – and then it became Papageno's song from *The Magic Flute* which had been Ruth's Christmas treat since she was eight years old. He played 'The Skater's Waltz' to which she'd whirled round the ice rink in the Prater and moved down to the bass to mime the deep and solemn bells of St Stephan's summoning the people to midnight mass. And he ended with the piece he had played for her every year on the Steinway in the Felsengasse – 'their' tune: Mozart's consoling and ravishing B Minor Adagio which he had been practising when first they met.

Then he closed the lid of the piano and got to his feet.

'Ruth,' he said huskily, 'I liked your present, but there is only one present I want and need – and I need it desperately.'

'What?' said Ruth, and her heart beat so loudly that she thought he must be able to hear.

'You!' said Heini. 'Nothing else. Just you. And soon please, darling. Very soon!'

And Ruth, still caught in the wonder of the music, moved forward into his arms and said, 'Yes. It's what I want too. I want it very much.'

Quin's Christmas Eve was very different.

He had walked since daybreak and now stood on the top of the Cheviots looking across at the rolling slopes of blond grass bent by the wind and the fierce storm clouds gathering above the sea. Tomorrow he would do his duty by his parishioners, read the lesson in church, and accompany his aunt to the Rothleys' annual party – but this day he had claimed for himself.

Yet when he began to apply his mind to the problem which had brought him up here, he found there was no decision to be made. It had made itself, heaven knew when, in that part of the brain so beloved of Professor Freud.

Instead of thought came images. A steamer to Dar es Salaam . . . the river boat to Lindi . . . a few days with the Commissioner to hire porters. And then the long trek across the great game plains on the far side of the Rift. He had dreamt of that journey when he was working in Tanganyika all those years ago – and if Farquarson was telling the truth . . . if there really was an outcrop of fossil-bearing sandstone in the Kulamali . . .

As he saw the landscape, so he saw the people he would take. Milner, of course, and Jacobson from the museum's Geology Department . . . Alec Younger, back from the East Indies and longing to be off again . . . Colonel Hillborough who'd had his fill of administration and would harness the resources of the Geographical Society to the trip . . . And one other person; someone young to whom he'd give a break. One of the third years, perhaps. It would depend on the exam results, but young Sam Marsh was a possibility.

Africa had been his first love: the bone pits of Tendaguru had set him on his way professionally and if

381

this was to be his last journey it would be a fitting end to his travels. There were other advantages in going to Kulamali. The territory was British ruled and from it one could go through other protectorates back to the sea. No danger then, if war came, of being locked up as a foreigner. He'd be able to make his way back home and enlist.

Another decision, seemingly, had already been made in some part of his mind. This was not a journey to be packed into the summer vacation. He was leaving Thameside, and leaving it for good.

24

'I must say sometimes I wish the human heart really was just a thick-walled rubber bulb, don't you?' said Ruth to Janet, with whom she had stayed behind to draw a model of the circulatory system kindly constructed for them by Dr Fitzsimmons.

Nearly two months had passed since Christmas, and Heini's passionate plea that they should be properly together was about to be answered at last. Ruth had not delayed so long on purpose. She wanted to be like the heroine of *La Traviata* who had sung about living utterly and then dying and she knew that in giving herself to Heini she was serving the cause of music. Heini, who was studying the Dante Sonata for the competition, had become very interested in the composer's private life and Liszt (who was famous for being demonic) had already been through a number of countesses by the time he was Heini's age, so that it was entirely understandable that Heini did not feel able to do justice to his compositions while in a state of physical frustration.

All the same, it hadn't been easy. The opportunities for being demonic at Number 27 were nonexistent and they couldn't afford a hotel. So she had turned to Janet, who had so completely got over being a vicar's daughter, and Janet had come up trumps.

'You can have my flat,' she had said. 'We'll have to find out when the other two are away, but Corinne goes home most weekends and Hilary quite often works all day Saturday; I'll let you know when it's safe.'

And the day before, Janet had let her know. The very next Saturday, Ruth could have the whole afternoon to be with Heini. Now, looking at her friend, Janet said: 'You don't have to, you know. No one has to. Some people just aren't any good unless they're married and it seems to me you may be one of them.'

'It's just cowardice,' said Ruth, rubbing out a capillary tube which was threatening to run off the page. 'If you can do it, so can I.'

Janet's reply was a little disconcerting. 'Yes, I can and I do. Someone started me off when I was sixteen and I was ashamed because my father was a vicar and I wanted to show I wasn't a prig. And once you start, you go on. But I'm twenty-one and I'm a bit tired of it already and sometimes I wonder what the point of it all is.'

It was as they were packing up their belongings that Ruth, looking sideways at Janet, said: 'Do you think I ought to read a book about it first?'

'Good God, Ruth, you do nothing *but* read books! You must know more about the physiology of the reproductive system than anyone in the world.'

'I meant . . . a sort of manual. A "How to do it" one, like you have for mending motorbikes.'

'You can if you like. If you go to Foyles and go up to the second floor you can read one free. They've got half a dozen of them in the Human Biology section. The assistants won't bother you; they're used to it.'

So on the following day, Ruth went to Charing Cross in her lunch hour and Pilly insisted on accompanying her. Ruth had not meant to burden Pilly with the ecstatic experience she was about to undergo, but Pilly had been so hurt when Ruth had secret conversations with Janet that she had let her into the secret. Pilly had been very admiring; 'You are *brave*,' she said frequently, but she had taken to bringing along cod-liver oil capsules in her lunch box and urging Ruth to swallow them, and this was not quite the image Ruth had in mind.

'I won't come upstairs with you,' said Pilly. 'I'm sure I won't be able to understand the diagrams and there are probably going to be a lot of names. I'll wait for you in Cookery.'

Pilly was right. There *were* a lot of names and the diagrams were deeply dispiriting. One would just have to rely on living utterly.

'It'll be all right, Ruth,' said Janet when they got back to college. 'Honestly. I'll take you to the flat tomorrow and show you where everything is. There's just one thing you want to be careful of.'

Ruth swallowed. 'Getting pregnant, you mean?'

'No, not that – obviously Heini will see to that. It's about his socks.'

'What about them?' said Ruth, feeling her heart pound at this new threat.

Janet laid a hand on her arm. 'Try to make sure that he takes them off early on. A man standing there with nothing on and then those dark socks . . . it can throw you a bit. But after all, you love him. There's really nothing to worry about at all.'

Janet's flat was in Bloomsbury, in one of those little streets behind the British Museum. Had she climbed down the fire escape which led from the kitchen, Ruth would have found herself a stone's throw from the basement where Aunt Hilda worked. Hilda wouldn't be shocked by what she was about to do. The Mi-Mi were very easy going; everyone in Bechuanaland took love lightly.

But her parents . . .

Ruth forced her mind away from what her parents would think. She had so hoped that the annulment would be through by now – then she could at least have got engaged to Heini. But it wasn't and that was her fault and another reason for not keeping him waiting any longer.

The flat was very Bohemian; the furniture was sort of tacked together and there wasn't much of it and everything was very dusty. Still, that was a good thing. Mimi had been a Bohemian, arriving with her candle and her tiny frozen hands and not fussing any more than the heroine of *La Traviata* about being married. She had died too, of course, clutching her little muff, but not from sin, from consumption – one had to remember that.

Heini should be here any moment now. She had cleaned the sink and swept the kitchen floor and unwrapped the wine that Janet had brought her as a good luck present. Ruth had been worried about this – Janet was dreadfully hard up – but Janet had waved her protests away.

'It was a special offer from the Co-op,' she said.

The wine would be a big help, Ruth was sure of that, remembering what it had done for her on the Orient Express.

Fighting down her nervousness, she opened the door of Corinne's room which was the one Janet suggested they use. It had a double bed – well, a double mattress – covered in some interesting coloured sacking. Corinne was an art student; there were drawings tacked round the wall which she had done in life class. All the women had breasts which soared upwards and Doric-looking thighs. Heini was going to be very disappointed – perhaps it would be best to make the room properly dark. But when she began to draw the curtains, the bamboo rail came clattering down on to the floor and she only just had time to replace it before the doorbell rang.

'Heini! Darling!' But though he embraced her, Heini

did not look happy. 'Is everything all right? Did you get them?'

'Yes, I did in the end, but I've had an awful time. The slot machines were right up against each other and the instructions had been ripped off so the first time I put a sixpence in I got a bar of chocolate – that revolting stuff with squishy cream in the middle.'

'Oh, Heini; how awful!' Heini never ate chocolate in case it gave him acne.

'Then I tried the other one and the money got stuck. I had to hit it with my shoe while some idiot came past and sniggered. I never want to go through that again!'

Guilt surged through Ruth. Heini had asked her to go to the chemist and see to 'all that' and it was true that her English was much better than his, but there were words one wasn't absolutely sure about, even if one looked them up in the dictionary. *Particularly* if one looked them up in the dictionary. At the same time, she wondered if he had brought the chocolate. She had missed her lunch, but it was probably better not to ask.

'Anyway, we're here,' she said, helping him off with his coat. And then bravely: 'Would you like a bath?'

Heini nodded – he must have read the same book as she had; the one which said that a bath beforehand was a good idea – and followed her into the bathroom where she lit the geyser and turned on the tap.

The effect was dramatic. There was a loud bang, gusts of steam erupted, and a purple flame.

'Good God, we can't use that!' said Heini. 'It's worse than Belsize Park.'

'You don't think it'll calm down?'

'No I don't.' Heini had grabbed a towel and was holding it to his nose. 'Emile Zola was killed by a leaking stove.'

'Well, never mind,' said Ruth, turning it off. (Not all the books had recommended hot baths. Some believed in naturalness.) 'Let's go and have some wine.'

They returned to the kitchen and she poured a glass for Heini and another for herself.

'We'd better drink a toast,' she said.

Heini smiled: 'To our love!' he said.

It was at this moment that they heard a series of frantic, high-pitched squeaks outside on the fire escape. Ruth opened the door and a black cat ran into the room, carrying a bird in its mouth. The bird was a sparrow and it was not yet dead.

'Oh, God!'

'Shoo it out for heaven's sake!'

'I think it lives here. Janet said something about a cat.'

'It doesn't matter if it lives here or not.'

Heini rose, chased the cat out, and bolted the door.

'We should have killed it,' said Ruth.

'I can't kill cats without a gun.'

'Not the cat. The bird.'

Feeling distinctly queasy, she lifted her glass and drank. Sour and chill, the wine crashed into her stomach. Seemingly there was wine and wine . . .

'Come on, Ruth! Let's go into the bedroom.'

'Yes. Only Heini, I'd like to get into the mood a bit. Couldn't we have some music?'

'I *am* in the mood,' said Heini crossly. But he followed her into the sitting room where a pile of records was heaped untidily onto a low table.

'Oh, *look!*' she said delightedly. 'They've got *Highlights from La Traviata.*'

But, of course, musicians do not listen to highlights – it is not to be expected – and Heini was beginning to look hurt.

'You do love me, don't you?'

'Heini, you know I do!'

He held out both hands, boyish, appealing. She put hers into them. They made their way into the bedroom. And he was taking off his socks – someone must have warned him! It was going to be all right!'

'Oh, damnation! This place is a tip! I've got a drawing pin in my foot.'

He had subsided on to the bed, clutching his left foot from which, sure enough, a drop of blood now oozed.

'It's not the part you pedal with,' said Ruth who could always read his thoughts. 'It's right on the side. But I'll get a bit of plaster.'

'And some iodine,' called Heini as she made for the door. 'The floor must be knee-deep in germs.'

She found some iodine in the bathroom and a roll of zinc plaster, but no scissors. Carrying the plaster into the kitchen, she searched the drawers but without success. Eventually she took a kitchen knife and started to hack off a strip.

390

'It's stopped bleeding,' called Heini. 'If you just disinfect it, it'll be all right.'

Carrying the iodine into the bedroom, she anointed the sole of Heini's foot. Heini was being brave, not wincing.

'We'll have to wait for it to dry.'

'It won't take long,' he said. 'Why don't you get undressed?'

'I'll just take the iodine back. It would be awful if we spilled it.'

She went past the life class pictures, past a small grey feather dropped from the breast of the little bird, and restored the iodine bottle. Returning, she found that Heini was in bed.

It could be postponed no longer, then – the living utterly. Ruth crossed her arms and pulled her sweater over her head.

On the same afternoon as Heini was learning to be demonic in Bloomsbury, Quin made his way to the Natural History Museum to confer with his assistant about the coming journey.

'I'm afraid I have bad news for you,' said Milner, climbing down from the scaffolding on which he was attending to the neck bones of a brontosaurus.

But he was smiling. Since Quin had told him they were off in June, he had been in an excellent mood.

'What kind of bad news?' asked Quin.

'I'll tell you in private,' said Milner mysteriously, and together they made their way through the echoing dinosaur hall to Milner's cubbyhole in the basement.

'It's Brille-Lamartaine,' he went on. 'He's got wind of your trip and he wants to come! He's been lurking and hinting and making a thorough nuisance of himself. I haven't said a word, but something must have leaked out.'

'Good God! I thought he was in Brussels.'

Brille-Lamartaine was the Belgian geologist whose spectacles had been stepped on by a yak. It isn't often that a member of an expedition is a disaster without a single redeeming feature, but Brille-Lamartaine had achieved this distinction without even trying.

'I wonder how he heard?'

'He's been spending a lot of time at the Geographical Society. Hillborough's totally discreet but something may have leaked out.'

'I'll tell you what,' said Quin, 'if he brings up the subject again, tell him I'm bringing a woman. One of my students. A young life-enhancing woman greedy for experience with the opposite sex.'

Milner was appreciative. Brille-Lamartaine was terrified of women and convinced that every one had designs both on his portly frame and his inheritance from a maiden aunt in Ghent.

'I shall like to do that,' he said.

But as he left the museum, Quin knew that he could no longer postpone telling his staff that he was leaving. The Placketts could wait till the statutory term's notice at Easter, but to let Roger and Elke and Humphrey hear the news from others would be unpardonable.

As it happened, Roger was in the lab, using the

weekend to catch up with his research, and the look on his face when Quin spoke was hard to bear.

'It'll be a desert without you,' he said and turned away to hide his distress. 'Elke thought this might happen, but I hoped . . . Oh, hell!'

'If it's any consolation to you, I think next year may see us all scattered,' said Quin. 'This war, if it comes, won't be like the last one. I've seen some pretty weird contingency plans, but few of them involve leaving scientists in peace in their universities.' And as Roger still stood in silence, trying to deal with his sense of loss, Quin put a hand on his arm and said: 'I'll take you to Africa, Roger, if you can get away. I'd be glad to. It's not strictly your line of country, but I think you'd enjoy it.'

'Thanks – you know how I'd love it, but I can't leave Lillian. We're supposed to be taking delivery of an infant at the end of May, sight unseen. A Canadian dancer who's got into trouble. Lillian thinks it'll do *entrechats* as soon as we get it; she's really thrilled.'

'I'm glad!' said Quin warmly. 'And if you've got a vacancy for a godfather, perhaps you'd consider me?'

Roger's face lit up. 'The job is yours, Professor.'

Crossing the courtyard after his talk with Roger, Quin encountered Verena accompanied by Kenneth Easton, carrying a squash racket and clearly in the best of spirits.

'You look very fit,' said Quin when it was evident that she would not let him pass.

'Oh I am, Professor!' said Verena archly. She did not

actually invite him to feel her biceps, but this was not necessary. Bare-armed and in shorts, the state of her musculature was evident to anyone with eyes to see. And then: 'I was wondering what you thought of the Army and Navy Stores? Would you recommend them as the best outfitters before an expedition?'

'Yes, indeed. They're excellent – I always use them; you'll find everything you want there. If you mention my name to Mr Collins, you'll find him very helpful.'

'Thank you, I'll do that. And flea powder? Do you recommend Coopers or Smythsons?'

Quin, who had vaguely gathered that Verena was off on some kind of journey with her Croft-Ellis cousins, came down in favour of Coopers and made his way to his room, leaving Kenneth in a state of deep depression. The sacrifices he had made for Verena were considerable. He travelled fourteen stations on the Underground to partner her in squash; he had stopped saying 'mirror' and 'serviette' both of which, it seemed, were common, and been corrected when he mispronounced Featherstonehaugh. And yet every time she saw the Professor, Verena bridled and simpered like a schoolgirl. There were times, thought Kenneth, when one wondered if it was all worthwhile.

'I am leaving,' announced Heini. 'I'm going to look for another room.'

Leonie stared at the wild-haired youth who had come back in a towering rage after spending Saturday in town.

'But why, Heini? What has happened?'

'I can't discuss it, but I have to leave. I'm too upset to stay here. I can't even play.'

This was not strictly true. Heini had been home for half an hour and had considerably decreased the life expectancy of the hired piano by crashing through the Busoni Variations so as to send the dishes rattling on the sideboard.

'Does Ruth know?' asked Leonie nervously.

'Not yet. But she will not be surprised,' said Heini darkly.

'Oh, dear. If you've quarrelled . . . I mean, that does happen.'

'Not this,' said Heini obscurely. 'This does not happen. I'll leave as soon as I've found somewhere to go.'

Warring emotions clashed in Leonie's breast. Ruth would be upset and Leonie would do anything to spare her daughter pain. Yet the thought of Heini being elsewhere rose like an image of Paradise in her mind. To be able to wander in and out of her sitting room at will, to be able to put her feet up in the afternoon . . . To be able to get into the bathroom!

Not knowing what to say, she retreated into the kitchen where Mishak was looking at the pages of a gardening catalogue lent to him by the lady two houses down.

'Heini says he is leaving. I think he and Ruth have had some dreadful quarrel.'

Mishak looked up. 'Where will he go?'

'I don't know. He says he's going to look for another room.'

'And how will he pay for it?'

Heini had, of course, been living rent-free; the money he had brought from Budapest having been used up long ago.

'I don't know. But he's very determined.'

In Mishak's mind, as in Leonie's, there rose a vision of Number 27 without Heini. He imagined hearing the blackbirds in the morning, the rustle of wind in the trees.

'Do you think he'll want any supper?' asked Leonie, preparing to mix the pancakes which, when filled with scraps of various sorts, could fill up large numbers of people at very little expense. 'He was very upset.'

'He will want supper,' said Mishak, and was proved right.

It was Ruth who did not want supper. Ruth who phoned to say she would be late . . . and who was walking the streets wringing her hands like a Victorian heroine. Ruth who felt disgraced and shamed and wished the earth would open up and swallow her . . .

For after all, it had happened, the thing she had dreaded that night on the Orient Express. It was prophetic, all the reading she had done there on the Grundlsee. They had not minced their words, those behavioural experts with their three-volumed tomes: Havelock Ellis and Krafft-Ebing and a particularly alarming man called Eugene Feuermann. It was not for nothing that they had devoted chapter after chapter to one of the great scourges of those who seek fulfilment in the act of love.

Anything would have been better than what had happened. There were chapters on nymphomania too, but Ruth would have settled for that. Nymphomania might end badly, but it sounded generous and giving. Someone with nymphomania might expect to live utterly and die whereas . . .

Why me? thought Ruth, when I was so much looking forward to being with him. And what would Janet say? Could one even mention it to Janet who was so bountiful in the backs of motor cars?

The word drummed in her ear – the dreaded word which branded her as ice cold, as having splinters in her heart as if the Snow Queen herself had put them there. It had begun to drizzle and she pulled up the hood of her loden cape, but the bad weather suited her. Why should the sun shine ever again on someone who was the subject of two whole chapters and a set of tables in Feuermann's *Sexual Psychopathology*?

Ruth walked for one hour, and two . . . and then, tainted or not, she made her way to the Underground. Sooner or later she would have to face Heini and to add cowardice to coldness would solve nothing.

'Come in.'

Fräulein Lutzenholler sat in her dressing-gown drinking a cup of cocoa with a wrinkled skin, which she had made earlier, spilling the milk. Above her hung the portrait of the couch she had used to see patients in

Breslau, a small blue flame hissed in the gas fire, and she was not at all pleased to see Ruth.

'I am going to bed,' she announced.

Ruth entered, her hair in disarray, her eyelids swollen. 'I know; I'm sorry. And I know you can't help me because I can't pay you and psychoanalysis only works if you pay the person who's doing it.'

'And in any case I am not permitted to practise in England,' said Fräulein Lutzenholler firmly.

'But I thought you might know if there's anything I can do.' It had been difficult to come into the analyst's uninviting room and after her remarks about the lost papers on the bus, Ruth had sworn never to consult her again, but it seemed one couldn't escape one's fate. 'I am so unhappy, you see, and I thought there might be something I haven't understood about my childhood. Something I have repressed.'

Fräulein Lutzenholler sighed and put down her cup. 'Is it true that Heini is moving away?' she asked.

Ruth nodded, and something that was almost a smile passed over the analyst's features, lightening the moustache on her upper lip.

'It is not so simple, repression,' she said.

'No. But I know that if you see something awful when you are small . . . if your parents . . . you know if you find them making love. But I never did. When Papa had his afternoon rest everyone crept about and my mother sat in the drawing room with her embroidery like a Grenadier Guard shushing everybody. And anyway our flat had double doors, you couldn't hear

398

anything. And on the Grundlsee I always fell asleep very quickly because of all that fresh air and though the maids told me about Frau Pollack always wanting gherkins before she let her husband come to her, I don't think it was a trauma and anyway I haven't repressed it. And I can't think –'

Fräulein Lutzenholler frowned. The good humour caused by the news that Heini was leaving had evaporated and she was worried about her hot-water bottle. She had filled it half an hour before and liked to get into bed while it was still in peak condition.

'What are you talking about?' she said, spooning the cocoa skin into her mouth. 'I don't understand you.'

Ruth, who had shied away from the word all day, now pronounced it.

There was a pause. Fräulein Lutzenholler looked at the clock. 'Ruth, it is a quarter to eleven. I cannot discuss this with you now. It is a technical problem and there can be very many causes; physiological, psychological . . .'

'Oh, please . . . please help me!'

Fräulein Lutzenholler stifled a yawn.

'Very well, tell me what happened.'

Ruth began to speak. Her words tumbled over each other, tears sprang to her eyes, her hair fell over her face and was roughly pushed away.

To these outpourings of a tortured soul, Fräulein Lutzenholler listened with increasing and evident displeasure. She put her soiled cup back in its saucer. She frowned.

'Please understand, Ruth, that technical terms are not there as playthings for amateurs. There is nothing I can do to help you and I now wish to go to bed.'

'Yes . . . I'm sorry.'

Ruth wiped her eyes and rose to go. She had reached the door when Fräulein Lutzenholler uttered – and in English – a single sentence.

'Per'aps,' she said, 'you do not lof 'im.'

A few days later, Heini announced that after all he would stay. His stint of room hunting had shaken him: rents were exorbitant, there were absurd restrictions on practising and, of course, no one provided food. With the first round of the competition only six weeks away, he owed it to everyone to provide himself with the best conditions for his work. There was also Mantella. Heini's agent had planned an interview with the press at which Ruth was to be present. If Heini could not altogether forgive her, he was determined not to harbour a grudge and as the spring term moved towards Easter, a kind of truce was established in Belsize Park.

Among Verena's many excellent qualities could be numbered a thirst for learned gatherings, especially those with receptions afterwards at which, as the daughter of Thameside's Vice Chancellor, she was invariably introduced to the participants.

Her reason for attending a lecture at the Geophysical Society was, however, rather more personal. The subject – Cretaceous Volcanism – was one which she was certain would interest Quin, and seeing the Professor out of hours was now her main objective.

But when she took her seat in the society's lecture theatre, Quin was nowhere to be seen. Instead, on her left, was a small, dapper man with a carefully combed moustache and slightly vulgar two-coloured shoes who introduced himself as Dr Brille-Lamartaine, and showed a tendency to remain by her side even when she moved through into the room where drinks and canapés awaited them.

'An excellent lecture, I think?' said the little man, who turned out to be a Belgian geologist of some distinction. 'I expected to see Professor Somerville here, but he is not.'

Verena agreed that he was not, and asked where he had met the Professor.

'I was with 'im in India. On his last expedition,' said Brille-Lamartaine, taking a glass of wine from the passing tray but rejecting the canapés, for prawns, in this country, were always a risk. 'I was instrumental in leading 'im to the caves where we 'ave made our most important finds.'

He sighed, for Milner, that morning, had told him something that distressed him deeply.

'How interesting,' said Verena, who was indeed anxious to hear more. 'Did you enjoy the trip?'

'Yes, yes. Very much. There were accidents, of course . . . my spectacles were destroyed . . . and the provisions were not what I would have expected. But Professor Somerville is a great man . . . obstinate . . . he would not listen to many things I told him, but a great man. Because I have been on his expedition, they have made me a Fellow of the Belgian Academy of Sciences. But now he is finished.'

'Finished? What on earth do you mean?'

'He takes a woman on his next expedition! A woman to the Kulamali Gorge . . . one of his students with whom he has fallen in love. I tell you, this is the end. I will not go with him . . . I know what will happen.' He took a second glass of wine and mopped his brow, pursued by hideous images. A naked woman with loose, lewd hair crawling into the safari tent . . . hanging her underwear on the line strung between thorn trees . . . She would soon hear of his private fortune and make suggestions: Somerville was known to be someone who did not wish to marry. 'I have great respect for the Professor,' he said, draining his glass and drawing closer to Verena who was not at all like the Lillith of his imagination . . . who was in fact very like his maiden aunt in Ghent, 'but this is the end!'

'Wait a minute, Dr Brille-Lamartaine, are you sure he is taking one of his students? And a woman?'

The Belgian nodded. 'I am sure. His assistant told me yesterday – he is completely in the Professor's confidence. The Professor has fallen in love with a girl in his class who is very high-born and very brilliant. It is a secret because she must not be favoured, but in June he will declare 'imself. I tell you, women must not go on these journeys, it is always a disaster, I hav' seen it. There is jealousy, there is intrigue . . . and they wear

402

nothing underneath.' He drained his glass and wiped his brow once more. 'You will say nothing, I know,' he said. 'Oh, there is Sir Neville Willington – you will excuse me?'

'Yes,' said Verena. 'Yes, indeed.'

She could not wait, now, to be alone. If any confirmation was needed, this was it! Not that she had really doubted Quin, but his continuing silence sometimes confused her. But how could he speak while she was still his student? Only last week a Cambridge professor had been dismissed because of his involvement with an undergraduate: she had been foolish all along imagining that Quin could declare himself at this stage. And she wasn't even going to demand marriage before they sailed. Marriage would come, of course, when he saw how perfectly they were matched, but she would not make it a condition.

So now for her First and for being even fitter – if that was possible – than she had been before!

Frances usually came down to London only twice a year; in November for her Christmas shopping and in May for the Chelsea Flower Show.

This year, however, the wedding of her goddaughter – the niece of Lydia Barchester who had come to grief when retreating backwards from Their Majesties – brought her to London at the end of March. She came under protest, as the result of fierce bullying by Martha who had decreed that she needed a new dress and, in particular, new shoes.

'Nonsense,' said Frances. 'I bought some shoes for the Godchester christening.'

'That was twelve years ago,' said Martha.

Frances detested buying anything for her personal adornment, but if it had to be done then it had to be done at Fortnum's in Piccadilly. Displeased, she took Martha's shopping list and headed south with Harris in the Buick. Beside her on the seat was a cardboard box padded with wood shavings and containing a dozen dark brown bulbs which, after some hesitation, she had dug out of her garden on the previous day.

When in London, Frances did not stay with Quin, whose flat she regarded as faintly disreputable and liable to yield French actresses or dancing girls. She dined with him, but she stayed at Brown's Hotel where nothing ever changed, and sent Harris to his married sister in Peckham.

Her day had been carefully planned, yet when she found Harris waiting the next morning with the car, the instructions she gave him surprised even herself.

'Take me to Number 27 Belsize Close,' she said.

Harris raised his eyebrows. 'That's Hampstead, isn't it?'

'Nearly. It's off Haverstock Hill.'

Now why? thought Frances, already regretting her impulse. She was seeing Quin that evening – why not give the bulbs to him to pass on to Ruth?

The streets as they drove north became meaner, shabbier, and as Harris stopped to ask the way, they

404

were given instructions by a gesticulating, scarcely comprehensible foreigner in a large black hat.

Number 27 was all that she had feared; a dilapidated lodging house, the door unpainted, the wood sagging in the window frames. A cat foraged in the dustbins; the paving stones were cracked.

'I won't be long,' she told Harris, and made her way up the steps.

Leonie, enjoying the calm of her sitting room, for Heini had gone to see his agent, heard the bell, went downstairs and saw an unknown, gaunt lady in dark purple tweeds, and behind her an unmistakably expensive, though ancient, motor car with a uniformed chauffeur.

'I can help you?' said Leonie – and then: 'Are you perhaps the aunt of Professor Somerville?'

'Good heavens, woman, how did you know?'

'There is a look . . . and Ruth has spoken of you. Please come in.' Then, with the sudden panic which assails women the world over at an unexpected apparition: 'There is nothing wrong at the university? All is well with the Professor . . . and with Ruth?'

'Yes, yes,' said Miss Somerville impatiently, wondering again why she had come. The house was appalling: the worn lino, the smell of cheap disinfectant . . . 'I brought some bulbs for your uncle. You are Mrs Berger, I take it? Ruth mentioned that he liked autumn crocus and I have more than I know what to do with. Would you please give them to him?'

'For Mishak?' Leonie's face lit up. 'Oh, he will be so

pleased! He is in the garden now, you must of course take them yourself – he will want to thank you. And I will make us a cup of coffee. No; tea, of course . . . I forget!'

'No, thank you. I won't stay.'

'But you must! First I will show you the garden . . . it is best to go through the house because the side door is stuck.'

Frances followed her reluctantly. Now it was going to be impossible to get out of an invitation to drink tea. Foreigners could never make it properly and she would probably be expected to eat something sickly with a spoon.

Mishak was digging his potato patch – and as he straightened and turned towards them, Frances was gripped by a fierce, an overwhelming disappointment.

I have come to fetch you, he had said to Marianne, opening his briefcase, lifting his hat, and she had imagined a dapper little man in an expensive overcoat, a man of the world. But this was an old refugee, a foreigner in a crumpled jacket and cloth cap, shabby and poor and strange. It was all she could do to force herself to approach him.

Leonie explained their errand and Mishak leant his spade against the fence.

'Autumn crocus?' he said. 'Ruth told me how they grow under the cherry tree.'

He took the box, pushed aside the shavings. His hands, as he searched for the bulbs, were earth-stained, square and stumpy-fingered. Hands that planted and

406

mended, that hammered and turned screws. Not really foreign; not really strange . . .

'Yes,' said Mishak, touching a bulb. 'How I remember them!' He didn't even thank her; he only smiled.

The tea was excellent, but Frances could not stay.

'I have to shop,' she said wearily.

Leonie's eyes lit up. 'Where do you go?'

'Fortnum's in Piccadilly.'

'Ah, that is a wonderful place,' said Leonie wistfully. 'You buy a dress?'

Frances nodded. 'And shoes.'

'What kind of shoes?' It was Mishak who spoke, and Frances glared at him as shocked as if it was a tree which had dared to interest itself in her concerns.

'The same as I always buy,' she said testily. 'Brown strap shoes with a side button and low heel.'

'No,' said Mishak.

'I *beg* your pardon?' Frances was unable to believe her ears.

'Not strap shoes. Not low heels. Not buttons,' said Mishak. 'Fortunati pumps with a Cuban heel, in kid. From the Milan workshops; they use a different last.'

Leonie nodded. 'He knows. He worked for many years in my father's department store.'

Frances was in no way appeased. 'Certainly not! I wouldn't dream of it. I've had the same shoes for years and I haven't the slightest intention of changing now.'

'You have a high arch; it is a gift,' said Mishak. He felt in his pocket for his pipe, remembered that it was

407

filled with the stumps of cigars which Ziller brought from the Hungarian restaurant, and abandoned it.

'Anyway, no one sees what I wear up there,' said Frances, still glowering.

'God sees,' said Mishak.

Ruth, coming in late from the university, heard about Miss Somerville's visit and was instantly transformed.

'Oh, what did she say? Tell me, Mishak – tell me everything she said! Did she talk about the garden?'

'Yes, she did. They've had a hard winter, but the alpine gentians are almost out, and the magnolias.'

'What about glassing in that bit of the south wall by the sundial? Is she going to do it? She wanted to see if she could grow a lapageria so far north – everyone said she couldn't and you can imagine the effect that had on her!'

'I believe she means to; yes.'

He exchanged a glance with Leonie. They had not seen Ruth look like this for weeks.

'Oh, Mishak, it was so beautiful up there, you can't believe it! It's so *clean* and everything has its own smell, completely distinct, and the air keeps moving and moving. There must be more air there than anywhere in the world! Did she tell you whether Elsie has got on to the WEA course in Botany?'

'No, she didn't. Who is Elsie?'

'She's the housemaid. She's really interested in plants and so nice! And what about Mrs Ridley's grandmother – I told you about her – she was going to be a hundred in February.' She looked up, suddenly afraid. 'She's still alive, isn't she? She *must* be – she was so looking forward to her telegram from the King.'

'We didn't speak of her either,' said Mishak.

'I suppose the lambs will just be being born – John Ridley said the end of March. They're like sheep in the bible up there, so clean, and you can hear them cropping the turf . . . And it's full of rock roses; and the birds . . .' She shook her head, but it wouldn't go away; sometimes she thought it would never go away, the vision of blond grass and blue sky and the white horses of the sea.

'But she told me about the little dog,' said Mishak. 'She's keeping it and they're calling it Daniel. She said I should tell you and you would understand.'

'Daniel? Oh, yes – of course.' So Miss Somerville had not betrayed her foolishness on the journey to the Farnes. 'After Wagner's stepdaughter – you know, Cosima von Bülow's daughter, Daniella, only it's a male, of course. Yes, that's good! He looks like a Daniel – God help any lions if he gets into their den; he's really fierce!'

Leonie, who had been listening to this conversation with increasing puzzlement now said: 'But, Ruth, you see Professor Somerville every day. Why don't you ask him about these things yourself? Whether the old grandmother is dead or the lambs are born? He must know.'

Ruth flushed. 'I wouldn't talk to him about Bowmont;

it's none of my business – and anyway he's always working; he's incredibly busy this term.'

Busy and abstracted and not at all friendly . . . And there were rumours that he was leaving.

She took out her lecture notes, but before she could settle down to work, the door opened and Heini came in. It was a quarter to ten, too late to practise without incurring the wrath of Fräulein Lutzenholler and he now went to sit disconsolately on the sofa, avoiding Ruth's eyes. It was a fortnight since the meeting in Janet's flat and he had still not forgiven her properly, but as she pushed back her notes and went to make him a cup of cocoa, Ruth understood what she had to do. For it was not only Mishak and Leonie who had learnt something from Miss Somerville's visit. Ruth herself had obtained rather more insight into her own mind than she cared for – and now it was necessary to act.

And this meant changing the way she had been thinking. It meant repudiating her goat-herding grandmother and the consolations of her mother's Catholic faith. It meant saying goodbye to the Baby Jesus in his crib and the consoling angels with their feathered wings, and calling on her other heritage: the stern, ancient and mysterious Jewish faith where the word of the rabbis was law and it was the God of the Ten Commandments and not of the Sermon on the Mount who reigned supreme. It was there that she would be cured of her disability and find her way back to Heini. She had not quite wanted to admit kinship with those black-bearded, shut-off figures in their skull caps . . . the

Hassidim wandering poverty-stricken through Polish forests, the thirteen-year-old boys who studied and chanted like old men, ruining their eyes. Yet it was in the traditions of just those people that she would find deliverance.

The laws of England had failed her – or she, with her carelessness had failed them. Mr Proudfoot could not give Heini what he needed, but there were other and older laws she could evoke.

It would take courage – a great deal of courage – but she knew now what she had to do.

25

She tried not to run . . . tried to keep to a decorous walk, but it was impossible because she *had* to get there quickly. To Quin's flat while her resolution held . . . to Quin who even now might save her.

She was beside the river, on a path between the Thames and the road with its busy end-of-the-day traffic. The lamps had just been lit, their reflections shone on the water, for the tide was high and the current raced out towards the sea.

'Oh, God, let him be in,' she prayed. 'Let him be in and alone!'

But what right had she to pray? She wasn't even a proper sinner who was entitled to the Almighty's ear; she was a cold rejective failure. God hated the mean in spirit, she was sure of that. Or would he have understood about Krafft-Ebing and Havelock Ellis and the terrifying Eugene Feuermann? Would he think of her as simply ill and heed her after all?

It had been raining ever since she came out of the

Underground; fine, slanting rain which soaked through her loden cape. Leonie had taken the hood off for relining; the cloak was dreadfully shabby, and her hair too was sodden. Not that that mattered – perhaps the rain would wash her clean once more.

A street sign opposite said Cheyne Walk, and she saw the crescent of Regency houses and the shapes of the fine trees in the gardens.

'Henry the Eighth had a palace there,' Quin had told her in Vienna, talking about his London home. 'You can see a mulberry from my window that's supposed to have been planted by Elizabeth the First. Not likely, but a nice idea.'

All the trees in the gardens of the tall houses looked as though they might have been planted by a queen. There were streaks of orange and amethyst still in the west, and turning she could see the necklace of lights on the Albert Bridge. It was a beautiful street. Well, of course. Quin was rich, he could live where he liked whereas she and Heini had had to make do with Janet's flat. Perhaps that was why it had all gone so wrong.

But it was no good blaming anyone. The fault lay in herself. Only not entirely, perhaps. If Quin would only do what she asked it might still come right.

She was passing the wrought-iron gates of the houses now; the elegant carriage lamps, and the graceful fan windows which sent semicircles of light out onto the steps. There was no need to peer at house numbers. She had seen the Crossley at once, parked outside the door. Best to get it over then – and she walked resolutely up to the door and rang the bell.

Quin put down his pen, frowning. He had counted on a couple of hours' work before dinner. It was Lockwood's weekend off; he'd taken the phone off the hook and planned to finish his paper for the museum journal.

'Good God! Ruth!' And seeing her face, 'What is it?' Are you in trouble?'

She shook out her hair like a dog and followed him upstairs. 'Yes, I am. I'm in very serious trouble.' She spoke in her native language, her words gaining an extra and metaphysical weight.

'Come in and get warm.'

He took the sodden cloak from her shoulders and led her into the drawing room, but though the curtains were drawn back, she did not go to the window, nor to the grate where a bright fire was burning. Instead she held out her hands to him, the palms upwards in the age-old gesture of beseechment.

'I can't stay. I just want you to do something for me. Something terribly important.'

'What is it, my dear? Just tell me.'

Her head went up. Her entreating eyes held his.

'I want you to divorce me. Completely and absolutely. This minute. *Now*.'

There was a pause. Then Quin, schooling his expression, said carefully: 'I will, of course, do anything I can to help you. But I'm not quite clear how I can divorce you *now*. Dick Proudfoot is doing –'

'No!' she interrupted. 'It's nothing to do with Mr

414

Proudfoot and documents and things. It's much more fundamental than that. It's to do with undoing a curse.'

'I beg your pardon?'

'I'm sorry. I don't mean that our wedding was a curse. But I knew when we said those words before witnesses . . . I mean, you might think if someone has bunions and cuts the sides out of their slippers it wouldn't feel like a wedding, but bunions can't stop oaths from mattering. So you have to absolve me and I know how you can do it because I asked Mrs Weiss. She wasn't good about Hanukkah, but she knew about divorce and so did Paul Ziller, and anyway I knew before that. All you have to do is say "I divorce you, I divorce you, I divorce you", three times. With your hand on my shoulder, I think, but I'm not sure about that. It's an old Jewish law, truly, and it dissolves the marriage then and there. You should say it in front of a rabbi, but just saying it and really meaning it is what counts. Really repudiating me and wanting to be free. Only *you* have to say it – the man – because the old Jews were like that; it was the men who counted. And I know if you did it, things would get better. They might even be all right.'

She subsided, running out of breath, and as Quin was silent: 'You will do it, won't you?' she begged. 'If you said "I divorce *thee*" it might be better. More biblical.' And as Quin moved towards the door, she added anxiously: 'Where are you going?'

Quin did not answer. She heard him cross the landing; then he came back carrying a large white towel.

'Come here,' he ordered. 'Sit down on the sofa. Next to the fire.'

She came, puzzled but obedient, and sat down.

'What are you going to do?'

'Bend your head.'

'But –'

'You came to your wedding with wet hair. At least you can come to your divorce with it dry.'

As he spoke he began to towel her hair – but this was not what she wanted. This was not right. There was nothing in Old Testamental lore about having your hair dried by a husband who was putting you away and she tried to pull back, but it wasn't like that. It was very peaceful and his hands . . .

But as he moved away from her scalp and down to the loose hair on her shoulders she became angry. For she could *see* his hands now and they had been a trouble to her from the start. When she was five years old, her father had brought back a book of Donatello sculptures from Italy and one night when she wasn't well, he had shown her the plates.

'A person can't have made that,' she had said, sitting on his knee. 'It's too beautiful. It must have come from a shop.'

It was the left hand of John the Baptist she had been looking at: the long fingers, one crooked to hold a scroll in place, the sinewy line leading to the wrist.

Now it was all going on again as Quin towelled her hair . . . as it had gone on in the museum when he helped her sort the cave bear bones . . . on the Orient Express when he cracked a walnut and laid it on her plate . . . and endlessly when he jabbed, poked at, emptied and almost never lit his pipe.

'No, please, you must *stop*.' She put up her arm to seize his wrist, but that was a mistake. Quite a big one really.

Quin folded the towel, carried it out of the room, and returned with a small glass containing a liquid the colour of a Stradivarius.

'Now,' he said. 'Drink this. It'll warm you. And then tell me very quietly what all this is about.'

Ruth took the glass, sniffed, drained the Grand Armagnac. A small 'Oh!' of appreciation escaped her. She repressed it, called on her resources.

'What it is about,' she said, putting up her chin, 'is . . . frigidity.'

Quin's expression did not change. Only his eyebrows rose a fraction as he waited.

'Proper, awful, medical frigidity, like in a book. Like I was reading about on the Grundlsee. Like in Havelock Ellis and Krafft-Ebing and Eugene Feuermann. I must have had a premonition because why would I read about it when I could have been reading *Heidi* or *What Katy Did*?'

'One does wonder,' murmured Quin.

'I think I've always dreaded it most of all. Being cold. Not responding. Lying there like a log.'

'Is that what you did?'

Now his expression *had* changed; the nails bit into his palm, but Ruth was looking at the floor.

'Not exactly, because I didn't *lie*. But effectively.'

'This is Heini, I suppose? That is what we are talking about?'

Ruth nodded. 'I told you Heini had changed his mind about Chopin and the études and he is preparing for this very important competition and he is going to play Lizst's Dante Sonata which is all about the Eternal Feminine and he wanted . . . love. He said so on Christmas Eve and it was very moving. And when I left the annulment papers on the bus, it didn't seem any good waiting till we could be married, so I arranged everything and Janet was very helpful and lent us her flat. She even gave me a bottle of wine – it was a Liebfraumilch from the Co-op, but it didn't taste like the wine we had on the Orient Express.'

'No,' said Quin gravely. 'It wouldn't do. I have to say that Liebfraumilch from the Co-op might make anyone frigid.'

But to speak lightly was an effort. He wanted to strangle Heini slowly and with his bare hands.

'Oh, please, it isn't funny! It's a frightful condition. Krafft-Ebing says the causes are often psychological, but how could I ever afford to find out what awful thing I saw my parents do – and Fräulein Lutzenholler is a dreadful woman. She's supposed to be a professional and all she can do is drink cocoa with the skin on and babble about love. And if it's physical that's worse because you *know* how complicated the nervous system is and I don't want to have operations.'

Quin had mastered himself. 'Look, Ruth, the first

time people make love is often a disaster. It's a thing that has to be learnt and —'

'Yes but how *can* it be? How can it be learnt if people are so frigid that there never *is* a first time? If they take their sweater off and then put it on again and run away down the fire escape? How can they ever get it right when they don't even *do* it?'

Quin rose and went to the window. It struck him that the view was the most beautiful, possibly, in the world, and that he must be careful not to smile. 'You mean you never got as far as making love at all?'

'No. And it's so awful because Heini took such trouble getting the contraception things from the machine and getting cream chocolate instead and then I rushed out into the night like a frightened hen. He's scarcely spoken to me since and you can't blame him.'

Quin came back and sat down beside her on the sofa. 'And why do you think me saying "I divorce you" three times would make it better?'

Ruth looked at her empty glass, then down at the carpet. 'You see, I want to be liberated and giving and, of course, I love Heini very much. But my family . . . it's difficult to get away from one's upbringing and they *are* old-fashioned and marriage has always been . . . marriage. Even ones like ours that aren't proper ones. And I thought, maybe it isn't just my nervous system being deformed or having seen something horrible in a haystack on the Grundlsee. Maybe some part of me is going to go on running down fire escapes till I'm *un*married. Which is why I want you please to do this thing now. It's perfectly valid, I promise you.' She looked about her and her eyes rested on two silver candlesticks on the mantelpiece. 'We could light some candles,' she said. 'That would make it more solemn.'

'So we could,' he said. He got up, carried the fluted candlesticks to the low table, lit a match.

'Now,' he said.

She turned to him. 'Now you're going to do it?' she asked breathlessly.

'Well, no,' he said apologetically. 'What I'm going to do now is not exactly that. What I'm going to do now, is kiss you.'

'Oh, God – you mustn't go away! I shall die at *once* if you leave me.'

He turned to where she lay beside him on the pillow. The window framed the night sky and the constellations named for the heroines of legend: Andromeda, the Pleiades . . . She belonged in their company now, this gallant girl who had taken her first journey into love.

'I was going to get us something to eat,' he said. 'It's nearly midnight. You must be starving.' He ran his fingers down the curve of her cheek, her throat; gathered a handful of her tresses. '*I am looped in the loops of her hair*,' he murmured, his face in the hollow of her shoulder.

'Miss Kenmore didn't teach me that,' said Ruth, not pleased with this gap in her education.

'No. We have rather moved out of Kenmore country.'

A long way out of it. He had evidently decided against killing her by getting out of bed and as she folded herself against him, she realized that she must be careful not actually to *become* him, which would be impractical. Then suddenly she drew away.

'Quin, something terrible has happened! I haven't had my *tristesse*!' She gazed at him, her eyes huge. 'You know, the thing you have afterwards. Total despair. *Postcoital tristesse*, it's called. It's in all the books! It's when you realize that in spite of everything, every human soul is tragically and hopelessly alone, and I don't feel it at all; I feel absolutely marvellous. I *told* you I wasn't like other people.'

'No,' he said rather shakily. 'You're not in the least like other people. If you were, all the gods would come down from Olympus and proclaim Paradise on Earth.' And presently: 'We'll eat later.'

But later, quite suddenly, he fell asleep and she followed him into his imagined dreams as he twitched, chased into a Utrillo landscape of rich green trees and hounds and huntsmen in scarlet – and she vowed to keep awake because she must miss nothing of this night, not one instant . . . but she did sleep in the end, briefly, and woke up in wonderment because she understood now what people meant when they said: 'She slept with him.' That it was part of the act of love, this sharing of oblivion.

When he too woke it was suddenly and with contrition. 'Now you *shall* eat, my poor love,' he said, and they went into the kitchen hand in hand because she

421

wasn't prepared to be separated from him even for as long as it took to cross the hallway, and had a picnic of bread and cheese and a wine that was not very much like the Liebfraumilch that she had drunk in Janet's flat.

'Oh, I'm so *hungry*,' said Ruth, and she seemed to be tasting food for the first time. And pausing with a hunk of Emmentaler in her hand: 'Do you think it will come later, the *tristesse*? The terrible, tragic hopelessness – the feeling that everyone is really alone?'

'I am not alone,' said Quin, coming round behind her, holding her. 'And nor are you. We shall never be alone again.'

When they had eaten, they opened the French windows and stood looking out at the sleeping city and the river which never slept. Wrapped in Quin's dressing-gown, feeling his warmth beside her, she took great breaths of the night air.

'*Sweet Thames run softly till I end my song*,' she quoted. 'I may not know improper poems about people's hair, but Miss Kenmore taught me a *lot* of Spenser. I love it so much, this river.'

'I too,' said Quin. 'As a matter of fact I think I might go in for some bottle-throwing on my own account. I shall go out tomorrow and buy a thousand lemonade bottles and put a note in each and every one and drop them from the bridge.'

'What will they say, the notes? What will you put in them?'

He turned his head, surprised at her obtuseness. 'Your name, of course. What else?'

Hand in hand, still, they wandered back to bed. 'It's strange,' said Ruth. 'I thought love would be like the slow movement of the Mozart Sinfonia Concertante . . . or like one of those uplifting paintings my mother used to take me to look at with putti and clouds and golden rays . . . or even like the sea. But it isn't, is it?'

'No. Love is like itself.'

'Yes.' She sighed . . . curled herself, warm and relaxed and pliant against his side.

But when presently she indicated that in spite of her deep frigidity and the *tristesse* which she expected at any moment, she was, so to speak, *there*, and he gathered her into his arms, he did not use any of the endearments in either of the languages which they spoke.

Clearly and quietly in the darkness, Quin said: 'My wife.'

26

He had dropped Ruth off at the corner of her street soon after it was light. Now, punctually at nine o'clock, he parked the Crossley outside the elegant premises of Cavour and Stattersley, Jewellers, since 1763, to His Majesty the King, and made his way up the steps.

It had come to him unbidden – this uncharacteristic desire to buy her a present that was sumptuous beyond reason; a useless, costly gift that would blazen his love to the skies. Uncharacteristic because there was no such tradition at Bowmont – no family tiara stowed in the bank and brought out for high days and holidays; no Somerville *parure* handed down through the generations. His grandmother had kept her Quaker faith and her Quaker ways; Aunt Frances possessed one cameo brooch which appeared, listing slightly, on the black chenille on New Year's Eve.

But now for Ruth – for his newly discovered wife – he wanted to make a gesture that would resound through the coming generations, a proclamation! The times were against it, his conscience too: as he passed through the wide doors held open by a flunkey, the orphans of Abyssinia, the unemployed, stretched out imaginary hands to him, but to no avail. Later they would be sensible, he and Ruth: they would plough and sow and make rights of way; they would sponsor yet more opera-loving cowmen, but now, instantly, he would send a priceless, senseless gift to his beloved, and she would rise from her bed and *know*!

Thus Quin, walking lightly up the steps between the little box trees in tubs – and Mr Cavour, seeing him coming, metaphorically licked his lips.

'What had you in mind?' he asked when Quin had been shown to a blue velvet chair beside a rosewood desk. In the show cases, lit like treasures of the Hermitage, were Fabergé Easter eggs, earrings trembling with showers of crystal, a butterfly brooch worn by the exiled Spanish Queen. 'What kind of gems, for example?'

Quin smiled, aware that he was cutting a slightly absurd figure: a man willing to mortgage himself for a gift with only the haziest notions of its nature. What gems *did* he have in mind? Diamonds? Sinbad had found a valley filled with them; they were lodged in the brains of serpents and carried aloft in eagle's bills. The Orlov diamond had been plucked from the eye of an Indian idol . . . the Great Mogul, the most famous jewel in antiquity, was the favourite treasure of Shah Jahan.

Were diamonds right for Ruth, with her warmth, her

425

snub nose and funniness? Was there too much ice there for his new-found wife?

'Or we have a ruby *parure*,' said Mr Cavour. 'The stones are from the Mogok mines; unmatchable. The true pigeon's blood colour. They were sold to an American by the Grand Duchess Tromatoff and they're just back on the market.'

Quin pondered. Mogok, near Mandalay . . . paddy fields . . . temples . . . He had been there, making a detour after an earlier expedition and had seen the mines. Why not rubies with their inner fire?

'And there is a pearl and sapphire necklace which you would be hard put to match anywhere in the world. Someone is interested in it, but if you wished to make a definite offer . . .' He flicked at an underling. 'Go on down to the safe, Ted, and get Number 509.'

Quin's mind was still in free fall, pursuing he knew not what. The Profane Venus was always painted richly dressed in a fillet of pearls. It was the Celestial Venus that they painted naked, for they knew, those wise men of the Renaissance, that nakedness was pure. Either was all right with him: Ruth in her loden cape, loaded with jewels; Ruth without it at midnight, eating a peach.

The box was brought, snapped open. The necklace was superb.

'Yes . . . it's very beautiful,' said Quin absently.

Then suddenly it came, the clue, the allusion . . . the thing he had been waiting for: Ruth, barefoot with windblown hair, coming towards him on Bowmont

426

beach, cupping something in her hand. 'Look,' she was saying, 'Oh, *look*!'

He rose, waved away the necklace. 'It's all right,' he said. 'I know now what it has to be. I know exactly!'

His next errand did not take him long.

Dick Proudfoot had returned from Madeira, sun-tanned and pleased with life. He had also produced four watercolours of which only three displeased him. Now, however, he looked down at the complicated document, with its seals and tassels – a replica of the first which his clerk had brought in when Professor Somerville appeared unexpectedly in the office – and up again at Quin.

'*What* did you say?'

'You heard me! I want you to tear the thing up. I'm stopping the annulment. I'm staying married.'

Proudfoot leaned back in his chair and folded his hands behind his head.

'Well, well. I can't say I'm surprised.' He grinned. 'Allow me to congratulate you.'

It struck him that he had not seen Quin look so relaxed and happy for a long time. The volcanic craters were missing; there was peace in those alert, enquiring eyes. Proudfoot pulled the document towards him, tore it in two, dropped it in the wastepaper basket. 'Quite apart from anything else, it's a great relief – we were on pretty dodgy ground all along. Will you be living at Bowmont?'

'Yes. She fits the place like a glove – she was only

427

there a few days, yet everyone remembers her: the shepherd, the housemaids . . . it's uncanny!' For a moment, a slight shadow fell over his face. 'The trouble is, I've set up this trip to Africa.'

But even as he spoke, Quin realized what he would do. The climate on the plains was healthy; the trip was not hazardous – and in an emergency Ruth could always stay with the Commissioner and his wife at Lindi.

'Do you want me to write to Ruth?'

'No; I'll tell her myself. And thanks, Dick, you've been splendid. If you send your account to Chelsea I'll settle it before I go.'

He had reached the door when Proudfoot called him back. 'Have you got a minute?'

Though he was impatient to be gone, Quin nodded. Dick went to a bureau by the wall, opened a drawer, took out a small painting: a feathery tamarisk, each brush stroke as light as gossamer, against a mass of scarlet geraniums.

'I did it in Madeira. Do you think she'd like it? Ruth?'

'I'm sure she would.'

'I'll get it framed then and send it along.'

Out in the street, Quin looked at his watch. Ruth should have received his gift by now – Cavour had promised to send it instantly. Light-headed from lack of sleep and the conviction that he would live for ever, he turned his car towards the museum. It shouldn't be difficult to book an extra cabin on the boat, but he'd better put Milner on to it right away. And how very agreeable to know that Brille-Lamartaine, if he chose to make further enquiries, would learn nothing but the truth. For he *was* taking along a woman, one of his own students . . . and one with whom he was passionately in love!

Ruth had not expected to go to sleep after she left Quin. She had crept in and climbed into her bed only wanting to relive the whole glorious night again, but she had fallen instantly into deep oblivion.

Now, as she woke and stretched, it was to a transformed world. The bedroom she shared with her Aunt Hilda, with its swirling brown wallpaper, had never seemed to be a place in which to let the eye linger, but now she could imagine the pleasure the designer must have felt in being allowed to wiggle paint about. And Hilda herself, as she brushed her sparse hair, seemed to Ruth the personification of the academic ideal – devoted all her life to a tribe she never saw, made ecstatic by a chipped arrowhead or drinking cup. How good Aunt Hilda was, how grateful Ruth was to be her niece!

She swung her feet over the side of the bed, smiled at the shrunken head. She was walking now over the buried biscuit tin containing her wedding ring, her marriage certificate. Soon – today perhaps – she could dig it up and take it to her mother.

'I'm married, Mama,' she would say. 'I'm married to

Professor Somerville and I love him terribly and he loves me.'

She slipped on her dressing-gown and went to the window and here too was a beauty she had never perceived before. True, the gasometer was still there, but so was the sycamore in the next-door garden and, yes, the bark was sooty and one of the branches was dead – but oh, the glory of the brave new leaves!

On the landing she encountered Fräulein Lutzenholler, glowering, with her sponge bag.

'He is in the bathroom,' she said.

There was no need for Ruth to ask who. It was always Heini who was in the bathroom. But this morning she did not rush to Heini's defence, she was too busy loving Fräulein Lutzenholler who had been so right about everything: who had said that we lose what we want to lose, forget what we want to forget . . . who had said that frigidity was about whether you loved someone or not. Ruth, in her dramatic nonfrigidity, beamed at the psychoanalyst and would have kissed her but for the moustache and the knowledge that, so early in the morning, she could not yet have cleaned her teeth.

'Hurry up, Heini,' called Ruth.

The thought of Heini did halt her. Heini was going to be badly hurt and for a moment her joy was clouded by apprehension. But only for a moment. Heini would find another starling – a whole flock of them in years to come. It was music he loved, and rightly – and what had happened last night was beyond anything one could be sorry for. It was a kind of metallurgical process, a welding of body and soul; you couldn't argue about it.

Oh, *Quin*, she thought, and hugged herself, and Fräulein Lutzenholler, furiously waiting, looked at her, startled, remembering the existence of something she seldom came across in her profession: joy.

Giving up hope of the bathroom, Ruth went into the kitchen where all of them, since Heini's arrival, kept a spare toothbrush. Her mother was laying the breakfast and Ruth stood for a moment in the doorway watching her. Leonie looked tired these days, there were lines on her face that had not been there when they left Vienna, and strands of grey in her hair, but to her daughter she looked beautiful. And with the love that enveloped Ruth, with the ecstasy of her remembered night, there came an overwhelming gratitude, for now she would be able to help her parents, help Uncle Mishak . . . pay back at last.

Her mother would not want to live at Bowmont – Ruth smiled, thinking of the surging sea, the cold wind, the draughts. Her parents would visit, but they would want to stay in town and now they should do so in comfort. She would be an undemanding wife – no grand clothes, certainly no jewels or trinkets which she did not care for anyway. She would learn to be frugal and sensible, but there were things she would ask Quin for and that he would grant in their shared life, she knew that. A cottage for Uncle Mishak – Elsie had shown her an empty one in the village – sanctuary for her friends when they needed a place to rest or work . . . and she might just mention the problem of the sheep! And she, in exchange, would not whine to be taken on his journeys. It was not easy to see how she was supposed to live away from him for months on end, but she would – somehow she would.

Now she embraced her mother who said: 'You look very happy. Did you have a good time with Pilly?'

'Yes, I did. A lovely time.'

Ruth blushed, but it was her last lie. They had not made plans in the night – it was a night outside time – but when they did she would announce her marriage and then she would never need to lie again!

It was as she was cutting herself a slice of bread that she came out of her dream of happiness to notice that Leonie was clattering the crockery in a way which had boded ill in Vienna.

'Is anything the matter, Mama?'

Leonie shrugged. 'I'm silly to be surprised – I should have expected it from the stupid, pop-eyed Aryan cow! But even so one couldn't quite imagine that she would treat him like that after all he did for her and that loutish family of hers. When you think how she chased him in the hospital – a junior nurse as thick as a plank – and the way she showed off about being a Frau Doktor.'

'Is this Hennie? Dr Levy's wife?'

Leonie nodded. 'She's written to say she wants a divorce on racial grounds. You should have seen him yesterday; he looks ten years older – and even so he won't hear a word against her. The man's a saint.'

Ruth was silent, cupping her hands round her mug, in sudden need of warmth. How could anyone hurt this modest, gentle man – a brilliant doctor, a generous friend. She had seemed to love him, the foolish Hennie, echoing his words, basking in his status. Was it so strong, the pull of her family with their pernicious views?

'Aren't you going to college?'

'Not till later.'

Quin had told her to be lazy, to have the morning off. It had surprised her, but she would heed him. When she did go, she would have to be careful not to levitate in the lecture room and float over the carafe of water into his arms. Levitating during lectures was almost certainly bad manners and she could only repay the gods now by being very, very good.

She was still sitting dreamily over a second cup of coffee when the doorbell rang, insistent and shrill. For a moment she thought it might be Quin and in an unconscious gesture of coquetry, she shook out her hair, making it into an offering. But that was silly; Quin had left her saying he had something important to do. He had sounded mysterious, almost preoccupied. He wouldn't, in any case, have followed her to Belsize Park – not till they had decided what to do.

'Go down, darling,' said Leonie. 'Ziller's out – he's gone to the Day Centre.' She brightened. 'Perhaps it's the rodent officer!'

But it was not the rodent officer. A messenger stood there in a dark blue pageboy's suit and a peaked cap.

433

He must have come in the van that stood parked near by, also dark blue, with scrolled writing saying *Cavour and Stattersley* and surmounted by a crown.

'I've a package for Miss Ruth Berger. It's got to be delivered to her personally.'

'I'm Ruth Berger.'

'Can you give evidence of identity?'

Ruth, in her dressing-gown, sighed. 'I can go up and get a letter or something. But I'm not expecting anything. Are you sure it's for me?'

'Yes, I'm sure. It's a special delivery. Got to be handed over personally and had to get here first thing – *and* came in an armoured car, and that only happens when we're delivering stuff that's worth a fortune!'

'I think you must have got it wrong,' said Ruth, puzzled.

But the driver now leant out of the van and said: 'It's okay, I've got a description. You can hand it over – just get her to sign.'

Ruth took the parcel and signed her name. The delivery boy looked at her, impressed. 'We haven't had to hustle like that since we delivered a tiara to the Duchess of Rockingham before the state visit of some bigwig. I wish it was me going to open the box.'

Ruth, still bewildered, said: 'I'm sorry, I don't have anything to give you – but thank you all the same. Only if there's a mistake . . . ?'

'If there is, just get in touch with Cavour and Stattersley. They can change it for you maybe . . . shorten it or something. But you won't want to mess about with what you've got in there!'

The van drove away. Left alone, Ruth opened the box.

She didn't, at first, take in what she saw: a necklace of green stones, each ringed by diamonds and linked by a golden chain. Emeralds, green as the sea, as the eyes of the Buddha and perfectly matched.

Then suddenly she understood.

This was a gift . . . a gift hurried to her through the London streets so that it should reach her the morning after the bridal night. Obscenely valuable, because Quin was generous and would not buy her off with anything cheap, but unmistakable in what it signified.

'The word comes from the Latin *matrimonium ad morganaticum*,' Quin had told her in the Stadtpark, explaining the concept of a morganatic marriage. 'It's a marriage based on the morning gift with which the husband frees himself from any liability to his wife. A morganatic wife doesn't share any of her husband's duties or responsibilities, and their children don't inherit.'

That was why he had urged her to stay home this morning; so that she would be certain to receive it. So that she should understand at once that she was not wanted at Bowmont. A girl with tainted blood might be fit to share his bed, but not his home. A refugee, a foreigner, part Jewish . . . of course, it was unthinkable. If it could happen to Dr Levy, that saintly man, then why not to her?

435

She shut the box, hid it in the pocket of her dressing-gown. How physical it was, this kind of pain, like being terribly ill. Why couldn't one stop the shivering, the giddiness? And if one couldn't, why didn't the next part follow – the part that would have made it right again? Just dying? Just being dead?

'Look at this!' said Lady Plackett. 'It's outrageous! Professor Somerville must be informed immediately and take the necessary steps!'

Unaware of Verena's expectations over Africa, she was no longer so pleased with Quinton who seemed to be doing nothing to further his involvement with her daughter.

Verena, taking the newspaper from her mother's hands, entirely agreed. She had not been able to find anything to pin against Ruth, but there were things that still niggled on the edge of her mind. Why had Ruth been carried to the tower at Bowmont where no one else was allowed to go? What *was* the Austrian girl's connection with Quin before she came?

'The impression is one of lewdness,' she remarked in her precise voice, and felt a glow of satisfaction, for if the Professor still harboured protective feelings for the foreigner, this photograph would surely banish them.

'I shall ring his secretary now,' said Lady Plackett.

Thus Quin, on the way back from the museum where he had arranged Ruth's passage, and still treading on air, found a message from Lady Plackett and made his way to the Lodge.

'We feel that you would wish to be informed of how one of your students conducts herself in her spare time,' said Lady Plackett, and opened the newspaper.

Quin did not consider how the *Daily Echo* had got through the august portals of the Vice Chancellor's Lodge. He did not stop to consider anything because the picture – a half-spread on the centre page – hit him a blow for which he was entirely unprepared.

It was of Ruth and Heini side by side and very close together. They were not entwined, not lolling on a sofa – not at all. Heini sat by a grand piano and Ruth was leaning across, one arm in a curve behind his curly head and her face, as she followed the instructions of the photographer, turned directly to the camera. Her wide mouth, her sweet smile, thus stared out of the page, trusting and happy and Heini, gazing up at her adoringly, was brushed by a straying tendril of her hair.

The caption said – of course it said – *Heini and his Starling*.

'I'm sure you will agree that this kind of exposure in the gutter press is quite unacceptable,' said Lady Plackett.

'And that isn't all,' said Verena. 'She has endeavoured to bring the university down with her. Thameside is specifically mentioned. She is referred to as one of its most brilliant students.'

Quin was silent, bewildered by the effect the picture had on him. He would have found it less painful to have seen her photographed with Heini in bed. People went

437

to bed for all sorts of reasons, but the homage and devotion with which she bent to the boy was devastating.

'She seems to have been the victim of a somewhat unscrupulous journalist,' he said.

He spoke no less than the truth. It was after the débâcle in Janet's flat that Mantella had sent for Ruth and confronted her with Zoltan Karkoly, a Hungarian journalist now working for the *Daily Echo*. Karkoly had explained that his article would be one of a series devoted to the more outstanding competitors in the Bootheby Piano Competition and the music they would play, and had drawn her out skilfully on her favourite topics. He thus found himself in possession of a great deal of information about the livestock favoured by Mozart: not only the starling bought for thirty-four kreutzers in the market, but a subsequent canary and the horse which the composer had ridden through the streets of Vienna. His questions about Ruth herself and her relationship with Heini were thrown in casually and answered trustingly. Yes, she worked in the Willow; yes, she loved Thameside – and yes, she would follow Heini to the ends of the earth, said Ruth who had left him in a tumbled bed and escaped down the fire escape. And yes, she would pose for photographs if it would help Heini's career.

So they had adjourned to the Bechstein in the Wigmore Hall and Karkoly had taken several photographs, but printed only the last one in which she turned her head a little, asking if it was over, and her hair tumbled forward over Heini's shoulder so that only an idiot would fail to catch the allusion to the painting *By Love Surprised* which hung in every other drawing room.

Ruth had not seen Mr Hoyle's article about the Willow and she had not seen Karkoly's piece in the *Echo* – no one had money for newspapers in Belsize Park. But Quin now, staring down at the fulsome words of adoration put into her mouth, found himself crushed by a jealousy so painful that it must have shown him, if nothing else had done, how utterly he was committed to this love.

'We take it you will speak to her?' said Lady Plackett.

'Yes; I shall certainly do that.'

By the time he drove back over Waterloo Bridge, Quin was calm again. The article was certainly days old; he himself knew of the tricks and distortions practised by journalists, but the joy and wonder had gone from the day and, for the first time, he saw the unlikeliness of what had happened. A man who has known countless women marries a girl out of chivalry and finds in her his true and only love . . .

He let himself into the flat and found Lockwood back from his weekend.

'There's a message for you from Cavour and Stattersley,' he said. 'It was Mr Cavour what rung. You're to ring him back when you get in; he'll be there till 6.30. The number's on the pad.'

'Thank you.'

Now what? Surely they couldn't have made a mistake

– he'd been absolutely clear about Ruth's address, and his instructions.

He went to the telephone. Dialled . . . sat down; a thing he didn't generally do when he phoned.

'Ah, Professor Somerville. I'm glad I've caught you. Something very strange has happened. The necklace has been returned to us.'

'What?'

'At lunchtime. Miss Berger came in herself and handed it back.'

'For alterations? It's too long?'

'No, not for that, not to be exchanged. I thought she might prefer different stones. Green is considered unlucky by some people, you know. I had a client –'

'Yes, yes. Just tell me what happened. What did she say?'

'She appeared to be very angry. She said I was to tell you that she didn't want it. She was only in the shop a moment. Very upset she seemed to be. We'll keep it here, sir, awaiting your instructions. It can stay in our strong-room till then – only we'd appreciate hearing from you soon; something as valuable as that is best kept in the bank.'

'Yes.' One must be polite. One must thank Mr Cavour. One must eat the supper Lockwood had prepared.

Was it really that, then: that old, old story? Using an experienced man to teach you the arts of love so that you can return, unafraid, to your lover? Not such a bad idea, really. She had probably read it in a book.

440

No, that wasn't true. It couldn't be true. 'I shall die if you leave me,' she had said not twenty-four hours ago. But she had said other things too. She had said, 'I would follow Heini to the ends of the earth.'

Resting his forehead against the glass of the window, he struggled for belief, for the conviction of her goodness which alone made life worth living. He would see her tomorrow. She would come to his lecture; there would be an explanation. It couldn't be real, this descent into hell.

'Oh, God – give me faith!' begged Quin, reduced by this unfamiliar agony to the prayers of his childhood.

But God was silent and the Thames, as Ruth had bidden it, flowed on and on and on.

Ruth sat in the Underground and stared at the advertisement opposite.

Have you got chill spots?
Yes, a lot.
Have you got chill spots?
No.
Why not?
Cos Mr Therm is raving hot
And drives all chill spots from the spot.

Mr Therm, a sort of flame on legs, would have had to work very hard to drive the chill spots from her heart . . . from her very soul. It wasn't true that she hadn't slept – after she'd returned the necklace, she'd gone back home and told her mother she had a migraine and got into her bed and pulled the blanket over her head and she *had* slept, because being dismembered made one extremely tired. It wasn't the sleeping that was the problem, it was the waking – the whole cycle of agony repeated every hour: it cannot be true, I cannot have mistaken what went on that night. And the green stones snaking into her dreams . . .

But in the morning she had decided to go to college.

'Ruth, you're not fit to go,' said Leonie, looking at her daughter's drawn face and quenched eyes.

'I must, Mama. It is the last day of term and Professor Somerville's last lecture.'

She had said his name. She had been British like Lord Nelson on the column.

But in the Underground, she faced the truth. It wasn't courage, it was the impossibility of not being where he was, and it was then, staring at Mr Therm and the Phonotas girl who would come weekly to clean and sterilize your telephone, that the abject, crawling thoughts came back again. For she had pleased him a little; she knew that. If she accepted his terms, if she kept away from Bowmont and his public life . . . if she got a job somewhere here in London and found a flat . . . a cheap flat like Janet's where he could come sometimes? The annulment could go ahead, he could marry some girl of his own world if he wished, but she would be there. Just to see him once in a while . . . just to know that she didn't have to be pushed forward into grey deserts of time without him.

No, it wouldn't work. Secret love nests were for people in control, not for people who thought they would die if someone got out of bed to fetch a glass of water. She loved him far too much for that, she would make scenes and demands. There was only one thing to do – finish her degree and get right away for ever.

When she got out at the Embankment and made her way to the lift, she found that Kenneth Easton had been on the same train. Kenneth was usually unfriendly, copying Verena's attitude, but today he seemed to want to walk with her and Ruth saw that he looked pale and wretched, so that their reflections, in the mirror of a shop, showed a pair of weary, green-faced wraiths.

'You look a bit tired,' said Ruth, as they made their way to the bridge.

'Yes, I am,' said Kenneth. 'I am very tired. I didn't sleep at all.'

'It's been a long term,' said Ruth. 'You'll be able to take it easy after tomorrow. And you've been playing a lot of squash – that's tiring.'

Kenneth turned to her, his long face showing signs of gratitude, for she had given him the lead he wanted.

'Yes, I have been playing a lot of squash and it's a very expensive occupation. And in other ways too . . . you may think it's easy all the time to say napkin instead of serviette and that Featherstonehaugh is pronounced Fanshaw, but it can be quite a strain and my mother doesn't always understand. In Edgware Green a toilet is a toilet and if you suddenly start saying loo people look at you. But it didn't matter, nothing mattered because I really thought that Verena might grow to care for me.'

They had reached the river and Ruth, for a moment, lost concentration. ('I shall buy a thousand lemonade bottles and put a note in each and every one . . .')

When she could hear Kenneth again, he was admitting to his foolishness. 'I sort of declared myself. It was last night after squash and we were having a drink together in the club and it was so companionable. I completely forgot that my father was a grocer. He's dead, of course, but that only makes it worse. If he'd lived he might have gone on to other things, but now he's a grocer for ever.'

'And Verena turned you down?'

'Yes, she did. And she told me about Professor Somerville and that seemed to make it worse. I knew she cared for him, of course, but I thought it might just be one-sided – only when she told me about Africa, I realized –'

Watch the water, Ruth told herself. Water heals . . . it carries away pain. 'What about Africa?'

'That the Professor is taking her. She knew before, but she didn't say anything because it's a secret – and yesterday she went to the Geophysical Society and the Professor's assistant had just been to arrange for a special cabin. No one's supposed to know – I shouldn't be telling you. You won't say anything, will you, Ruth? Promise?'

'No, Kenneth. Of course I won't.'

'I should have understood. They always stick

together, the upper classes. People like us are all right for them to amuse themselves with, but when it comes to the point we're nowhere. My father's a grocer, that's all there is to it. I never had a chance.'

No. I never had a chance either. My father is something worse than a grocer. Well, at least she was spared the humiliation of offering herself to Quin as a kind of concubine. The African journey was bound to be a long one and it was unthinkable that he wouldn't marry Verena at some point. Kenneth had done her a good turn by severing the last shreds of hope.

She managed a few words of comfort, and together they made their way through the arch and into Thameside's courtyard. Facing them, a confirmation of everything that Kenneth had told her, stood Quin and Verena in animated conversation beneath the walnut tree.

Quin lifted his head; he looked directly at her, and though she had thought in the night that nothing could get worse, she had been wrong: for what she had to do now was *not* to run towards him, not to throw herself into his arms and beg him to release her from this nightmare, and that was worse. It was impossible, but she had done it; she had plucked at Kenneth's arm, she was pronouncing words.

'Kenneth, I've decided not to go to the lecture – Heini wanted me to come to the practice rooms and I feel I ought to go. Will you tell Professor Somerville and make my excuses? Tell him I have to be with my fiancé

– be sure to tell him that – and ask Sam to let me borrow his notes.'

Kenneth, suffering also, managed a magnanimous gesture. 'I'll let you have my notes, Ruth. My hand-writing is far more legible than Sam's.'

Quin had seen her come; had seen her bright head, her gallant figure in its worn cape, and his heart had leapt for now, in the morning, he knew it was impossible, what he had thought in the night – and he waited for her to walk towards him, relieved and grateful for the return of sanity. And then she checked and turned and went away, and even before Kenneth gave – verbatim – Ruth's message, pronouncing the word fiancé in a way which was displeasing to Verena, the pain struck and clawed, and incredulity became belief. He had been used and betrayed.

But Quin, as he went to his room, had an escape which men have perfected and Ruth had yet to learn. Anger. An all-enveloping fury, a rage which consumed him: rage against Heini, against Ruth, against himself for having been duped. Tearing his gown from its hook, marching blindly to his lecture, he let it have its way – this torrent of fury which was so much less agonizing than the pain.

27

Ruth spent the Easter vacation working. It was the work which, she assured her mother, accounted for the rings under her eyes, her loss of appetite and a certain greenish tinge under her skin.

'Then you must *stop*!' yelled Leonie, unable to endure the sight of her lovely daughter reduced to the kind of person one saw crawling out of bombed houses in newsreels of Canton or Madrid.

'I can't,' said Ruth and (inevitably) quoted Mozart who had said he went on working because it fatigued him less than it did to rest.

If Ruth was exhausted, Heini was in excellent spirits. He and Ruth had been completely reconciled. She had come to him and asked his pardon and he had wholeheartedly forgiven her.

'It's not your fault, darling,' he'd said. 'That flat would put anybody off. Only Ruth, if you'd help me now, if you'd be beside me, I *know* I can win! I won't ask for anything physical – when I'm established we can be married and have a honeymoon in some splendid hotel. You see, Mantella thinks he can get me to America if all goes well and if he does, you have to come with me! You have to – I couldn't go alone.'

'America! Oh, Heini, that's so *far*!'

What he had said then, standing in his shirtsleeves looking out at the grey, slanting rain, had shaken her badly.

'Far?' said Heini. 'From where?' – and she had seen what he saw in her adopted country: the shabby lodgings, the poverty, the unfamiliar language and ill-cooked food. But she struggled still.

'I couldn't leave my parents.'

He'd taken both her hands then, looked into her eyes. 'Ruth, you're being selfish. We can bring them over as soon as I'm established. Everyone says there's going to be a war – what if London is bombed?'

'Yes.' He was right. She was being selfish. She could help her parents best that way . . . and help herself. Three thousand miles of ocean should ensure that she was never tempted to crawl cravenly back to Quin and the remembrance of happiness.

'All right, Heini; if you win and Mantella can arrange it, I'll come. And I'll help you all I can.'

That had been two weeks ago and Ruth *had* helped. She glued Heini's tattered music; she massaged his fingers; she sat beside him as he mastered the dreaded arpeggios of the *Hammerklavier*.

She helped Pilly too, travelling to her house and writing even more revision notes to paste on her bedroom wall, till even Mr Yarrowby, shaving each day under diagrams of *Reproduction in the Porifera* or graphs of *Dinosaur Distribution in the United States*, became quite a competent zoologist. And she continued to work at the Willow.

Just before Easter, Professor Berger, whose tenure in Manchester had been renewed for three months, moved into a larger room and asked Leonie to join him. Torn between her husband and her daughter, Leonie became distracted and it was Ruth who bullied her.

'You must go, Mama,' she insisted. 'I'm fine. I have Mishak and Tante Hilda and it's only a few weeks. When the competition is over, and the exams, we'll have a marvellous holiday.'

So Leonie went and Ruth, freed from the constraints of maternal care, worked even harder and felt even iller – and then it was time for the beginning of the summer term.

Quin's lectures had ended at Easter. In the weeks before the final exams he only gave two revision seminars, spending the rest of the time in the museum.

He had been quite prepared to deal with Ruth when he saw her: anger had been succeeded by an icy indifference. The past was done with; Thameside itself, as the day of his departure grew nearer, was growing shadowy. In the event, his studied indifference, the cool nod he meant to bestow on her, were not needed. Ruth cut his seminars and managed never to be anywhere that he might be. This was not the game of invisibility she had played at the beginning of the year; this was a sixth sense bestowed on those who love unhappily and one which seldom failed her. She knew when Quin was in college – even before she saw the Crossley at the gates she knew – and took the necessary action. That her work suffered was inevitable, but that no longer seemed to matter. Survival was what mattered now.

Her friends, of course, saw that she looked ill; that she had lost her appetite.

'What is it, Ruth?' Pilly begged day after day – and day after day Ruth said, 'Nothing. I'm fine. I'm just a bit worried about Heini, that's all.'

From being a girl tipped to get a First, she became someone whom the staff hoped would simply last the course. Dr Elke wanted to speak to her and then, for reasons of her own, decided against it and Dr Felton, who normally would have made it his business to find out what ailed her, was himself struggling through his days, for the Canadian ballet dancer, to everyone's consternation, had produced twins. The babies were enchanting – a boy and a girl – so that Lillian, after years of frustration, achieved in one fell swoop a perfect family, but among their accomplishments, the babies did not number an ability to sleep. Night after night, poor Dr Felton paced his bedroom and thought wistfully of the days when his wife's thermometer was all he had to contend with. He knew that Ruth was unwell, that her work was slipping, but he too accepted the general opinion: that she was anxious about Heini, that her work at Thameside was now second to her life with him.

There was only one treat which Ruth allowed herself during those wretched weeks, and it arose out of a conversation she had with Leonie before her mother went north.

'That old philosopher,' Ruth had asked. 'The one who used to meditate on the bench outside the Stock Exchange. What happened to him?'

'Oh, they locked him away in a Swiss sanatorium years ago. He was completely batty – when they came to clear up his flat they found it full of women's underwear he'd stolen from the shops, and he treated his housekeeper like dirt.'

That settled it. A man could be mad and one could still heed his words; even being an underwear fetishist could be forgiven – but ill-treating one's housekeeper was beyond the pale.

And then and there, Ruth gave up her long struggle to love Verena Plackett.

The results of the first round of the piano competition were a surprise to no one. Heini was through, as were the two Russians and Leblanc; and the second round confirmed the general opinion that the winner must come from one of those four. But the Russians, though exceedingly gifted, had been shut away in their hotel under the 'protection' of their escorts and Leblanc was a remote, austere man whom it was difficult to like. By the time of the finals in the Albert Hall, Heini, with his winning personality and his now well-known romance, was the public's undoubted favourite.

'I feel so *sick*,' said Ruth, and Pilly, beside her, pressed her hand.

'He'll win, Ruth. He's bound to. Everyone says so.'

Ruth nodded. 'Yes, I know. Only he was so nervous. All last night he kept waking up.'

All last night, too, Ruth had stayed awake herself, making cocoa for Heini, stroking his head till he slept, but not able to sleep again herself. Not that that mattered much: sleep was not really one of her accomplishments these days.

A surprising number of people had come to the Albert Hall for the finals of the Bootheby Piano Competition. Of the six finalists, three had played the previous day: one of the Russians, a Swede, and Leblanc whom Heini particularly feared. Today – the last day – would start with the pretty American girl, Daisy MacLeod, playing the Tchaikovsky and end with the tall Russian, Selnikoff, playing the Rachmaninoff – and in between, came Heini. Heini had been disappointed when they drew lots: he had hoped to play at the end. Whatever people said, the last performer always stayed in people's minds.

The orchestra entered, then the conductor. To get Berthold to conduct the BBC Symphonia for the concertos was a real coup for the organizers. Heini, rehearsing with them in the morning, had been over the moon.

On Ruth's other side, Leonie turned to smile at her daughter. She had come down from Manchester and meant to stay till the exams the following week. Her anxiety about Ruth, who was clearly unwell, was underlain by a deeper wretchedness for she knew that if Heini won it meant America and the idea of losing Ruth was like a stone on her chest.

'You must not show it,' Kurt had said. 'You must want it. She'll be safe there and nothing matters except that.'

Since March, when Hitler, not content with the Sudetenland, had marched into Prague, few people believed any more in peace.

The whole row was filled with Ruth's friends and relations. Beside Pilly sat Janet and Huw and Sam. The Ph.D. student from the German Department was there, and Mishak and Hilda . . . even Paul Ziller had come and that was an honour. Ziller was very preoccupied these days; the chauffeur from Northumberland was pursuing him, begging to be heard – there was pressure from all sides for him to lead a new quartet.

It was hot in the hall with its domed roof. Leonie, dressed even at three in the afternoon like a serious concert-goer in a black skirt and starched white blouse, fanned herself with the programme. And now Daisy MacLeod came onto the platform with her dark hair tied back with a ribbon and her pretty blue dress and shy smile, and a storm of clapping greeted her. The Tchaikovsky suited her. She was very young; there were rough passages and once or twice she lost the tempo, but Berthold eased her back and the performance was entirely pleasing. Whether she won or not, she was assured of a career.

The applause was loud and prolonged, bouquets were carried onto the stage; the judges wrote things down and nodded. Ruth liked Daisy, liked her playing, but: 'Oh, God, don't let her win.'

And now the culmination of all those weeks of worry and work. Heini came on the platform with his light, springing gait; bowed. Ruth had searched the flower shops of Hampstead for the perfect camellia, Leonie had ironed each ruffle on his shirt, but the charm, the appealing smile, owed nothing to their ministrations. His platform manner had always been one of his strong points, and Ruth looked up at the box where Mantella sat with Jacques Fleury, the impresario, who as much as the judges held the keys to heaven or hell. Mantella was important, but Fleury was god – he could waft Heini over to the States, could turn him into a virtuoso and star.

Berthold raised his baton; the orchestra went into the tutti . . . the theme was stated gently by the violins, taken up by the woodwind . . .

And everybody smiled. Mantella had been right. The audience was ready for this music.

When the angels sing for God they sing Bach, but when they sing for pleasure they sing Mozart, and God eavesdrops.

Heini waited, looking down at the keys in that moment of stillness she had always loved. Then he came in, stating the theme so rightly, so joyfully . . . and she let out her breath because he was playing marvellously. Obviously he had been nervous only to the necessary degree: now he was purged of everything except this limpid, tender, consoling music which flowed through him from what had to be heaven if there was a heaven anywhere. He had performed this miracle for her the first time she heard him and she would never tire of it, never cease to be grateful. All her past was contained in the notes he played – all her life in the city she once thought would be her home for ever. No wonder she had been punished when she forsook that world.

The melody climbed and soared, and she climbed with it, out of her sadness, her wretchedness, the discomforts of her body . . . out and up and up. Ah God, if only one could stay up there; if only one *could* live like music sounded – if only the music never stopped!

The slow movement next. She was old enough now for slow movements, she was immemorially old. It must be possible to love someone who could draw such ravishment from the piano. And it was possible. She could love Heini as a friend, a brother, someone whose childishness and selfishness were of no account when set against this gift. But not as a man – not ever, now that she knew . . . and suddenly the platform, Heini himself, grew blurred in a mist of tears, for it was a strange cross that Fate had laid on her, ordinary as she was: an inescapable, everlasting love for a man to whom she meant nothing.

The last movement was a relief, for no one could live

too long in the celestial gravity of the Andante – and here now was the famous theme! It would have to be a very unusual starling to have sung that melody, but what did it matter? Only Mozart could be so funny and so beautiful at the same time! Everyone was happy and Ziller was nodding his head which was important. Ziller didn't like Heini, but he *knew*.

Then suddenly it was over and Heini rose to an ovation. People stamped and cheered; a group of schoolgirls threw flowers on to the stage – there were always schoolgirls for Heini – and in his box, Jacques Fleury had risen to his feet.

'I'm sorry I said he was too long in the bath,' said Leonie, dabbing her eyes. 'He was too long, but I'm sorry I said it.'

He had to have won. There could be no doubt . . . not really.

But now Berthold returned, and the tall Russian, Selnikoff, to play the Rachmaninoff.

And, God, he was good! He was terrifyingly good, with the weight of his formidable training behind him and the outsize soul that is a Russian speciality.

Ruth's nausea was returning. Please, God – oh, please . . . I'll do anything you ask, but let Heini have what he so desperately wants.

The dinner, as always at Rules, had been excellent; they'd drunk a remarkable Chablis, and Claudine Fleury, in a little black dress which differed from a little chemise only on a technicality, had made Quin a much-envied man.

Now she yawned as delicately as she did everything. 'That was lovely, darling. I wish I could take you back, but Jacques is here for another week.'

'Of course, I quite understand,' said Quin, managing to infuse just the right amount of regret into his voice. Claudine's father was notoriously easy-going, but there is an etiquette about such things. She had rung him a few days earlier to suggest dinner before he left for Africa and he had been ready to take the evening any way it suited her, for he owed her many hours of pleasure, but the temporary return of Jacques Fleury to attend to business was not unwelcome.

'How is Jacques? Has he snapped up any more geniuses?'

'As a matter of fact, he has. He called just before I left. He's signed up an Austrian boy – a pianist whom he's going to bring to New York and turn into a star! There was some competition today; he wanted me to come, but three concertos in one afternoon – no thank you!'

'He won, then, this Austrian?'

'No. He tied with a Russian and he wasn't too pleased, I gather. Jacques thinks the Russian is more musical, but you can't do anything with Russians; they're so guarded – whereas he can get the Austrian boy over almost straight away. He's going to bring his girlfriend over too – apparently she's very pretty and absolutely devoted . . . worked in some café to pay for

Radek's piano or something. Jacques thinks he can use that at any rate till they're married; she photographs well! There was some story about a starling . . .'

She yawned once more; then stretched a hand over the table. 'I suppose we won't meet again before you go?'

'No, I'm off in less than three weeks. And Claudine . . . thanks for everything.'

'How valedictory that sounds, darling!' Her big brown eyes appraised him. 'Surely we'll meet again?'

'Yes. Of course.'

For a moment, he felt the touch of her fingertips, light as butterflies, on his knuckles. 'I shall miss you, *chéri*. I shall miss you very much, but I think you need this journey,' she said. 'Yes, I think you need it badly.'

The news that Quin was leaving Thameside, which the Vice Chancellor received officially on the first day of the summer term, had affected Lady Plackett so adversely that Verena had been compelled to take her mother aside and make her acquainted with the real state of things.

'There is no doubt, Mummy, that he means to take me to Africa, but the matter has to be a secret for the time being. I can trust you, I know.'

Lady Plackett had not been as pleased as Verena had hoped. It was a proposal of marriage that she wanted from Quin, not the use of her daughter as an unpaid research assistant. She was still busy bringing Thameside's morals up to scratch and had managed to get two

458

first-year students sent down who had been caught in flagrante in the gym, so that her daughter accompanying a man, however platonically, to whom she was not married, was far from agreeable. But Verena had always done what she wanted, and Lady Plackett, accepting that times had changed, continued to be civil to Quin and to invite him to the Lodge.

Verena's preparations, meanwhile, were going well. She had acquired a sunray lamp; she had been to the Army and Navy Stores for string vests and khaki breeches; she rubbed methylated spirits, nightly, into her feet. Some people might have wondered why the Professor was taking so long to inform her of his plans, but Verena was not a person to doubt her worth, and if she had felt any uncertainty, it would have been quelled by Brille-Lamartaine whose increasingly fevered descriptions of the academic *femme fatale* who had ensnared Somerville fitted her like a glove.

Nevertheless, with the final exams only a week away, Verena felt she could at least give the Professor a hint. He had praised her last essay so warmly that it had brought a blush to her cheek, and the intimate discussion she had had with him on the subject of porous underwear seemed to indicate that the time for secrecy was past.

So Quin was invited to tea, and aware that it was his last social engagement with the Placketts, he set himself to please.

It was a beautiful early summer day, with a milky sky and hazy sunshine. The French windows were open;

the view was one Quin had enjoyed so often in previous years when Charlefont was alive and the talk had been easy and unaffected, not the meretricious academic babble he had had to endure from the Placketts.

'Shall we go out on to the terrace for a moment?' suggested Verena, and he nodded and followed her while Lady Plackett tactfully hung back. Leaning over the parapet, Quin let his thoughts idle with the lazy river, meandering down to the sea.

'You always live by water, don't you?' the foolish Tansy Mallet had said, and it was true that he lived by water when he could and was likely to die by it, for he still had his sights set on the navy.

But it was not Tansy he thought of now, nor any of the girls he had once known.

They had collected a lot of rivers, he and Ruth. The Varne which she had intended to swim with a rucksack . . . The Danube which had brought Mishak his heart's desire . . . and the Thames by which they'd stood on the night he thought had set a seal on their love. Once more he heard her recite with pride, and an Aberdonian accent so slight that only a connoisseur could have detected it, the words which Spenser had penned to celebrate an earlier marriage. Had she known it was a prothalamium, a wedding ode, that she spoke, standing beside him in the darkness? Had Miss Kenmore told her that?

And suddenly Quin was shaken once more by such an agony of longing for this girl with her lore and her legends, her funniness and the dark places which the evil that was Nazism had dug in her soul, that he thought he would die of it.

It was as he fought it down, this savage, tearing pain, that Verena, beside him, began to speak, and for a moment he could not hear her words. Only when she repeated them, laying a hand on his arm, did he manage to make sense of her words.

'Isn't it time we told everyone, Quin?' she asked – and he recoiled at the intimacy, the innuendo in her voice.

'Told them what?'

'That you are taking me to Africa? I know, you see. Brille-Lamartaine told me that you were taking one of your final students and Milner confirmed it. You could have trusted me.'

Horror gripped Quin. Too late he saw the trail of misunderstandings that had led to this moment. But he was too fresh from his images of Ruth to be civil. The words which were forced out of him were cruel and unmistakable, but he had no choice.

'Good God, Verena,' he said, 'you don't think that I meant to take *you!*'

The final examinations for the Honours Degree in Zoology took place in the King's Hall, a large, red-brick building shared by all the colleges south of the river. An ugly, forbidding place, its very walls seemed steeped in the fear of generations of candidates. Dark wooden desks, carefully distanced each from the other, faced a high rostrum on which the invigilators sat. There were

461

notices about not smoking, not eating, not speaking. A great clock, located between portraits of rubicund Vice Chancellors, ticked mercilessly, and the stained floorboards were bare.

To this dire place, Ruth and her friends had crawled, day after day, their stomachs churning . . . had waited outside, pale with fear and sleeplessness, trying to crack jokes till the bell rang and they were admitted, numbered like convicts, to shuffle to the forbidding desks with their blue folders, the white rectangles of blotting paper which they would see in their dreams for years to come.

But today was the last exam, if the most important. In three hours they would be free! It was the Palaeontology paper, the one in which Ruth would have hoped to excel, but she hoped for nothing now except to survive.

'It'll be all right, Pilly.' Wretched as she was, Ruth managed to smile at her friend, glad that whatever else had gone wrong with her life she had not neglected to help Pilly. 'Don't forget to do the "Short Notes" question if there is one; you can always pick up some marks on those.'

The bell rang. The door opened. Even on this bright June morning, the room struck chill. The two invigilators on the platform were unfamiliar: lecturers from another college whose students also had exams this morning. A woman with a tight bun of hair and a purple cardigan; a grey-haired man. Not Quin, who was sailing in a week, and Ruth was glad. If things went wrong, as they had before, she wouldn't want him watching her.

'You may turn over your papers and begin,' said the lady with the bun in a high, clear voice.

A flutter of white throughout the hall . . . 'Read the paper through at least twice,' Dr Felton had said. 'Don't rush. Select. Think.'

But it would be better not to select or think too long. Not this morning . . .

What do you understand by the Theory of Allometric Growth? She could do that; it was a question she'd have enjoyed tackling under different circumstances – the kind of question that enabled one to show off a little. *Discuss Osborn's concept of 'aristogenesis' in the evolution of fossil vertebrates.* That was interesting too, but perhaps she'd better do the dunce's question first – Question Number 4. *Write short notes on a) Piltdown Man b) Archaeopteryx c) The Great Animal of Maastricht* . . .

Clever candidates were usually warned against the 'short notes' questions; they didn't give you a chance to excel – but she wasn't a clever candidate now, she was Candidate Number 209 and fighting for her life.

Verena had started writing already; she could hear her scratching with her famous gold-nibbed pen. Verena frightened her these days. Verena was solicitous, her eyes bored into Ruth.

But Verena didn't matter. Nothing mattered except to get through the next three hours of which seven minutes had already passed.

The Theory of Allometric Growth, which quantifies the relationship of small animals to large ones, wrote Ruth, deciding to take a chance.

Pilly scratching out her views on Piltdown Man, whose reconstructed skull mercifully hung above her father's shaving mirror, looked up, saw Ruth's bright head bent over her paper, and exchanged a relieved look with Janet. The clock jerked forward to the first half-hour. One question done, thought Ruth; four more . . . The short notes, then, because it was beginning; it was getting quite bad, actually, but she would fight it off; she would take deep breaths and it would pass. Oh God, I've worked so hard, she thought, suddenly swamped by self-pity. It can't all be wasted!

The Great Animal of Maastricht was discovered in 1780 in the underground quarries of St Peter's Mountain, wrote Ruth, her pen moving very fast because nothing mattered except to get something down for which someone could give her a mark. If she failed this paper, she would fail her degree . . . there could be no resits in December; not for her.

But there was no way of writing fast enough. She could feel the sweat breaking out on her skin, the dizziness . . . Another deep breath.

Ruth put up her hand.

On the dais the lady with the bun looked up, said something to the man beside her, and made her way slowly, agonizingly slowly, between the desks.

'Yes?'

'I need to go to the toilet.'

464

'So soon?' The lady was displeased. 'Are you sure?' She looked again at Ruth, at the beads of sweat on her forehead. 'Very well. Come with me.'

Everyone watched as Ruth was led out. It was a complicated procedure, taking out a candidate – no one could go unwatched. It was like escorting a prisoner, making sure there was nothing secreted behind the lavatory seat – no file to saw through the bars, no crib giving the geological layers of the earth's crust.

Pilly bit her lip. Huw and Sam exchanged worried glances. Ruth had had to go out before, but never so early.

Then Verena, too, put up her hand.

This wasn't just inconvenient; this had the making of a minor crisis. No candidate could leave the room unattended – on the other hand at least one invigilator had to be present at all times. Up on the rostrum, the grey-haired man frowned and pressed a bell beneath his desk. A secretary from the Examination Office appeared in the doorway and was directed to the desk where Verena, still writing with her right hand, continued to hold her left arm aloft.

'I wish to be excused,' said Verena.

The secretary nodded. Verena rose – and the incredulous gaze of all the Thameside candidates followed her to the door. It was hard to believe that Verena even *had* bodily functions.

The gold hand of the great clock jerked forward . . . three minutes . . . four . . .

Then Verena returned. She looked pleased and well,

and immediately took up her pen again. Of Ruth Berger there was no sign.

It'll be all right, thought Pilly frantically. Ruth had had to go out in the Physiology exam too, and in the Parasitology practical . . . but never for as long as this. Never for twenty minutes . . . for half an hour . . . for forty minutes . . . Ruth was clever but no one could miss so much of an exam and still pass.

The woman with the bun had returned long ago; she was conferring with the grey-haired man, they were looking at Ruth's empty desk.

Three-quarters of an hour . . . an hour . . .

And then it was over and still she had not come.

28

She was the most famous ship on the Atlantic route: the *Mauretania*, still Queen of the Ocean with her luxurious salons, her cinema, her glamorous shops. Film stars travelled on her and Arab princes and business tycoons. Even now a woman in a fantastic fur coat was coming up the gangway, pursued by photographers for whom she turned and produced a dazzling smile. Heini too had been photographed as he left on the boat train; his life, since the competition, had been completely transformed. Even half the prize money had enabled him to leave Belsize Park and move into a small hotel. He could have travelled First Class too, but Fleury was bringing Ruth over and that meant travelling Tourist. Having made that sacrifice made Heini feel benign – and actually even the Tourist accommodation was luxurious enough. Leaning on the rail watching for Ruth, who should have been here by now, Heini let his eye travel over the bustle of the docks – cranes loading mysterious packages, vans bringing last-minute cargo – and

467

drank in the smell of tar and rope and seaweed. The *Mauretania* might be a kind of floating grand hotel, but she was still a ship, and a dockside the world over catches at the heart strings with its promise of adventure.

It was all beginning, his new life, the life he knew from childhood was really his. America and fame! And he would share it with Ruth, young as he was. There would be many women who would want him – Heini, without conceit, knew that – but a musician needs roots and a wife. Horowitz's playing had taken on a new depth when he married Toscanini's daughter; Rubinstein's wife protected him from all disturbance. Ruth would do that for him, he knew.

Only where was Ruth? He looked at his watch, for the first time a little anxious. He had respected her wish to make her own way to the docks – in fact he had been rather patient with all Ruth's moods and foibles in the month since the end of her exams. The results weren't out yet, but he sympathized with her disappointment. Having gastric flu during the finals was rotten luck and having missed almost the whole of the last paper was a real blow to a girl as ambitious as Ruth. The most she could hope for now was an aegrotat and that wasn't worth much, but he didn't see that it mattered greatly now that her life was linked with his.

Only an hour before they sailed. Some of the relatives and friends who'd come on board were leaving. Perhaps he'd given Ruth too much freedom? She'd insisted on making her own arrangements for her visa and he'd given way over that too, but he hoped in general that she wasn't going to be obstinate.

A poor family, obviously immigrants from the East – the men in black wide-brimmed hats, the women in shawls, pushing children, made their way up the gangway to the steerage – bound for some sweatshop in Brooklyn perhaps. Two old women belonging to them waited on the quayside, waving and keening: steerage passengers were not allowed to bring relatives on board to see them off. There'd have been plenty of weeping and wailing in Belsize Park as they said goodbye to Ruth; he was glad he'd missed all that. He'd have to be a bit careful about Ruth's determination to bring her family over. He'd promised to do it and he would do it, but there were expenses to take care of first: a decent apartment, a Steinway, insuring his hands . . .

Ah, thank God, there she was, making her way through the crowd. She wore her loden cape, buttoned up even on this warm day, and carried her straw basket so that she looked even more like a goose girl on an alp, and for a moment he wondered if he had made a mistake . . . if she would fit in with the sophisticated life he was bound to lead. But Mantella thought the world of her, and Fleury . . . and his father ate out of her hand. He had never met a man who didn't like Ruth, and now as she came up the gangway, a sailor walking down turned his head to look at her.

'Ruth!'

'Heini!'

They were in each other's arms; he felt her hair against his cheek, the warmth, the familiarity.

'You've been crying, darling.' He was solicitous, wiping a tear away with his fingers.

'Yes. But it doesn't matter. It's all right now. And I've brought us a present. A lovely present. It was a chance in a million, finding them in the summer, but look!'

She bent down to the straw basket and took out a small brown paper bag which she put into his hands. Heini felt the warmth before he opened it, and smiled.

'*Maroni!* Oh, Ruth, that takes me back!'

He took out a chestnut, almost too warm to hold, gazed at the split skin, the wrinkled, roasted flesh – drank in the delicious smell. Both of them now were back in the city they had grown up in, wandering along the Kärntnerstrasse, dipping into the bag . . . sharing . . . sniffing . . . Ruth had carried them in her muff for him, walking to fetch him from the Conservatoire . . . Once they had eaten three bags of them, driving in a sledge through the snowbound Prater.

'I'll peel one for you,' said Ruth – and she freed it deftly from the skin and held it out to him – as she had held out wild strawberries on the Grundlsee, a piece of marzipan pilfered from her mother's kitchen.

'Shall we take them down below?' he suggested.

'No, let's eat them here, Heini. Let's stay by the sea.'

So they stood side by side and emptied the bag and threw the skins into the water, where they were swooped on – and then rejected – by the gulls.

470

'Is your luggage aboard, then?' asked Heini. 'We sail in less than an hour.'

'Everything's taken care of,' said Ruth. She put her arms round him and once again he felt her tears. 'Only listen, darling – there's something I have to tell you.'

No one ever forgot where they were on the morning of the 3rd of September.

Pilly, who had joined the WRNS without waiting for the result of her exams, heard Chamberlain's quavery voice in the naval barracks at Portsmouth. Janet heard it in her father's vicarage the day after which, to everyone's amazement, she had become engaged to his curate.

The inhabitants of Number 27 heard the news that Britain was at war with Germany clustered round the crackling wireless set in Ziller's room and as they listened the expression on every face was strangely similar. Relief that the shillyshallying and compromise were over at last, and with it the realization that they were cut off finally from the relatives and friends that they had left behind in Europe.

And from Ruth. From Ruth who had been five weeks in America and had not yet written – or probably had written, but the letter with the uncertainty of the time had not arrived. And now every mail would be threatened by U-boats, every telephone line requisitioned for the war.

'Oh, Kurt,' said Leonie, coming to stand beside her husband.

'Just think that she is safe. That's all you have to think of; that she is safe.'

Almost before Chamberlain had stopped speaking came the air-raid warning, and with it a taste of things to come as Fräulein Lutzenholler dived under the table and Mishak went out into the garden so as to die in the open air. A false alarm, but it made it easier for Leonie to heed her husband's words. Ruth *was* safe – the *Mauretania* had berthed without mishap; they had rung the shipping office. She herself had said it might be a while before a letter reached them, but oh, God, let her write soon, thought Leonie. She knew how disappointed Kurt had been in Ruth's exam results: the aegrotat she had been awarded was almost worthless – and in something about Ruth herself which had held them at a distance before she sailed, but he suffered scarcely less than she did at this separation from the daughter he loved so much.

Quin heard the news three days later in a manner which would have done credit to a Rider Haggard yarn. A horseman, galloping across the plains towards him in a cloud of dust, reined in and handed him a letter.

'So it's come,' said Quin, and the African nodded.

One by one the men who had been working on the cliff put down their tools. There was no need to ask what had happened. The Commissioner at Lindi had promised to inform them and he had kept his word.

'We're going home, then?' asked Sam – and filled his

eyes with the blue immensity of the sky, the sea of grass, the antelopes moving quietly over the horizon.

Quin put an arm round the boy's shoulder. Sam had proved his worth out here and would never be free now of the longing to return.

'Yes,' he said. 'Straightaway.'

The first weeks of the war saw a number of crises in Belsize Park, but none was due to enemy action. The old lady two doors down collided with a lamp post in the blackout and was taken to Dr Levy, now permitted to practise his profession and established in a surgery on Hampstead Hill. An officious air-raid warden reduced Miss Violet to hysterics by hammering on her bedroom door and accusing her of being a German spy because a chink of light was visible between her curtains. Leonie, now employed in the kitchen of a service canteen behind Trafalgar Square, was reprimanded for spreading margarine too thickly on the soldiers' sandwiches. Leaflets were showered on the populace: they were told to Dig for Victory, to remember that Careless Talk Costs Lives, to Carry Their Gas Masks at all times. Evacuated children from the slums of London screamed in the silence and safety of their country billets.

Only at sea had the war started in earnest. Ships travelled in convoy and in secrecy, escorted by destroyers; even so the U-boats claimed victim after victim – and every boat sent to the bottom could have carried

473

the letter Ruth had written to assure her parents that she was safe and well.

But when at last the longed-for letter came from New York, it was not from Ruth, but from Heini, and by the time she had read it, Leonie was a shivering wreck clinging to the edge of the table.

Heini wrote to thank them for their hospitality throughout the years and he enclosed a message for Ruth.

'I don't want to reproach her,' he wrote, 'I suppose it was honest of her to say that she did not love me and did not want to share my life. But you can imagine how I felt, sailing alone to an unknown land. Fortunately, as soon as I arrived, everything went splendidly. The Americans are as warm-hearted as one hears and my debut at the Carnegie Hall was a triumph. Will you tell Ruth this, and tell her too that someone else has now entered my life – a very musical woman, a little older, who uses her influence to help me and who insisted that I move into her apartment – a dream-like place with picture windows overlooking Central Park. So Ruth must not feel guilty – but she must not think either that I shall take her back. I shall always remember her with fondness, as I remember all of you, but the past is past.'

Leonie had collapsed into a chair, trying to still the trembling of her limbs. 'God, Kurt, what has happened? Where is she? Why didn't she tell us?'

'Hush, hush. There will be an explanation.' But as he stroked his wife's back, the Professor himself was fighting for control. This couldn't happen twice, his beloved daughter lost in the Underworld.

'We must tell the police. They must find her,' said Leonie.

'We will see first what we can discover for ourselves.'

But they discovered nothing. Pilly, to whom they telegraphed, had not heard from Ruth, nor had Janet and everyone at Thameside believed that Ruth had sailed on the *Mauretania*. Once more, Leonie stifled her sobs under the pillow and drearily promised God to be good, but before she could make herself seriously ill, a letter came by the afternoon post with which Hilda hurried to the Willow, where Miss Maud and Miss Violet, their windows taped, their doors suitably sand-bagged, were carrying on as usual.

'It came just now – that's Ruth's handwriting, I'm sure.'

Silence fell in the café as the envelope was opened. Silence was maintained as Leonie and her husband read what Ruth had written.

'She is safe,' said Leonie at last. 'She is safe and in England. In the country. And she has a job.'

'So why this long face?' enquired von Hofmann. 'Why are you not dancing on the tables?'

Things had gone well with him since the outbreak of war. A whole spate of anti-Nazi films were lined up by the studios and he had secured the part of an SS officer who said not only *Schweinehund* but *Gott in Himmel* before dying a very nasty death.

'She wants to be alone.' Leonie's lip trembled as she tried to embrace this extraordinary concept.

'Like Greta Garbo?' enquired the lady with the poodle.

Leonie shook her bewildered head. 'I don't understand . . . she says she must be independent . . . she must learn to grow up by herself. Later she will come back, but now she must discover who she is. Twice she says this about the discovering.'

'Everybody goes through such times,' said Ziller. 'Times when they need to find out who they are. It is natural.'

Mrs Weiss disagreed. 'So she finds out who she is?' she said, spearing a piece of guggle with her fork. 'What has she from that? Myself, it is bad enough that I *am* it, but to find out, no!'

Mrs Weiss's views, rather surprisingly, were shared by Miss Maud and Miss Violet who said they thought it didn't do much good to go delving about in one's self, but were sure it wouldn't last.

'You'll see,' said Miss Maud, 'she'll be back soon enough. It's feeling she's failed you with the exams, perhaps, and breaking with Heini.'

'There is no address,' said Leonie wretchedly. 'And I can't read what is on the stamp. But in the post office they will read it and tell me. We *must* find her, Kurt; we must!'

Professor Berger put down the letter in which his daughter had begged for their understanding. 'No,' he said curtly. 'We will respect her wishes.'

'Oh, God – I don't want to respect her wishes, I want *her*!' cried Leonie.

'We have spoken enough of this,' said the Professor – and she looked up, silenced, aware of a hurt even deeper than her own.

'No go home?' begged Thisbe, as Ruth pushed her pushchair back down the rutted lane.

'Thisbe, we have to go home. It's teatime.'

The little girl's face puckered; she let out a thin wail. Ruth bent down to her. The wind was getting up, the tops of the fells were wreathed in mist. However much both she and the three-year-old Thisbe preferred to be out of doors, there were limits. The Lake District in late autumn was beautiful, but it was hardly suitable for alfresco life.

'No soup?' begged Thisbe, shifting her ground.

Ruth sighed. She felt sympathy with Thisbe who dreaded a return to the domestic hearth: to the cold stone floors of the tiny shepherd's cottage, the chaos, the screams of her two brothers as they returned from school. Progressive child-rearing did not suit Thisbe, who was no trouble as she and Ruth plodded through the countryside conversing with sheep, picking berries, chatting on stone walls, but became almost ungovernable at home.

Ruth had been two months now with the lady weaver whose children she had looked after on Hampstead Heath. Penelope Hartley was kind enough in a vague way, and offering Ruth bed and board in exchange for help with the children was generous under the circumstances. When war became inevitable and she had transferred her loom to Cumberland, Ruth had gone with her. There was certainly plenty of wool which Penelope gathered from the hedges, often in a less than appetising state, and carded and dyed . . . and out of the appalling muddle in which she worked, there did, surprisingly, emerge some rather pleasant and occasionally saleable rugs. But Mr Hartley, some years ago, had sought consolation elsewhere, and Penelope had rather let things go.

Inside the small, dark cottage with its oil lamps and view of a sheer scree, they found something nameless bubbling on the stove. Not a sheep's head broth, for Penelope did not eat meat, but a vegetable equivalent: a stew of mangelwurzels, old carrots, the tops of Brussels sprouts caught by the first frost, which nevertheless managed to suggest the presence of bristles and teeth and protruding eyes.

'No *soup!*' repeated Thisbe, and lay down on the floor, ready to start a tantrum.

'No, we'll find some bread and butter.'

Rationing had not yet affected them here, so far from the towns; there was plenty of food in Cumberland or there would have been if there had been any money to buy it with and not all the villagers turned away from Ruth; some had been helpful. But, of course, Penelope believed in 'Nature', not realizing how very unnatural good husbandry really is. Three damp chickens which did not lay wandered into the house, soiling the flagstones; old milk, dripping through discoloured muslin, failed dismally to turn into cheese.

The boys now returned noisily from school. Peter, whom she had pleased by hitting him on the leg in the far-off days on Hampstead Heath, and Tristram, a year older.

'Oh God, not mother's muck,' said Tristram. 'I won't eat it, and she needn't think it.'

Ruth, fetching bread, butter and apples from the larder, reassured him. If only it didn't get dark so soon. When they'd first come, she'd been able to go out with the boys after supper while they kicked a ball around or searched for conkers, but now they all faced an interminable evening sitting round the smoking Aladdin lamp. Even so she could manage if only Penelope stayed next door at her loom. They could play dominoes or ludo – at least they could if the pieces weren't lost again; she wasn't as nimble as she had been at crawling round the floor looking for missing toys after the children were in bed.

But, of course, Penelope did come in, concerned for her motherhood, and within minutes the boys were at each other's throats and Thisbe was lying on the floor drumming her heels. Too many sages had made their way into Penelope Hartley's head: Rudolf Steiner who said children should not learn to read till their milk teeth were shed; the Sufi chieftain who set Penelope to her meditations instead of the washing up; A. S. Neill with his child-centred education. The poor, confused children of Penelope Hartley were so child-centred that they almost imploded each night in the confines of the tiny cottage – and tonight, as so often before, Ruth who was supposed to finish her work at seven, carried Thisbe upstairs and eased her into her nappies and sat with her till she slept.

And then the long evening began when she went to her attic under the eaves which was at least her own and looked out at the darkness and the rain, and longed for her mother and the lore and certainties of her own childhood and the painted cradle, now splintered wood, in which her baby should have lain.

But she wouldn't yield. It wasn't so long now – less than two months. She would see it through on her own. *Not whose I am, but who I am, there lies my search* . . . The lines of some half-remembered poem ran again through her head.

Only who *was* she? Someone who had loved and been rejected; a daughter who had caused her parents disappointment and pain . . . and now, soon, a mother who knew nothing.

And yet she had no regrets. She blamed no one, not even Verena, hissing her ultimatum in the cloakroom, threatening to expose her condition unless she left Thameside then and there, and for ever. In a way Verena had done her a service, bringing home the contempt and disgust with which the world might now regard her state. If her father, so strict, so upright, had turned his back on her as a fallen woman, Ruth couldn't have borne it: she'd have revealed the marriage and then it would have all have begun . . . finding

Quin, letting him know . . . begging for a place in his life . . . And Verena had kept her own side of the bargain; no one at college knew what had happened or where she was.

Nor had Quin carried her dreamily from his sofa to his bed. He had said: 'Wait; there are things to be attended to.' He had said it very gently, very lovingly, cupping her face in his hands, but firmly: he had begun to leave her, and it was she who had clung on to him and said: 'No, no, you mustn't go!' . . . because even then she couldn't bear to be away from him. 'It's absolutely safe,' she'd said. 'It's my completely safe time; I *know* because of Dr Felton's wife and the thermometers. It's as safe as houses!'

She hadn't been lying; she'd believed it and he'd believed her. Only houses, these days, were not so very safe: houses in Guernica and Canton and Warsaw toppled like cards as bombs fell on them, and she'd been wrong. She'd been a whole week out in her calculations and that was another mark chalked up to Fräulein Lutzenholler and Professor Freud. She wasn't usually sloppy about dates – it was that damnable thing way below the level of reason which all along had wanted nothing except to belong to this one man.

And even now, an official 'unmarried mother' from whom the older villagers averted their eyes, even now when Quin had unmistakably rejected her, there was, deep down below the anxiety and fear for the future, an unquenchable sense of joy because she was carrying his child.

Only the child itself had lately disconcerted her. This fishlike creature still unable to breathe or eat except by her decree, had developed a will of its own. Ruth did not need the doctors in the antenatal clinic to which she travelled once a fortnight on innumerable buses, to tell her that her baby was fit and well, but what about its mental state – its obstinacy? It disagreed completely with Ruth's careful plans and was profoundly uninterested in her voyage of self-discovery.

Bowmont is only sixty miles away, it said, twisting its foot merrily round her spinal nerves. *You* may be an upstart and an outcast, but *I'm* half a Somerville.

I want, it said, my home.

At the end of November, Leonie received a visit from Mrs Burtt who had left the Willow to work in a munitions factory and was greatly missed by the customers. Smartly dressed in a new brown coat and a hat with a feather, she was carrying a small parcel wrapped in silver paper and seemed a little shy and tentative which was not her usual state.

'I'm sorry to be bothering you,' she said, 'but . . . well, I thought you wouldn't mind; you wouldn't take it amiss.'

'How could I do this?' asked Leonie. 'I am very happy to see you.'

She led Mrs Burtt into the sitting room, in which one could actually sit once more now that the piano had been sent back, and offered coffee which Mrs Burtt refused.

'I don't want to pry,' she said, after asking rather oddly if they would be undisturbed. 'But well, I really like her, you know, and people sometimes say things, but I know Ruth is as good as they make them. And her going off like that to have it on her own . . . well, it's like her. Not wanting to bother anyone. But I want her to know that whatever she's done I know she's a good girl and I'd like you to give this to her. Afterwards. Not before, because that's bad luck, but when it's all over. I knitted it myself.'

She laid the parcel on the table, and Leonie, who was having trouble with her breathing, stretched out her hand. 'May I see?' she said.

Mrs Burtt removed the wrapping paper. Pride shone for a moment on her face. 'Took me hours, that did. It's a brute of a pattern. It's those scallops, see? But it's come out nice, hasn't it? I kept it white to be on the safe side, but she can put a blue ribbon through it or a pink when it's all over.'

Leonie was still having difficulty with the business of drawing air into her lungs. 'Thank you – she will be so pleased. It is the most beautiful jacket. I will see that she has it . . . and tell her . . . what you have said.'

Mrs Burtt nodded. 'I don't want to know any more now,' she said. 'It's not my business. Just to know she's all right and the baby's safe.'

Leonie, swallowing the unbearable hurt her daughter had done her, said: 'Did she tell you . . . herself . . . about the baby?'

Mrs Burtt shook her head 'Bless you, no. She's no

blabber. But I was one of four daughters and I've three girls of my own. I guessed soon enough. There's ways of being sick that's a bug in the tummy and there's ways that isn't. And she got so tired. I came out with it and I think it was a relief she could talk to someone.'

'And . . . where she was going . . . her plans? Did she tell you about that?'

'No. And I didn't ask her. I knew it wasn't Heini that was the father, so there wasn't any more for me to say.'

Leonie lifted her head. 'How did you know?' she asked.

'Well, you could see she didn't love 'im, couldn't you? Tried too hard all the time . . . And if it wasn't him, I wasn't going to go nosing around.'

'I didn't see . . . as well as you,' said Leonie out of her deep despair.

Mrs Burtt's work-roughened hand rested for a moment on her own. 'You was so close, the two of you,' she said. 'You loved her so much. It's a real killer, love is, if you want to see.'

Left alone, Leonie sat as still as a statue, holding the exquisite, tiny garment in her hands. Ruth had not trusted her. She had confided in a lady who washed dishes and not in her. She had gone off alone.

Professor Berger, returning home, found her still in a state of shock.

'What has happened, Leonie? What have you got there?'

'It's a baby's jacket.' She traced the scallops on the

collar, the lacy frill, with blind fingers. 'Mrs Burtt brought it for Ruth.'

She watched as her husband's face changed; saw the incredulity, the dismay . . . then the tightness of anger.

'My God, that scoundrel, Heini. I'll *force* him to marry her,' he said furiously.

'Oh, Kurt, it isn't Heini's child. If it was she'd have gone with him.'

This was worse. His beloved, protected daughter a fallen woman, the bearer of an unknown child. Pitying him as he paced the room, Leonie had no energy to retrieve him from his conventional hell of moral outrage. What is it I have not understood? she thought. What is it that is missing here? And if I was right all along, how could it have come to this?

The doorbell rang, shrill and insistent. Neither of the Bergers moved.

'What are you going to do?' asked the Professor – and the sudden helplessness of this proud man did touch her.

'I'll tell you what I'm going to do,' she began.

A second ring . . . and now Fräulein Lutzenholler's door could be heard opening, and her indignant footsteps as she made her way downstairs. The easing of laws against refugees at the onset of hostilities meant she was allowed to practise her profession and, incredible as it seemed, people came to her room and paid to have her listen. Answering the doorbell would annoy this exalted person very much.

She returned, as displeased as Leonie had antici-
pated, and with her was a red-faced man in some kind
of uniform.

'It's the rodent officer,' said Fräulein Lutzenholler –
and as Leonie stared blankly at this man she had
awaited with hope and passion for month after month:
'He has come about the mice.'

'Oh, yes . . . thank you . . .' Leonie rose, tried to collect herself.

'Please go where you will. They are everywhere. The
kitchen is bad . . . and the back bedroom.'

'That's all right, ma'am. I'll just get on with it. Looks
like a sizable infestation you have here – I may have to
take up some boards.'

He left the room and they could hear him moving
about, tapping the walls, opening cupboards.

'I'll tell you what I'm going to do,' said Leonie, turning back to her husband. 'I'm going to take Ruth's letter
to the post office and make them tell me where it comes
from and then I'm going to go there and find her.
And when I have found her I'm going to bring her back
here and look after her and after my grandchild. And if
the father's a chimney sweep I'm going to do it.' She
swallowed. 'Even if he is a *Nazi* chimney sweep,
because if Ruth gave herself to him it's because she
loved him and she is my blood and yours also, so you
will please *not* –'

A knock at the door and the rodent officer reappeared.

'I found this under the boards in the back room,' he

486

said – and deposited on the table a large, square biscuit tin covered in mouse droppings and adorned with a picture of the Princesses Elizabeth and Margaret Rose patting a corgi dog.

She had come by bus as far as Alnwick, but there were eight miles still to go before she reached Bowmont. She'd have walked it easily enough in the old days, but not now, and she spent some of her meagre stock of money on a taxi as far as the village. It would have made sense to be set down by the house itself, but she couldn't face that. She didn't want to sweep up as a claimant – it was sanctuary she sought at Bowmont, not her rights.

The driver was worried; she had a suitcase, the afternoon was grey and chill, but she reassured him.

'I'll be all right,' she said. 'I need some air.'

She certainly looked as though she needed something, thought the driver, turning his cab, watching the bundled figure in its shabby cape set off up the hill.

There was nobody about and that was a blessing; there might have been people who recognized her and till she knew her fate she wanted to speak to no one. And her fate depended on a ferocious old woman known for her sharp temper and her strict and old-fashioned views.

'I hope you're satisfied,' she said bitterly, addressing her unborn child. She had fought a long battle, pitting her pride and independence against the creature's blind, stubborn thrust towards what it considered to be its home, and she had lost. Now, trudging up the hill, she tried to face the consequences of rejection. Where would she go if she was turned away? It was growing dark, she could hardly go back to Penelope whose advice she had ignored . . . whom, in a sense, she had left in the lurch. She was mad, coming here like this at the eleventh hour.

'Oh God, why did I listen?' she thought, for the sense of dialogue between herself and the child had been with her from the start.

But she knew why. Even now, in the bitter cold of a raw December day with the storm clouds massing in the west and the light withdrawing itself in readiness for an endless winter night, she walked through a heart-stopping beauty. The wind-tossed trees, the tumble and thrust of the waves against the cliffs and Bowmont's tower etched against a violet sky, brought a sudden mist of tears to her eyes – and that was not very sensible nor very practical. She had to find her way, not stumble, for she was not alone.

Yet memories, as she made her way up the last stretch of road, came unbidden to weaken her further. The incredible clarity of the stars; the dazzling silver of the morning sea the first time she had walked towards it; the enfolding, unexpected warmth and fragrance of the garden – and she thought that if she was sent away again she would not know how to bear it.

She was on the gravel drive now and still she had encountered no one. Then as she reached the steps and put down her suitcase, she knew with certainty that her quest would fail. Aunt Frances hated refugees, she hated foreigners; she belonged to a bygone age. There was no sanctuary here, no safety, no hope.

She could hear the clang of the bell echoing inside the house. Would Turton even announce her, seeing her state? She belonged at the back door or in one of those dark genre paintings of banished women staggering out into the night.

The bolt was drawn back slowly . . . so slowly that Ruth would have had time to turn away down the steps.

'Yes? What is it?'

It was not Turton who stood there, not any of the servants. It was Aunt Frances herself, barring the way, showing no welcome, no inclination to move aside – not even when she recognized who it was that stood on her threshold.

'What on earth are you doing here?' she went on, horrified. 'This is no place for you!'

Ruth drew breath, lifted her head. *Not I, but thou* . . . She must fight for her child. But the words she brought out were halting, inadequate; she was suddenly so exhausted that she could hardly stand.

'Please . . . I beg you . . . Can I stay?'

'Stay here! Stay *here* in your condition! Really, Ruth, I know all foreigners are mad but this goes beyond everything. Of course you can't stay.'

'There is an explanation . . . There is a reason.'

'Explanations have nothing to do with it. You can't stay here, absolutely and definitely not, and that's the end of the matter.'

Ruth looked up at the gaunt fierce woman she had nevertheless hoped was her friend. As she pulled her cloak tighter, struck by a deathly cold, the first flakes of snow began to fall.

29

It had been Pilly's ambition, when she joined the WRNS, to be employed as a cook, but the third-class degree which made so little impression in academic circles secured her a status she did not really seek. She was deployed as a driver and by the end of November was carrying signals to and from the docks and senior naval officers about their business.

But the officer she had been asked to collect from the destroyer *Vigilantes* at an outlying berth some ten miles from the base was a mere sublieutenant and it was better not to ask why he rated a car or why the ship, supposedly on Atlantic convoys, was being refitted in this obscure and inconveniently sited dock on the South Coast. There were a lot of things one did not ask this first winter of the war.

It was a raw December afternoon; the quay was deserted except for the two sailors guarding the barrier, but Pilly, standing beside her car, waited contentedly. Her instructions were clear; her passenger would come.

But when he did come, a lone figure carrying a duffel bag, and she saluted, the result was unexpected.

'Good God, Pilly!' Quin peered, moved closer in the dusk. 'It is you, isn't it?'

'Yes, sir.'

'Well, well, this is amazing!' He threw his bag into the back and climbed into the front seat. 'I had no idea you were in the same outfit. How do you like it?'

'I absolutely love it!'

Quin smiled at the enthusiasm in her voice and at the change in the nervous girl who had peered so sadly at her specimens. Pilly was slimmer, the uniform suited her, and as they turned inland, he saw that she handled the big car with confidence and skill.

'My instructions are to take you to the station,' she said, 'but it wouldn't take a minute to call in at the mess if you wanted to pick up your mail?'

'No, thanks.'

The mail was of no interest to him now. He had put a moratorium on his past life. In the forty-eight hours before his next assignment, he was going down to a pub in Dorset to walk and eat and sleep. Mostly to sleep.

'Janet's in the ATS,' Pilly said, for she knew she must ask him nothing personal, 'though she's getting married soon, and Huw is in the army. And Sam's going to join the RAF.'

Quin turned his head sharply. 'He could have got deferment with a Science degree. I told him.'

'Yes – but he wanted to be part of it. He really hates the Nazis and not just because he was so fond of Ruth.'

She changed down and they began to climb up the slope of the Downs. Well, it was inevitable that the girl who had followed Ruth like a shadow, should mention her name. Impossible, now, not to proceed.

'Have you heard from Ruth?'

'Yes, I have. I heard two weeks ago.'

'And how does she like America?'

No answer. They had reached the top of the hill and she turned left between trees. Thinking she might need to concentrate on the dark stretch of road, he waited, but when she still did not answer, he repeated his question.

Pilly made up her mind. 'She is not in America,' she said.

'You must be mistaken.' His efforts to keep his voice neutral were only partly successful. 'She sailed with Heini on the *Mauretania* at the end of July.'

'No, she didn't. Heini sailed, but Ruth didn't. She told me in her letter.'

'Where is she, then?'

Another decision to make . . . but this new and confident Pilly made it.

'She's somewhere in the North of England working as a mother's help.'

'What! No, you must have got that wrong.'

Pilly shook her head. 'I haven't. And I'm very worried about her. I don't understand what's happening. She keeps saying she's all right, but she isn't – I know she isn't. She's unhappy and in a mess . . . and I think she's being *silly*.'

'What do you mean?'

Pilly, waiting at a crossroads, tried to explain. 'I love Ruth,' she said. 'I really love her. It's because of her I got my degree, but that isn't why. She made life . . . big for me. For all of us. Important, not petty. But sometimes suddenly she'd behave like someone in a book or an opera. Like she did when she was trying to give herself to Heini. All that business about being like *La Traviata* or that girl with a muff. Love isn't about operas,' said Pilly – and smiled for she had met a petty officer who had promised to marry her and take her away from Science for ever.

They had driven for several minutes before Quin spoke again.

'Do you have her address?'

'No, I don't. She didn't give it in her letter. That's why I think she's being someone in a book again. A sort of Victorian heroine going out into the snow.' She glanced sideways at her passenger. He had been a famous scientist and would, if he survived, most probably be a hero with a medal, but he was still a man and the suspicion that she and Janet had harboured could not be voiced to him. 'It's not because she hasn't gone with Heini that I'm worried. Obviously she didn't love him and –'

'Really? That was not my impression.'

God, don't let it start again, he thought, looking out at the winter trees. There was no rage to call on nowadays; just a relentless sense of bereavement lying below his conscious thoughts as dark and heavy as stone.

'I'm going to try and find her,' said Pilly. She had switched on the headlights; they were turning into the road which led to the station. 'The trouble is, my next leave is not for three months.'

'How can you find her without an address?'

'I think she's in Cumberland – the postmark looked as though it might be Keswick.' Pausing at a traffic light, she turned to look at him. 'I've got the letter in my locker back at headquarters, if you had time to look – you're good at deciphering things. And if it is Keswick, that's not *so* far from Bowmont, is it? So if you were going north –'

'But I'm not. I've got exactly forty-eight hours and it takes a whole day now to go north, as you know.'

Pilly sighed. Probably Dr Elke had been wrong. Probably she herself was mistaken. 'If she was a dinosaur's tooth you'd find her,' she said. 'And she isn't; she's *Ruth*.'

The car drew to a halt in front of the station. Quin reached for his duffel bag – and dropped it back on the seat.

'All right, Pilly, you win. We'll go and look at your envelope.'

But when Pilly hurried back to him in the hallway of the officers' mess carrying the letter, she saw that Ruth's cause was lost. Quin was staring at a telegram in his hand and his face was ashen.

'Thank God we called in here,' he said. 'My aunt's been taken ill. I'll have to go to her at once.'

He handed her the message which had been waiting with the *Vigilantes'* mail.

COME IMMEDIATELY WARD THREE NEWCASTLE
GENERAL HOSPITAL URGENT SOMERVILLE.

There was no chance to sleep in the crowded, blacked-out train; nothing to eat or drink. There were only the dragging hours in which to recall, in unsought detail, the services his aunt had performed during her life and to realize the blow her death would deal him.

They reached Newcastle at ten in the morning and, still in his rumpled uniform, he snatched a few minutes to wash and shave in the station cloakroom before jumping into a taxi. He'd sent a cable before he left; giving his name at the hospital reception desk, he was directed to the first floor.

As he entered the ward, the Sister came towards him. 'Ah yes, we've been expecting you. It's not visiting time, but I understand the circumstances are exceptional. I'll take you to your aunt.'

Steeling himself to face what awaited him, Quin followed her to the door of a small day room which she opened.

Aunt Frances was not ill and she was certainly not dead. As she saw him she rose and came towards him – and she was laughing. Not the reluctant smile she occasionally allowed herself at the foibles of mankind, but the full-bodied laughter of intense amusement.

'Oh, thank goodness!' She embraced him, but her

shoulders still shook. 'Only . . . don't worry,' she managed to say. 'It's just a few days and then it'll disappear. He'll lose it completely – isn't that so, Sister?'

Sister agreed that it was.

'Lose what?' said Quin, completely bewildered.

'The resemblance. The likeness. Oh dear, I wouldn't have believed it! Go and see! She's in the end bed on the left.'

Walking in a dream, Quin made his way up the ward. Girls were sitting up in bed, some talking, some knitting – but all watching him as he passed.

Then suddenly there was Ruth, her hair mantling her shoulders. Ruth as he remembered her . . . warm . . . feminine; somehow both triumphant and unsure.

But he didn't go to her at once. At the foot of the bed, as at the foot of all the beds, was a cot. And inside it – lay Rear Admiral Basher Somerville.

The baby wasn't *like* the Basher. It *was* the Basher – shrunk to size, a little more crumpled, but identical. The Beethovian nose, the bucolic, livid face, the double chin and pursed-up mouth.

Quin could not speak, only stare – and his son moved his ancient, wrinkled head, one eye opened – a fathomless, deep blue, lashless eye . . . the mouth twitched in a precursor of a smile.

And Quin was undone. In an instant, this being of whose existence he had been unaware five minutes earlier, claimed him, body and soul. At the same time, he knew that he could die now and it did not matter because the child was there and lived.

Only I must not hold him back, he thought. He is himself. I swear that I will let him go.

Then he looked up at Ruth, watching him in silence. But not her, he thought exultantly. Not her! I shall never relinquish her – and he moved, half-blind, to the head of the bed, and took her in his arms.

The Sister had said: 'Half an hour, but no more, since you're on leave.' She had drawn the cold blue curtains round the bed, but the lazy December sun touched them with gold. Inside was Cleopatra's barge, was Venus' bower as Quin touched Ruth's face, her hair.

'I can't believe it. I can't believe you could have been so stupid. I just wanted to give you something lovely and priceless.'

'I know . . . I was an idiot. I think I didn't believe I should be happy when there was so much suffering in the world. And there was Verena. She told everyone that you were taking her to Africa.'

'Ah, yes. An unpleasant woman. She's going to marry Kenneth Easton and teach him how to pronounce Cholmondely, did you know?'

Ruth liked that. She liked it a lot. But Quin was still shaken by the risk he had taken when she came to him that night. 'When I think that you went through all that alone.'

'Well, actually I didn't,' said Ruth a trifle bitterly.

'Not at the end. All I can say is that your aunt may have left *you* alone but she certainly didn't leave me!'

And she described the moment when Aunt Frances had appeared in the doorway at Bowmont, apparently barring the way. 'She said I couldn't stay and I was desperate, but she meant I couldn't stay in case we were cut off by the snow and the ambulance couldn't get through. She just bundled me into the car and took me down to Mrs Bainbridge's house in Newcastle and even when my parents came, she didn't let me out of her sight. I think she was worried because of what happened to your mother.'

Quin took one of her hands, laced her fingers with his.

'Thank God for Aunt Frances,' he said lightly – but he was still troubled by his carelessness that night in Chelsea. Or was it carelessness? Would he have believed any other woman as he had believed Ruth? Hadn't he wanted, at one level, to be committed as irrevocably as now he was?

But Ruth was asking a question, holding on to him rather hard in case it was unjustified.

'Quin, when you give Bowmont to the Trust, do you think it might be possible to keep just one very small –'

'When I do *what*?' said Quin, thunderstruck.

'Give Bowmont to the Trust. You see –'

'Give it to the *Trust*? Are you mad? Ruth, you have seen that baby – you have seen the fists on him. Do you seriously think I'd dare to give away his home?'

Ruth seemed to find this funny. She found it very

funny, and her remarks about the British upper classes were so uncomplimentary that Quin, slightly offended, prepared to seal her lips with a kiss. But when he'd cleared away her hair to obtain a better access, he found that her brow was furrowed by a new anxiety.

'Quin,' she said into his ear, 'I seem to have become a mother rather quickly, but I want so much to be . . . you know . . . a proper loveress. The kind that wiggles a gentleman's cigars to see that the tobacco is all right and knows about claret.'

He was entirely shaken, not least by the way that her adopted language had suddenly deserted her.

'Oh God, you shall be, my darling. You shall be a loveress to knock Cleopatra into a cocked hat. You are already! We shall love each other on beds and barges, in bowers of lilies and on the Orient Express. It owes us, that train!'

He drew her closer, feeling that never again would he have enough of her, and at that moment the child began to cry. At once he loosed his hold, schooled himself. He must relinquish her though soon he would leave her, perhaps for ever. He must take second place for that was the law of life.

But it was not her law. He felt her responding to the thin, high wail . . . felt the cord that bound her to the child – and would bind her till she died – draw tighter. But when she stretched out her hand, it was to press the bell beside the bed.

'Would you take him to the nursery just for a little

while?' she asked the nurse who came. 'He can't be hungry yet and my husband doesn't have . . . very long.'

It seemed to him then that she had given him a pledge of which he must be worthy as long as they both lived – and as he laid his head against her cheek, he felt her tears.

'Quin . . . about swimming . . .'

'Yes?'

'I mean, you're good at it, aren't you? Very good? So whatever happens, even if . . . I mean, it's only the Atlantic or the Pacific. It's only an *ocean*. You'll just keep on swimming, won't you? Because wherever you land, on whatever shore or island or coral reef, I'll be there waiting. I swear it, Quin. I swear by Mozart's head.'

It was a moment before he could trust his voice to do his bidding. Then he said: 'Of course. You can absolutely rely on it. After all, it isn't as though I'll be wearing a rucksack.'

And then they held each other quietly until it was time for him to go.

EPILOGUE

It was a day of extraordinary beauty: a day that perfectly matched the mood of Britain's citizens as they celebrated the end of the war in Europe. The soft blue sky was cloudless, the May-green trees spread their canopy of tender leaves. Strangers embraced each other, children feasted; bonfires were lit – and in the bombed squares round St Paul's, the people danced.

There were some, of course, who preferred to rejoice without external displays of agitation. At Bowmont, Frances and Uncle Mishak spent the day working in the garden and arguing about the asparagus bed. The need to feed the populace had enabled Mishak to plant asparagus in a place under the south wall which Frances now wanted to reclaim for her day lilies. Not that the outcome was in doubt for a moment: everyone who worked at Bowmont knew that the bandy-legged old gentleman who seldom spoke could twist Miss Somerville round his little finger.

But in the Willow Tea Rooms, everything was carnival and joy. Ruth had intended to celebrate V-E Day at Bowmont, but her son had different ideas.

'I think I ought to go to London and see the King and Queen,' he said.

Questioned further, the five-year-old Jamie said he thought that they had done well to stay at Buckingham Palace throughout the bombing, and to keep visiting the troops, and he wanted to tell them so.

'But, darling, there'll be thousands and thousands of people there waiting for them to come onto the balcony. You won't be able to see them alone.'

James said he didn't mind. A handsome child with dark eyes and his mother's light, abundant hair, he had retained only one feature from his great-grandfather: the Basher's iron and indomitable will.

So they went to London and where James went there went his little sister, Kate – and once it was clear that this was to be a grand reunion, Ruth accepted the offer of Miss Maud and Miss Violet of a party in the Willow. London was really one great party that halcyon May day – there were trestle tables out on the pavements of Belsize Square and Belsize Lane and Belsize Avenue, so why not in the Willow – and Mrs Burtt, though she was very grand now (a floor manager in the munitions factory) had offered to come with her son, Trevor, and lend a hand.

All the same Mrs Weiss, arriving in the café, was not at all pleased.

'*Mein Gott*,' she said disgustedly. 'So many children!'

There were a lot of children. Six years of war had had a startling effect on the birth rate. Dr Felton and his twins had joined Professor Berger and Jamie in the expedition to Buckingham Palace, but Janet, up from the country, had deposited her pugilistic two-year-old so that she could go and look at the crowds. Dr Levy, now a consultant at Hampstead Hospital, was on duty, but his new young wife was rocking their infant daughter while Thisbe – back from Cumberland – trotted at Ruth's heels. And sitting on Leonie's lap, surveying the uproar from the safety of her grandmother's embrace, was Katy Somerville.

'So that is why the Lutzenholler has not come,' said Mrs Weiss grimly, manoeuvring herself on two sticks to her usual table by the hat stand and taking out her horsehair purse, for it was only by pretending that this was an ordinary session in the café that she could endure what was going on.

But she maligned the psychoanalyst. That people could actually pay good money to bring their troubles to the soup slayer of Belsize Park continued to surprise everyone, but it was so. Established in a smart area of St John's Wood, she was even on this historic day attending to patients who could not face the world without a session on her couch.

There were other absentees – von Hofmann had said *Schweinehund* to such effect that he now said it in Hollywood and the lady with the poodle nursed a shivering chihuahua for the poodle had succumbed to old age.

But almost everyone else was there and Ruth, in her role of waitress, was kept busy running to and fro.

'And Pilly?' asked Leonie, as her daughter passed with Janet's baby on her hip and a tray of cakes. 'Is she coming?'

'She said she'd try. Sam's picking her up in Portsmouth. Only Mama, you mustn't matchmake!'

'Why mustn't I?' asked Leonie, who was convinced that the growing attachment of Sam and Pilly could be laid at her door. She had kept open house for all Ruth's friends on the top floor of Number 27 which she had turned into a comfortable flat. The year when Pilly's petty officer had been lost at sea and Huw was killed at Alamein had been a hard one, and she had seen for herself how well those two would suit.

She took a cake from Ruth's tray and pressed it into the hand of her granddaughter. The anxieties that Ruth and Quin felt about letting their children go forth in freedom had not affected Leonie. Children, perhaps: grandchildren, no.

But at three o'clock Ruth handed the baby to Miss Maud and went upstairs to keep a tryst with the four men who all through the war had travelled, clad in the khaki of the Pioneers, to bring music to soldiers in outlying barracks, to tired office workers and housewives in the Blitz . . . and who today were performing in a ruined church in a ravaged city in England's heartland to celebrate the peace.

She turned the knob of the wireless, and they were

playing the Schubert Quartet which she had heard that night at Thameside when she believed a miracle had happened and Biberstein was, after all, alive.

And yet . . . Perhaps, it had occurred, this miracle. It was the chauffeur from Northumberland who now took the melody from Ziller, but as the ravishing, transcendent music filled the room, Ruth seemed to see a plump and curly-headed figure who leant out from heaven and lifted the bow of his Amati in salute – and smiled.

Making her way back into the café through the kitchen, she checked on the threshold and her hand went to her heart. He was coming! He hadn't been sure if he could get away, but here he was walking across the square, and she knew that there could be no greater happiness in the wide world than seeing him come like this towards her.

But others had noted the arrival of Commander Somerville. Katy slid off Leonie's knee and came to pluck at her mother's skirt; even the children fell silent. Ruth had not thought it necessary to keep her husband's exploits to herself. Everyone knew that the circles of gold braid on his sleeve denoted an ever-increasing eminence; that he had been twice torpedoed; that he had housed twelve Jewish orphans and an experimental sheep at Bowmont and been awarded the DSO.

For such a hero something was due and Mrs Weiss was against the hothouse family embrace she could see developing. Stilling Ruth with a wave of the hand, she manoeuvred herself to her feet – and as Quin entered, she pointed at him with her rubber-tipped walking stick.

'I buy you a cake?' said Mrs Weiss.

A selected list of titles available from Macmillan Children's Books

The prices shown below are correct at the time of going to press. However, Macmillan Publishers reserves the right to show new retail prices on covers, which may differ from those previously advertised.

Eva Ibbotson

A Song for Summer	978-0-330-44498-9	£6.99
The Secret Countess	978-0-230-01486-2	£6.99
A Company of Swans	978-0-230-01484-8	£6.99

Guus Kuijer

The Book of Everything	978-0-330-44113-1	£4.99

Celia Rees

The Wish House	978-0-330-43643-4	£5.99

Jaclyn Moriarty

Feeling Sorry for Celia	978-0-330-39725-4	£5.99

All Pan Macmillan titles can be ordered from our website, www.panmacmillan.com, or from your local bookshop and are also available by post from:

Bookpost, PO Box 29, Douglas, Isle of Man IM99 1BQ
Credit cards accepted. For details:
Telephone: 01624 677237
Fax: 01624 670923
Email: bookshop@enterprise.net
www.bookpost.co.uk

Free postage and packing in the United Kingdom